Mae Van Dorn's Perfect Storm

Sheila Athens

QUIET COAST PRESS, INC.

Chapter One

Mae Van Dorn stood in the parking lot beside her beat-up Toyota, doing her best to delay the inevitable. She'd rather eat a live lizard than walk inside the Tallahassee nonprofit where she'd been fired four days ago.

But Janice from payroll had insisted that an employee's last check was always a live one, whether the person had direct deposit or not. So here was Mae, about to trudge into the headquarters of Into the Florida Wilds, her employer for the last three years. She'd thought she'd found her dream job when she'd started working for the organization. After all, it created opportunities for low-income children to get out into nature, whether that was to the beach or the mangrove forests or the wetlands.

But she'd gradually learned that all that goody-two-shoes mumbo jumbo was just a front. In reality, most who donated to their organization wanted two things: to make more money and to preserve their own hunting grounds.

"Mae? Is that you?"

The voice came from behind her. She turned to see Matthew, from the legislative affairs department, all dressed up like he'd been over at the state capitol that day. Maybe if he didn't spend so much time wining and dining people, he could answer an email every now and then. On the other hand, he'd obviously done a few things right. He was in his late twenties—maybe five years younger than Mae—and already hobnobbed with some of Tallahassee's most influential people. More importantly, he still had a job.

She raised her hand in a less-than-enthusiastic wave. She'd hoped to get in and out without anyone seeing her except the receptionist and Janice from payroll. "Hey."

"That sucks, what happened to you," he said as he approached. "I mean, it's not like the rest of us don't think the same things."

She scoffed, though she appreciated his kindness. "I was just the one dumb enough to say them out loud."

He gave a sympathetic nod. "With a hot mic nearby."

"And Channel Seven in need of a good story." It had been the perfect storm. Her words, broadcast into the meeting room where the press conference had just ended. The sound man for the local station still recording everything that took place there.

She'd criticized Steven Borowski, the entitled ass who also happened to be the organization's largest donor. Her exact words, in response to an intern who'd asked pointed questions about a recent news article about Borowski's company, recorded and rebroadcast that night for all of Tallahassee to hear: *They've clear-cut more acreage than anyone else in Florida. But if he donates to an organization like ours, he can convince the masses that he cares about the environment. And the land where the kids visit? He saved it so he could go duck hunting there.*

"Did Patricia give you a chance to explain yourself? I mean, before she fired you?"

"Is that what they said? That I was fired?" So much for employee confidentiality. Whatever happened to the diplomatic "Mae is no longer with the organization"?

Matthew's gaze moved everywhere but her face. He clearly didn't want to look her in the eye. "Well, not in so many words, but you know how everyone talks."

A sad resignation cascaded through her body. She would have done the same thing if she were still on the inside. Still a part of that cozy little PR team that had been her only family over the last few years. But none of them had even texted her since it happened. Her gaffe had gotten her kicked out of that circle as swiftly and surely as a cleaver severing a finger.

And then she'd gotten home that day and . . . She squeezed her eyes closed before the repulsive image could return to her mind's eye. The image she couldn't forget. The image she would likely *never* forget.

She looked up at the two-story office building that had been funded, in large part, by Steven Borowski and his company. She wanted to flip it the bird, but even as pissed as she was, she was still going to miss this place—the closest thing she'd had to a home in recent years.

"I'll bet you get an even better gig, though," Matthew said. "I mean, you did good work here."

She gave him a sly grin. "Only because I'm bossy as hell and don't put up with anyone's bullshit."

He cocked his head to the side. "I heard we had a pretty weak PR department until you got here. You get results, and that's what counts."

"But not as much as criticizing our biggest donor."

"Something else will happen soon—some legislator will sleep with the governor's wife or whatever—and everyone will forget all about what happened with you."

"Let's hope so." She had only a couple of thousand dollars in savings and no place to live, so she needed to find a new job fast.

"I heard the Florida Institute of CPAs is looking for a PR person."

She squinched her nose. "Does that mean I have to understand accounting?" It was a joke, but the truth was, she'd apply anywhere that might employ her.

He laughed. "Good point. Listen, I have to get to a meeting. Let's stay in touch, okay?"

She nodded, though she knew they wouldn't. He was a good guy, but they'd never been close. It was just a thing people said—a robotic response, shallow and insincere, like the majority of interactions in the workplace.

She gave him a minute to get inside the building and through the lobby. No need for people to witness her moments of shame as she picked up her last paycheck.

Thankfully, the lobby was empty when she plodded inside.

"I'm here to see Janice," she said, trying to ignore the receptionist's pitying look. "I told her I'd be here between nine and nine-thirty."

The woman motioned toward the notebook that held the visitor log. "Sorry, but you've got to sign in. And Janice told me Patricia has your paycheck."

Mae's gaze snapped to the receptionist's. "What? Why?" She'd planned to be in and out of the lobby in under three minutes. And she most definitely did *not* want to see the executive director of the organization. Her boss's boss. The one who treated Steven Borowski like Florida's mild winters were created solely for him—not that he hadn't acted like that already. Even though Mae had reported to Amanda, Patricia had taken it upon herself earlier in the week to conduct Mae's termination meeting. She'd pulled rank so that she could be the one to say, "You're fired."

The receptionist shrugged. "Janice just said I was supposed to call Patricia when you arrived."

Mae looked up at the ceiling, defeated, then down at her clothes. Had she known she would be seeing the head honcho instead of the payroll person, she would have dressed in something other than shorts, flip-flops, and a form-fitting tee. At least she'd showered that morning and spent the five minutes it took to blow dry her brown pixie. Without any makeup on, her riot of freckles was on full display.

"Mae Van Dorn is here for you," the receptionist said into her phone, then waited a second for the response. She placed the receiver back in its cradle. "She said I could send you on up."

Mae's ID badge had been confiscated from her within minutes of her returning to the building after the ill-fated press conference. But now they trusted her to walk through the building by herself? Maybe Patricia had calmed down a bit. Maybe she even planned to apologize for the tirade she'd unleashed on Mae that afternoon.

Fat chance. Patricia had berated her for forty-five minutes straight, defending the guy who had talked down to the receptionist, come on to Amanda, and bragged to Mae, every single time she'd met him, about the size of his boat—and why? Because the guy signed Patricia's paycheck.

Mae tried not to make eye contact with anyone as she made her way past rows of cubicles and up the open staircase toward the executive director's office. Whispers and stares followed her through the building like a snake's tail end, slithering behind her.

Patricia waited outside her office. She wore a slim, teal-colored pantsuit and the *I'm in charge* attitude she never seemed to take off. The older woman let her gaze slowly take in Mae's attire. She didn't say anything, but the pinched look on her face showed her distaste.

Screw her. "I understand you have my paycheck?"

Patricia motioned to the interior of her office. "Come in for a minute, won't you?"

Do I have a choice?

Patricia followed behind as Mae entered the office. The older woman closed the door quietly, like what they were doing might be a secret, then went to stand behind her large desk. Outside her window, the state capitol gleamed in the Florida sunshine.

Mae refused to sit. She was not here to be lectured again. Scolded for embarrassing the organization and the man who had meant so much to their funding. Mae had taken those thrashings earlier in the week, and that was *after* Patricia had told her she was fired. Mae's boss, Amanda, had sat quietly in the background, a surprised look on her face.

No, Mae had heard enough from Patricia. "Can I have my check, please?"

Patricia extracted an envelope from the center drawer of her desk and tapped it on the palm of her opposite hand. Like she wanted Mae to know she had it, but she wasn't yet ready to hand it over to her. "Let's chat for a minute first, shall we?"

"Is Amanda going to join us?"

"It's going to be just the two of us." Patricia came around the desk to stand closer to Mae. With Mae's height and Patricia's heels, they stood eye-to-eye. "A little heart-to-heart talk."

Mae let out a frustrated huff but kept her mouth shut. Whatever this was, she wanted to get on with it.

Patricia rested her hips on the desk and studied Mae for several seconds before speaking again. "I've realized over the years how important it is for more experienced women to mentor others through their careers."

Mae held her tongue. She was thirty-four years old, for God's sake. The younger women in the organization had often come to *her* for advice.

Patricia continued. "If women are ever going to be on equal footing with men in the workplace, we've got to pass our collective knowledge on to those who follow in our footsteps. So I'm going to share some words of wisdom with you. You may not agree with them now, but if you go home and think about them . . ."

If only I had a home to begin with.

". . . I think you'll realize their importance."

Mae tried to give Patricia her best I'm-so-bored-with-you look, but the woman didn't seem to notice.

Instead, Patricia smoothed a wrinkle in her pants and continued. "I've seen a lot of really smart people over the years who didn't get as far in their career as you would expect because of how they conducted themselves in the workplace. I don't want that to happen to you, but I'm afraid your attitude"—Mae could tell she was choosing her words carefully—"could limit you if you don't get it under control. It's really none of my business where it came from or how long you've had it, but sometimes it *screams* that you're a difficult person to get along with. I mean, we all see the problems with this organization. We know Steven Borowski can be a jerk. We know his intentions aren't always as honorable as he'd like us to believe. But we also know we've got to play the game. If we're going to continue to get funding, we don't call those things out. We don't gossip about them to other staff members, and we certainly don't tell the interns about them in public places."

When the Channel Seven mic is still on. The unsaid words hung silently in the room. Mae didn't want to admit it, but she knew she'd messed up. Her words—her bad judgment and bad timing—had created a termination-worthy PR catastrophe for the organization.

The older woman gave Mae a sympathetic look. "You've got *a lot* going for you. You're bright and efficient, and you connect the dots when other people can't. You could have a good career at whatever you choose to do, but not until you get that attitude under control."

"Until I swallow all the bullshit and learn to play the game," Mae deadpanned.

Patricia nodded. "Until you begin to get along with others in the workplace."

But Mae's coworkers had liked her just fine. She'd never had a problem with any of them. "So when exactly did you cave?"

Patricia looked confused. Or frustrated. Or both. "Pardon me?"

"When did you become one of them? When did you start playing by *their* rules and stop trying to make things better and fairer and—"

"You can't accomplish anything if you don't have a seat at the table. And you earn that seat by showing them they can trust you to have professional behavior." Patricia's voice had become sterner.

"So telling the truth isn't professional behavior? I mean, isn't that how the Steven Borowskis of the world get to do whatever they want—because they've convinced everyone to sit down and keep their mouths shut?"

Patricia jabbed a finger in Mae's direction. "See, it's that bluntness that gets you into trouble."

"Yeah. We established that earlier in the week. Can I have my check now?"

Patricia pushed herself up from the edge of the desk and stood tall, her anger building. Her skin took on a tinge of silver—like a faded Tin Man—a phenomenon Mae often saw when other people had bad intentions. She'd long ago gathered—after conversations with Mama and her brother, Cole, and a couple of her childhood friends—that not everyone saw this, and it was best to keep her mouth shut whenever it appeared on another person's skin.

Patricia's jaw tightened. "I assume you know that little stunt with the mic is going to have a big impact on your career."

"I'm pretty sure it already has." Mae met her gaze, refusing to look as desperate to get ahold of that paycheck as she actually was. She'd worked the hours, so they had to pay her, regardless of what Patricia thought of her, right? She could barely concentrate over the rippling sensation under her right eyebrow, which always happened when someone with the silver tinge stood close. It felt like someone's fingers running down the piano keys one by one—all the way to the end, then back again. Repeatedly.

"I'm talking about an impact beyond our organization. Even beyond Tallahassee."

"What do you mean?" The words popped out of Mae's mouth before she had a chance to swallow them. She wanted to appear as calm and aloof as Patricia, but she was failing miserably.

Patricia walked around to stand behind her desk. Apparently the friendly-advice portion of the chat was over. "Surely you know how small this industry is. People talk. Your chances of getting another job with a nonprofit in this town are slim, and that likely extends to the rest of the state too."

Mae ran her finger over her rippling eyebrow—a delay tactic because she wasn't sure what to say. She'd never had any indication that people could actually *see* the rippling, but the pain and distraction made it hard for her to concentrate.

So Patricia would kill Mae's chances of working for another nonprofit, especially in Tallahassee? Mae would get a job in corporate PR then. Everyone knew there was more money there anyway.

Patricia continued, her skin now as bright as polished silver. "And you're as good as dead in the PR world too. I mean, who wants to hire a PR professional who *hurts* an organization's image rather than helps it?"

Mae's anger now matched Patricia's. "You never made any mistakes in your career?"

"We're living in a different world than when I came up through the ranks. Nowadays, if a hiring manager is interested in a candidate, the first thing the recruiter does is google them. Maybe they'll find some pictures from some drunken New Year's Eve party. Or an old, buried post with discriminatory comments that make the organization stay as far away from that person as possible. But for you? They're going to find an entire segment from the Channel Seven news. All two minutes and thirteen seconds of you throwing our benefactor under the bus."

"I've already apologized. I don't know what else you want me to say."

"You got your moments of fame." Patricia leaned forward, her palms flat on the desk. Her voice lowered to a sinister whisper. "And they're going to follow you around *forever*."

Chapter Two

Mae's hands still shook as she uploaded a picture of her pay-check into her bank's app on her phone. Maybe by the time the funds became available, she'd have figured out where she was going to live.

On the other side of the bedroom door, Rocco banged around in the kitchen. She would really miss his cooking, but finding him six inches deep in the server from the nearby wing joint had put an end to their two-year relationship.

To make matters worse, Mae had discovered the little tryst on the same day she'd been fired. When Patricia had finally finished yelling at her, Mae had gone home in the middle of the day—unemployed and ready to crawl into her bed—only to find Rocco and Miss Hot-n-Spicy-Wings already tangled in the sheets. And because the tiny bungalow Mae and Rocco lived in had belonged to his late aunt, it meant Mae would be the one to move out. When she had the funds. And when she knew where the hell she was going and where she would work.

Why had she not paid more attention to the silvery tinge that had started to color his complexion a few weeks ago? It had been mild at first, and she eventually attributed it to the fact that he'd lost a few hundred dollars in the poker games their new downstairs neighbor had started hosting every Friday night. When Rocco had trouble coming up with his share of the rent, he'd finally confessed his losses. But Mae didn't know there had been more going on underneath that silvery glow.

He now knocked on the door of the spare junk room, where Mae had moved all her stuff once Miss Hot-n-Spicy had gotten dressed and sauntered off.

"Come in," Mae said.

He opened the door and looked around. She had once found the dark, side-parted hair that flopped in his eyes endearing, but now it looked disheveled. He'd had a guilty expression ever since *the incident* the other day. "You want me to move my surfboard to the back porch?" he asked. It was wedged diagonally—floor to ceiling—against one wall. It loomed precariously above the air mattress she'd used as a bed for the last few nights.

"I'm okay." She crawled onto her makeshift bed and leaned her back against the wall. It was the only place in the room to sit.

"I'm making some manicotti. I'm happy to share." He'd gotten all his recipes from his grandmother, who lived in the Little Italy section of Fort Lauderdale.

Mae ignored her empty stomach and picked at a thread on the old blanket beneath her. "No, thank you."

"Babe," he said for the two-hundredth time in the last few days.

Her gaze snapped to him, daring him to speak.

He held out his hands in a beseeching manner. "She doesn't mean a thing to me."

"Yet you managed to sleep with her ten or fifteen times."

He shook his head. "I really don't think it was that many."

But that's not what the girl had said as she'd slipped on her deep-cut leopard print bra while Mae had stood there, unable to move. Unable to forget the sight of Rocco's hands cupping those oversized breasts. Unable to process all that she'd seen when she'd come home early that day and flung open the bedroom door. "I'm not really in the mood to haggle over the exact number," she said.

All Mae knew was that he was a cheater. A liar and a cheat. Why had she ever believed he was different from everyone else who had let her down? She made a mental note to figure out where she could get tested for STDs for free.

He banged his fist against the door jamb. "Who are you going to believe? Me or her?"

Mae's cell phone rang, saving her from having to answer that ridiculous question. "I've got to get this."

He grunted as he turned to go back to the kitchen. "The manicotti will be done soon, if you want some."

"Will you shut the door the way you found it?" she called after him as she lifted her phone to look at the screen. *Ugh.* Her brother's number. Half-brother, technically, because they had different fathers, and the only sibling she had. Cole had called to check on her each of the last three days. They'd rarely talked before that, but he'd happened to call on what she'd come to think of as her *really bad day.* She'd cried and blabbered to him about everything that had gone wrong . . . and now she wished she'd kept her mouth shut.

But why had he become so caring all of a sudden? Where was this caring brother years ago, when he'd left her—a scared and hungry thirteen-year-old—to fend for herself when their party girl mom disappeared for days? Why had he bolted from their Central Florida home when he was nineteen, leaving her behind, even though he knew the appalling environment where they'd both been raised?

He'd resurfaced Mae's senior year of high school, only to vanish again for more than a decade after that.

But now he wanted back in her life, as if nothing had happened? How dumb did he think she was?

"Hey, Sis," he said when she answered the phone.

"You don't have to check on me every day, you know." She didn't mean to sound snotty, but it wasn't like they had a relationship that needed to be preserved.

"I'm calling with something better than a check-in." Cole sounded unusually jovial.

"Oh, yeah?" She had subzero expectations for something better.

"My roommate got a work assignment overseas and will be gone for three months. He says it's okay for you to live in his room while he's gone."

How is that better?

She'd never even been to Jacksonville Beach, where her brother had apparently lived for a few years now. And besides, why would she want to live with the guy who'd ditched his little sister when she needed him most? She'd crafted her life around not needing anyone. She'd been a fool to move in with Rocco. Until then, she'd rarely had roommates and had certainly never lived with a boyfriend. Because life had shown her how unreliable people usually were.

"So what do you think?" he asked, enthusiasm still lacing his voice.

"I don't know." Maybe she should let him down lightly. Because he *had* been trying to connect with her these last couple of months. He'd been there for her on her *very bad day*, when her so-called friends had disappeared. She and Cole didn't have to be pals, but they could at least have a civil, maybe even familial relationship.

"Where else do you have to go?" he asked.

"I live in Tallahassee."

"But you don't have to. I mean, you don't have anything keeping you there, right?"

She got it—no job, no boyfriend, no housing. Her few friends from work—the only friends she had in town—had been coolly distant since she'd been fired. "How much is the rent?"

"My roommate was going to have to pay it all to keep his spot, so he said he'd be happy if you pay four hundred per month."

"And it's just you two who live there?" She didn't normally do roommates, so if she considered this—and that was a big *if*—she'd be making an exception for her brother that she'd rather not make. And she certainly didn't want to live with some random dude she'd never met, but the truth was, she trusted her brother even less than a stranger.

"It's just me. And I'm at work most of the time."

"You know, I still haven't forgiven you about the laptop." After four years away, he'd shown up again—all smiles—during her last semester of high school. She'd started looking up to him again. Even started to trust him a bit, then *boom*! He'd stolen her school-issued computer and disappeared. The fact that she couldn't turn it back in meant she couldn't walk in the graduation ceremonies with the rest of her class. Not that it mattered, really. There wouldn't have been any family members there to see her. But it would have meant something to her.

He remained silent for several seconds. "Look, I was a jerk back then. And high about ninety percent of the time. But I don't do that shit now. Hell, I don't even drink anymore, and I *really* don't do any drugs."

But why would she believe him? Why believe Cole or Rocco or the mother who left her child in the car at a bar while she snorted lines of coke with whatever lowlife she called her current boyfriend? Everyone Mae had ever cared about had let her down. And those experiences had taught her one of life's basic tenets: that people are crap.

Add to that an internal alarm system that gave a silvery glow to anyone with bad intentions, and she sure as hell knew that the human race was no good. Sure, people *acted* like they cared or like they had other people's interests in mind, but Mae knew better. Whether she liked it or not, the strange biology that lived inside her body sussed out a person's deepest thoughts and advertised it on their skin plain as day, though no one else seemed to see it. That glimpse of people's private agendas only reinforced Mae's most negative views about the human race.

And though her internal alarm system had never worked on blood relatives like Mama or Cole, she knew better than to trust her brother. No way would she move in with someone who'd taught her that lesson more vividly than anyone. It was a matter of self-preservation. "I'm going to see what I can find in Tallahassee."

"Really? Why would you turn down such a great deal?"

Because I don't want to get hurt again. "This is where I live. My friends are here." Friends who hadn't reached out to her in days.

"I thought moving to a new town would be good for you. A place where everyone hasn't—you know—seen you on the news."

He had a point, but she wasn't going to open herself up to Cole again, regardless of how desperate she was. "I've got to go."

"Okay, but think about my offer."

She said a quick goodbye and hung up the phone. She scooted down the wall until she lay flat on the air mattress, staring at the ceiling. Maybe if she kicked that massive surfboard that loomed over her, it would dislodge, fall on her head, and put her out of her misery. She considered the physics of it all, but it hurt her head to think too much.

Her phone pinged. She searched through the blankets until she found it. A text from Cole.

If you don't say yes by Wednesday night, I've got to let one of my roommate's buddies rent the room while he's gone.

Mae closed her eyes and burrowed under the covers. Jacksonville Beach sat on the Atlantic coast, just below the Georgia border. Maybe three hours due east of Tallahassee. That distance would undoubtedly lessen Patricia's circle of influence in the job market.

But Mae *really* didn't want to consider going there. She did *not* want to move in with Cole. She barely knew her brother anymore, and what she did know of him, she didn't like.

Wednesday was two days away. She'd better come up with some other options *fast*.

Or she'd have no choice.

CHAPTER THREE

After forty-eight hours of scrambling, Mae hadn't come up with any options—no decent job leads, no available apartments within her budget, no old friends offering their couches for even a few nights. And so, she'd had no choice but to text Cole to let him know she'd take over a portion of his roommate's rent for the next three months.

She'd left Tallahassee early the next morning, piling all of her belongings into her beat-up, old Toyota and not leaving so much as a goodbye note for Rocco, who'd already gone to work for the day.

Three hours later, she pulled into the driveway of a small concrete block house on the inland side of Third Street, the main thoroughfare running through Jacksonville Beach. She guessed this neighborhood sat maybe three or four miles from the ocean. Aside from a few scruffy sabal palms, it could have been anywhere—Des Moines or Little Rock or Hoboken.

Spots of dirt or mildew dotted the faded white paint on Cole's rented house. A medium-sized dog stuck its nose through the missing slats of the neighbor's backyard privacy fence.

She turned off the car, leaned her head against the headrest, and closed her eyes. She wanted a few minutes of solitude before her new life began. She wouldn't even *be* there if she'd had any other options, but there she sat—in a town she'd never visited—about to move in with the brother she didn't trust and hadn't seen in years. So much for finding the home she'd expected to establish for herself well before she'd hit her mid-thirties.

Something slapped on the car's roof, jarring her. Her eyes flew open. Cole stood outside her window, a look of anticipation on his face.

He swung the door open the second she unlocked it. He held his arms wide. "Baby sister."

She didn't remember him ever being this demonstrative before. Their fractured little family had been more the keep-a-safe-distance-away type. She held her hands up, palms facing forward—a wall to keep him away. "I'm not a hugger."

His face fell, followed by his outstretched arms. He took a couple of steps back. "Oh. Sorry. It's just been so long since I've seen you."

Yeah. And whose fault is that? He'd gotten back in touch a month or so ago, but it had been ten years before that. Even longer since they'd seen each other in person. Sometimes she'd had no idea where he was.

"You look good," she said as she stood. He'd filled out. Seemingly less gaunt than before. But she hated the way he tucked his longish brown hair behind his ears. Maybe he thought it was cool, but it looked unkempt to her. She tried to ignore how much his hazel eyes looked like their mother's.

"You too." The lie slid from his mouth too easily.

Dark circles had rimmed her eyes ever since her breakup with Rocco, regardless of how much concealer she slathered on. A huge, stress-induced zit bulged on her forehead. And her raggedy pixie was in bad need of a cut.

Her once shapely body now veered toward "ample," but what did she care what a bunch of judgy people thought of her? Besides, Rocco used to compliment her "gorgeous curves." Of course, he'd now outed himself as a grade A liar.

Cole's eyes widened as he looked through the back window of her car, which was stuffed full with everything she owned. "I hadn't thought about how much stuff you might bring," he said.

"Yeah, well. I didn't have anywhere else to leave it." She didn't want to spend any of her few precious dollars on a storage unit in Tallahassee.

He made a lifting motion toward the hatchback. "Well, open it up. Let's find a place for all this to go."

She raised the door to the back and things immediately tumbled to the ground—a milk crate filled with mismatched bedding, a laundry basket full of her dirty clothes. Her coffee maker teetered on the edge. The machine didn't fall out, but the glass carafe hit the ground and shattered. She did her best not to see it as a precursor of how this new living arrangement would likely work out. "You got a broom?" she asked.

"I'll clean it up while you unpack." He picked up the dirty T-shirts and shorts that had fallen out of her laundry basket but left the bra and underwear for her to retrieve. "Let's get the rest of this stuff to your room," he said.

They each grabbed what they could of her belongings, and she followed Cole inside. The small house had obviously been built before open-concept floorplans had become a thing. A pair of swinging, saloon-type doors separated the narrow living room from the kitchen. A bistro table with mismatched chairs, wedged into a corner near the fridge, aspired to be a breakfast nook.

He waved for her to follow him. "The bedrooms are back here."

"Back here" meant two steps beyond the living room, where a short hallway came to an end at three doors side by side. He started at the left and pointed to each in succession. "Bathroom. My room. Your room."

She hadn't thought about the fact that she might have to share a bathroom with her brother. So much for privacy. And if he was anything like Rocco—who had left his little black beard hairs all over the sink—she was *not* looking forward to it.

Mae hoped Cole had gained some cleaning skills along the way. Their party girl mom hadn't owned a vacuum cleaner. Mae didn't remember her ever cleaning the shower drain. On the few occasions Mae had been forced to have a roommate, she'd lived in fear that it would become apparent she was unaware of some all-important cleaning regimen that everyone else in the world knew about.

Cole opened the door to what would be her bedroom. A bare mattress on a steel bedframe filled most of the room. Two mismatched dressers stood beside each other on the far wall. "I found that black one by the curb the other day. Figured you'd need a place to put your clothes. And I had Ryan squish all his stuff to one end of the closet so you'd have room for your hang-ups."

"Thank you," she said, wishing she'd confiscated some cleaning supplies from Rocco's house before she left. She'd been the one to buy most of them, so they were hers to begin with.

After she and Cole had each brought in four more armloads of stuff, Cole left her to sort everything out while he went to sweep up the glass in the driveway.

She surveyed the room, not sure how to fit her entire life into a space that still held the belongings of someone else. She opened the closet door. Ryan had, in fact, moved all of his stuff to one end. She sniffed the air inside, then looked for the source of the faint foul odor. Maybe it was the pair of scuffed work boots on the floor? Or the contents of the gym bag on the shelf above the hangers? Or the fishing pole wedged into one corner? She didn't want to know if there were fish guts or a part of a worm or something else hanging on the hook.

She picked up the sleeve of a flannel shirt and held it to her nose. It had a definite outdoorsy scent . . . and not the good marshmallows-around-a-cozy-campfire smell. More of a foul wild-animals-poop-here aroma.

Her first order of business, though, was to find a hiding spot for the red plastic pocket folder she'd hidden inside her only suitcase. She turned from the closet and considered the room. Where could she hide the folder so that Cole would never find it? He'd been cagey about his current relationship with their mother, and Mae wasn't going to risk Mom finding out she had it.

Last Mae knew, Mom had been in Texas with a guy who bartended at a local honky-tonk. The two had apparently met in Baton Rouge, though Mae had no idea why her mother would have been in Louisiana. Nor did she care. Mae had learned long ago that the less she cared about her mother, the less she got hurt. If she had no expectations of dear ole Mom, then her expectations could never be shattered.

She inched open one of the dresser drawers. The interior looked fairly clean, but she'd rather be sure before she put her clothes inside. The piece may have sat in someone's garage for months before they finally moved it to the curb, and garages in Florida were fair game for every palmetto bug or lizard that wanted to move in.

She grabbed a washcloth from the old canvas beach bag that held her bathroom supplies and went to wet it in the sink. The tiny bathroom had very little counterspace—only a one- or two-inch band surrounding the single chipped sink. Specks of toothpaste or spit or some other liquid she didn't want to think about dotted the mirror.

Would there be room to put her makeup and face soap under the sink? She opened the door to the single cabinet and peered inside. She felt guilty snooping, but she'd chalk this up as gathering important information. Finding out more about the brother who had once stolen from her in order to fund his drug habit.

Two pill bottles sat beside a dusty bottle of cough syrup. One bottle—filled a couple of months ago and definitely in Cole's name—was for Rosuvastatin. She pulled her phone from her pocket and googled. Medicine to treat high cholesterol—a reminder that she and Cole were approaching middle age.

The other bottle—Amoxicillin—had been prescribed to Cole more than a year ago. During college, the doctor at the campus health clinic had given her Amoxicillin for strep throat. It was an antibiotic, so it could be for anything—an ear infection, a toothache, something like that.

Maybe what Cole had said about not being on drugs anymore was true. Then again, if he knew he would share a bathroom with her, he would have removed any damning evidence, right?

She rummaged through the cabinet some more—three kinds of shaving cream, an old Ace bandage, a bottle of generic ibuprofen. She moved an empty box that had once held a thousand Q-tips. Behind it was . . . a box of tampons . . . ? Did Cole have a girlfriend who stayed here on a regular basis? *Ugh.* Mae didn't want to hear her brother getting it on with some girl through the bedroom wall. Hopefully the girlfriend had been Ryan's.

Beside the tampons, she found a bottle of strawberry shampoo and a little canvas makeup tote. Mae pulled the canvas bag out from under the sink and unzipped it to find a tube of lipstick and a hair tie. Definitely girly things. She zipped them back inside and turned the pouch over. The embroidered word "Angie" decorated the other side.

Ahhhh. More information, indeed.

Somewhere in the house, a screen door slapped shut. Mae quickly placed the makeup pouch back under the sink, returned the empty Q-tip box to where it had been in front of the tampons, and closed the cabinet door. She turned on the faucet and stuck her washcloth under the tap.

Cole appeared in the doorway to the bathroom within seconds. "You finding what you need?"

She nodded as she wrung out the rag. "Just wiping out the inside of that dresser before I put my clothes inside. Thanks for getting it for me, by the way." Maybe she should try to see it as a sweet gesture, but that didn't mean she trusted him.

"Anything other than the coffeemaker that needs to go to the kitchen?" he asked. "I can start finding room for it."

She shook her head automatically, though she really hadn't thought it through. Her mind was still stuck on who Angie might be.

Cole stepped aside so Mae could head back to the bedroom. "Maybe we can find a another coffee pot at a Goodwill or something."

That sounded way better to her than having to buy a brand-new replacement. She needed to be as frugal as possible, especially since she'd have to move out before Ryan returned in three months. A new apartment would require first and last month's rent, plus a security deposit—way more money than she had now.

Assuming she found a job here that she liked, would that mean she'd find an apartment in Jacksonville or Jacksonville Beach? Was this her new home now? Was she leaving Tallahassee behind the same way she'd left Ocala and Tampa? Might this be the place where she'd finally establish a home?

She'd passed a lot of large businesses on her way through Jacksonville and Jacksonville Beach. The bridge over the intracoastal waterway seemed to be the dividing line between the two seemingly connected towns. Two large campuses—one a Mayo Clinic and the other some huge megachurch—sat close to the intracoastal.

She opened a drawer and started wiping the inside. "So how'd you end up here, anyway?" she asked.

He shrugged. "A buddy of mine from Jacksonville needed a roommate and I was between jobs, so I thought, 'What the hell? It's as good a place as any.'"

She grunted. "Seems to run in the family."

"By the time he moved to Colorado with his girlfriend, I'd met another buddy who lived in Jax Beach, and I moved in with him."

"Jax Beach? Is that what they call it?"

He reached up and straightened the top of the cheap-looking blinds. "They'll know you're not a local if you don't call it that."

"And where does Ryan come in?"

"I started sharing this place with him after that."

So Cole moved around as much as their mother did. Or, for that matter, as much as Mae did. Would any of them ever have a stable, stay-in-one-place kind of life? Would any of them ever have a real home?

She'd envied those classmates who'd been in school with the same kids since kindergarten. Who went to the same summer camp their parents had attended. Or, hell, who'd gone to any summer camp at all. Mae and Cole's mom had left them at home to fend for themselves, usually with an empty refrigerator. "Any house rules I need to be aware of?" she asked.

He barked out a laugh but then seemed to ponder her question. "If I'm working the morning shift, I've got to get up by five a.m. in order to get the smoker started by six." He'd told her a while back that he worked at a nearby barbecue joint and that he worked some morning shifts and some night shifts. "So the only rule I've got is don't make a bunch of noise after I go to bed."

She closed the top dresser drawer and pulled out the one below it. "Fair enough. I think I can do that." She shook out her rag and started to wipe again.

"And, listen." He hesitated. Moved the laundry basket around on the bed. Sat down in the empty space he'd just created on the mattress. He was stalling.

She looked up at him. "Yes?"

"I'd prefer you not answer my phone if it rings. Even if I'm in the shower or out mowing the grass or whatever."

She froze so she could look at his face. His solemn expression told her how important this topic was to him. His skin maintained its normal color. No silver tinge in sight, but then she'd never seen it on him, even in the days and hours before he took off when they were teenagers, or later when he'd stolen her school-issued laptop. The silver tinge seemed to signal everyone else's bad intentions, but she'd never seen it on Cole or their mother, despite the many times they'd treated her poorly. Perhaps because they all shared the same blood? She'd asked them both over the years if they saw it in other people, but each time they'd acted like she was introducing them to an imaginary friend. Some made-up entity. Or maybe like Mae needed a cranial examination. Or worse. Eventually, she'd stopped asking them about it at all.

Cole's insistence that she not answer his phone seemed like a warning flag, despite the normal color of his skin. "Keeping secrets, are we?" she asked.

He scrubbed his hand down his face. "It's just that . . . we haven't been close for a while, and it's going to take some getting used to. Having you here and all."

She couldn't argue with that, but what was he hiding? "Are you in some kind of trouble? You owe somebody money or something? Your drug dealer, maybe?"

He jumped to his feet and paced the room. "I told you I'm not using anymore. Do you think I could get up before dawn to go to work if I was getting high all the time?"

Her well-honed survival instincts kicked in. She'd been protecting herself for years. "Will I be in danger while I'm staying here?"

He slapped his open palm on the top of the other dresser. "Do you think I'd invite my baby sister to stay somewhere that wasn't safe?"

She crossed her arms. "I don't know." He'd left her alone with their mother when Mae was still in middle school. Why should she expect anything different now? "I barely know you now."

He rolled his eyes and let out an exaggerated sigh. "Just don't answer my phone, okay?"

She hesitated, unsure of how much to push the conversation. After all, she'd gotten through all the shit he and Mom had laid on her when she was young. This place—his house—was just a temporary landing spot. A momentary blip in her life. He wasn't any different from anyone else who might have provided a room for her to rent. She didn't need to know the details of his life any more than he needed to know about hers.

But the tampons under the sink did make her curious. "Can I at least ask who Angie is?"

His face paled. "How do you know about Angie?"

She didn't answer right away. She wanted to study his face. To see if he'd offer any kind of information, but he just stood there, a terrified look in his eyes.

"There's a makeup bag with her name on it under the bathroom sink," Mae finally said.

A look of relief crossed his face. His shoulders relaxed. "She's just a friend."

He'd been a terrible liar as a kid too. "Your friends leave entire boxes of tampons under your bathroom sink?" she asked.

His attempt at a casual-looking shrug was unconvincing. "She stayed here a while back. She must have left them then."

But Mae wasn't buying it. "Why did you look so scared when I asked about her?"

He squared his feet and faced her directly. "I'm not talking about her, Mae. You got it?" He slashed a hand through the air to emphasize his point.

"So *three* rules, then," she said. "Don't make noise at night. Don't answer your phone. And don't ask about Angie."

"That's right," he said, then stalked out of the room.

She understood the first rule, but the second two were sketchy at best.

Good thing she hadn't planned to trust her brother again.

Not now.

Not ever.

Chapter Four

Mae padded to Cole's kitchen in her pajamas—an oversized *I Hate Peopling* T-shirt and a pair of loose-fitting gym shorts. The good thing about her brother going to work before dawn most days was that she had the house to herself. His twelve- to fourteen-hour shifts at the barbecue place were a luxury, at least for her. He came home dog-tired and smelling of burnt meat, so not such a good deal for him.

The tension between her and Cole still permeated the air every time they were both in the house at the same time. Like Tuesday afternoon—his only day off so far—when he'd tried to get her to go to the beach with him. How could he not understand that every waking hour needed to be dedicated to her job search? When she'd turned down his invitation, he got all weird and pouty but ended up making a batch of her favorite beverage—three-quarters sun tea, one-quarter lemonade—just the way she'd liked it when they were both still living with Mama all those years ago.

Of course, he was being nice. Trying to be the good guy he imagined he was. The problem with Cole was that at some point he always stopped trying, and then he disappeared or stopped communicating, or worse. His failed attempts to be the good guy littered her past. She wouldn't fall for it again.

She poured herself another cup of coffee from the old-fashioned percolator that belonged in a museum somewhere. She hadn't had time to replace the carafe she'd broken on her Mr. Coffee. She couldn't waste time trawling through thrift shops until she'd found work.

But four straight days of applying for jobs had gotten her absolute zilch. The bigger employers in town—the banks and insurance companies and medical facilities—all required online applications. And they'd only let people apply for their PR department if they had a specific opening at that time. They didn't allow applicants an opportunity to say, "Here's my résumé for your future consideration." What a load of administrative bullshit.

She'd stopped by to introduce herself at a couple of nonprofits and PR firms, hoping they'd turn her down less quickly if she showed up in person, but none of them seemed to be hiring . . . or at least that's what they told her. She knew enough about the job-search game to know that if an organization didn't want to hire you, they'd make up some bogus excuse instead of admitting to the real reason—not cute enough or not poised enough or "this is the woman Patricia Knight warned us about." Would she ever really know if Patricia's influence had travelled across I-10 to tank her chances of getting a job in Jacksonville?

She stirred a couple of sugar packets into her coffee and returned to her bedroom. She settled on the floor with her computer on her lap and returned to the online job board that seemed to offer the most Jacksonville-based openings. But she wasn't qualified for many of the posted positions—welder, actuarial, sous chef, physical therapist.

She scrolled past the opening she'd seen every day since she'd started looking—receptionist for the Pathway to Abundant Life Ministries in Jacksonville Beach. She'd seen that megachurch as soon as she'd crossed the bridge over the intracoastal waterway when she'd first arrived in town. The behemoth main building had a sculpture inset at the peak of its towering roofline—two praying hands set against a palm tree. Five or six other buildings of similar architecture and color surrounded the church to form a campus of sorts. A school, maybe? Or just places for various church-related activities?

Mama had tried to send Mae to Vacation Bible School one year, probably to get her daughter out of her hair for part of each day. But Mae had refused to go back after two days, embarrassed that the other kids had made fun of her. Apparently, all the other children had known about some dude who talked to a burning bush . . . and thought it was ludicrous that she'd never heard of him.

Mae's only other times in churches had been at friends' weddings. One of the couples had already divorced, and the other one's husband had died of a rare form of brain cancer within nine months of the honeymoon.

Both of those reasons epitomized why she would never be on #TeamGod. How did people believe in an all-powerful deity when husbands cheated on wives and twenty-five-year-old newlyweds passed away, not to mention school shootings and deadly earthquakes and bad haircuts? No, she was pretty sure she'd been an atheist before she even knew the word.

But since none of the other jobs she'd applied for seemed to be panning out, maybe she should apply at the Pathway to Abundant Life Ministries, aka PALM. The online ad *did* say that they preferred applicants who believed in Jesus Christ as their savoir, but how would her co-workers ever know what went on inside her head and heart? Surely Google could get her up-to-speed on the whole burning bush thing that seemed so important to their kind. Surely, she could find a YouTube video that would outline the basic tenets of their religion.

Armed with a little Christ-infused knowledge, she could almost certainly cover up her nonbeliever status. She'd had two acting classes in high school. How hard could it be?

She took another sip of her coffee as she pondered whether to move forward. She had her student loan payment to make every month. In addition to the partial rent she'd agreed to pay here, she needed to buy some groceries. As much as she enjoyed the leftover brisket that Cole brought home some nights from the restaurant, a meat-only diet wouldn't cut it for her. He ate most of his meals at work, and there hadn't been a fruit or vegetable in the house when she arrived. Most of all, though, she needed to have several thousand dollars saved up before his roommate, Ryan, returned, meaning she'd have to find somewhere else to live.

Damn Rocco.

Damn Patricia.

Damn Channel Seven news.

But at this point, Mae had nothing to lose.

She set down her coffee cup and clicked the button to apply.

***

Three cars—all headed in the opposite direction on the narrow street in downtown Jacksonville—honked at Mae, a cacophony of noise in an already frustrating morning. One of the drivers waved frantically as his car passed hers, but she had no idea what had him so worked up. Her shoulders tensed. She passed through the shade created by the track of the overhead people mover, but—just as quickly—the sun glared again on her dirty windshield, making it difficult to see.

About half a block ahead, a man stepped off the sidewalk and onto the edge of the street. He waved his arms in wide circles and shouted something at her. She cracked her window so she could hear him.

"Wrong way!" he yelled as she slowly rolled by. "It's a one-way street!"

She looked around, suddenly more aware of her surroundings. At the stoplight ahead, all three lanes had a car in them, each facing her direction.

Damn it.

Her heartbeat pummeled the wall of her chest. Without looking, she whipped her car into the right-hand lane and turned onto the next street—her only option to avoid colliding head-on with one of the cars that faced her.

A long row of empty spaces lined the curb of the new street. "Loading Zone," the sign said, but there were no vehicles in it. She really needed to find somewhere to pull over and calm herself down. She'd already maxed out on her daily quotient of stress . . . and she hadn't even left her car.

She'd been trying to find the headquarters of a nonprofit that had advertised an entry-level program coordinator position. The duties were about two levels down from Mae's position at Into the Florida Wilds, but desperation had set in.

Maybe this brush with death, though, was the universe telling her to stick with jobs at the beach. That she didn't need to work in downtown Jacksonville, with its one-way streets and   rush-hour   traffic   and where-the-hell-did-you-park-if-you-worked-down-here-any-way?

The shrill ring of her phone jangled her nerves even more. She pulled into the loading zone and answered.

"Is this Mae Van Dorn?" The man on the other end sounded very official.

Her heart still hammered in her chest. She tried to calm her breathing. "It is."

"Is . . . everything okay? You sound . . . distressed."

"Just a little scare, but I'm fine now. What can I help you with?"

"This is Walter Miller. I'm the operations director at Pathway to Abundant Life Ministries. You may know us as PALM."

She sat up taller in her seat. Maybe things were looking up after all. "Yes?"

"I know you applied for the receptionist role at our church, but I've got another opportunity I'd like to talk with you about. Can you meet with me this afternoon at, say, four o'clock?"

She glanced at the clock on her dashboard. That was less than two hours away. She could easily make it back to the beach in that length of time, but she had yet to watch any YouTube videos to see what she needed to know about Jesus people. She'd assumed she'd have at least a night to bone up on her biblical knowledge if they called her in for an interview. "It's another position? Different from receptionist?"

"It is." His voice held an air of false intrigue.

"What position is it?"

He hesitated. "I'd rather we talk in person."

She panicked for a moment, wondering if he wanted her to knock on doors and hand out literature to unwitting strangers. But did those people get paid? She'd always thought they were members of the congregation, putting in their hours to earn bonus points with God.

But did she really *care* what the position was as long as it helped to pay the bills? No one else had called her from any of the places where she'd applied. It was in Jax Beach, close to Cole's house. Away from the traffic and confusing one-way streets of downtown Jacksonville. If she could just bluff her way through this first interview, she could watch some YouTube videos tonight. "Four o'clock, you said?"

"I'm in the administration building. It's right behind the main church, connected by a breezeway."

"Can you tell me your name again?" She hated to ask, but she *had* been in distress when her phone had rung.

"Walter Miller. I'm the director of church operations."

"Thank you, Mr. Miller," she said. "I'll see you then."

***

Less than two hours later, Mae waited nervously in the administration building of the Pathway to Abundant Life Ministries. The receptionist desk sat empty, but a white woman in her late twenties—about five years younger than Mae—had stepped out from an office down the hall to greet Mae when she'd first arrived. The woman's arms displayed several flower-themed tattoos, and her nose sported a septum ring. Maybe church employees weren't as prim and proper as Mae had envisioned them to be.

The woman reappeared in the reception area. "Walter is still tied up on the phone."

Mae smiled. "That's fine. I'm good." It was already twenty-five minutes past her appointment time, which would have normally pissed her off, but Patricia's words echoed in her head. *You could have a good career if you would lose your bad attitude.*

"You sure you don't want some water?" the woman asked.

"No, thank you. But can I ask you a couple of questions?"

The woman glanced nervously down the hall. "Ummm. Sure."

"Do you know what position I'm here to interview for?"

"This is the only one we have open right now." The woman tapped the empty desk beside her. "We filled the accounting role last week."

"I applied for receptionist, but Mr. Miller said he wanted to talk to me about something else."

The woman's eyes narrowed. Again, she glanced nervously down the hall, in the direction of the other offices. "I don't know then."

Maybe there was something the staff had yet to be told? That didn't bode well for the kind of workplace this would be. She placed a hand on her chest. "I'm Mae, by the way."

"I know. I greeted you when you first came in." The woman's tone was flat, like she wanted to discourage Mae's friendliness. She certainly didn't offer her own name, like Mae had hoped she would.

"What do you do here at the church?" Mae pushed. She wanted to know everything she could about the inner workings before she met with Walter Miller.

The woman jabbed a thumb behind her. "I'll see if Mr. Miller's phone call is over," she said before she disappeared down the corridor lined with offices.

Two minutes later, a short, balding Black man rushed down the hall, his hand extended. Nervous energy vibrated off of him, like a battery-operated toy grinding away in a corner. "Mae. So sorry to keep you waiting. I'm Walter Miller."

She stood and shook his hand.

"I thought that would be a quick call, but those board members sometimes get a little verbose," he said.

Noted, but would members of the board be involved in whatever job Walter Miller wanted to talk to her about?

He motioned for her to join him in walking down the hall. Most of the five or six offices were empty, but a couple held middle-aged white women, typing away at computers on their desks.

He led her to the last office on the left and motioned for her to sit in one of the guest chairs at his desk. He closed the door behind them and then sat in his chair. "Thank you for coming in on such short notice." He leaned toward her, his forearms braced on the flat surface. "I happened to see your résumé for the receptionist role, but as I said on the phone, I want to talk to you about a different position."

"Which is . . . ?" She had little patience for the fake intrigue. The more he stalled, the more skeptical she became.

"Halsey Green, the founder of our ministry, has a personal assistant." He paused, as if waiting for her reaction.

Ahhhh. So she now understood why her résumé had been plucked from the stack. It wasn't a career path she would have willingly pursued—not after her first nightmarish go-round as a personal assistant—but she was desperate for a job.

Walter continued. "It's separate from the administrative staff that I oversee, but I help him hire for the position."

"And that position is open now?"

He crossed and uncrossed his fingers in rapid succession. "It will be. Soon."

So someone was about to get fired. She wondered what that person had done to displease the minister, but she kept her mouth shut. Diplomacy and tact would likely be necessary to help Halsey Green keep his life in order. She needed to display those now. "Can you tell me more about it?"

"It's what you might expect—a lot of personal errands for both Halsey and his wife, Dawn. Overseeing the household staff. Fielding phone calls. Knowing which ones to put through and whom to make go away—in a nice way, of course." Walter paused and smiled. "Halsey would need your utmost discretion." He peered at her over his glasses. "And your utmost loyalty."

"How many household staff members are there?" Managing other people had been the least favorite part of her jobs in recent years. She had enough of her own crap to deal with without having to worry about other people too.

Walter looked up at the ceiling as if trying to remember. "I'd say maybe three or four housekeepers. A nanny. A couple of gardeners. I think the pool care is contracted out, so maybe six or seven staff members on the full-time payroll. Oh, and there's a personal chef who prepares dinner for the family a couple of nights a week."

Good Lord. Weren't clergymen supposed to take a vow of poverty or something like that? How did a minister afford such a lavish lifestyle?

Walter continued. "You'd be in charge of the household finances too—the payroll, the groceries purchased by the personal chef, the cost of the kids' activities, payment of the contractors, that sort of thing."

"I assume I would get to meet the Greens before I took the job?" She'd seen a picture of Halsey on the church's website. He appeared to be maybe mid-forties—a little older than her—with a full head of dark blond hair, longish on the top and combed to one side, with the sides cut short. His suit looked tailored to his slim, athletic frame. His perfect teeth could have been caps. He looked more like a gameshow host than any minister she'd ever seen. But Mae didn't remember seeing any pictures of his wife, Dawn.

"Meeting Halsey and Dawn would be step two of the interview process, but let's not get ahead of ourselves." He shuffled some papers on his desk until he found what he was looking for.

She leaned forward to look. A copy of her résumé.

"I want to ask you about your time with Ms. Summers," he said.

Of course he did. Hannah Summers had been one of the biggest mistakes of Mae's life. Mae had snagged an interview with the recently retired Olympic gold medalist—a native of Tallahassee—as part of her Women in Leadership course during her sophomore year of college. The two had hit it off and young Mae had been flattered when the thirty-five-year-old media darling had asked her to become her personal assistant and travel companion. How stupid Mae had been to give up a full-ride scholarship to follow this . . . unbalanced person . . . on her speaking engagements around the country.

Mae had managed Hannah's antics behind the scenes for several months. Had done her best to not let anyone discover how wild her boss had become after years of unwavering discipline in the pool. But it wasn't until Hannah's infamous spectacle on national TV that the world knew just how unstable she'd become. The screaming and howling and groping the male host on the network's morning show had been the end of Hannah's speaking career. And no speaking career for Hannah meant no money to pay Mae's salary.

By then, Mae's full-ride scholarship had vanished. She'd worked a full-time job as a receptionist in a dentist's office while taking classes at night to finish her degree. Paying for her classes on her own, because Mama sure as hell didn't have any money to help her with it. It had taken Mae seven years total, but she was proud of her degree.

She'd taken an entry-level job at a marketing firm and fought her way into PR from there. But Walter Miller didn't need all those gory details. "What would you like to know about my time with Hannah?" she asked.

"Without . . . divulging any secrets, tell me the kinds of things you had to manage behind the scenes for her."

"I did most of the things you mentioned earlier—fielded phone calls, turned away fans, decided which business opportunities were worth her consideration, worked with the accountant on her expenses, booked her travel—"

"Anything . . . unusual?" Again, Walter Miller peered at her over his glasses, his gaze filled with intensity.

You mean, other than batshit crazy?

"She could be 'difficult'"—Mae made quotation marks in the air—"at the venues where she spoke. I prepared the staff members in advance and smoothed things over with them after we'd left. Your basic damage control."

"Until the whole fiasco on the morning show."

Mae nodded. Until Hannah Summers imploded her own life, along with Mae's. But she needed to appear confident now, not to wallow in how things had gone so wrong, so fast. "That job taught me a lot about the importance of public personas and how to make someone look good on social media." The minister would need that, too, no? She'd seen enough megachurch leaders on TV to know they were public figures. Actors. Showmen. "It was really the start of my career in public relations."

"And that's why I thought you might be a good candidate for the position with Halsey—part personal assistant, part guardian of his public image."

"Can I ask why the previous person left the position?" Not that the woman knew she was leaving yet. Walter had already made that clear.

"She"—Walter seemed to be choosing his words carefully—"didn't always embrace the Greens' way of doing things. And when she disagreed with their approach, she made it known."

Mae nodded. Knowing when to keep her mouth shut had been a lifelong struggle for her too. Patricia would have categorized it under *bad attitude*.

Walter continued. "We need someone who can exercise good judgment. Someone who knows when to keep quiet, regardless of her personal feelings and beliefs."

Mae's cheeks heated. She hoped her skin hadn't turned too dark a shade of red. "Sounds exactly like my job with Hannah Summers."

"And why did you leave your job with Into the Florida Wilds?"

A wave of anxiety cascaded through her. Did Walter Miller know what had happened in Tallahassee? "My brother lives in Jax Beach. We haven't spent a lot of time together in recent years, and I wanted to mend that. Family is important, you know." She motioned to a couple of pictures on the nearby bookshelves.

He chuckled. "That I do know. Those are my grandchildren, Thomas and Delilah."

"They're adorable."

"Thank you," he said. "Have you found your church home since you've moved here?"

She uncrossed one leg and crossed the other, then forced herself to stop fidgeting. "I've only been in town a week or so, but I plan to attend Sunday's service at PALM."

He smiled and stood. "Well, we'd be honored to have you join our congregation." He extended his hand. "We'll be in touch soon about the job."

She stood, too, and shook his hand, thankful the interview was over.

He made his way to the office door and opened it. "Are you in town the next few days?"

She had no money to go anywhere, so she was stuck in Jax Beach for the foreseeable future. "Yes, sir."

"I need to see when Halsey would be available for an interview, but I know he's eager to get the position filled."

"So you're recommending me to move on to the next step?" she asked.

He smiled. "I am, indeed."

"God bless you," she said, giving him her sweetest fake-Christian smile.

The rest of the world lied to get what they wanted, so—dammit—she could too.

Chapter Five

"Halsey Green?" Cole asked two mornings later when Mae was in the kitchen with him, up before dawn. "Why the hell would you interview with *that guy*?" Cole hadn't been cross with her since their discussion about Angie's makeup bag.

"He's the founder of—"

"I know who he is. His face is on billboards all over town." Cole's tone held a derisive edge.

"And what's wrong with him?" She poured a cup of coffee from the old percolator. She missed her mornings when Cole was already at work by the time she woke up.

"Do you even *go* to church?" he asked.

"No, but I wouldn't be working for the church, anyway. I'd be his personal assistant. They're calling this a 'working interview,' whatever that is."

Cole scoffed. "Yeah, well, I'd hold out for something better if I were you."

The problem was, not one of the other places she'd applied had even responded. Whether she liked it or not, Halsey Green represented her best hopes of getting a job. So she'd spent a couple of hours last night studying the PALM website and watching some YouTube videos about the basic beliefs of the

Christian faith. "You still haven't told me what's wrong with him."

Cole turned to face her, like he wanted to make sure she paid attention to what he was about to say. "First of all, everyone in town thinks he's a shyster."

"Except for the huge crowd that fills that ginormous church every Sunday?"

Cole ignored her sarcasm. "And second of all, I was flipping through the channels a couple of weekends ago, looking for the NFL pre-game show, and I ran across his church service on TV."

"And?"

"I never saw so much writhing and moaning and carrying on."

Mae laughed. "On TV? During a church service?"

"I'm telling you, it was more drama than I'd seen in a long time. He kept running from one side of the stage to the other, holding up his hands and crying, and he had on one of those headset mics like Beyonce wears during a concert. And people kept falling down in the aisles, and they probably started talking in tongues after I turned the channel, but I had to find out what ESPN had to say about the Jags defense." Cole poured the rest of the coffee into a king-sized thermos.

"So there's nothing wrong with going to work for him? I mean, he may be a little overly dramatic, but he's not a perv or anything."

"The worst part was, he kept asking for money over and over again. Sending the ushers through the aisles with the offering plates and flashing the phone number of their 'donation line' on the screen, like raising funds to pay for that huge campus of theirs was all they were interested in."

Mae barked out a sarcastic laugh. "I thought you were just flipping through the channels. Sounds to me like you watched the entire thing."

"I kept going back. I mean, it was like a bad reality TV show. I couldn't look away. The way they were acting would've been funny if it hadn't been so frightening."

"Well, I don't have a lot of other options. If I go to work for him, I'll be sure to stay away from the scary little church ladies." She said the last few words in a meek, squeaky voice.

"You joke now, but that dude is trouble. I'm telling you."

At least Mae could rely on what she'd come to think of as her internal warning system—that odd quirk that allowed her to see—right on a person's skin—when they had less-than-honorable intentions. She wished that quirk didn't come with the pounding in her eyebrow, but still, she felt more grateful for it than anything. Since people in general were crap, her "gift" served her well.

Cole took a final swig from his coffee mug and headed toward the back door. "I've got to get to work."

Mae leaned against the counter, glad he was gone. Glad she hadn't told him that the interview was actually at Halsey Green's *house*. No telling what her brother would have had to say about that one. Whatever it was, she didn't want to hear it.

When Walter Miller had called yesterday, he'd said the entire Green family would be there this morning—Halsey and Dawn and their two elementary-aged children, whom the nanny would be shuttling off to school.

The early morning "working interview" was necessary be-cause Halsey was scheduled to appear live on the morning show of one of the local TV stations, which would require him to drive into downtown Jacksonville. And since he and Dawn planned to leave later in the day for a weekend away, 6:30 a.m. was the only timeslot available for Mae's interview. Was he always up at that time of day? Would a 6:30 start time be the norm? She added these to her mental list of questions.

She took the last sip from her mug, then cursed Cole for taking the rest of the coffee she'd brewed. Of course, she'd known he was selfish. Why else would he have left his little sister with a mother whose *raison d'être* was to collect low-life, pervy boyfriends? Thank God Mae had gotten out of there before one of them went beyond creepy leers to actually touch her.

Back in the bedroom, it took her a few minutes to tie her pink paisley scarf so that the big snag in the woven fabric didn't show. She'd worked hard the night before to figure out an outfit that might be conservative enough for a minister. She would be glad when she could afford to buy some new clothes.

Finally, she was ready. She typed the address she'd scribbled down yesterday into the maps app on her phone and went out to her car.

All the beach communities ran together, and Halsey's town was the next one down from Jax Beach. The words Ponte Vedra Beach still didn't roll off Mae's tongue the way it did for the locals, but she was getting better at saying it. It was apparently where a lot of the rich people lived and even had its own famous PGA golf tournament on TV every year. Mae's closest encounter with the sport had been when she and David

Pollack had stolen a golf cart at the Alachua County Fair, years ago. Mama had been off God knows where that weekend, but luckily David's dad had talked the sheriff out of pressing charges.

Mae followed the directions her phone gave her until she reached Roscoe Boulevard. Pines and palm trees lined the two-lane road, making the scene look almost rural, but almost every lot off to her right held a large house. These mansions—some with ornate security gates—sat far back from the road. Others had garages and what appeared to be guesthouses out front, closer to the street.

The sun lightened the cool gray sky, but patches of fog lingered off to her right, back by the houses set deep on their lots. Finally, she glimpsed a boat hoisted high inside a boathouse, farther away than the main house. *There was water back there.* The intracoastal waterway? The geography seemed to make sense. The body of water ran the entire length of Florida.

She slowed and looked at the address in her phone again. Was this really Halsey Green's street? These huge houses seemed better suited for CEOs and hedge fund managers and professional athletes than for ministers.

His address was, in fact, on Roscoe Boulevard. Only 1.8 miles ahead, meaning he lived in one hell of a neighborhood. Surely his house was on the non-water side of the street. Otherwise, he'd have to justify to his congregation why their minister—the guy on *their* payroll—lived in such a high-dollar location.

And didn't these mansions epitomize one of the many things wrong with people? All these rich bastards waking up in houses like this while millions of other people worked two or three jobs just to pay the bills? She and Cole had eaten restaurant leftovers each of the last four nights, which allowed her to save some of her grocery money for the security deposit on her next apartment. Cole didn't seem to have a lot of money to spare, either. He'd been promoted to manager a while back, he'd said, but what that meant was longer hours with no additional pay since he now held a salaried position.

Yes, a big divide separated people like her and Cole from people who . . . well . . . lived on this road. But if Halsey Green had this kind of money to throw around, maybe he'd slide her a bonus every now and then. The salary Walter Miller had told her over the phone was decent, but not Roscoe Boulevard-worthy, based on what she saw from the street.

Her GPS warned her that her destination was one hundred feet ahead on the right. So Halsey's house *was* on the water side of the street. She turned between two off-white pillars that had to be ten feet tall. They, like the three-car garage to her right, were made of coquina—a mixture of shell fragments and corals cemented together to create a definite Florida feel. The main house that sat on the back of the property looked more like a boutique hotel than a single-family residence. The modern design combined the same coquina exterior with sharp angles, wood accents, and a multitude of glass.

The circular drive held a maroon SUV and a black BMW. Mae pulled behind the Beemer and watched a moment as a woman in denim shorts and a tank top rearranged the contents in the back of the SUV.

Mae got out of her car and approached the woman. "Excuse me? Ms. Green?"

The young woman's shiny black ponytail swished behind her as she turned. She let out a light-hearted chuckle. "Oh, no. I am not Dawn." She was Asian and had a slight accent from another country, but Mae couldn't place it. "I am Akira, the nanny."

"I'm Mae. I'm here to interview for the personal assistant job." She would have stuck out her hand, but Akira's arms were full of baseball bats and a volleyball.

"Yes. So sad about Joy, but . . ." Akira shook her head—an indication that she wouldn't continue speaking—then turned to place the baseball bats inside the SUV.

"Was she the personal assistant before?" *The one who got fired?*

Akira turned back to face Mae. She motioned with her chin toward the house. "Go up the front steps and knock. They are in the kitchen waiting for you."

Mae turned. The imposing double doors were a couple of car-lengths away. Bold, teal-colored wood framed large panes of intricately beveled glass. The teal stood out against the exterior walls—a burst of color in an otherwise flawless field of ivory. "It was nice to meet you," she said without returning her gaze to Akira.

The other woman didn't answer, and Mae heard a car door shut behind her. Just as well. Mae's focus needed to be on what awaited her beyond those big, statement-making doors. She took a deep breath, blew it out slowly between her lips, squeezed her shaking hands open and shut a couple of times, then walked up the three wide stairs and knocked.

Inside, two figures—blurred by the beveling of the glass—sat toward the back of the house. One stood and headed her way. She willed her heart to stop pounding so hard.

The door swung open, and a mid-forties blond gave her a wide smile. She wore turquoise yoga pants and a matching form-fitting workout shirt.

Mae took a step back—an involuntary reaction to the deep silver hue that ran along the woman's jawline. But the rest of her made-up skin had the smooth flawlessness of a cover model. Mae might have thought her internal alarm system had short-circuited, but the telltale rippling in her eyebrow told her it worked just fine.

"You must be Mae. Come in, come in." The woman's accent was from Southern Georgia, if Mae had to guess. She stepped aside so Mae could enter. "I'm Dawn, Halsey's wife. Can I get you some coffee?"

"No, thank you." She didn't want to appear jittery during the interview, and her hands already shook.

A dark, furry thing—a scraggly, balding cat?—scampered through Mae's feet and down the hallway. She halted her step mid-stride so as not to trip over it. A surprised noise escaped her throat.

Dawn gave a dismissive wave. "Don't mind him. Billy Graham takes *stranger danger* very seriously."

Down the hall, the cat disappeared inside a doorway tucked underneath the staircase.

"Your cat's name is Billy Graham?" At least the Greens had a sense of humor.

"Yes, and don't worry. He's on a couple of different meds. It's a nervous condition. He won't stop licking himself. It's like . . . nonstop. And he's peeling all his fur off."

Mae glanced in the direction the bedraggled cat had run. She'd only seen him for a fraction of a second, but she'd guess that pale gray skin was exposed on half of his body. Uneven patches of black fur covered the rest. Poor little guy.

Dawn's sandals clicked on the hardwood floor, which made Mae realize she should follow. They walked past a formal dining room toward the back of the house, which was large and open. Two-story-tall windows showcased a swath of the intracoastal waterway as wide as two city blocks—much wider than most of the lots Mae had seen as she drove down Roscoe Boulevard. A boathouse sat off to one side so as not to spoil the view. A swimming pool filled much of the yard between the house and the intracoastal.

The light-colored great room had the vibe of an upscale beach house with a large but cozy living room with a tiled fireplace, the biggest kitchen Mae had ever seen, and a round four-top table that sat in an all-glass corner—a breakfast nook of sorts.

Halsey rose from the table and came toward her—the silver on his thin, angular features mimicking the Tin Man even more than most people.

The rippling under her eyebrow felt, as always, like someone's fingers running up and down a piano keyboard, only this time it hurt like hell. Like needles prickling along her browbone.

She tried to tamp down the apprehension that buzzed through her body. If she hadn't needed the job so badly, she might have left right then.

"Mae." He smiled and extended his hand. He looked exactly like the pictures she'd seen on the church's website. Well, except the pictures on the website hadn't included the silvery sheen.

She tried not to stare at his too-perfect teeth. "Nice to meet you, sir."

He poured himself another mugful of coffee and made his way back to the round table, motioning for her to join him.

"I'm glad you could come so early this morning," he said.

She glanced around the big room one more time before she sat, taking it all in. Everything seemed staged—from the books artfully displayed on the coffee table to the pristine kitchen countertops to Dawn's bright pink nails and perfectly-coifed hair. As in the pictures on the church's website, Halsey's suit appeared to be tailormade.

Mae folded her fingers into her palms as she sat, hiding her ragged nails. "Thank you for seeing me this morning."

He lowered his long, lean frame into the chair across from her. Dawn busied herself in the kitchen—not part of the official interview but close enough so she could overhear it.

"Walter gave me his notes from his interview with you," he said. "Sounds like you had quite the work experience with Hannah Summers."

Walter Miller hadn't written down a thing during their interview, but what did Mae care? Whatever he'd told Halsey, it had landed her this interview. "Yes, sir. I had my hands full with that job."

"Just so you know, neither Dawn nor I plan to behave that way on national television." He smiled good-naturedly at his wife.

"Do you actually *appear* on national television?" Mae asked. Maybe he was a bigger deal than she thought.

He winked at her. "Not yet, we don't."

All three of them gave a polite laugh. Mae wondered if he was an optimist or just full of shit.

"So, tell me, Mae." Halsey took a sip of his coffee. "How much of your time with Ms. Summers did you spend as a personal assistant and how much did you spend on public relations?"

Her gut continued to tell her to leave, but her brain intervened, reminding her that she had no other job leads. "My job with Hannah changed over time. At first, it was personal assistant tasks—travel arrangements, making sure the organizers of her speaking engagements had her photo and official bio, answering emails from fans, making sure they weren't filling every hour she was in town with lunches or cocktail hours or dinners or whatever because she needed some down time. Things like that. But over time, as she became less . . . stable . . . that's when I started having to cover for her more and more."

He quirked an eyebrow upward. "You think public relations is having to cover for people?"

She rushed to correct herself. "No. I mean, not solely. It's making people look good. Putting the best spin on things. Protecting someone's image."

He raised his chin—not really a nod, but almost—and shared a knowing look with Dawn, who still stood in the kitchen, behind Mae's back. Mae wondered what part of his image needed to be protected. Did a lot of people have the same reaction Cole had to Halsey's preaching style? Or maybe there were parts of Halsey's life he didn't want the public to know about?

"And how does one protect the image of another person, particularly someone who's a public figure?" he asked. Like Walter Miller, he took no notes. The only thing on the table between them was his coffee mug and a large vase filled with yellow tulips.

"You make sure that everything going out for public consumption—photographs, interviews, social media posts—is in keeping with the desired image. A minister, for example, would have a different image than, say, a rock-and-roll band."

Again, he smiled over Mae's head to his wife. "Let's hope so."

"Everything needs to be consistent with the brand." The more relaxed Mae got, the cockier she felt.

"So I'm a brand now?" He seemed amused.

She shrugged. "In a way, yes. Do you not agree?" She wished she could see Dawn's face. It was hard to read the room while looking only at him. Maybe she was pushing too much. Sharing too many of her own views. Walter Miller had said the previous personal assistant hadn't done a good job of keeping her opinions to herself.

Halsey's gaze briefly moved the pool deck out the window as he seemed to think about her question. "I guess I am a brand of sorts. The church has a brand, and I'm an extension of that."

Dawn walked up behind Mae and put a hand on her shoulder as she leaned in and placed an unopened bottle of cold water in front of her.

"Thank you," Mae said.

Dawn smiled and nodded.

"Tell me about a time your loyalty to Hannah Summers was tested," Halsey said.

Interesting question. Walter Miller had talked about loyalty too. Why was that such an important topic for these people?

Mae gazed out onto the water, buying time. Wondering why Halsey seemed more interested in her ability to defend him in the public eye than her skills as a personal assistant, which was technically what the job was supposed to be for. "How was my loyalty to Hannah tested?" she repeated his question as memories of that awful time in her life flashed through her mind.

She raised her thumb to indicate her first answer. "For starters, I had people try to bribe me for access to her or private pictures of her in bed or whatever. Obviously, I didn't take the bribes." Mae raised another finger. "The wilder she got, the harder my job got, but I stuck with her until the very end." Mae now realized how stupid that had been. Her workload had doubled, her stress level had quadrupled, but her pay never changed. "Until all of her speaking engagements and sponsorships had been cancelled."

"Was there anything else?" he asked.

He was undoubtedly testing her. Making sure she wouldn't spill Hannah's secrets the way he wouldn't want her to spill his. But, oh, she had so many examples to share. Like how Mae had lied to the police after Hannah had torn up the ladies' room at a bar in Austin. Or how Mae had had to return an antique letter opener Hannah had stolen from a benefactor's house "for the fun of it."

Mae cleared her throat and squirmed in her chair. "I promised to protect Hannah's privacy, so I prefer not to share more specific examples, even though there are . . . plenty."

He slid a side-eyed look to his wife, then returned his attention to Mae. "And you would give me those same assurances?"

She nodded once. "I would."

"And to me?" Dawn's voice came from behind her. It was more stern, less friendly, than before.

She turned to look at the woman. "I would." Mae jerked back around—startled by the scrape of Halsey's chair scooting across the hardwood floor.

He stood and downed the rest of his coffee. "Then let's get to the working part of the interview. You came prepared?"

She stood too. "I'm not sure what I'm supposed to be prepared for." She looked from Halsey to his wife and back again, suddenly as nervous as when she'd first arrived.

He leaned down toward her. "A personal assistant needs to be prepared for anything." His coffee breath washed over her as he spoke. "Surely your time with Ms. Summers taught you that."

Chapter Six

Mae stood alone in the Greens' kitchen as Dawn walked Halsey to his car. She would google his morning TV interview later in the day—a bit more research on her prospective employer.

She used the time alone to take in more of the details of this expensive-looking space. The large, open concept great room consisted of the kitchen breakfast nook and living room.

In the kitchen, two ovens flanked the wall to her left—on the other side of an island the size of a large dining table. The huge refrigerator, which Dawn had opened earlier, hid behind ivory-colored cabinetry that matched the rest of the kitchen. A long faucet-looking thing came out of the wall over the cook-top. Mae had seen something like that when she'd thumbed through *Southern Living* in the grocery store checkout line a while back. A pot filler, they'd called it. Apparently rich people couldn't be bothered to lug pans of water from the kitchen sink like the rest of the population.

The focal point of the living area was the massive floor-to-ceiling fireplace made of flat brownish stones, stacked one on top of the other. Pops of yellow pillows accented the blues of the upholstery. Instead of a TV, wall-to-wall bookshelves filled the room. She walked over to browse the Greens' collection—everything from JFK biographies to Harlen Coben novels. The biggest surprises to Mae: a bunch of spicy romances and an entire section of books on how to make money. What was a minister doing with well-worn copies of *Think and Grow Rich* and *Key Strategies of Multimillionaires?* She pulled a title from the shelf that caught her eye—*We Should All Be Millionaires.* Hell, Mae would be happy to be just a hundredaire. Anywhere but in her current financial rut. She turned the book over. Ha! The author photo on the back cover showed Rachel Rodgers, a Black woman. At least the good minister didn't limit his financial advice to a bunch of old white guys. Still, the location and size of his house likely meant that Halsey Green had bypassed millionaire status some time ago and now aimed at some goal beyond that.

The front door opened, startling Mae. She dropped the book and it thumped to the floor. Her face heated as she bent to pick it up. "I am so sorry."

Thank God it was a hardback. At least the cover wasn't damaged. She stood, avoiding eye contact with Dawn as she replaced it on the shelf. "Y'all have a great library."

Dawn poured herself another cup of coffee, apparently not angry at Mae's *faux pas.* "Are you a reader?"

"Well, I haven't gotten a library card here yet, but I will soon."

Dawn took a carton of milk from the hidden fridge. A row of silver still covered her jawline. "What do you like to read?"

"Love stories, mainly. Either romance novels or fiction that has a love story woven in." Mae knew it contradicted her generally sour attitude about the human race, but something inside her wanted to believe in happy endings. She barely admitted it to herself—much less talked about it—but maybe she could gain some bonus points with Dawn, whom Mae assumed was the romance reader in the house.

"So, let's get started on your tasks for the day," the other woman said.

Mae stiffened. She still didn't know if she was getting paid for today. Did the Greens expect free labor? And was it even legal to have her work without being on the payroll? "Walter told me I'd be here for about four hours?" She raised her voice at the end, making it a question.

"Something like that. We want to see how quickly you catch on to things. How resourceful you are." She motioned for Mae to follow her. "We don't need a personal assistant who has to have her hand held every step of the way."

"I'd be working for both of you?" Mae said to Dawn's back as they entered a hallway near the front of the house. She wanted to confirm what Walter Miller had told her.

"Mainly Halsey—he's got the most demands on his time—but I'd have things for you to do too."

They passed a wide door with buttons next to it. "Is that an elevator?" Mae asked. *An elevator?* In a personal home?

Dawn waved a dismissive hand as she stopped at the next door in the hallway. "It mainly gets used by the chef or the housekeepers when they're bringing in groceries or other supplies. I try to use the stairs. Gotta get my steps in every day, you know?" She smiled as she opened the door behind her.

Mae followed her into a laundry room the size of Cole's kitchen. The center island was filled with a mishmash of items—plastic shopping bags and boxes and new gift bags still folded flat. The same creamy ivory cabinetry as in the kitchen lined the walls. The granite countertop dipped to form a lower, built-in desk. A laptop sat closed on its surface.

Dawn placed her hand on the back of the ladder-back chair that was pushed under the desk. "This would be your workstation. The internet is all connected and the email already set up. Your address would be Assistant—all spelled out—@Ha lseyGreen.com."

So the minister had his own domain, separate from the church. Perhaps a way to make money from his name, like TikTok influencers who got sponsorships based on how many followers they had? A minister would have followers, but in a different sense of the word. Mae made a mental note to look him up on social media.

Dawn frowned. "Did you not bring a pad and pen to write things down?"

Mae's face heated. "No, ma'am. I wasn't sure what to expect."

The woman sighed and rummaged through the desk drawer. She withdrew a scrap of paper and a pen. She handed them to Mae and repeated the email address slowly so Mae could write it down.

Then Dawn turned and indicated the contents of the island. "This is one of your projects for the day. The ladies from my tennis league are coming over for lunch later in the week, and each one will get a gift bag while they're here." She expanded one of the decorative bags and plucked some items from the boxes on the island. "Each woman gets a candle, a jar of this lotion from Paris, and a box with a silver bracelet inside. Let's leave the bracelets in the boxes. And *make sure* you take the price tags off of everything before you stuff them in the bag."

Mae lifted a candle from the box and turned it over. Fifty-eight dollars? For a candle the size of a beer can? She swallowed. "Yes, ma'am."

"Then top off each bag with a couple of sheets of tissue paper and tie one of these ribbons around the handles." Each piece of the ensemble had the same magenta-and-green motif. A matching set. Definitely not from the dollar store.

Dawn moved to the other side of the island and lifted a sheet of paper. "Once all the bags are put together, here's the list with everyone's name on it. Use this glittery pen to write a name on each of these tent cards." She held up an ivory card with a green border and showed Mae how to fold it in half. "I'll set the table with their bags and their place cards the morning of the luncheon."

Mae nodded. "Got it." Maybe Dawn expected her to write down some notes, but how hard could this be? Still, she needed to impress the woman. She moved a box on the island, set her piece of paper down, and wrote. *Candle. Lotion. Bracelet. Price Tags. Name Cards.*

Dawn gave a possibly fake smile when Mae looked up. "There's something upstairs I need to show you." She waggled her fingers for Mae to follow.

They passed the elevator and front door as they walked to the other side of the house, where a staircase led them to a light-filled second floor sitting area with a TV. Game controllers sat on the coffee table in front of the couch.

Dawn motioned toward the three doors leading off the sitting area. "These are the kids' rooms, plus the nanny's room.

And this is your next project." She lifted a crooked shade off a contemporary-looking lamp—one of two that sat on the table behind the couch. "Gretchen was bouncing her volleyball around up here and Griffin swatted at it and one of my favorite lamps got broken."

Mae schooled her features, trying not to frown at Dawn. Did the woman expect her to be a handyman *and* a personal assistant?

Dawn continued. "The problem is, this model is no longer being made, so you're going to have to search to find another one. Maybe eBay? Or some high-end consignment shop online? The thing is, we bought it in Denmark, so I guess you'll need to figure out the Denmark version of those places."

Mae's jaw clenched. All within today's four-hour gig? "This is where you test my resourcefulness." She said it with a smile, but what she really wanted was to ask why the hell lamps from Target weren't good enough for the children's game room.

Dawn grinned and tapped the end of Mae's nose with her forefinger, like she was a fricking puppy. "You got it."

"Anything else for me to do today?" Surely this had to be the end of it.

Again, Dawn waggled her fingers for Mae to follow. She headed back down the stairs. "Figure out when the Bolles spring break is and—"

"Wait. Bowls? Like in bowling alley?" Mae said to Dawn's back as they descended to the first floor.

Dawn giggled. "You *are* new to town, aren't you? It's Bolles. B-O-L-L-E-S. It's a private school."

Of course it was. Why would a minister's kids go to a lowly public school?

"Anyway," Dawn said as they entered the kitchen. "Figure out when their spring break is, then find us potential villas to stay in out in Aspen. Four or five bedrooms—Akira will go with us. It has to be ski-in, ski-out. We've always gone to Vail, but we want to give Aspen a try this year. I've got a call in to the Woodruffs to see where they stay out there, but I haven't heard back."

"Is there, like, a price range you're looking for?"

"Don't worry about that for now. You're not booking anything. You're just sending me what's available for those dates." The woman pointed her bright pink nail to the sheet of paper in Mae's hand. "Send a list of the links to DivaDawn@d mail.com. The email address should auto-populate from the assistant email address you'll be using."

Mae couldn't stand it any longer. "Am I getting paid for my work today?"

A look of confusion crossed Dawn's face. "It's a working interview."

"Yes, and . . ." Mae held the other woman's gaze, unwilling to back down.

"You'll need to work that out with Halsey."

"Who isn't here right now." Mae kept her voice even, but her insides roiled. Granted, she had nothing else to do that day, but she sure as hell didn't like being taken advantage of. And she wouldn't save the money she needed for her own apartment if she spent her hours working for free.

She took a deep breath as Patricia's words about getting control of her bad attitude echoed in her brain.

Dawn stepped into what looked like a butler's pantry and came out with a purse. She hung it on her shoulder. "Okay, well, I've got to get to an appointment. The housekeepers will be here in a couple of hours, in case any questions come up."

Mae's mouth gaped. "You're just going to leave me here? Alone in your house?"

Dawn gave her a duh look. "You've got work to do."

"You just met me."

Dawn's expression softened. She placed a hand on Mae's arm. "Honey. We're Christian. We believe the best in people."

So Diva Dawn was either stupid or naïve or both. Mae wouldn't steal anything, but maybe she should, just to teach them a lesson. A lot of other people would if left alone in a fancy house like this.

"Don't do anything that makes a lot of noise," Dawn said. "No loud music or anything like that. We need to keep Billy Graham as calm as possible. And maybe check on him every now and then? He pretty much stays in his bed in that closet under the stairs."

And what—exactly—would Mae do if the cat looked upset? She didn't even know Diva Dawn's phone number to call in case something in the cat's demeanor looked amiss. But the sooner Dawn left, the sooner she'd stop assigning Mae new tasks. "Will do."

Dawn opened a cabinet door near her head and took out a pill bottle. The silver tinge now covered her entire face. "If something agitates him, give him one of these kitty Xanax."

Seriously? This morning got worse by the second. Mae wondered if she could down a few kitty Xanax to help with her *own* agitation.

Dawn opened a door and punched a button on the wall. The garage door raised behind her. "Halsey will be in touch about the job. It was nice to meet you."

Mae raised a hand in goodbye and waited for the sound of the garage door to go back down, then looked around again. She usually made snap decisions, but this one had her stumped. Did she do the work with no guarantee of payment? Or did she go outside, get in her car, and leave the silvery wannabe multi-millionaires behind?

CHAPTER SEVEN

Forty-five minutes later, Mae set the next to last completed name card beside the others on the laundry room island. She'd done her best to make sure each letter was perfect. She'd learned early on that the glittery magenta ink smeared at the slightest provocation. After having to throw out three ruined place cards, she had one card and one name left. Hopefully, Diva Dawn wouldn't care that there weren't any extras after Mae finished.

Mae glanced at the time on her phone as she picked up the last name card. She'd placed a call to Walter Miller at the church before she'd started working, but he had yet to return her call.

She picked up the last card and the glittery pen. Her jaw locked—a sure sign of her concentration on the task in front of her—as she set pen to paper.

J-E-N-N-I-F-

A loud, grating noise ripped through the air. Her hand jerked, causing the pen to skitter off the card at the top of the second *E*. Magenta ink bloomed on the white quartz countertop.

"Mother F—" She stopped herself. She was, after all, in a minister's home. She didn't want any nanny cams ratting her out for foul language.

She worked up a ball of spit on her tongue and ran her thumb through it, then scrubbed at the ink on the countertop. Luckily, it came off, but the last card lay ruined.

And what the hell was that noise?

She rushed to check on Billy Graham, who sat ready to pounce in the little, slanted-ceiling closet under the stairs. His large round eyes signaled fear, but he hissed and swatted at her when she bent to comfort him.

Mae backed away from the cat and marched toward the kitchen, following the offensive, repetitive sound. Outside the wall of windows, a white-haired man with a jackhammer pounded away at a corner of the patio, leaving a pile of sandwich-sized concrete pieces in his wake.

The decibel level jumped as she opened the back door and rushed outside. "Whoa. Whoa. Whoa," she yelled.

The man didn't hear her, so she ran up to him, circling her arms in the air to get his attention. Finally, he turned off the machine and lifted the protection off one ear.

"What are you doing?" she asked, exasperated.

The older man looked at her like she was an idiot. "I'm busting up this concrete."

"But you can't—"

"Can I help you?" A stern male voice came from behind her.

She turned. A thirty-something white guy in faded jeans, a Lynyrd Skynyrd T-shirt, and scuffed work boots marched toward her. His dark brown eyes blazed below close-cut copper-colored hair.

"Why is he doing that?" She motioned wildly with one arm toward the grizzled guy bent on demolishing the Greens' patio.

"We can't put the new deck in until the old patio is gone." The redhead's deep voice had a rich Southern drawl.

"Do you have the right address? I mean, are you supposed to be at the Greens' house?" Dawn had mentioned only the housekeepers—not that some work crew would be here to destroy their backyard. And surely she would have mentioned that when she talked about Billy Graham's need for peace and quiet.

The man narrowed his eyes. "Who *are* you, anyway?"

Though his words challenged her, no silver tinge lingered on either of these men. She placed her hands on her hips and squared her stance. "Who are *you*?"

As he opened his mouth to answer, a black and gray streak shot out the open door of the house and around the corner. "Oh, shit. Billy Graham!" She turned to the men. "See what y'all have done? Their cat got out." She turned back to the fence in time to see Billy Graham slide between two wrought iron rails and escape to the front yard. She took off at a run and yelled behind her. "He has some kind of nervous condition. He's supposed to remain calm."

She reached the fence, which had to be more than six feet tall with a pointy finial on top of each vertical rail. There was no gate on that side of the house, so she ran back to the patio.

The men just stood there, staring at her like she was some kind of circus act.

"Can you at least help me get him back inside?" she barked.

"You keep at it, Joe," the younger man pointed to the jack-hammer. "I'll help her find the cat."

She turned to face the younger man head on. "Really? He can't take a break for five minutes? All that noise is going to scare the cat away."

"Seems to me like the cat's already gone." The older man spit a stream of tobacco onto the lawn as Mae turned to glare at him.

"Five minutes," she said, looking from one man to the other. "That's all I'm asking."

The younger man—the redhead—blew out a frustrated breath. "Take a break, Joe."

"Thank you," she said, though her sarcastic tone wasn't nearly as gracious as her words.

She cut through the house and out the front door with the redhead behind her. His heavy work boots clunked onto the wooden planks as she surveyed the long, expansive front lawn from the elevated porch. There was no sign of Billy Graham, but then multiple beds of tightly-packed plants and bushes filled the yard—the perfect place for a cat to hide.

Tension and anger wound through her body. "I can't believe he ran out."

"That's what happens when you leave the door open." He gave her a sideways glance.

"If you two hadn't been making all that noise—"

He made a T with his hands—the symbol for a time-out. "Shouldn't we find the cat now and argue about this later?"

She let out a frustrated groan, hating that he was right. "You look under the bushes over there. I'll look on this side of the yard."

That sounded like a great idea, but a football field's length of land lay between the house and the road. And the more time Billy Graham spent outside, the more time he had to get farther from home.

The two split up. She looked under the white pickup truck now parked in the driveway. The side read *Ezra Watts – Construction Project Management.* No sign of the cat under there, so she continued on to the beds of orange hibiscus and neon purple bougainvillea and large clusters of sawgrass.

Calling "Here, Billy Graham" proved too much of a mouthful, so she reverted to "Here kitty, kitty, kitty, kitty." She heard the man doing the same from the other side of the yard.

Moisture gathered on her scalp and at the base of her neck. Her blouse stuck to her back. Thank God she'd shed her pink scarf in the laundry room. It would have made her even hotter. She leaned against a live oak and took off her ballet flat to dump the sandy soil out of it. This whole finding-the-cat fiasco only added to the time she'd need to spend at the Greens' house, and it wasn't even calculated into the initial four-hour estimate. When the hell was Walter Miller going to call her back?

She took an extra second while she was in the shade to glance toward the man on the other side of the lawn. He squatted at each bush and shook it a bit, making sure Billy Graham wasn't hiding underneath. The guy might have a bad attitude, but at least he seemed to really care about finding the cat. Maybe he had a pet at home that meant a lot to him?

She had just bent over to take her second shoe off when he yelled across the yard. "Taking a break over there?"

She held up her ballet flat. "Getting the sand out of my shoe. Didn't know I was going to be four-wheeling it today." His work boots were better suited for this task.

He gave a dismissive wave and walked to the next bed of plants on his side of the yard.

A few minutes later, the jackhammer roared to life in the backyard. She spun to glare at the man who helped her search for Billy Graham. He raised his arms as if to say, "What did you expect?" and made no movement to stop the noise. There was no way the cat would come back home with that racket.

Thirty minutes later, the pair had reached the front of the Greens' property but still hadn't found the fugitive. If he'd left the yard, then he could be anywhere—in a neighbor's yard, in the empty field across the street. Mae's skin and temper were both about to boil. Halsey and Diva Dawn would have to pull out all their Christian forgiveness if Mae lost their stupid cat. She could feel this job—her only current hope of an income—slipping away.

She was walking toward the redhead, who crouched under a bush, when a car slowed on the other side of the ten-foot-tall pillars that flanked the driveway.

The window rolled down and an older woman called to them. "Excuse me."

The man stood and looked at the car.

"Yes?" Mae asked.

"Are y'all looking for a black cat?"

Mae couldn't believe this stroke of luck. She took a step toward the car. "We are."

"He ran across the road right in front of me." She laid a hand on her chest. "I'm so glad I didn't hit him."

"And where was that?" the man asked.

"Right in front of the Crawfords' house."

"The Crawfords'?" Mae asked.

The old lady looked surprised. "Carl and Emma. Surely you know the Crawfords."

Mae shook her head.

"They're the ones with the beautiful Christmas lights every year."

"Which house is it?" Mae asked.

"They had all blue lights last year, with the one bright yellow star all the way at the top."

Why could this woman not answer a simple question? Mae's jaw clenched. She ground out her words in slow, deliberate syllables. "Listen. I already told you I don't know—"

The man rested a hand on her arm as if to calm her down. Or was it to shut her up? She didn't need some stranger governing her communication with other people.

"Can you point out which house it is, please?" he asked the woman in a syrupy sweet tone that accentuated his Southern accent. "Maybe how far down it is? Or what kind of architecture it has?"

Mae glared at him, though she had to admit that with all the custom-built homes on this street, a brief description would identify where the Crawfords lived. Maybe he could finally get some useful information out of the old biddy.

The lady pointed to the waterfront side of the street, behind her. "It's the all brick with the stained glass above the front door."

"Got it. Thank you very much." He dipped his head to her. "Have a good day, ma'am."

His hand now encircled Mae's arm right above her elbow. He started walking—with her in tow—toward the Crawfords' house. "It's not going to do you any good to piss off the one person who's seen the cat."

She jerked her arm away. "Let go of me or I'm going to call Ezra Watts and tell him you're accosting the clients."

"I'm pretty sure you're not a client."

"Yeah, well, that doesn't make your behavior any more acceptable."

He stopped walking and turned to face her. "Who *are* you anyway? I don't remember seeing you at Halsey's house before."

"I'm . . . doing some work for the Greens." No need for him to know about her working interview—whatever that was. The more she thought about working off the payroll, the stupider she felt.

"You have a name?" he asked.

"Mae Van Dorn."

They took a few steps in silence.

"And you?" she asked. "Don't *you* have a name?"

He stopped walking and stuck his hand out. His mischievous gaze caught hers. "Ezra Watts. It's nice to meet you."

She rolled her eyes and grunted, then begrudgingly shook his big, calloused hand before they resumed walking. At least she could see the house the old woman had described up ahead. They walked in silence until they turned into the driveway. Thank goodness the large security gate stood open. Without speaking, the pair split up and started searching the yard, calling for the cat.

"Mae." Ezra called to her a few minutes later. He stood at the base of a large live oak. He put a forefinger to his lips, then pointed upward.

She couldn't see anything up in the tree but walked gingerly in his direction, not wanting to scare Billy Graham. "Is he up there?" she whispered when she'd reached him.

Ezra took a step toward her and pointed upward. He had a sweaty-but-recently-showered scent about him—not at all unpleasant. "About twenty feet up. Right next to the trunk."

She still didn't see the cat, but she took a step back, uncomfortable with her reaction to Ezra's closeness. She looked toward the house. "You think we can borrow a ladder?"

He jumped and grabbed the lowest branch with both of his hands. "Don't need one."

His arm muscles bulged against the sleeves of his T-shirt as he pulled himself up to sit on the branch. Then he scrambled up to stand on it and started to climb. She enjoyed the view of his backside as much as she had his arms.

Her phone rang. She stepped away as she pulled it from her pocket. He didn't need to overhear her conversation, regardless of whom it might be.

"Don't mind me. I won't fall," Ezra called in a sarcastic tone.

What, did he think she would be his spotter? He'd certainly skedaddled up there without any hesitation. Just another ludicrous man being ludicrous.

She chose to ignore him and answered the phone. "Walter, I'm glad you called."

"I'm...uh...returning your call. How's it going at Halsey's this morning?"

"Okay, I guess. The cat got out, but some construction guy is helping me get him down from a tree now."

Walter made a sound of delighted surprise. "It's not Ezra Watts, is it?"

"Ummmm. Yeah?" She glanced over at the tree. Ezra had climbed about halfway up it now, but Mae still hadn't spotted the cat. "You know him?"

"Haven't seen him in years, but Halsey told me he'd hired him to redo his dock."

Ahhh. So she'd been right about these men being trouble. "They're not anywhere near the dock. They're busting up the patio in the yard."

"Yeah. Same project. But that's not why you called me, is it?"

She turned her back to Ezra and the tree. "No, actually I called to ask about my interview this morning."

Walter's tone got more serious. "What about it?"

"Well, other than the fact that they left me at their house alone . . ." She paused, reining in her attitude. "It seems kind of . . . odd . . . that they expect me to work this morning without getting paid."

"Did Halsey not give you money before he left for the TV station?"

"No." Her voice held more vehemence than she'd intended.

"Maybe he's testing you. Seeing how assertive you are."

She'd already tired of these little games and she didn't even work for them yet. Not to mention the silvery warning her internal alarm system had provided. "Yeah, well, if I'm going to spend half my day knocking things off their to-do list, I'm going to need to get paid for it."

"Point taken. I'll make sure you get a check. Is there anything else?"

"No." As much as she dreaded it, she would do her best to find the discontinued lamp and the villa in Aspen. She needed this job, regardless of how ridiculous these people were.

"Well, do a good job at whatever they asked you to do. And tell Ezra I said 'Hi.' My boys played baseball with him for years. He's a good guy."

Mae thought he was a smartass, but that was beside the point. "I'll let you go. I've got a list of things I'm supposed to do before I leave." And she couldn't get back to them until Billy Graham was safely back inside.

"Come to my office day after tomorrow. Maybe around noon? I'll make sure to get you some money, and I should know about the job by then."

They said goodbye and hung up, then Mae walked back to the tree. About twenty feet up, Ezra lay flat on a branch, one arm outstretched toward Billy Graham, who had crawled out to the much thinner end. There was no way Ezra could climb out to get him. The end wouldn't support his weight. She wished she could help in some way.

He said soft, soothing words as he slowly inched away from the trunk. She couldn't tell what he said, but his deep voice sounded melodic, comforting. For a split second, she almost felt jealous. When was the last time a man had spoken to *her* that way?

Billy Graham crept toward Ezra's outstretched hand, but the man didn't grab for him. Instead, he waited for the cat to come closer, sniff his hand. He scratched under Billy Graham's chin. The cat raised its head, offering Ezra better access.

"Grab him," Mae said in a stage whisper.

But instead, Ezra's large hand moved to Billy Graham's ears, cupping his head and rubbing both ears at the same time. The cat luxuriated under his touch, offering different parts of his head and chin for Ezra's ministrations.

Finally, Mae couldn't take it any longer. "Will you hurry it up? I have things to accomplish this morning." Maybe Ezra Watts, construction project manager, could goof around with this cat all day, but Mae Van Dorn, unemployed PR professional, could not.

The thought jarred her. Could she even claim to be a PR professional anymore? Her only interview since her move had been for a personal assistant position. A glorified secretary. With a desk in a laundry room, of all places. Even if she got the job, she'd be embarrassed to tell her PR friends back in Tallahassee about it. Not that any of them had stayed in touch with her. Further evidence of the many ways the human race had let her down.

Ezra's voice pulled her back to the situation at hand. "I can't just grab him. He needs to think it's his decision to come to me. Have you never had a cat before?"

She gave a frustrated grunt instead of answering. Like it or not, she was at Ezra's mercy when it came to getting Billy Graham out of the tree.

Slowly, Ezra reached out and placed his hand underneath Billy Graham's front armpits. He pulled the cat into his chest and nuzzled him with his chin—the sound of his deep murmurings barely audible to Mae. She had never seen Rocco move so gently in the entire two years they'd been together.

Finally, Ezra tucked Billy Graham into his chest and started their descent. Mae stepped to the side. Ezra had only one hand with which to climb, and she certainly couldn't catch a two-hundred-pound man if he fell. No way was she going to get injured for a family who had yet to employ her.

Things were going far better than she expected when suddenly Billy Graham let out a murderous screech and swatted a paw at Ezra's face.

Then, like a slow-motion parachutist, the black cat plummeted through the air, twisting as he fell. His side ricocheted off a wide branch and he changed direction, claws extended, headed straight for Mae.

Chapter Eight

Billy Graham seemed to fall from the tree in slow motion, twisting and turning as he tried—and failed—to grasp each limb he bypassed. Mae watched in horror as the cat headed straight toward her, its desperate howls mingling with Ezra's curses from above.

Miraculously, the cat landed like a loaf of bread in her outstretched arms—an ESPN-worthy catch, though she had no idea how it had actually happened. She quickly trapped the scared animal against her chest. He twisted and tried to climb up her shoulder, scratching the hell out of her arm in the process, but she grabbed the back of his neck and tucked him under her other arm, his legs pinned close to her body so he couldn't get any traction. She'd seen her friend Ashlyn Bradley's brother trap a stray like that when she was a kid and had never dreamed she'd be so rough with an animal. But there was no way she would let Billy Graham escape again.

"Nice catch," Ezra called as he continued his descent.

"Nice fumble," she said.

He lowered himself from the tree so that he stood next to her. "He clawed the shit out of my face." He turned to show her a deep, bloody scratch that started next to his eye and continued about six inches down his cheek.

She held out her forearm to show the big gash the cat had left on her too. "At least one of us was man enough to take it and not let go."

He grunted. "Man enough, my ass."

She motioned with her head in the direction of the Greens' house. "Let's get back before he shreds both of us to death."

Ezra studied her. "Tell me again how you fit in at Halsey's house?"

"I didn't tell you before, but I'm interviewing to be his personal assistant." She didn't like admitting to it. She was a PR professional, for God's sake. Not someone's glorified secretary. She tucked Billy Graham tighter against her and started walking.

Ezra caught up and walked beside her. "It probably doesn't help your chances that you let the cat escape."

Her gaze snapped to his. "No one told me there would be construction workers here, even when they talked about how important it was for Billy Graham to not get agitated."

"Stupid name for a cat."

She snorted. "Yeah. No kidding. What do you know about them anyway?"

He shrugged. "The Greens? Not much. This is my first project working for them."

"Isn't Halsey kind of Jacksonville-famous, though?"

Ezra swiped a hand over his forehead, then wiped the sweat on his jeans. "I knew who he was, sure, but I don't go to his church or anything like that. Do you?"

She barked out a laugh. "No. I just moved to town."

The closer they got to the Greens' house, the louder the sound of the jackhammer.

"Pretty sweet job for a newcomer," he said.

She slid him a sideways look. "Maybe none of the locals want to work for him."

He chuckled. "I guess that could be true." He seemed to be enjoying their banter as much as she did.

"I mean, you'd think there'd be someone from his congregation who'd want the job."

"Maybe he doesn't want someone he knows that close to his private affairs. I mean, bank accounts and business dealings, not—you know—mistresses and whatnot."

He wouldn't be the first minister to have committed adultery. "You think he has something to hide?"

Ezra held his hands out in front of him. "Whoa. I didn't say that."

"Well, I'm good as long as he doesn't turn out to be a raving lunatic. I already worked for one of those."

"Sounds like there's a good story there."

"Aren't all bosses horrible people?" she asked.

"I kind of take issue with that. I'm a damn good boss. My guys are like family to me."

She grunted. Patricia probably thought she was a good boss too.

"Are you always this cynical?" Ezra asked.

She gave him a fake grin. "I'm usually a delightful mix of hope and happiness."

The cat squirmed in her arms. Ezra reached out and took it from her, careful of those lethal claws.

"How long have you had your own company?" she asked once Billy Graham had settled in his arms. Ezra looked to be about her age. She wished she'd started her own PR firm years ago so that she no longer had to work for other people.

"About a decade." He gave her a proud smile. "I got my contractor's license the day after my twenty-sixth birthday. We specialize in docks, decks, patios."

A droplet of sweat slid down her spine. "Must be big business in Florida."

"That's the plan." He reached up and gently touched the big scratch on his face.

"Did the Greens not mention to you that their cat can't tolerate loud noises?"

He frowned. "How am I supposed do a construction project without making some noise every now and then?"

She looked over at the partially bald cat whose eyes darted around as if eager to find an escape. Its little feline mouth hung open as it panted. "Well, the least you can do is help me give him his kitty Xanax when we get back to their house."

"What? No. I've already spent too much time dealing with that stupid cat."

She reached over and scratched behind Billy Graham's ear, hoping to give the poor guy some comfort. "It's what you get for making me leave the back door open."

"I need to get back to work," he said as they turned into the driveway and walked past the pillars that marked the edge of the Greens' property. The jackhammer stopped in the distance.

"Can you call that guy and tell him to keep it quiet until we get Billy Graham inside?"

"You're kind of a pain in the ass," Ezra said, but he handed the cat to her, pulled his cell from his pocket, and called Joe to tell him to take another break until Ezra got back to the patio.

"So will you help me or not?" she asked once he'd hung up. "I've got to get him calmed down before the Greens get home."

He glanced up at the sky as if pondering his answer, then returned his attention to her. "If I help you give him the pill, will you leave me alone after that?"

She smiled and nodded. "I will."

He let out a long, slow breath. "I'm only doing this because you might become Halsey's assistant."

She leaned toward him conspiratorially. He smelled of soap and man. "You want me to put in a good word with the boss?" she teased.

"If you're gonna be paying my invoices, I want to be on your good side."

She stood straight again, increasing the distance between them. A sting of rejection flashed through her. She'd thought she'd sensed a spark of attraction between them, but apparently he only appreciated her as a potential payer of bills.

Well, fine. It wasn't like she needed another boyfriend so soon after Rocco anyway. She still desperately needed the job with Halsey Green, even if Ezra Watts didn't want to flirt with her under the minister's nose.

CHAPTER NINE

Mae looked at the clock on the computer screen and groaned. She'd been at the Greens' house for four hours and was just now sitting down to research villas in Aspen. She hadn't even started trying to locate the discontinued lamp, but at least she and Ezra Watts had—miraculously—gotten a pill down Billy Graham's throat. The cat had hissed, taken another couple of swipes at each of them, then slinked off to his little room under the staircase. But that damn jackhammer had pounded outside since then, and when Mae had last checked on the cat, he'd been licking his fur like it was on fire and only his saliva could put it out.

The jackhammer bothered Mae, too, with its constant pounding. The ache in her head moved to her shoulders when she saw the results of her first Google search. One night in a ski-in, ski-out condo cost more than her entire month's rent in Tallahassee. The more she learned about this family, the more she became convinced that Halsey Green ran a moneymaking business, not a church.

Down the hall, the front door opened.

"Miss Mae? It's me, Klara, the housekeeper. I didn't want to scare you."

Mae rose and exited the laundry room. A short, fifty-ish-looking white woman stood in the foyer holding three or four plastic grocery bags. Her accent indicated she wasn't from America. Maybe Eastern European?

"Hi, I'm Mae."

"Miss Dawn texted and told me you would be here. Is there anything I can get for you?"

"No, I'm fine, but thank you." She started to return to the desk, then stopped. "Actually, can I ask you a few questions?"

"Sure. I try to answer them if I can." Klara bustled into the kitchen. Mae followed her.

"Ah, I see the workers are here." The older woman placed the bags on the counter and started unpacking the groceries. "Mr. Halsey will be happy."

Yes, as long as he didn't know about Billy Graham's earlier escape.

"Do you like working for them?" Mae tried to sound casual, but this would likely be her only chance to talk to another employee in private before she'd have to decide about the job.

Klara took three lemons from a bag and smiled. "They are good people."

Not based on the silvery tinge on both Halsey's and Dawn's faces earlier that day. Mae's internal alarm system was almost always spot on. The recent episode with Rocco had proven that. She unpacked some groceries—a tray of organic chicken, a head of cauliflower, a package of Oreo cookies—and set them on the counter for Klara to put away. "How long have you worked for them?"

The woman looked off into the distance, as if trying to remember. "Seven, maybe eight years. There are three of us who work here, all from Bosnia. They took me in when I first got to this country." She picked up a carton of eggs and opened the fridge.

It was the first real evidence of Christian values Mae had seen that morning. "So this personal assistant job. It's a good one?"

"I think so, yes."

"The previous woman—Joy Do you know why she left?"

"Mr. Halsey is an important man. He has much to accomplish."

"And that's why Joy left?" That didn't make any sense.

Klara shook her head. "I do not know Joy's business."

Mae stayed silent for a moment as she contemplated her next question. Outside, Ezra paced back and forth, a phone pressed to his ear.

Klara finally spoke. "When Mr. Halsey makes a decision, he expects everyone to follow." She wagged her forefinger back and forth in front of her face. "No questions. No trouble."

Mae studied the older woman's face, trying to see if her expression would reveal anything further, but Klara turned away and busied herself in the pantry, clearly finished with the conversation.

"I appreciate the information. Thank you." Mae headed back to the laundry room.

No questions. No trouble.

But Mae knew herself well. People had let her down too often for her to put up with anyone's bullshit. That often meant asking questions. Challenging people. Calling them out when they were evasive or not telling the truth.

It sounded like she and Halsey Green might clash, but she had to make this work. Her living situation with Cole wasn't as bad as she'd expected, and the rent on Ryan's bedroom cost less than she'd be able to find anywhere else.

Her internal alarm system had done her a favor that morning. The silvery hue on Halsey's face had shown his true colors—literally—so she knew to proceed with a high degree of caution. But she had plenty of practice keeping her guard up. Protecting herself.

Yes, it was exhausting to never be at ease. To always be at the mercy of whatever bad intentions the human race chose to display on any given day.

She'd long ago accepted this as her fate.

And still she marched on, because—really—what other choice did she have?

***

Walter Miller lowered himself into the chair behind his desk in his office at PALM. He motioned for Mae to sit across from him.

"I've got good news," he said as he slid two one-hundred-dollar bills across the desktop toward her.

Her eyes widened. She looked up at him, then back down at the money, then back at him.

"Your payment for the other day," he said. "At Halsey's house."

"Both of them?" she asked, then wished she'd kept her mouth shut.

He smiled and nodded.

She slid the bills out from under his fingers and tucked them inside her purse. She wasn't sure what she'd expected from this meeting, but it wasn't this. Either the amount or to be paid under the table. But then, she wasn't an employee, so they couldn't exactly cut her a payroll check, either. "Thank you. I appreciate it." She started to rise from her chair, but he made a motion for her to stay seated.

"I told you I'd make sure you got paid," he said.

"And I appreciate it." She quickly did the math in her head. She'd stayed at their house for seven hours—three more than she'd planned—so this was twenty-seven or twenty-eight dollars an hour. She'd definitely take it, especially given that her income had been a big fat zero since she'd left Tallahassee.

Walter sat back in his chair and crossed his fingers over his large belly. "But the good news is, they want to offer you the job."

"Really?" She tried to look excited, though she had mixed feelings. Sure, it was an income—and a pretty decent one if they paid twenty-seven or twenty-eight bucks an hour—but the work itself annoyed her. Behind-the-scenes secretarial work for a bunch of high society tennis club women? *No, thank you.* A wild goose chase for a lamp made in Denmark when the Target in Jax Beach sold perfectly good lamps that worked just as well? Worst of all: That silver tinge that was especially pronounced on Halsey Green's face two days ago. Sure, people with bad intentions existed everywhere. She'd learned to never trust people whose skin had the silvery sheen to it, but a *minister*? Still, regardless of that dangerous omen, she needed to make some money. "That's great news. When can I start?"

He shoved a few pieces of paper in her direction. "You'll be working directly for Halsey, but he uses the church's application process. You'll need to fill it out so they can run a background check before you start."

She looked up, confused. "They already left me alone at their house." Seemed ridiculous to do that and *then* run a background check.

"It's just a formality. Part of the hiring process." He frowned. "Is there something you're worried we'll find out about?"

"No. No. Nothing to worry about." She smiled to reassure him. Luckily, she'd rarely been caught doing things that could have resulted in a criminal record. And, besides, what teenager didn't drink beer or smoke a joint every now and then?

"You'll have access to some of Halsey's bank accounts, so they'll be running a credit check too."

"Is bad credit a crime?" She said it jokingly, but the thought of them delving into something so personal made her angry. Her shoulders tensed as she waited for Walter to answer.

"I guess the theory is that if someone is desperate for cash, they're more likely to make bad decisions."

Whatever happened to Dawn's statement? *We're Christians, honey. We believe the best in people.*

"I'm not going to steal anything from them, if that's what you're saying. Money or otherwise." She held his gaze, making sure he understood that she meant it.

"I didn't think you would."

But Mae couldn't help herself. "Don't some people have bad credit because their kid got cancer or their husband lost his job in some big corporate takeover or whatever? I mean, bad credit doesn't equate to bad character, does it?" Not everyone could live in a huge house on the intracoastal and take ski trips to Aspen. Some people—like her—got dealt shitty parents and an even shittier life and they struggled just to make it all work, but that didn't make them dishonest.

But then she remembered Klara's words: *No questions. No trouble.*

She raised her hand, palm facing toward Walter. "You know what? I shouldn't have said that. I understand why a credit report is part of the process, especially for people with access to money."

He smiled, apparently relieved that he didn't have to defend their application process. "We'll let you know if we have questions about anything that shows up in the report. You can't start until the results are back, and that will take a few days."

A few days? After taking so long to find a job, she couldn't afford any more days without an income. If she was a thief, she could have stolen things from their house when they'd left her there alone. But she couldn't be too pushy. Not with the man who represented her only current possibility for a paycheck. "Is there anything else I need to know?"

Walter fidgeted with a pen on his desk. He rearranged a stack of papers. Finally, he leaned forward, his palms together, his fingers pointing toward her. "In any organization the size of this one"—he chose his words carefully—"there are factions of people. Cliques, if you will. Halsey is clearly the leader of our church, but some people may . . . speak out against him. Try to get information from you they might think could damage his reputation. You need to know, above all else, that you work for him and that he expects your utmost loyalty. Those are the rules I live by, and those are the rules you'll need to live by as well."

She swallowed. This job sounded way more contentious than she'd imagined. Perhaps the conflicts with other people arose from whatever bad intentions had turned Halsey's face the bold metallic color. "Is he a good guy? I mean, does he deserve that loyalty?"

Walter nodded once. "Without question." Great confidence echoed in his voice.

She gave a fake smile. "Then I guess I can do it too."

He stood and shook her hand, then escorted her out to the lobby.

She trudged to her car, dazed. The last time Mae had given an employer blind loyalty, it had tanked her career. Mae had defended her boss's image, even as Hannah Summers's behavior veered more and more off the rails. Even when the reality became darker and more inexplicable. The disastrous ending had left Mae without a job and wondering what she could have done differently to protect Hannah. To protect herself.

How stupid could she be to promise that same blind loyalty to Halsey Green, a man she barely knew and who seemed suspicious at best? And why did it feel that—within the four walls of that church—she'd just made a pact with the devil?

Chapter Ten

A week later, Mae sat in the breakfast nook of the Greens' home, sipping a cup of coffee on her second morning of work. Though she'd been nervous about what Walter Miller might find on her credit report, he'd said nothing about it. He'd simply called, said her background check had come back okay, and asked if she could start the next day.

Klara, the housekeeper, had been there both days and had been friendly enough, but she had her own tasks to do in the rest of the house while Mae had been either glued to the computer in the laundry room or out running errands. She'd gotten the instructions for her first day's activities during brief conversations with Dawn, who had popped in and out throughout the day.

Mae had entered all the church's activities for the next three months onto both Halsey's and Dawn's Google calendars. Had cropped some family photos into squares to make them Instagram-ready. Had picked up an absurdly expensive white chocolate raspberry cake at a custom bakery in the historic Riverside neighborhood of Jacksonville and some fabric samples at a furniture upholsterer in nearby Atlantic Beach. She'd even found a replacement for the Danish lamp at the online estate sale for a property in Purchase, New York. Once she got Dawn's approval and credit card number, she'd buy it and have it shipped to them.

The one thing Mae *hadn't* done was see Halsey Green. She had, after all, been hired as *his* personal assistant.

But Klara had told her when Mae arrived this morning that he'd be downstairs in a few minutes and would like to meet with her. She'd given Mae a cup of coffee and asked her to wait for him in the breakfast nook.

She took another drink of her coffee—a custom blend from a small-batch roaster, according to the package of beans she'd seen Klara grind. The deep, rich flavor tasted a lot better than the store brand Mae usually bought.

Outside, Ezra dismantled a cabana that provided some shade to the pool deck. He'd nodded to Mae when he'd first seen her through the windows, but now he faced away from her, his faded green T-shirt pulled tight across his broad shoulders. Each time he picked up an armload of discarded wood to toss into the back of his pickup, his arm muscles bulged against the sleeves.

She cleared her throat and rotated her chair a few degrees so she no longer faced outside. The last thing she needed was for Halsey Green to come down the steps and catch her ogling the construction crew.

The sound of footfalls on the stairs made her sit up straighter. A few seconds later, Halsey strode into the kitchen, his hair wet and his gray suit impeccably tailored. Silver tinged his skin near his hairline. The rippling underneath her eyebrow felt more like an itch than a pain. Perhaps that meant he had better intentions than he'd had the other day?

"Good morning," he said in a commanding voice she could imagine booming over a microphone throughout the congregation.

"Good morning," Mae said. "Klara told me to wait for you here."

"Yes. I thought we should meet. An orientation of sorts."

She'd brought a legal pad to take notes. She waited while he poured himself a cup of coffee and added a splash of milk from the refrigerator hidden inside the cabinetry. He stepped out of the kitchen into the hallway and looked around, as if making sure no one else was nearby, before sitting across from her.

He took a sip of his coffee. "Let's address the 'Klara told me to wait here' comment first. Yes, Klara passed on a message from me to you, but keep in mind that you're her boss, not the other way around. She won't be telling you what to do."

"Understood." If he could see the disarray in her room at Cole's house or the stack of dirty dishes she'd left in his sink, Halsey would know she had no business overseeing a housekeeping staff. Thank God Klara seemed to know what she was doing and to be conscientious about it. "I oversee Klara and she oversees the rest of the housekeeping staff?"

He nodded. "That's right. Now, I wish I had more time this morning for us to get to know each other a bit, but I've got a busy day at the church, so I have to rush right into the ground rules for this job. Anything you see or hear stays with you. If I ever hear of you discussing any part of it with someone else, you will be fired immediately."

Not exactly the opening message she expected from a minister, but whatever. "Yes, sir."

He leaned to the side and pulled his wallet from his back pocket. "I'm going to give you our credit card and banking information, but this piece of paper never leaves this house. You don't buy anything that isn't for our family, and you move money out of the accounts only to pay our bills and expenses." He slid a piece of paper out and handed it to her.

She didn't unfold it. She could look at it later. She'd seen both Quicken and Bank of America icons on the computer in the laundry room but hadn't dared to click on them until he asked her to. "Yes, sir."

"I'm putting a lot of faith in you. Trusting you not to do anything that could . . . get you in trouble."

This felt like a reprimand, though she'd done nothing wrong. Anger bubbled from deep inside her, but she quashed it down. This guy obviously had a lot of money, and he had to be careful about who could access it. "I would never use the accounts for . . . unauthorized purchases."

"All the bank information feeds into Quicken, so why don't you go in there this morning and look around a bit? Familiarize yourself with the bills we pay, the ledger categories we've set up, that kind of thing. You'll need to put all of our purchases into the correct category—clothes or household items or utilities or whatever, so you can tell us how we're doing against our budget, which is also in Quicken. Walter said you did that sort of thing for Hannah Summers?"

"I was responsible for her business accounts." But Mae had never been given access to Hannah's *personal* finances. The thought of having access to Halsey's made her nervous. What if she made a mistake? "I deposited the money from the speaking engagements, paid the bills, that sort of thing."

He smiled. "Good. Anytime you get into most of the apps, it will send me a code—two-factor identification. I'll text you that code as soon as I get it, assuming I'm not somewhere I can't look at my phone."

So he'd know anytime she accessed their financial information. His way of keeping an eye on her. It made sense. She nodded.

"You should get the mail every day, throw away any junk or solicitations, pay any bills a couple of days before their due date, leave anything with a handwritten envelope—like birthday cards or invitations or whatever—on the kitchen counter for us to see when we get home that night. Any questions?"

"Does Dawn have a job too? I mean, you said 'When *we* get home that night.'"

He gave a little chuckle as he rolled his eyes. "She doesn't have a job, but she stays busier than I do most days. She oversees several committees at the church and is part of a tennis league, a garden club, a couple of book clubs, and on the board of several charities. She may be here some during the day, but not often."

"Should I prioritize any specific kind of work over anything else?" What she really wanted to ask was if the tasks he assigned to her should be completed before the ones assigned by Dawn, but that seemed too old-fashioned. Yes, he had a paying job—someone had to pay for this mansion—but Mae was too much of a feminist to imply that the man's work was more important than the woman's.

He seemed to ponder the question as he sipped his coffee. "I like the way you think, and, yes, anything to keep the house running smoothly and the finances in line takes precedent over the . . . fluffy stuff."

Like tennis league gift bags. Got it.

He stood and walked to the sink, placing his cup in it. "Any other questions?"

She stood too. "None for now. Thank you for your time this morning."

He took a pad and pencil from a nearby drawer and wrote something. "Here's my cell number and Dawn's. Don't share them with anyone. If someone needs me, give them the number to the church." Again, he wrote on the pad, then tore off the top sheet of paper.

"I appreciate the opportunity you've given me," she said.

"I appreciate having you here to make my life easier." He handed her the sheet of paper but didn't let go when she tried to take it from his fingers. "And your loyalty." He held her gaze longer than necessary, as if drilling those last words into her conscience.

She looked away, uncomfortable with his overly long eye contact. That word—*loyalty*—kept coming up in conversations about him. Like he expected people to be unquestioningly devoted to him. But she'd been betrayed too many times to hand out blind trust just because someone thought they deserved it.

Finally, he let go of the sheet of paper and turned to take his keys off the hook near the door. "Call me if you think of any questions."

She held up the paper. "I will."

When the door to the garage closed, she let out a long breath, grateful to be alone again. Away from the overbearing gaze of her new boss. He'd given her the same vibes she'd first gotten from "Scary Larry" Milstead, her eighth-grade science teacher, who intimidated her at first but ended up being one of her favorite teachers. Maybe Halsey would grow on her too. Of course, Scary Larry had never had silvery skin or custom-made suits.

She took one last glance out the windows toward Ezra, then made her way back to the laundry room, where she logged into Quicken, waited for Halsey to text her the code, then browsed through the last couple of months of expenditures. Where *did* a minister get that kind of money? The kids' schooling alone cost more than Mae had made in six months at Into the Florida Wilds. But there were also significant deposits from PALM and other entities with names that told her nothing, like LRC Enterprises or the Kearney Family Trust. But whatever—none of that was her business.

After sitting at her desk for an hour or so, she got up to stretch. She hadn't heard Klara in a while, so she wandered into the kitchen, which stood empty.

Mae went out on the front porch and stood there, breathing in the scent of the gardenias as she pretended this house belonged to her . . . or rather, a scaled-down version of Halsey's house. She'd never need a place that large. Since people were intolerable, her goal would always be to live alone. To live a simple life in a quiet house, away from the complexity and pain of other humans.

The front door opened behind her and Akira, the nanny, stepped onto the porch. "I wondered where you'd gotten off to," the other woman said.

Mae still couldn't place the woman's slight Asian accent. "I got the job."

Akira smiled. Her twentysomething skin was olive-toned and flawless—not a hint of silver in sight. "Yes, I know."

Mae held out her hand. "We met the other day, but I'm Mae."

The woman shook it, then withdrew her hand quickly. "Akira. I figured we should . . . get to know each other."

"How long have you worked here?"

"About a year, year and a half."

"Do you like it?" Mae would take all the inside intel she could get.

Akira inclined her head and gave a pointed sideways look at the doorbell.

Mae immediately understood the woman's message—the built-in camera captured everything they said, just as it would capture a delivery person or other visitor to the front porch.

Akria's smile appeared fake. "I *do* like it here. The kids are sweet. Much better than the little monsters I nannied for in Atlanta."

"Well, I look forward to working with you." Mae's words sounded stiff, but she now felt like an actor performing for Halsey's doorbell.

"I've got a couple of errands to run before I pick up the kids, so I'll see you later." Akira pulled a set of keys from her purse and headed toward the maroon SUV she'd packed with sporting goods the other morning. "Let me know if you ever need help with anything."

Mae waved, happy to have connected with the young woman. "Will do." Maybe Akira's experience with the Greens could help Mae along the way.

As soon as the nanny drove off, Mae went back into the house, retrieved her sunglasses, and started the trek up the long driveway toward the mailbox.

Only a couple of cars—a jeep with surfboards on top and a blue PT Cruiser—passed along the road as she approached it. Roscoe Boulevard was, in many respects, like living out in the country, though the elaborate PGA Headquarters and famous TPC Stadium Course were only a couple of miles away.

The blue PT Cruiser came up the road again—this time from the opposite direction—as she got closer to the mailbox. It slowed as she neared the road. Her step stuttered for a minute. A female jogger had been dragged into a car a few weeks ago in Tallahassee, but this was Ponte Vedra Beach, one of the ritziest parts of the metro-Jacksonville area. She continued walking, determined to look confident. To hide her fear and anxiety.

The car pulled off onto the shoulder on the opposite side of the road as she passed through the tall columns that flanked Halsey's driveway.

A fortysomething white man in khakis and a fitted golf shirt got out and waved. His small, thin stature eased Mae's nerves. She could probably take him if he tried to do her harm.

"Good afternoon," he called. "I'm Rob Lassiter."

She raised her hand as little as possible to return his greeting, while at the same time trying to convey that she had no interest in chatting with him. The sun's glare, plus his position on the other side of the road, made it impossible to see his skin clearly, but still, he made her uncomfortable. She reached the mailbox and opened it, taking out several envelopes and a couple of catalogues.

"Are you Halsey Green's new assistant?" the man called from behind her, still on the other side of the street. "If so, I've got a few questions I'd like to ask you."

CHAPTER ELEVEN

Mae turned from the mailbox to look at the man who'd just asked if she was Halsey's new assistant. Who was this guy? And what could he want from her? She shaded her eyes with her hand, hoping to get a better look at his skin, but he remained on the other side of the road—too far away for her to see much detail.

She stood there, not saying a word. Waiting to see what his next statement might be.

He apparently took her response as an affirmation. He strode across the street toward her. "Are you aware of the accusations being made against your new boss?"

"I haven't told you what kind of work I do, so I don't know how you'd know who my boss is." She did her best to buy some time. To figure out what this man's angle might be. Despite his challenging words, his skin remained a pale pink. *Interesting.*

He gestured toward the mansion with the notebook in his hand. "This is Halsey Green's house. Well, at least the house the church provides for him to live in. And Joy Jones left as his personal assistant a couple of weeks ago." He paused and raised his sunglasses to the top of his head. They nestled into his thinning brown hair. "By the way, do you know how I can get ahold of her? I haven't been able to track her down online."

"What was your name again?" she asked.

He dug a business card out of the front pocket of his shirt and handed it to her. "Rob Lassiter with Channel Ten, News of the First Coast."

Mae had assumed when she'd first moved to the area that so many company names included "First Coast" because it was the first region southbound travelers on I-95 came to when they crossed into the Sunshine State. But she'd learned that the region had been the first place in the continental United States that Europeans had settled. St. Augustine, just south of there, was the oldest continuously inhabited European-established city in the nation.

Either way, she was new to Jacksonville. She'd never heard of—much less seen—Rob Lassiter's TV station. "Well, it was nice to meet you." She turned and headed toward the house.

He rushed to follow her. She pivoted at the sound of his footsteps and let her gaze rest on where he stood, then back to where the Greens' property met the road, then back to his feet—making sure he knew he was trespassing. She'd learned at her old job that managing the media meant keeping them in their place.

"I just want to ask a few questions," he said, then rushed to finish before she could respond. "Have you heard about the growing contingent of PALM members asking about the church's finances? Some are even suggesting that an outside accounting firm that specializes in religious organizations be brought in to study—"

Mae held her hand up to stop him but softened it with a sweet, albeit professional smile. Perhaps this was the reason her internal alarm system had warned her about Halsey. "I'd be happy to pass on any questions to Mr. Green that contain names and verifiable facts, but it sounds to me like you're dealing in rumors and innuendo."

The man's eyes narrowed. "So you *are* his new assistant."

"I simply said I could pass on some questions to him."

He raised his notepad in front of him and slid the pen from the spiral binding. "Can you give me your full name, including the correct spelling?"

She hesitated. She *really* didn't want to get involved in whatever Rob Lassiter was alleging, but she figured this came with the territory of being Halsey Green's personal assistant. Walter Miller had, after all, plucked her résumé from the stack because of her experience protecting Hannah Summers's image and reputation. It might now be her job to fend off any journalists that tried to get to Halsey Green, but that didn't mean she had to give him her name. "Just refer to me as a bystander." She glanced again at the property line. "Someone present when you trespassed on the Greens' property."

"Are you a member of the congregation at Pathway to Abundant Life Ministries?"

She gave him an are-you-kidding-me look. She wasn't about to share any personal information with this guy. "My religious affiliation is none of your concern."

"Are you aware that some church members are asking why such a large percentage of the church's funds go to Halsey Green? They want to know why he has such an extravagant lifestyle." He pointed toward the house behind her.

Crap. She'd known something was up with the Greens. She steeled her expression, a small smile hardening on her face. "Again, I'll be happy to pass on any questions to Pastor Green that contain names and specific allegations."

"A good journalist doesn't divulge his sources."

"And a good employee doesn't expose her boss to unfounded accusations." She made a mental note to find out if the church had some kind of internal audit process. Maybe a finance committee that oversaw the church's money. Given the ample size of the PALM campus and the square footage of Halsey's house, there had to be a lot of cash coming from somewhere. And, besides, a good PR professional always understood the ins and outs of her client's business so she could intelligently answer any question that came her way. It was becoming more and more apparent why Halsey Green had hired a PR professional under the guise of a personal assistant.

Lassiter pulled his sunglasses down over his eyes. "I've got interviews scheduled with some of the church's administrative leaders next week."

Then why the hell are you bothering me? She couldn't decide which was worse—a potentially smarmy pastor or a pushy journalist. She had no respect for either. "Have a good day, Mr. Lassiter."

He took a step toward her. "Have you ever seen anything you would consider a misuse of church funds?"

She barked out a quick laugh. "I run errands for Halsey's wife—things like picking up birthday cakes and fabric samples. Neither of those could be considered high finance." But the figures she'd seen on the computer a while ago might be a different matter.

He stuck the pen back into the spiral of his notebook and took a step backwards. Despite his obnoxious behavior, his skin hadn't changed. It now glistened with perspiration but remained a definitive pink. "It's been nice to meet you. Maybe I'll stop by to see you again." He gave her a teasing wink.

"It's private property, Mr. Lassiter." She turned and walked toward the house.

"You might want to check the property records," he called after her.

She had no idea what he was getting at, and she didn't care. She raised her hand in a wave but didn't turn around again.

***

Mae waited nervously for the sound of the door from Halsey's garage to open at the other end of the house.

She'd texted him earlier:

A TV reporter showed up at the house asking questions about the church's finances. I've put him off for now but wanted to make sure you knew about the conversation.

He'd answered her back almost immediately:

Was coming home for a late lunch, anyway. Let's discuss in person. I'll be there about 1 p.m.

Now Mae nibbled on the chicken salad sandwich Klara had brought her, eager to impress Halsey with the way she'd held Rob Lassiter at bay. It had felt good to use her professional skills again—to use her brain to deal with the media. It sure as hell beat picking up fabric samples or stuffing gift bags for a bunch of tennis ladies.

Finally, the door to the garage opened. She rose, grabbed her plate, and headed toward the kitchen.

Halsey gave a nervous smile when he saw her. She didn't know him well, but he almost looked . . . a little panicky . . . ?

"Can I get you some chicken salad, Mr. Green?" Klara asked.

"Yes, thank you, Klara. Mae and I will be at her desk, so bring it to me in there, please." Once the housekeeper had turned her back to open the fridge, he made a quick, furtive motion toward the laundry room.

Mae got the distinct impression that he didn't want Klara to hear their conversation. She nodded, placed her plate in the sink, and returned to her desk at the other end of the house.

He followed her and shut the door to the laundry room behind them.

She leaned against the island, thinking perhaps the boss should take the only chair in the room, but he stood too.

"This TV reporter, was he a scrawny, little guy?" He held his hand up to indicate shoulder height on him. "Not much hair on top?"

"Yes. Rob Lassiter. He gave me his card." She dug it out of her pocket and handed it to Halsey.

"He just knocked on the door and asked to speak with me?" Halsey's expression had gone from tense to angry. His skin—which had been a normal pink when he'd first arrived home—now glowed with silver. Even his eyebrows had changed color.

She shook her head. "He stopped to talk to me when I went out to the mailbox. I saw him drive by before that, then come back from the opposite direction."

Halsey slapped his open palm on the big island in the middle of the room. "Damn it."

Mae startled, then took a step back, not ready to share the contents of her conversation with the journalist until Halsey calmed down.

"If he ever steps foot on our property, tell him he's not welcome. What kinds of questions did he ask you?" Halsey's eyes widened. "And, oh God, what did you say?"

They both turned at the sound of a soft knock at the door. Halsey jerked it open. Klara handed him a plate with a tiny scoop of chicken salad and a small helping of mixed fresh fruits. No wonder the guy was so trim. Klara had given Mae a heaping sandwich on a croissant and some barbecue chips on the side. Mae couldn't see the housekeeper, but a bottle of water, a napkin, and a fork appeared in the crack in the door.

Halsey thanked Klara, then shut the door, making sure it closed tightly. He turned, set his plate on the island, and nodded toward Mae. "Tell me about the conversation."

"He asked if I knew that members of the congregation were questioning some of the church's finances."

Halsey shoved his plate away from him. A purple grape rolled off of it and onto the floor near his feet. He didn't move to pick it up.

"And he wanted to know if I'd ever seen any evidence of misuse of church funds."

Halsey barked out a sarcastic laugh. "On your second day on the job?"

"I didn't tell him who I was or how long I'd worked for you. I tried to share as little information as possible."

Halsey placed both hands flat on the island and leaned toward her. "I was hoping you wouldn't have to deal with all this until later, but here's what's going on: There's a member of the church, Bull Williams. He's a local businessman used to getting his way on things—past president of the Rotary Club, big in the Gator alumni group, knows everyone in town. He wanted to use a portion of church funds to support a public school in a low-income part of Jacksonville, but that's not in keeping with the church's primary mission, so I turned him down."

He bent to pick up the grape before he continued. He set it on the island next to his plate. "So now he's trying to convince other church members that I've misused funds. It's all in retaliation for me not agreeing to his pet project, which, by the way, he only wanted to do because his daughter teaches at that school."

Interesting. So even the minister had enemies. She wondered if there was any truth to what Bull Williams was alleging. After all, she'd been suspicious from the get-go of how a minister could live in a neighborhood like this . . . and that was before she'd seen the silvery, telltale sign of someone who was up to no good.

Maybe what Rob Lassiter had to say was true. Maybe the "misused funds" paid for Halsey's kids' expensive private school and the family's vacations in Aspen. From the little she knew about Jesus, wouldn't he have wanted Halsey to give all that money to the poor and downtrodden? People like her, for example? "Mr. Lassiter said he's interviewing members of the church staff next week."

Halsey let out a long breath and paced one side of the room. This was apparently the first he'd heard of that. Finally, he stopped to face her. "Listen, the main reason I hired you was because of your experience with Hannah Summers. I'm going to need you to keep the wolves at bay for *me* the same way you did for her."

Mae nodded, though she felt angry at being duped. This was far more than a simple personal assistant job, and she did *not* want to be in the middle of two warring factions. Living through the Hannah Summers debacle had taught Mae that she didn't want a job that required her to defend someone's personal behavior. She made a mental note to get back on the job boards tonight. The Jacksonville area had a million people. Surely another job existed out there for her.

He looked at his watch. "I've got to get back to the church for a two o'clock meeting. Are we square now?"

"We're square." She'd sort through her anger later. Figure out what—exactly—she'd say to him about it once she'd calmed down. Old Mae would have immediately demanded a raise, but Current Mae knew she needed to gather her thoughts before opening her mouth. Maybe she'd absorbed more of Patricia's advice than she'd thought.

He left the room, leaving his plate behind. He hadn't eaten one bite of the food Klara had prepared him. So coming home for lunch had been a ruse. He'd wanted to talk face-to-face with Mae about her encounter with Rob Lassiter. That meant he took the accusations seriously.

Maybe there was some truth to what Bull Williams alleged, but what did she care? It was all just part of the job. Other people did worse things to support themselves.

Besides, if Halsey Green really had misused church funds, he'd been doing it before she came along, and he'd be doing it long after she left. It wasn't like she'd be here forever. If another job came along, she would gladly leave Halsey and Diva Dawn behind. In the meantime, though, she had to make this one work.

Back at Into the Florida Wilds, she'd opened her mouth about a smug, deceitful donor and had ended up getting fired over it.

She wouldn't be that stupid again.

Chapter Twelve

As if Mae's life wasn't bad enough already, she'd realized that morning that her car was 460 miles over the number on the little time-to-change-your-oil sticker on the upper lefthand side of her windshield. She didn't have any extra cash for an oil change, but she *really* didn't have the money for a costly repair if she let it go too long without being changed.

Maybe a local could give her a recommendation on where to get it done. She slid the sliding glass door open and stepped out onto what remained of Halsey's patio. "Hey there."

Ezra turned, and what appeared to be a genuine smile crossed his face. "Hey, what's up?"

"Do you know the cheapest place to get an oil change around here? I mean, I'd take some shade tree mechanic who'd do it on the side for not a lot of money."

He rubbed the back of his neck as he looked out over the intracoastal waterway, thinking. "There used to be some guy who lived over by the baseball fields—"

"Ezra." Halsey came out the sliding glass door and marched toward them. He must have just gotten home.

He looked cool in a crisp linen shirt and khakis—a stark contrast to Ezra's sweaty, end-of-the-day T-shirt and jeans.

Though it was past 6 p.m., heat and humidity still hung in the air, making it seem more like the middle of the day. Summer in Florida didn't end until sometime around the end of October.

Halsey got closer and peered at Ezra's cheek. "What happened to your face?"

Ezra reached up and touched the still-tender scratch. "A run-in with someone's cat." His gaze slid to Mae's.

But Halsey didn't seem to care. He jabbed a thumb in the direction of the driveway. "Are you aware there are a couple of Black kids messing around in your trailer out front?"

"That's Rodney and LaShawn. They're packing everything up for the night."

"They *work* for you?" Halsey asked.

Ezra nodded slowly, as if trying to figure out why Halsey looked so surprised.

"I haven't seen them before," the minister said. "And I didn't see them when I came home for lunch today."

Mae had seen them a couple of times, though not as often as the adult members of Ezra's crew.

Ezra took off his baseball cap and ran his fingers through his hair. "They're sixteen years old. One of their older brothers drops them off after school."

"And they work for you?" Halsey repeated.

Again, Ezra nodded slowly. He looked as stymied as Mae about the fact that Halsey didn't seem to grasp this. "They do."

Mae looked from one man to the other, gauging the reaction of each of them. Surely the minister didn't look down on the boys because of their race?

"You couldn't get *real* construction workers? Is that the deal?" Halsey's voice grew louder as he spoke. His face grew red. Beads of perspiration formed at his hairline. "I don't re-member your contract saying you were going to use underaged labor or—"

Ezra held up a hand, stopping Halsey's tirade. "I've got plenty of qualified workers. Some of the best in the business."

He'd told Mae the other day that some of them had worked for his father way back in the day. He'd seemed proud of his team.

Halsey flailed an arm in the direction of the front drive, where the boys worked. "So those kids are—what—here to do the grunt work? They're not actually working on my dock, are they?"

Ezra took a deep breath, as if to quell his anger before he answered. "I've got five or six high school kids working for me at any given time. It's how I give back to the community—by helping at-risk kids learn a trade they might use later."

Mae cocked her head to study Ezra, impressed by his altru-ism.

Halsey's mouth twisted in distaste. "'At-risk kids?' So they're all Black?"

The minister's words shocked Mae. She felt her eyes widen.

Ezra's steady gaze challenged Halsey. "Not necessarily, but would it matter if they were?"

The minister seemed to realize how his behavior must have looked. His posture softened. "No, of course it wouldn't."

"I didn't think so." Ezra ground out his words.

Mae wasn't sure she believed Halsey.

The sad fact about the South—and this northernmost part of Florida was definitely the South—was that many people still shared the same racist views of their ancestors. The younger the person, the more open-minded they often were, but there were still pockets of people who acted like they were raised in the era when Black people had separate restrooms and weren't allowed to eat in most restaurants.

Again, Halsey waved his arm toward the front yard. "Why am I paying for a bunch of unskilled labor? Wouldn't my project be less expensive without this little program of yours? If you didn't include those boys on the job?"

"That's not an option. It's how my company works." Ezra glanced toward the monstrosity of a house behind Halsey.

Mae wondered if he wanted Halsey to get the message: Surely a guy who lived in a place like that wasn't going to nickel and dime him about paying some high school kids a few bucks an hour.

Halsey looked up the intracoastal waterway for a few seconds, like he was gathering his thoughts, then returned his attention to Ezra. "That's not the main reason I wanted to talk to you, anyway." His take-charge tone had returned.

Ezra's shoulders seemed to relax. "What can I help you with, sir?"

"You'd initially agreed to have this project finished by December first."

Ezra nodded.

"But I committed today to host a fundraiser for the governor on November tenth."

Ezra opened his eyes wide, but kept his mouth shut.

"All the movers and shakers of North Florida will be here," the minister said. "So I'm going to need you to have it finished by then. By November third, actually, so the landscaping crew has time after you're finished to get in here and replant the bushes and flowers before the party."

"That's a full month before our agreed-upon date." Ezra's steady voice conveyed a confidence in his position.

Halsey raised one eyebrow. "Is that a problem?"

Like the minister had done before, Ezra looked up and down the intracoastal waterway, as if buying himself time. Expensive docks and boathouses rimmed the water behind each home—a seeming reminder of the kind of work Ezra could get if he got a glowing referral from Halsey Green. "That would be a really tight schedule. I don't want to agree to a revised completion date and then not meet it."

"It's a fundraiser for the *governor*." A mix of arrogance and pleading snuck into Halsey's voice.

Given what Mae knew of Ezra, she guessed he had little respect for the current governor of their state, so the argument might not have the allure Halsey thought it did.

"Let me crunch some numbers tonight," Ezra said. "Look at the schedule for when the various parts of the job are scheduled for completion."

Halsey clapped his hand on Ezra's shoulder. "That's my boy."

The minister's actions reeked of good ole boy cajoling. Mae wondered what was going on inside Ezra.

"Just to be clear"—he called as Halsey walked back toward the house—"I haven't committed to revising the date. Not yet, anyway."

The minister stopped and turned to him, a smarmy smile pasted on his face. "I have faith in you, son. The Lord will show you the way."

Ezra held Halsey's gaze for several seconds. "You suppose the Lord knows how to operate a backhoe?"

Chapter Thirteen

Mae sat in her car in the third row of the church parking lot, knowing she should head inside. Halsey expected her to deliver the book she'd just picked up from the Bookmark in Neptune Beach before his weekly staff meeting, where they'd be celebrating Walter Miller's birthday. Apparently, Halsey hadn't thought of it until that morning but had become convinced that Walter needed an autographed copy of the latest Steve Berry novel as a birthday gift.

She checked the time: 1:42 p.m. Eighteen minutes before the staff meeting. But the suspicious-looking transaction going on two rows in front of her held her attention. Was it a drug deal? In a church parking lot? The old guy in navy blue coveralls wore a nametag of some kind. The younger kid, a teenager, looked like a typical surfer—long, stringy hair, board shorts, no shirt. The two stood next to a beat-up, old sedan.

The younger guy held out a large baggie half-filled with something reddish-brown. The older man looked around the parking lot before taking it, like he didn't want to be caught doing so. The pair chatted a minute longer, then the teenager opened the back door of the car and reached into a big box in the back seat. Mae tensed. There could be any number of dangerous things in there. Guns would have been her first guess, given the size of the box. Or maybe drugs?

The older man's mouth fell open. He reached his hands out eagerly toward whatever the surfer dude held close to his chest as he turned from the car. The younger guy's long hair obstructed Mae's view as he lowered his face to the khaki-colored object. Were they smoking a bong? Right there in the parking lot?

The two men laughed and the younger one held out the bundle. The other man took it and raised it to his face as it squirmed. A puppy?

Mae snorted. To think a puppy exchange was a drug deal in the making. *Good Lord.* What was wrong with her? She'd always been a misanthrope, but this was ridiculous, even for her.

Her phone vibrated against the console of her car. A text from Halsey.

Are you almost here? Staff meeting starts in seven minutes.

She grabbed her phone, got out, locked her car, and headed inside before she realized she'd left the book on the front seat. She rushed back to retrieve it, thankful the bookstore had complementary gift wrapping so she hadn't had to deal with that extra step. If she ever got any extra money, she'd go back to that cute little shop and browse for herself.

Headed inside now, she texted to Halsey as she hurried toward the church entrance for the second time. She smiled at the two men as they talked. Each scratched one of the puppy's ears.

A fiftysomething white woman met Mae at the doors to the church. "You must be Mae."

Mae nodded, not sure who this woman was.

"I'm Barb, the new receptionist in the church office." She motioned toward the wrapped gift. "Halsey wanted me to get the book from you and run it to him before the staff meeting starts."

Ahhhh. So this was the woman who'd gotten the job that Mae had originally applied for. And by handing Barb the gift at the door, Mae could avoid going into the church offices and having to make small talk with the people there. Even better. "It's nice to meet you." She handed Barb the package. "I'm Halsey's personal assistant, so I suspect we'll see each other from time to time."

Barb smiled as she held the book in the air. "I'd love to chat, but Halsey's impatient for this."

Mae raised her hand. "Talk to you later."

The older woman scuttled off in the direction of the administrative office, so Mae headed back into the midday sun. The two men still stood next to the car talking. The big baggie sat on the hood. Mae could now see it was filled with dry dog food.

Since the book emergency had now ended, she had more time. She walked closer to them. "Cute puppy. A yellow lab?"

"Probably not," the older man said. She hadn't realized it from a distance, but he was Asian. His church nametag read *Conrad*. "They would have tried to sell him if that was the case, instead of just dumping him."

Mae's heart sank. "Someone *left* him? Like on the side of the road?"

The kid nodded. "You know that land they just cleared at the end of Hodges Boulevard? I saw someone open their car door and throw him out, then just drive off."

Mae turned her attention to Conrad. "So you're going to keep him?"

"Not if you want him." He held the puppy toward her. "He's really a sweet one."

She scratched the little guy's ear but knew that wouldn't work. She was more of a cat person to begin with, and besides, she couldn't take on a dog while she lived at Cole's house. And apartment complexes these days charged a bunch of money for pet deposits and monthly pet fees, not to mention the cost of food and vet bills. No, a puppy was definitely not in her budget. "I wish I could, but I don't even have my own place these days."

The man's eyes narrowed. "Aren't you Pastor Green's new assistant?"

"Mae Van Dorn." She wouldhave held her hand out, but he had his own hands full of puppy. "And you work at the church?"

Conrad nodded.

The teen grinned. "When he's not saving puppies."

Mae looked from one man to the other, confused by the statement.

Conrad chuckled. "I'm known around here as the guy who'll take in strays. I nurse them back to health, take them to the vet if they need it, then try to find them a new home. Sometimes I find them a new family. Sometimes they stay with me."

"Doesn't that get … expensive?" Since he wore coveralls, she guessed he was the church janitor. He couldn't make much money. But then the minister at PALM lived in a huge house on the intracoastal waterway, so maybe the employees made above average pay?

He shrugged. "I live in a house that's been in my family for years. Never married. Never had any kids." He nuzzled the top of the puppy's head. "These little guys are my family, so I spend all my money on them."

"How many do you have at any given time?" she asked.

"Ten. Maybe twelve. It kind of varies."

"Where do you live, anyway?" the teen asked. "I mean, the people in my neighborhood would flip out if someone had that many dogs."

Mae could see the kid's point. Houses in the beach community sat jam-packed together, often within five or six feet of each other, making the most of the valuable real estate.

He pointed to the north. "I'm off of Girvin Road, behind that little cemetery on the east side of the road. I got about five acres of land and no HOA."

Mae had no idea where that was, but it made her happy to know a guy like Conrad existed. That he provided a home to dogs who would otherwise be unloved. Uncared for. "Sounds like the perfect setup."

The kid reached into his car and took out a faded blue T-shirt. He slipped it over his head. "I've got to get to work. Thanks for taking him." He scratched under the puppy's chin one more time. "You be a good boy. I hear Conrad will take good care of you." He took the baggie of dog food off the hood and handed it to the janitor, then got into the beat-up car.

"So people know you take in strays and they just . . . drop them off here?" she asked Conrad as the kid pulled away.

He swallowed and glanced furtively toward the church. "I . . . um . . . try to have people bring them to my house instead. Walter doesn't want me taking time away from work, but that kid sort of just showed up today. People do that sometimes."

Ahhhh. So that explained why he'd acted so secretive when she'd watched them from her car earlier. "How long have you been doing this?"

He shrugged. "I don't know. Maybe fifteen or sixteen years. My way of helping God's creatures, I guess."

Mae realized it was the first bit of true selflessness she'd seen on these grounds. She slid Conrad a sly smile. "Working with dogs sounds a lot better than working with people."

Conrad tucked his head and chuckled. "Ain't that the truth."

The kid's tires screeching out of the parking lot drew their attention to the road. A blue PT Cruiser had its blinker on, ready to turn into the church.

Rob Lassiter.

He'd told Mae he had interviews set up with some of the administrative staff members, but wouldn't they all be in the staff meeting right now? Maybe he'd lied to her. Or maybe he planned to show up when they weren't expecting him so he could catch them off guard.

"I've got to go," she said to Conrad before she realized how rushed she sounded. "And you need to get inside too."

He gave her a confused look.

"Don't look now, but there's a blue car about to turn into the parking lot. It belongs to a journalist who's been asking too many questions."

"About the church?"

It wouldn't be appropriate for her to share Rob Lassiter's specific accusations with a member of Halsey's staff. And, besides, she needed to get both herself and Conrad out of the line of fire. She headed to her car as she answered the older man's question. "Go on inside now, okay? He's trying to stir up trouble, and neither of us needs to be involved in that."

Chapter Fourteen

Mae fidgeted at her desk chair in the laundry room, nervous to meet with Halsey when he got home in a few minutes.

After fleeing the church parking lot earlier in the day so that Rob Lassiter wouldn't see her, she'd felt guilty about not warning Halsey of the journalist's arrival. It was—after all—her job to help protect her boss's reputation. And the last thing either of them needed was a journalist storming into a church staff meeting with accusations of misappropriated funds.

Mae had pulled into a nearby parking lot shortly after leaving the church's grounds and warned Halsey—via text—of Lassiter's arrival. But she had no idea if he'd seen the text during the meeting or what had happened when Rob Lassiter entered the PALM administrative offices.

His response to her text had come two hours later and with no mention of Lassiter: *Please stay at the house until I get home tonight. I'd like to talk to you.*

A hundred different scenarios had played through Mae's mind for the remainder of the afternoon. Rob Lassiter confronting Halsey in the church's boardroom. Conrad fessing up to Halsey that Mae had warned him away from the guy in the PT Cruiser. Halsey marching into the laundry room to fire her. It was all conjecture, but she hadn't been able to keep her mind off the possibilities.

At the other end of the house, a door opened. Mae's back stiffened and she cocked her head, eager to hear whatever might go on. Halsey's voice greeted Klara and the other two housekeepers who'd been working with her that day. The ice machine in the kitchen rumbled. Cubes tumbled into a glass. Bottles clinked at the nearby wet bar. The door to the laundry room creaked open.

Mae hadn't seen Halsey with an alcoholic drink before. Bourbon, it looked like, though she couldn't be sure. Had he had a bad day?

He flashed a brief smile as he settled his backside against the island in the middle of the room. The silver tinge of his cheeks pulsated like a heartbeat. She'd not seen that before. She reached up and smoothed her rippling eyebrow, hoping to ease the pain.

He wore his more casual uniform—slim-fitting khakis and a The Players Championship golf shirt. "Thanks for picking up that book and bringing it to the church."

She sucked in a quick breath, nervous that he'd immediately steered the conversation to *that* part of the day. "You're welcome. The Bookmark's a cute place."

He nodded and swirled the ice around in his glass.

She couldn't take the tension any longer. "Did your staff meeting go okay?"

"Walter really liked the book. Steve Berry's one of his favorite authors."

But that didn't answer her question. She felt like one of those live mice being lowered into the tank of a hungry snake.

"The reason I asked you to stay until I got home . . ." He tipped his head back and took a long swig from his drink. The tendons in his slender neck moved as he drank, pushing the live prey toward his digestive system.

She looked away, unable to watch any longer.

". . . is to ask you to drive down to Flagler Beach for me in the morning."

"Is that near here?"

"It's south of Palm Coast."

That still didn't mean anything to her. "Remember, I just moved here a month ago."

He let out a little huff, like he was put out to have to explain the geography to her. "It's about an hour and a half south of here. A little bit north of Daytona Beach."

Okay. That helped. She vaguely knew where Daytona was. "What am I going to do there?"

"You'll be making a deposit at a bank."

"You know most banks have an app now that . . ." She mimicked photographing a check with her phone.

"This will be a cash deposit."

She felt her eyebrows rise in surprise. Jacksonville—along with Charlotte—was a banking mecca of the South, and yet he needed her to drive an hour and a half away to make a *cash* deposit?

Maybe Rob Lassiter's accusations about misuse of funds had some truth to them. He'd been pushy and obnoxious, but her internal warning system hadn't shown any silvery alerts on his skin. Halsey, on the other hand, was a walking, talking Tin Man.

"I'll pay you for your mileage. And your time, of course. And you can find a nice little oceanfront restaurant to have some lunch while you're there. My treat." His smile reminded her of the used car salesman who'd sold Mae her last car—the one that needed a new transmission two months after she bought it. "So can you do it?"

She shrugged. "I guess. Let me make sure Dawn doesn't have anything planned for me."

"This is far more important than anything she's asked you to do." His voice had a hard edge to it, like it irritated him that Mae would even bring it up.

She sat back in her chair, still skeptical about this entire request. "Okay. Whatever you say."

"I'll leave a deposit slip with the cash in that drawer before I leave for work in the morning." He pointed to the built-in desk she used as her workstation. "The name and address of the bank will be on a sticky note with it."

Seemed simple enough. An entire morning of alone time in her car would actually be good. She loved alone time.

"And this is the important part," Halsey continued. "There's a teller there named Sherlene. You can't miss her. She's about six feet tall and has long jet black hair." He held his hand up until it was almost even with the top of his head. "She looks a lot like Morticia Addams. Do you know who that is?"

Mae nodded.

"She knows you're coming. Make sure you go to *her* teller line. I told her you'd be there between 10:30 and 11:30."

And what if Sherlene wasn't there? But Mae didn't ask. She'd deal with that problem if it came up tomorrow morning. The less she knew, the better. Because this all sounded way too fishy.

She still wanted to know if Rob Lassiter had confronted any of the staff members earlier in the day, but Halsey turned and took the three or four steps to the laundry room door.

He paused before he exited the room. "Make sure you get a receipt. If I don't see you late tomorrow afternoon, leave it right in that same drawer." He nodded toward the center of her desk. "And remember, this is nobody's business but mine and yours."

A question teased the tip of Mae's tongue, though she hesitated to ask it. Halsey's last personal assistant—Joy—had apparently been fired for opening her mouth too often. A shudder ran down Mae's spine as she thought of Patricia's monumental scolding after the faux pas with the hot mic—another instance when silence would have been best. Still, Mae's gut made her uncomfortable with this suspicious errand. Why would a cash deposit need to be made with a specific teller at a specific bank branch an hour and a half from Halsey's home?

She pushed Patricia's voice from her mind and gave herself permission to poke at Halsey with just one additional question. "Is this Dawn's business too?" She held his gaze, wanting to see whatever emotion flashed through his eyes.

"She'll know eventually." He glared at her. "But it's not your place to tell her."

And with that, he slipped out of the room, leaving Mae to wonder what she'd gotten herself into.

Chapter Fifteen

Mae stood in Cole's kitchen, her fingers wrapped around her warm coffee mug. After such a fitful night of sleep, she'd need a vat of caffeine to stay awake during the drive to Flagler Beach. The more she'd thought about it overnight, the more suspicious she became of the morning's errand—to get some cash Halsey had left for her, then drive seventy miles to deposit it with a specific teller at a specific bank branch.

She could hear Cole rummaging around in his bedroom as he got ready for work. Her gaze flicked to the clock on the microwave—5:47 a.m.—as she waited for him to come to the kitchen.

"What the hell are you doing up so early?" he asked a few minutes later as he headed toward the coffee pot. He'd tried to tame his rumpled brown hair with some water, but it didn't seem to have done much good.

"Couldn't sleep. Got a lot on my mind."

He slid her a side-eye as he scooped a spoonful of sugar into his mug. "Why do I get the feeling you want to talk about it?"

"Have you ever had a boss who asked you to do something that . . . didn't seem quite right?"

He grunted out a laugh. "I warned you about that guy." Then he rounded to face her, a look of anger on his face. "He's not . . . forcing himself on you, is he? Like . . . sexually?"

Mae grimaced. "God, no." Nothing about Halsey Green's too-slick demeanor had even *once* made her think of anything sexual. "But he does have a . . . business practice . . . that gives me pause." She wouldn't say any more than that, not with her pledge to Halsey about guarding his privacy. She wouldn't sacrifice her personal integrity for anyone, especially someone like him.

"Gives you pause? What the hell does that mean?"

"I'm just not sure it's . . . above board."

"I repeat: I warned you about that shyster from the get-go."

And Cole had no idea how Mae's internal alarm system shrieked every time she saw the guy. "Yes, I know, but so far no one else in Jacksonville wants to even *interview* me, much less hire me." Such an embarrassing fact to think about, much less say out loud.

"So give me some details. What's going on that makes you so uncomfortable?"

"I can't really say. I've promised to keep everything private."

Cole's eyes narrowed. "He's stealing from his congregation, isn't he?"

Mae looked away, unsure what her expression might convey to Cole. "I don't have any proof of that."

"But that's what you assume."

She hated that Cole was right. She'd wondered all night whether the cash Halsey would leave for her that morning had been taken from the PALM offering plates. "If Tallahassee taught me anything, it's to keep my mouth shut about rich guys who control my employment."

He motioned with his mug around the kitchen. "There are no live mics here. Talk away."

"Yeah, well, I have to live with myself if I open my mouth about something I'm supposed to keep confidential."

"So you're going to do it, aren't you? Whatever illicit thing he's asked you to do?"

She'd always thought of herself as a principled person. She hated that she'd tacitly agreed to become Halsey's accomplice to God knows what. She'd chastised herself all night, but the final answer never changed: She hadn't stood up to Halsey because she desperately needed the job. "I'm going to keep my head down and not ask any questions. The less I know, the better."

Cole's gaze held hers for a few seconds. He opened his mouth to say something, then apparently decided against it. He looked away. Paused for a few more seconds, then finally spoke. "You don't want to end up in jail, Sis. Or in trouble with the law in any way." His voice broke. "I care about you too much to watch that happen."

The emotion in his voice pierced Mae's heart like an arrow. He couldn't have faked it. She wanted to believe that he cared about her. She'd believed that for years when she was a kid. When he'd been her rock—the only point of stability in her otherwise chaotic life. But then he'd let her down. Left her behind. She'd only survived the intervening years because of her grit and determination, all the while growing the thick, hard shell that had protected her ever since.

She wanted to let him into her heart again, but he'd hurt her too many times to allow that happen. Better to keep the conversation superficial—focused on Halsey Green—than to dive into that pit of confusion and sorrow. "I'll be careful. I promise."

***

Mae's body thrummed as she punched the code to raise the door to the Greens' garage—the first step in making the bank deposit Halsey had requested. She already thought of it as her *ill-fated* trip to Flagler Beach, though she had yet to leave the Jacksonville area.

Klara's car sat in the drive, dashing Mae's hopes of getting inside to retrieve the cash from the desk drawer in the laundry room without anyone seeing her. If Halsey got caught committing some crime, she didn't want to go down with him.

She walked through the empty garage and into the house. Her shoulders relaxed when she found no one in the kitchen. She tiptoed toward the laundry room down the hall, but a horrible gagging sound came from the bathroom as she passed it. Her body stopped involuntarily midstride. She cocked her head to hear what was going on inside the room.

From the other side of the door, Klara's soft words seemed comforting, though Mae couldn't understand what she said. Another huge heave rose from someone's gut, though nothing splashed into the water of the toilet.

Klara often had a couple of younger housekeepers with her, though Mae rarely spoke to them. They'd apparently not been in the States as long as Klara and spoke very little English. Lejla looked to be about thirty-five—about Mae's age—and reminded Mae of a young, brown-haired Mrs. Claus. Her hearty laugh often boomed throughout the house, usually in response to something Klara had said in their native language.

Mae often thought that Ilma—the younger of the two women—belonged on a fashion show runway instead of on Halsey Green's housekeeping crew. Her tall, thin frame reminded Mae of the sandhill cranes that graced the banks of nearby ponds. But it was Ilma's startingly blue eyes that really stood out—twin pools of the palest aqua against her olive-toned skin. She seemed friendly enough, but those eyes always held a look of trepidation. Or maybe fear. Mae didn't want to think about the horrors Ilma may have seen during her childhood in her own war-torn country before immigrating to the United States.

But Mae didn't have time to think about that now. She needed to hurry to the laundry room, grab the cash, and get out of there while Klara and whoever remained in the bathroom. But just then, the bathroom door swung open. Klara startled, as surprised as Mae at the sudden appearance of another person.

Behind Klara, Ilma lay on the tile floor, looking gaunter than she normally did. Stringy strands of dark brown hair seemed stuck to her cheek. Her face—eyes closed—held a look of pain.

Klara pulled the door closed behind her, like she didn't want Mae to see anything inside.

"I am so sorry to bother you, Miss Mae," Klara said.

"It's no bother." Mae motioned with her head toward the bathroom. "Is she okay?"

"Just a little stomach problem. I get her glass of water."

But Ilma looked as weak and miserable as anyone Mae had ever seen. Mae rested her hand on Klara's arm. "You stay with her. It looks like she needs you. I'll get the water."

Klara hesitated. She gave Mae a questioning look that may have even been tinged with fear.

"It's not a big deal," Mae said. "I'll be right back." She plodded to the kitchen, her mission of retrieving the money from the desk momentarily set aside.

This wasn't the first time Ilma had appeared under the weather. A few days ago, Mae had come out of her laundry-room office to find her lying on the couch. She'd struggled to stand when she'd heard Mae approaching, then had a guilty look on her face.

And a few days before that, Klara had left midmorning and—after an absence of more than an hour—had returned with a peaked-looking Ilma, though Lejla had been at work at the Greens' since early that morning.

Mae took a glass from the cabinet and filled it with water as she wondered if Ilma—like Mama—had a drinking problem or maybe a drug problem. Was Klara covering for her? Maybe Klara felt the need to present Ilma as a good employee since she'd convinced the Greens to hire her? That would explain the look of fear Mae had seen on Klara's face. Klara didn't want Mae to tell Halsey that one of the housekeepers wasn't pulling her weight.

Mama'd had the same problem, losing job after job because of her drinking. Younger Mae had wondered why employers kept firing Mama, but as Mae grew older, she came to understand that Mama's unreliability meant she brought it on herself. Mae's adult mind now knew that alcoholism was a disease, but the frightened little girl inside her still had trouble accepting that. She'd read enough about the children of alcoholics to know that a lot of her own screwed-up-ness could be traced back to Mama.

She made her way back to the bathroom and knocked on the door, feeling less sympathetic than she had before.

Klara opened it, but shielded Mae's view inside with her body. "Thank you, Miss Mae. We get back to work soon."

"I've got to grab something from my desk, then I'll be out for a while." She couldn't really call it *running errands*. Driving to fricking Flagler Beach was more like a road trip.

Klara closed her eyes and gave a quick nod—a thank you of sorts—then slipped back inside the bathroom.

Mae took the remaining couple of steps down the hall and into the laundry room. She closed the door behind her and eased the desk drawer open to find a 9" x 12" white envelope with her name on it. A sticky note with the name and address of the bank in Flagler Beach also read "Deposit ticket is inside, so Sherlene will know which account to use."

The lumpiness of the envelope surprised Mae. She fingered the outside, curious about what might be inside, but the flap had been sealed shut. The contents seemed more like crumpled up tissue paper than neatly stacked bills.

A twenty-dollar bill lay in the drawer next to where the envelope had lain. The sticky note on it said, "Enjoy lunch on me—Halsey." Beside his name he'd drawn a smiley face.

A smiley face! Like his happy little emoticon might serve as consolation for having dragged her into this mess.

She huffed, ripped the sticky note from the twenty, and hurled it into the trash can below the desk. Another heaving sound came from the bathroom, reminding Mae she wanted to get out of there as quickly as possible. She stuffed the twenty in her pocket, picked up the envelope of cash, and bolted out of the house.

***

The drive to Flagler Beach took way longer than Mae had expected, but at least she was having a better day than the trucker who'd flipped his semi on I-95 South. The resulting traffic backup had Mae on edge. Halsey, after all, had said Sherlene expected Mae in her teller line between 10:30 a.m. and 11:30 a.m.

Mae glanced at her clock as she pulled into the bank parking lot—12:07 p.m. What if the woman had taken a lunch break by now? What if Mae got inside and no Morticia Addams look-alike was in sight? Should Mae simply turn around and walk out the door? Sure, nothing fishy about that.

But, really, she had no choice but to go inside. She grabbed the envelope from the seat beside her and thrust the car door open, not at all happy to be in this predicament. When she got inside, a fortysomething man in a suit stood near the front door—a sentry of sorts. Or was he a receptionist? The branch manager? Mae had only been inside a bank branch about four times in her life—not often enough to know how everything worked.

A fake smile spread across the man's face. "Good morning. What can we help you with today?"

Mae glanced around nervously, trying to take in her surroundings before she answered. A row of glass-walled offices behind him held single employees sitting at desks, but she knew that wasn't where she belonged. "I'm . . . uh . . ."

He pointed to the envelope in her hand. "You need something notarized?"

"What?" She looked down at her hands. "No."

Just then, a solid beast of a woman came out from behind a wall at what must be the teller stations. Her long jet-black hair hung like twin curtains on either side of her face. Halsey had said Sherlene was tall, but he'd failed to mention that she was built like a linebacker. But as big as Sherlene was, she moved with cat-like grace. Her deep purple dress flowed behind her like the frock of a priestess.

The woman raised her chin in an acknowledgment to Mae. *I've been expecting you*, it seemed to say.

Mae turned to the man whose fake smile still aimed at her like a flashlight beam. She pointed toward the woman on the other side of the bank's lobby. "I make a deposit over there?"

He held his arm out to indicate that direction, like an usher guiding her to her seat. "Sherlene will be happy to help you."

Yes. Mae gave herself an inward high five at the confirmation she'd found the person Halsey had sent her to see.

"Good morning," Sherlene said as Mae approached, greeting Mae with the same demeanor she might any other bank customer.

Mae followed the woman's lead, giving no indication that this cash exchange was a pre-arranged meet-up. She quickly ripped off the sticky note with the bank's name and address, then slid the envelope toward Sherlene. "I've got a deposit to make."

"I'm happy to help. This is your first time visiting us, no?" Sherlene's bold, impeccably applied makeup added to the exotic priestess vibe.

The woman's large hands turned the envelope over. She deftly slid a finger underneath the sealed flap and emptied the contents onto her workstation. Several hundred-dollar bills lay on the surface, neatly flattened and fanned out, as if they'd been stacked in a pile inside the envelope. But the majority of the money—twenties and tens and fives and ones—lay crumpled and unorganized, as it might have been when placed in an offering plate.

Mae heard herself gasp, then tried to cover it with a fake cough. She tried not to stare as Sherlene picked up each of the crumpled bills one by one and flattened them with the heel of her hand. She created a stack for each denomination.

Mae felt the need to apologize for the disheveled nature of the contents. She'd never have shown up with such a mess if this had been her own money. "I would have done that beforehand, but the envelope was sealed."

Sherlene looked up and smiled. "We appreciate your business."

The vague, almost out of place comment seemed odd to Mae, like the teller wanted to divulge as little as possible about the situation. Mae had trouble believing that Sherlene's involvement in Halsey's business was honorable, but she saw no hint of the silvery, telltale shine amid the woman's perfectly applied makeup.

Mae assumed the little white slip of paper at the bottom of the pile was the deposit slip. Sherlene picked it up, read it, and set it off to the side, making Mae wish she knew the name of the account that would receive all that cash.

Finally, Sherlene placed each stack of bills into a little machine that sat off to one side at her workstation. The machine whirred to life, fanning the cash in a brief burst of energy. It reminded Mae of that time a flock of ducks suddenly all took flight off a pond at once—an explosion of movement and sound.

After the machine counted each denomination, Sherlene recorded the amount onto a paper form in front of her, then—apparently—into her computer. With all the counting complete, she handed Mae a receipt, showing a deposit into an account titled Halsey Green. So a personal account, then. Without Dawn's name on it.

The amount deposited: $3,781—a huge amount of money in Mae's eyes. She'd never held a sum that large before, and she'd had no idea how much the envelope had contained while it had sat on the front seat of her car. She tried to hide her surprise as she looked from the receipt back to the teller.

Sherlene's smile appeared almost conspiratorial. "See you next time."

Mae flashed a fake smile and said goodbye, though she hoped to God there wouldn't be a next time.

"We appreciate your business," the overeager man in the suit said as she passed him on the way to the front door of the bank's lobby.

It's not MY business, she wanted to scream back at him. *I have nothing to do with this.*

But a realization followed her to the parking lot like an overpowering stench. She *did* have something to do with this. She might have just helped Halsey Green hide a boatload of cash—cash even his wife didn't know about. Mae had no idea where all that cash had come from, but she remembered going to church with Ashlyn Bradley's family a few times in elementary school. Young Mae had fantasized about how many ice cream cones she could buy with that big plate of cash that got passed through the pews. And now grown-up Mae wondered if the PALM offering plates provided Halsey Green with ready access to cash. Was that how he maintained such a lavish lifestyle?

But forget about Halsey. What about *her*? The Channel Seven incident back in Tallahassee already meant one black mark on her professional record. If she got pulled into some shady dealing for Halsey, she'd become even more unemployable. Yes, she needed this job—desperately, for now—but she didn't have to work for Halsey forever.

She slid into the seat of her car, hoping to never set foot in this parking lot again.

Maybe enough time had passed that her faux pas in Tallahassee had become old news. Maybe the Jacksonville job market had opened up a bit in the few days since she'd gone to work for Halsey.

In any case, she'd double down on her efforts to find another place to work. And until she found something else, she'd do her best to avoid being dragged into any more of his questionable dealings. Could she refuse to go to Flagler Beach again?

Should she start keeping notes of everything she did—the date and dollar figure of this morning's transaction, for example—in case the authorities ever questioned what she'd done while she worked for him?

In case the authorities ever questioned what she'd done.

She slammed the heel of her hand against the steering wheel. Maybe she was already in this too deep. Maybe she'd already done things that would haunt her forever. She'd known long before arriving in Jax Beach that people only looked out for their own good, so why had she let herself get into this mess?

And—most importantly—how was she going to get out of it?

Chapter Sixteen

Mae pulled into the Green's driveway, still mad at herself for running that morning's errand to Flagler Beach.

About a football field away—down the long drive—Ezra stood leaning over the hood of his truck, with the older guy, Joe, standing next to him. As she approached, it appeared they studied some kind of architectural plans for the deck and dock.

Ezra straightened and turned at the sound of her car, then returned his attention to Joe, who pointed at something on the plans as he talked.

Mae parked next to the truck and opened her door. Both men turned and nodded a greeting.

"You head on back to work," Ezra said to Joe. "I'll catch up with you in a minute."

Joe smirked but didn't say anything before heading toward the backyard.

"I thought maybe you'd been fired," Ezra said to Mae as she got out of the car.

"For letting the cat out? I told them you did that." She walked past him—close enough that she could smell his manly scent.

He scoffed. "Yeah. Right. How is the beast, by the way?"

"Mangy as ever." She turned to face him. "Please tell me you're not going to run a bunch of loud machines all afternoon."

He frowned. "We've been running them all morning already. This *is* a construction site, ya know."

"Well, let me get another pill down him before you start again."

"I thought you were supposed to give him those in the mornings. We've been at it all day."

"I had to go to Flagler Beach."

"Is that where you're from?"

She tensed and hoped he didn't notice. "I had to run an errand there."

"So not from Flagler Beach," he said under his breath, as if her lack of information offended him.

"Will you help me with the pill?"

He shook his head. "No way. The other day was a one-time deal. I'm not your personal vet tech."

She smiled, hoping to charm him. "No, but you might be Billy Graham's."

He snapped his fingers once in the air. "*That* was the stupid name I couldn't remember."

She leaned closer to look at his cheek. "What are you telling people about that big scratch on your face?"

He reached up to touch the still-tender mark. "That I wrestled an alligator."

She laughed. "So will you help me with the pill or not?"

He rolled his eyes, but seemed to be enjoying the banter as much as she did. "Can't one of those housekeepers help you?"

"One of them isn't feeling well."

"And? There's more than one of them in there. I've seen them through the windows."

She reached out and grabbed his hand, holding it in both of hers in a mock melodramatic fashion. "But you were so *good* the other day."

He grinned. "That's what all the women say."

"In your dreams," she retorted before pulling his hand—and him—into the house behind her.

A few minutes later, they both crouched on the kitchen floor, knees folded under them, just as they'd done the day before. He held the mangy cat between his thighs while she tried to pry its mouth open with her thumb and forefinger.

She bent over her unwilling patient, wishing the front of her purple T-shirt didn't fall away from her body the way it did. But wrestling Billy Graham required both of her hands. She couldn't use one to hold her shirt against her body the way she wanted to. At least she had on her good lacey pink bra.

Something sharp gouged her forefinger. She pulled her hand away from the cat's mouth and shook it. "He bit me," she said, before diving back in to try to open the fang-filled jaws.

Ezra leaned over the mostly bald animal, tightening his grip.

"You're not looking down my shirt, are you?" she asked while keeping her attention on the cat.

"It's like . . . gaping open right in front of me. Where am I supposed to look?"

She raised her head and looked at him. "The cat. The kitchen." She flung her arm behind her. "The frickin' intra-coastal waterway."

"I think you wore that shirt on purpose, then lured me in under the pretense of this cat needing a pill so you could—"

She motioned toward Billy Graham's back leg, which was as bare as a freshly plucked chicken. "Have you *seen* this cat? He's obviously in need of medication."

"Will you just give him the damn pill?" he gritted out.

Finally, she managed to wedge the cat's mouth open and jam the pill down its skinny little throat. "Keep ahold of him while I massage it down," she said in a soothing tone as she ran her thumb and forefinger down opposite sides of the cat's furry neck. "You're a good little kitty, aren't you, Billy Graham?"

She slid a bowl of water over in front of Ezra and the cat. "Now, let him go, gently. See if he'll get a drink to wash it down."

They'd both rested back on their rear ends—their mission complete—when the sound of the garage door opening rumbled nearby. Their gazes snapped to each other, eyes wide. The cat hissed and darted away.

Ezra stood, acting like a kid who'd been caught skipping school. "I'd better get outside,"

Mae grinned at his unease. He was a thirtysomething who ran his own business. A grown-ass man who'd done nothing other than help with a client's cat. "Relax. I'm not going to tell Halsey you looked down my shirt."

He chuckled as he walked toward the sliding glass door that led to the backyard. "And I won't tell him you keep distracting me from my work."

She watched as he pulled open the door and went outside. She might be a distraction, but based on the way he'd dismissed Joe in the driveway and their playful banter in the kitchen, she was pretty sure she was a *welcome* distraction.

Chapter Seventeen

Just moments after Ezra left Mae standing in the Greens' kitchen, Halsey entered from the garage and strode immediately to the sliding glass door. He slid the door open and called to Ezra. "Can you come inside and chat with me for a minute?"

Ezra nodded and made his way back to the door where he'd just exited.

Mae knew she should get to work in her desk in the laundry room, but she wanted to see what Halsey wanted with Ezra, so she busied herself with a stack of papers—a slide deck she'd prepared for a presentation Halsey would give to a conference of ministers later that week.

"It's way too hot to talk outside," Halsey said once Ezra had re-entered the kitchen. He narrowed his eyes and looked at Ezra's cheek. "Remind me again what happened to your face?"

Mae felt her eyes widen, but—luckily—Ezra didn't look her way.

"I had to help someone get a cat out of a tree," he said.

"Well, I hope they appreciated your efforts," Halsey said as he thumbed through some mail on the kitchen counter.

"I'm not sure they did." Ezra shot a playful glance in Mae's direction.

"Were you at least successful?" Halsey pointed to Ezra's face, as if it were proof that he'd somehow failed. "Did you get the cat back?"

Ezra gave a cocky smile. "Safe and sound. Just like she wanted."

Mae crossed her arms and gave him an exasperated look.

"You ready to talk about that November third deadline?" Halsey asked.

Mae saw Ezra's demeanor grow more serious. "*Proposed* deadline."

Halsey looked annoyed. "Are you going to agree to it or not?"

"I will *shoot* for it. But you have to realize that labor costs are going to go up. My guys will be earning time and a half for every hour after forty and those costs get passed on to you."

Halsey circled his finger in the air in front of him—the sign for *let's hurry up this conversation*. "Yeah. Yeah. Yeah. Increased labor costs. I get it."

Mae's anger grew. Clearly this was a big business decision for Ezra, but Halsey's reaction seemed to diminish its importance.

"And even *one day* lost to weather could throw the whole thing off," Ezra said. "It's that tight of a deadline."

"I've got an in with the Big Guy." Halsey winked as he pointed skyward. "I'll pray extra hard for no rain."

Ezra sliced the air in front of him with his hand, as if to emphasize his point. "We're going to *shoot* for the new deadline, but there's no way I can guarantee it. Not with so many variables involved."

Halsey let out a long sigh, apparently bored with the conversation.

Mae didn't know how Ezra put up with the man's arrogance.

But Ezra wasn't finished. "If my guys are going to bust their butts to try to meet an impossible deadline, we're going to need something from you in return."

One of Halsey's eyebrows crooked up. Mae's interest piqued.

"Assuming we *do* finish a month earlier than planned," Ezra said, "I want some free advertising out of the deal. The night of your big party, I want you to tell all the big donors that we refurbished your dock and deck. You make a little speech, telling everyone how pleased you are with our work and how you'd recommend us to them. We put a stack of my business cards on the bar or the buffet table or wherever makes sense."

Halsey held his hands out, palms up. "You haven't even finished the job. How do I know I can recommend your work?"

Ezra locked his gaze on Halsey's. "We do good work. That's why you hired us. My guys are the best in the business."

Halsey threw his hands in the air. "Fine. Whatever you need, but from now on, these are the kinds of things you discuss with her." He pointed behind him to where Mae stood.

"What?" Ezra and Mae said simultaneously, both apparently as surprised as the other.

"I'll be in and out of town over the next few weeks, but I want to make sure you stay on track to finish this project on time. So I want you to give *her* daily updates. You understand?"

Ezra's hands shot in the air. "Whoa. Whoa. Whoa. Daily updates? To her?" He, too, pointed in Mae's direction.

Finally, Mae spoke. "I know nothing about construction." She pointed to the dock. "And certainly not anything about construction *underwater*."

Halsey took a step back so he could look at both of them at the same time. He spoke slowly and softly, as if they might be dimwitted. "I need daily updates from him to you. And then you'll pass them on to me. Now what's so hard about that?"

Mae pointed at Ezra. "So I'm not . . . in charge of him or anything, right?"

"Damn right, you're not," Ezra said under his breath.

Mae continued. "I'm just . . . passing on information?"

"Yes." Halsey looked relieved, like his message had finally gotten through. "You're my personal assistant, right? So you keep me updated on projects that are on my plate. Didn't you do this sort of thing for Hannah Summers?"

Ezra looked at her, surprised. She could almost hear him think *Hannah Summers? The Olympic swimmer?*

Mae backed down, feeling reprimanded. "Yes, sir."

Halsey's gaze moved from her to Ezra and back again. "Now do you two need anything else explained to you?"

Mae shook her head.

"No, sir," Ezra said.

Halsey turned and walked up the stairs.

Ezra motioned with his head for Mae to follow him outside.

"God, how do you work for that guy?" Ezra said once they were both out on the patio.

"Not exactly the kindly minister type, is he?"

Ezra grunted. "No, but he's got a boatload of cash. And the donors at that party will too. They're exactly the kind of people who need the type of work my company does."

"You think you can actually finish by November third?" she asked.

He let out a long breath. "We'll try our best, but like I told Halsey, there are no guarantees."

"Then why did you agree to it?"

"Because I'd love to get in with the Roscoe Boulevard crowd. I mean, business is good, but I always want to have more projects in the pipeline. I always want to have plenty of work for my guys. They're like family to me." Ezra's voice cracked as he said it.

Mae looked at him, surprised at the sudden emotion. She waited for him to continue.

"Bobby's wife has breast cancer, which is costing him a boatload of money, even *with* our insurance. And Ricky's daughter is a helluva softball player. She's already been contacted by Division One schools and she's only a freshman. But that means travel ball almost every weekend, which gets ungodly expensive with all the hotel rooms and all."

"Sounds like . . . maybe they need time off instead of more work."

"I give them time off when they need it." His tone had an air of defensiveness. "But I also have a responsibility to make sure they can pay their bills. Life isn't cheap, you know?"

Mae snorted. "Tell me about it. What about you? Any kids? Ex-wives to support? *Current* wives?" She threw the last one in for good measure, though she was fairly certain he was single.

"No kids. No wives. Current or otherwise."

"Same," she said. "No kids. Never married. Do people look at you like . . . they're wondering what's wrong with you?"

He gave her a confused frown.

"I mean, they don't come right out and say it, but I get the feeling that people want to know why I'm in my thirties and haven't ever been married."

Ezra kicked at a bit of sod below his feet. "We're guys. We don't really talk about that stuff."

But Mae would guess that people thought it about Ezra. Just like they wondered what had kept her from finding a partner. "So you want to give me your update in person at the end of each day? Or send me an email or what?" The whole thought of it made her nervous. She might as well be passing on an update in quantum physics. She understood neither topic.

He looked out over the intracoastal while he thought. "Let's try it in person at first." He tossed her a smile. "Maybe you can learn a thing or two about construction along the way."

"Pass."

"You worked for Hannah Summers, the swimmer?"

"It's why Halsey hired me. I had experience as the personal assistant to someone famous. Kind of a personal assistant/public relations person all rolled into one."

Ezra snorted. "So Halsey thinks he's Olympic-level famous now?"

Mae was grateful Ezra didn't—like most people—launch into a discussion of Hannah Summers's unpredictable, public antics toward the end of her public speaking career. Maybe he hadn't heard about them. He didn't seem like the kind of guy who followed pop culture. "He's at least a little famous. Maybe hiring me was aspirational." She shot Ezra a grin. "He's going to need a good PR person when he takes over the world."

Ezra let out a long breath as he pulled his truck keys from his pocket. "Lord help us all."

Chapter Eighteen

Mae pulled open one of the intricately carved wooden doors she thought led from the outside of PALM into to the sanctuary. Instead, she found herself in a large, sun-filled entrance hall that reminded her of the wide foyers outside hotel ballrooms—where a cocktail reception or a breakfast buffet took place before a main conference event. The place looked more like a Ritz-Carlton than a place of worship.

Across the plush carpet, Halsey's microphoned voice spilled out of an open set of double doors. She made her way into the sanctuary, where the minister had told her they'd be rehearsing for that weekend's church service.

She stood at the back of the room, in awe of its cavernous size. Maple-colored pews filled the equivalent of four side-by-side movie theatres at the local Cinemark, not to mention the balcony, which wrapped around the entire space above. She made a mental note to look up the number of people this room would hold. Maybe a couple of thousand?

That many people, all willing to give up their Sunday mornings—not to mention their dollars—to hear Halsey speak? Parishioners probably came to church services for the Lord instead of Halsey, but couldn't they commune with the Big

Guy at home in their pajamas, without having to get dressed and come to such an . . . extravaganza? Did they really think all this glitz and technology was necessary to worship their God?

Two guys at the back of the sanctuary stood at a sound board bigger than the ones she'd seen at most of the rock concerts she'd attended. A spotlight beamed from somewhere in the balcony, illuminating Halsey at the podium in the front. A man wearing headphones hopped onto the stage and consulted with Halsey about something written on a clipboard. The show's director, perhaps? How much did all these people get paid?

A man's voice came from behind her. "Excuse me, Ms. Van Dorn?"

She turned to see a man in khakis and a golf shirt. She guessed him to be in his sixties, but she couldn't see him well in the dimly lit sanctuary. The only lights were aimed squarely at the stage. "Yes?"

He held out his hand. "Dr. Greg Wisely. I'm a member of the church's board of directors."

"Nice to meet you," she whispered, not wanting to draw attention from the front of the room.

The man pointed toward the door leading to the large foyer. "Might I have a word with you in private?"

She glanced to where Halsey stood a football field's length away. She still needed to deliver the envelope he'd asked her to bring from his house—concert tickets he planned to give to a friend since he and Dawn could no longer use them. But he seemed too tied up in rehearsals now, anyway, so she did have some time to kill. "Ummm. Sure," she said to Dr. Wisely, then headed up the inclined floor to the exit.

Dr. Wisely closed the sanctuary doors as he led her back out into the lobby. He kept walking until they'd reached the wall of windows farthest from the doors to the sanctuary. She waited, wondering what he could want with her. Walter Miller had warned her early on that the board of directors required a lot of his time, but this was her first interaction with one of them.

Dr. Wisely rubbed the side of his tanned nose. Above it, the whiter skin showed the outline of where his sunglasses would perch—a golfer, or perhaps a fisherman. Most importantly, Mae had to look *very* closely to see the silver tinge that ran along his receding hairline. She'd missed it at first, but a slight turn of his head made it visible in the bright sunlight of the atrium. She'd learned long ago that the lighter the color, the better the person's character. His intentions might not be good, but they likely weren't horrible, either. Still, Mae remained cautious.

He cleared his throat. "What I have to talk with you about is a . . . bit uncomfortable."

He didn't look at all uncomfortable, which made her wonder what he was up to. He looked more like a man who was used to getting his way. To bossing people around.

He glanced toward the closed doors of the sanctuary. "I wouldn't normally approach a stranger about this, but it's a pressing matter and you're in a unique position to help."

The man's serious demeanor made Mae more and more concerned.

He continued. "You see, the church has plans to build another classroom wing. Our congregation continues to grow, and that's a good thing. But as part of the loan application process, the lender required us to hire an external audit firm, and they're requesting documentation the church doesn't seem to have."

Mae had no idea why he thought she would be a part of this conversation. Halsey had mentioned Bull Williams, the board member who'd been unhappy when Halsey had turned down the pet project to help his daughter's school. Maybe Dr. Wisely and Bull Williams were in cahoots? Maybe Dr. Wisely was trying to bolster some kind of campaign against Halsey? "I pick up birthday cakes and find replacements for their broken lamps."

"And drive all the way to Flagler Beach to do their banking?" He crooked one eyebrow in a you've-been-caught look.

Oh, shit.

Mae wondered if he could hear her thundering heart, but she did her best to keep her exterior neutral. Her PR training had taught her never to let her reactions show. To remain calm until she'd gathered all the facts. She crossed her arms and straightened to her full height. "Was there something in particular you needed from me, Dr. Wisely?"

"The auditors found that the church has been paying large amounts each month toward Halsey's American Express bill, and we're not sure the charges are for church-related expenses."

"Sounds like you need to talk to Sharon Carroll." From what Mae had heard, the woman had been the CFO at PALM for years.

"It's Halsey's *personal* American Express card, so the contents of the bills are not part of the church's financial records. He only provides the first page of the statement, with no detail attached—no vendor names, nothing."

"So y'all are paying the bills, but you don't know what you're paying for?" *Jesus.* It didn't require an external auditor to know that wasn't right. She'd filled out enough expense reports over the years to know that backup documentation was like Accounting 101.

Dr. Wisely looked away and cleared his throat. "The board had no idea about this . . . irregularity until the auditors brought it to our attention."

She caught Dr. Wiseley's gaze and held it. "I've never seen an American Express bill at Halsey's house." Luckily, she could say that truthfully.

"You've only worked there a couple of weeks."

"Have you talked to Halsey about all this?"

"He's the one who refuses to provide the American Express statements. He says they're his private business."

But didn't they become the church's business once he expected the church to pay them? "Sounds like you've got a dilemma on your hands." She turned to walk away.

Dr. Wisely placed his hand on her arm. "I'd hate to see you caught up in all his misdeeds." He took a step closer. He smelled of coffee and bacon. "If he's skimming money off the collection plates—and we think he is—and you're helping him hide the stolen cash . . ."

He didn't have to complete his sentence. She knew the rest. She'd be an accessory to the crime. She swallowed. "What are you asking me to do?"

"You've got a cell phone. Take a snapshot of any American Express bills you can find—not only the front page with the total due but the other pages that list the vendor names and how much each charge was for." He pulled a business card from his wallet and scribbled something on the back, then shoved it in her hand.

She glanced down. A Gmail address. "There are likely nanny cams all over that house. You think I want to get caught taking pictures of his personal financial records?" A quick realization flashed through her mind—this vestibule likely held cameras, too, recording this very conversation.

He shrugged. "I'm sure you can figure something out."

She shoved the business card back at him. "I won't be able to help you."

He held his hands up, refusing to take it back. "There are pictures of you walking into that bank branch in Flagler Beach."

Good Lord. Did they have a private investigator staking out the bank? Or worse yet, *following her*? The zip of energy speeding through Mae's veins may have been anger. It may have been fear. "If you can figure out that I went to Flagler Beach, then surely you can get ahold of Halsey's American Express bills."

Dr. Wisely's demeanor softened. He smiled, but it didn't look sincere. "This is likely all a misunderstanding, but on the off chance he's mishandling funds . . ." He leaned closer to her. "Wouldn't you want to help redirect them back to those in need? Isn't that the Christian thing to do?"

She needed time to think about this conversation before she said anything else. "What kind of a doctor are you, anyway?"

"An OB/GYN."

Good to know. She'd avoid calling his office when she finally had enough money to schedule her long-overdue annual visit.

He nodded to the business card in her hand. "Keep this conversation between the two of us. You'll only cause a further rift if you tell him about it. The board is trying to keep things . . . congenial . . . while we get to the bottom of all this."

She wondered what *all this* was but didn't want to dig any deeper than she already had. "I work for Halsey Green, Dr. Wisely. I don't keep anything from him."

He gave her the same disappointed look a parent might give a misbehaving child. "I had hoped you'd be more helpful."

But it wasn't her job to help the board of directors shore up their accounting practices. It wasn't her job to double-cross Halsey Green, regardless of what kind of a grifter he might be. She gave Dr. Wisely a quick nod. "I've told you my stance. Have a good day."

He huffed and stormed away, crossing the long carpeted foyer toward the parking lot. She sank into one of the high-backed chairs that sat in little pods in the space, suddenly worn out from the conversation.

She now understood why Halsey had insisted on talking to her about loyalty, both in her interview and once she'd arrived on the job. Perhaps he knew the auditors and board of directors had questions about his personal expenses. Maybe he knew there would even be people who'd try to weasel information out of her.

She'd *told* Dr. Wisely that she'd tell Halsey about their conversation, and she fully intended to do so, but she was glad to have a few hours to let it all sink in.

If nothing else, one revelation had become clear: She wasn't the only one who had suspicions about Halsey Green's finances.

Her vow in Cole's kitchen now seemed more important than before. *I'll be careful. I promise.*

Chapter Nineteen

Mae stared blankly at the computer screen in Halsey's laundry room, desperately waiting for her second cup of coffee to kick in. She'd slept horribly the night before, unable to get the events of yesterday off her mind.

Of course, she wouldn't snoop around Halsey's house looking for his personal American Express bills, as Dr. Wisely had requested. If Halsey had wanted her to have access to them, they would have been part of the discussion when he'd shown her all the family bills he wanted her to pay.

On the other hand, wasn't their omission from that conversation cause for at least a little suspicion? She had to admit to herself that if she ran across an Amex bill by accident, she'd sneak a peek at its contents. See if anything seemingly inappropriate appeared there.

And she would definitely tell Halsey about Dr. Wisely's request. She'd promised her loyalty to the man, and she wouldn't sacrifice her personal integrity—not for Halsey, not for any employer.

Still, it concerned her that Dr. Wisely had a picture of her entering that bank branch in Flagler Beach. But why? Lots of people walked in and out of bank branches every day. And, besides, she couldn't be an accessory to a crime if she hadn't known a crime was being committed, right? Sure, it was irregular as hell to drive a wad of cash three counties away to deposit it, but people did odd things all the time. She'd just been doing what her boss—a minister, no less—had asked her to do.

She held her breath for a few seconds, listening for the presence of other people in the house. From upstairs, she heard the footsteps of Klara, Lejla, and Ilma as they bustled about the children's rooms. A shower came on—one of them cleaning a bathroom. A vacuum cleaner roared to life, muffled by the sound of the plush carpeting above Mae.

Ilma had looked peaked again when Mae had seen the housekeepers in the kitchen earlier. Must have been another drunken night in a long string of them, based on the girl's appearance each time Mae saw her.

Mae wasn't unfamiliar with the look. Her mind flashed to memories of her mother's face those dismal mornings—too hungover to pour cereal in the bowls for Mae and Cole. Too grumpy to care if they'd dressed appropriately for school. The smell of alcohol oozing from her pores as she clutched a cigarette and glared at her children as if they were unwelcome intruders. Mae pushed these thoughts aside and refocused her attention on Halsey.

Dr. Wisely had also accused him of skimming money off the collection plates. On the one hand, if that *was* happening, then it was stealing, plain and simple. And maybe that explained why he had so much cash on hand. And why he'd asked her to go to Flagler Beach to deposit it—far enough away so that a local bank teller wouldn't wonder where it all came from.

On the other hand, didn't the parishioners who worshipped at the Altar of Halsey willingly place their money in the collection plate as it made its way along each pew? Shouldn't they be smarter than to hand over that kind of cash to a man whose life held more glitz and glamour than a Miss America Pageant?

And if she was going to cooperate with anyone to make up for her involvement in all this, shouldn't it be the police or the FBI or someone like that? Not an OB/GYN playing financial overlord of a megachurch?

She glanced at the clock on her computer. 10:30 a.m. She hadn't gotten anything accomplished yet this morning, despite being on Halsey's clock since 8:30 a.m. Maybe the guy did have plenty of cash to spare, but it wasn't her nature to slack at work, regardless of who her boss might be.

She picked up her now-empty coffee cup and plodded toward the kitchen, ready for cup number three of the day. As she passed the large front door with its beveled glass, movement outside caught her eye—a maroon streak in the circle drive.

Mae walked to the door and looked out the glass, glad to see her suspicions confirmed. Akira's SUV had just pulled in. Mae quickly opened the door and bounded down the porch stairs, eager to have a conversation with the nanny *away* from any prying electronic devices.

Akira still sat behind the steering wheel, scrolling through her phone, when Mae reached the driver's side of the door. The nanny startled when she saw Mae, then quickly opened the door. "What's wrong?" Akira asked.

"Nothing. I didn't mean to scare you. I thought we'd just . . . talk. You know, away from any nanny cams that might be in there." She motioned with her head toward the house.

Akira stepped out of the car and closed the door. She wore black yoga pants, an orange T-shirt, and the same bright red Chuck Taylor sneakers she'd had on the first time they'd met. "The nanny cams don't work anymore. They had them at first, but I guess I've worked here long enough that they trust me." Akira shrugged. "Plus, the kids love me. And they're old enough now to tattle on me if I ever did anything wrong."

So *that* was how Ilma got away with lying around hungover all the time. "How do you know they don't work anymore?"

Akria gave a sly smile. "I dated their tech guy for a little while."

Mae laughed.

"If I had their kind of money, I'd have all kinds of security at my house," Akira said. "I mean, there are a lot of crazy people in the world."

Just another reason for Mae's general dislike of the human race.

Akria continued. "My ex-boyfriend—the tech guy—kind of hinted that they didn't like being recorded."

Mae frowned. "His church service is broadcast across the entire state and then some. Isn't that recorded?"

"Yeah, but that's, like, not his personal household."

Mae lowered her voice to a whisper. "Do you think they've got something to hide?" After the conversation with Dr. Wisely, she had *so* many questions, but she wouldn't tell Akira what he'd told her in the church lobby. Mae had, after all, promised loyalty to Halsey Green, and gossiping with another employee didn't seem to constitute loyalty.

"All I do is watch the kids," Akria said. "*You're* the one with access to all their personal information."

Mae looked off into the distance, not wanting Akira to see whatever glimmer of truth might show in her eyes. "Yeah. Good point."

The nanny pressed on. "So what do *you* think? Do *you* think they've got something to hide?"

Mae wished she'd kept her mouth shut. But she respected Akira. She respected anyone who got to the point quickly. "I haven't worked here long enough to know."

"Well, whatever they're up to, we're in this together." Akira laughed. "I feel like we should pinky swear or something."

Mae held up her little finger, and Akira wrapped hers around Mae's just as a beat-up, old pickup pulled into the long driveway. Both women turned to watch it approach.

"Do you know who that is?" Mae asked.

"I think it's that janitor guy. Conrad."

They walked back to the circle drive and waited for the faded red truck to reach them. Mae hoped Conrad wouldn't ask why she and Akira had been hanging out on the side of the garage.

As soon as Conrad's truck came to a stop, he flung open the driver's side door and jumped from the truck. He wore the same navy blue coveralls he'd had on each time she'd seen him. "I am *so sorry*, Miss Mae."

His jitteriness made her nervous. "For what?"

He grabbed a metal toolbox from the bed of his truck and acted like he might rush inside the house. "I was supposed to be here at eight, but one of my mama dogs was having her litter and having a really tough go of it, and I felt like I needed to stay to help her and—"

She put a hand on his arm, trying to calm him. "Relax. It's okay."

"But I told Mr. Halsey I would be here at eight." His eyes darted to Akira, as if trying to determine if she'd tattle about his tardiness.

"To do what?" Mae asked.

"He wanted me to take a look at the garbage disposal. Said it was making a funny sound."

Mae looked to Akira for confirmation that she read the situation correctly. The other woman also appeared calm. "So not an emergency, then?" Mae said. "No need to be in such a tizzy. It's not a big deal."

"I'm just . . . I don't want to lose my job. I've already been late a few times to the church, and they said—"

So he'd been late for work, but his intentions were good. That's why no silvery tone showed on his skin. It had taken young Mae a while to figure it out, but she'd eventually learned that her internal alarm system displayed a person's deepest thoughts—the private agenda they'd never willingly reveal to the world.

She leaned toward him, making sure he listened closely to what she said. "We're not going to tell anyone what time you got here." She moved her gaze to the nanny. "Are we, Akira?"

The younger woman checked a nonexistent watch on her wrist. "Looks to me like he got here at 8 a.m. sharp."

He blew out a long breath and stood silently for a moment, as if reassessing the situation. Some of the tension seemed to flow from his body.

"The puppies are okay?" Mae asked.

He smiled. "Five of them. Four males and a female."

Akira let out an "Awww."

"And the mama's okay?" Mae asked.

He shook his head, but the grin remained on his face. "I don't know how she did it, but she came through like a champ. She's a tiny little thing." He held his hands out to indicate the size of a loaf of bread. "But the father must be big, because she struggled a lot to get those babies out."

"Well, then you've done your good deed for the day, helping her." Actually, it sounded like he did good deeds every day, caring for those poor animals that had been dumped on the side of the road like trash.

He let out a single laugh. "She did all the work. I just gave her some comfort."

Mae smiled. That was what life *should* be all about, right? Providing comfort to others. Making their lives a little easier, if you could. Helping them find a little peace. Too bad the world didn't work like that. She'd learned that over and over again. "Let's get you a cup of coffee to celebrate."

He nodded once. "I'd like that, ma'am."

She walked toward the house, with him trailing behind. Akira opened the back door of her SUV and rummaged through a pile of things in the back seat.

"Did you get any breakfast during all the excitement at your place this morning?" Mae asked when she and Conrad had gotten inside. "The housekeeper made some chicken salad for all the employees to eat. Can I make you a sandwich?"

When she turned to look at him, he bowed his head, as if he didn't want to answer.

"Come on," she said, motioning for him to follow her to the kitchen. "There's plenty for everyone. I'm making you a sandwich. White, wheat, or croissant?"

"I don't want to trouble you," he said sheepishly.

"Croissant, it is. I don't know where they get them, but they're *delicious*." She pointed to the coffee pot. "The mugs are right above the pot. There's sugar and sweetener up there too. Spoons are in that drawer, and the milk's in here." She opened the fridge to get out the chicken salad. Before starting work for Halsey, she'd never been in a kitchen where the appliance stood hidden behind cabinetry that matched the rest of the room. She assumed this was true for Conrad, too, and she didn't want to embarrass him if he couldn't find the fridge.

They worked in silence for a minute or so—him making himself a cup of coffee and her preparing his sandwich. The muted voices of Klara, Lejla, and Ilma floated down from upstairs, though Mae didn't understand their native tongue. She heard the front door open, then watched as Akira's bright red Chucks walked up the stairs near the front of the house.

"I really should get to work," Conrad said as she handed him his plate.

"You have five minutes to eat a sandwich."

"But if Mr. Halsey—"

"Would you relax? No one's going to know what time you got here." She strode to the table in the breakfast nook and pulled out a chair. "Now, sit. Eat."

She got him a napkin, then fixed herself a third cup of coffee. The older she got, the more insomnia plagued her, but she really needed the caffeine after tossing and turning over the conversation with Dr. Wisely last night.

She joined Conrad at the table, hoping to make him feel more at ease. Outside, the construction crew worked, but there'd been no sign of Ezra so far that morning.

"They're building a new deck out there?" Conrad asked.

"And a new dock." She and Ezra had met three times now, in the late afternoons, so he could give her his daily update. Each time, she'd had to ask him what some construction term meant, but he seemed to enjoy explaining things to her.

"I wonder if this place floods when a hurricane blows through," Conrad said, interrupting her thoughts.

"On the intracoastal?" The other places she'd lived in Florida had suffered hurricane damage over the years, but they'd all been inland, away from the water.

He nodded. "Pretty much any body of water floods during a storm surge—the intracoastal, the St. Johns River, all the marshes. Some folks along Black Creek flooded so many times, they finally moved away."

Mae considered the topography she'd seen since moving to Northeast Florida. With all that water, no wonder people thought of the entire state as a swamp. She looked beyond the construction mess out to the intracoastal, trying to imagine what it might be like if that wide body of water got even wider, covering the kitchen floor with brackish water and whatever might come with it—alligators and snakes and dirt and germs. What a mess that would be to clean up.

"There are three or four storms out over the Atlantic right now, you know," Conrad said.

She didn't know. She did her best to avoid the negativity of the news as much as possible. "Any coming close to here?"

"Too early to tell." He took a bite of his sandwich and watched as Ezra's crew cut the straps off a bundle of pavers and sorted through them.

After a couple of minutes of companionable silence, she asked, "How often do you work here at the house?"

Conrad shrugged as he chewed the last bite of his chicken salad. "Maybe once a month. Sometimes more, sometimes less."

"What kinds of things do you work on?"

A second shrug from Conrad. "Stopped up toilets. A clothes dryer that wasn't heating up like it should. I even worked on their golf cart once."

"Do you bill him for your time? Like, does *Halsey* pay for it when you're out here doing work for him? Or does the church pay for it?" She hadn't meant to quiz the guy, but if Halsey skimmed off the offering plate, then maybe he skimmed in other ways too.

Conrad's eyes widened. His hands rose in front of him, palms facing her. "I don't want to get anyone in trouble."

She tried to appear nonchalant. The poor man already buzzed with tension. "I'm just trying to understand how things work around here. I mean, I pay Halsey's bills, so I need to know what to expect in terms of a bill from you."

He glanced out at the construction workers, like he was trying to decide how to answer. Finally, he returned his gaze to her. "I clock in at the church, like I do every day."

"You do that on days you come here to work?"

He answered quickly, as if defending himself. "I've never been here a full day. Maybe a few hours in the morning or the afternoon."

She held one hand in a *calm down* gesture. "It's okay. I'm not saying you're doing anything wrong."

He wiped his mouth with his napkin, then stood and picked up his plate. "I'd better get to work now."

She stood, too, and eased the plate from his hand. "I'll take this for you."

She rinsed his plate and loaded it into the dishwasher as he went to the foyer to retrieve his toolbox.

"Will the mama dog be okay all day without you there to help her?" she asked when he'd returned to the kitchen.

"I hope so." He set the toolbox on the floor and opened the cabinet under the sink. "Four weeks ago, she would have been giving birth out in the woods or behind a dumpster or somewhere like that. At least she's on a soft blanket inside my laundry room. I left food and water for her and made sure the puppies were nursing." His mouth held the hint of a smile as he seemed to remember the sight of the mother with her babies.

"The world needs more people like you," she said.

His cheeks grew red. "Just doing my part."

She laid her hand on his where it rested on the counter. "Thank you for that."

He nodded once—an acknowledgment—then slid his hand from underneath hers and bent to look under the sink.

She returned to her desk in the laundry room as the housekeepers clambered down the stairs, their various tools in tow. From down the hall, she heard Klara give Conrad a cheerful greeting.

Mae sat there, her hands motionless on the keyboard as she thought about how Conrad had stayed at home, comforting the mother dog through labor, despite his fear of being in trouble at work. About how a simple man who didn't seem to have a lot of money carried out this mission in life. Showed this kindness to another being.

He didn't need a mansion or a megachurch or a league of followers. He needed an old blanket and a bowl of water and a desire to leave the world a better place than he'd found it. Maybe Mae needed to find a mission like that. Maybe that would make her less calloused. Less jaded by humanity.

Too bad society didn't seek out and celebrate people with Conrad's kindness, his compassion.

No, the world was too focused on wealth and power and celebrity and greed.

The world was too busy rewarding people like Halsey Green.

Chapter Twenty

Mae came down the front steps at Halsey's house and headed toward her car. "Hey," she said to Ezra, who loaded tools in the back of his truck. "I've got to grab something from my car." They had yet to have their end-of-the-day update—the fourth since Halsey had implemented that ridiculous rule. The others had been uneventful. She'd written down Ezra's wording in her phone word for word—afraid she'd get something wrong since she didn't understand most of what he said—then passed the message on to Halsey via email. So far, so good, though she still had no idea why she had to be the intermediary between the two men.

She took a key from her pocket, opened the trunk of her car, and took out a small cooler. "I brought refreshments for our update tonight."

He glanced at the cooler in her hand and gave her a quizzical look.

She slammed the trunk closed, then shrugged as she walked past him toward the house. "I hear the sunsets over the intra-coastal are gorgeous. We might as well enjoy it since we're both working late."

"Refreshments?" he asked.

She paused and turned to look back at him. "Are you coming or not?"

He followed her as she made her way around the side of the house, through the gate, and onto the back deck, which stood partially complete.

She set the cooler down and opened the lid. "I've got Mich Ultra, a couple of different IPAs, and some bottled iced tea if you're not into beer." She'd taken the teas from Cole's stash in the fridge at his house.

She turned and dragged a deck chair from where it had been stored out of the way, under the eaves.

"Does the minister care if we drink beer at his house?" He hauled a second chair toward the first one.

"They're gone for the evening—some charity event. Plus, it's not like Halsey and Dawn don't drink. They've got an entire liquor cabinet in there." She nodded toward the house.

"An IPA, then. And thank you." His gaze met hers as they worked together to position the chairs so that they faced westward, toward the water.

She bent over the cooler, pulled out a can of Intuition I-10, and popped it open for him.

"Good choice," he said. "I visit their brewery anytime I have to be in downtown Jacksonville."

She got a Mich Ultra for herself, then settled into the chair closest to her. He sat in the other chair and took a big swig from the can.

She, too, took a drink of her beer. The cold bite of the icy brew reminded her of that first jump into Ichetucknee Springs on a hot summer's day.

The sun sat a few inches above the horizon on the other side of the intracoastal.

"I've been wanting to watch the sunset from here, so I figured I'd invite you to join me," she said.

His long legs were stretched out in front of him, his ankles crossed. "It . . . uhhhh . . . wasn't what I expected."

"If you don't want to do our daily update like this, I can take this back and . . ." She playfully tried to ease the beer from his hand.

"Whoa. Whoa. Whoa." He laughed as he tightened his grip on the can. "I didn't say that."

She pulled her feet up onto her chair, settling in. "I figured you might welcome a nice, cold beer after working all day out in the heat. I mean, is there any place hotter than Florida in the summer?"

He shrugged. "Beats sitting in a cubicle all day. No way could I ever survive cooped up in an office somewhere, even if I do smell like a goat at the end of the day."

She laughed. "I thought it was just all the manliness wafting off you."

He grunted. "Yeah. Something like that."

"So, what's the update for today?"

Ezra told her how the pavers had arrived ahead of schedule but couldn't be installed until all the heavy equipment had been in and out of the yard. How the pilings would be poured for the new dock tomorrow. How his normal electrician had broken his leg and would be out of work for six weeks, but Ezra had secured another, equally qualified one.

While he talked, her thumbs flew over the keyboard on her phone, typing the update she'd send on to Halsey. When Ezra was finished, she read silently over the text on her phone for a minute or two, checking for typos. "Okay. Send." She poked at her screen with her forefinger. "Now we're off the clock." She picked up her beer again and tapped it against his. "Cheers."

"How do you like working for him, anyway?"

"It's a job, I guess." One she'd gladly leave behind if—and when—something better came along.

"You don't enjoy it?"

"It's not exactly my dream job."

"So what *is* your dream job?"

"My degree's in public relations. And that's what I did before I came to Jax Beach."

Ezra looked like he might say something but then thought better of it. She was thankful for that. She didn't want to talk about how being Halsey Green's personal admin was miles away from the kind of PR job she wanted.

"What about you? What's your dream job?" she asked.

He spread his arms wide to indicate the construction project that surrounded them. "I'm doing it. This is it."

She chuckled. "Good for you, then."

"I like it all except the selling. The constant need to find new projects. Those Chamber of Commerce events where you have to go 'network' with other people are painful." He put air quotes around the word *network*.

She picked at the label on her bottle. "Yeah, I would guess that your typical construction guy and your typical sales guy don't have a lot of traits in common. Seems like it'd be hard to be both at the same time."

He gave her the side-eye. "I'm the owner of the company."

She sat back, reprimanded. "I didn't mean to offend you." But he'd come up through the ranks as a construction worker, no? "I mean, I wish I'd made different decisions in the past. I wish I'd started my own company years ago. Maybe I wouldn't be Halsey Green's assistant if that were the case."

He clinked his bottle against hers. "Well, I, for one, am glad you're here."

They shared a smile that had nothing to do with construction projects, then turned their heads to where the sun sank toward the horizon—a kaleidoscope of blue and peach and pink. She kept quiet, not wanting anything to disrupt the magnificence of the view.

After several minutes, Ezra spoke. "Do you know a guy named Bull Williams?"

She stiffened. "No, why?"

He barked out a single laugh. "Then why'd you have that reaction? You went all rigid when I said his name."

She took a long sip while she formed her answer. "You tell me what you know about him first."

"So you *do* know him."

"He's on the board of directors at Halsey's church, but—no—I've never met him." She returned her gaze to the horizon.

He scoffed. "Then Halsey needs to learn to keep his friends close and his enemies closer."

"What's that supposed to mean?"

"I ran into him at a Chamber event the other day. The guy kept giving me shit about doing the project out here. Said there was a good chance I wouldn't get paid and if I did, it'd be with money the little old ladies of Jax Beach offered up to the church. He acted like I was stealing their social security dollars or something."

She turned to face him, eager to hear more.

"You think it's true?" he asked. "You think there's a chance we won't get paid?"

She turned back to face the sunset, choosing her words carefully. "I . . . have no indication that he won't pay you."

"Then why would this Bull Williams say that?"

"Bull Williams's daughter apparently works in some underserved elementary school in downtown Jacksonville. Bull wanted PALM to adopt the school—to buy them supplies and books and whatnot—but Halsey turned it down."

"Because why would a church give money to poor people?"

She shrugged. "I guess they can't give money to every worthy cause out there." But it did seem like Halsey could spend a little less on himself and a little more on people who really needed it.

Ezra grunted. "So Bull Williams goes around town bad-mouthing Halsey because of it?"

"Apparently, but I've never met the guy."

"He badmouthed Halsey to me, and I'd never met him, either. And he's on the PALM board of directors?"

"Like you said, 'keep your friends close and your enemies closer.'"

He scoffed. "Yeah. No kidding."

She flicked a hand in his direction. "Now shut up about work. Let's enjoy the sunset."

They sat in silence as the bottom quarter of the sun dipped below the horizon. The sky seemed to ignite all at once—a fiery mix of bright orange and fuchsia and purple. She glanced over and caught him in a brief, unguarded moment. The childlike wonder on his face made her curious what he'd been like as a kid, a teen, even a younger man. She admired the way his crew meant so much to him, and she wanted to know more about that gentler side of him.

They watched for several minutes as the sun disappeared beyond the intracoastal waterway. Even when it was gone, they remained there, comfortable in the silence.

His hand hung limp off the end of the arm of his chair. She wanted to reach out and touch it. To intertwine her fingers with his. To see how he would react when her skin met his. She was pretty sure the attraction was mutual, but she couldn't be certain. After Rocco, she no longer trusted her instincts the way she once had.

"I guess we should go," she whispered in the dark. "The Greens would think it was creepy if they got home and found us out here just sitting in the dark."

"This was my favorite daily update." She could hear the smile in his voice.

"I thought it might be."

And still, they sat in silence a few more minutes, listening to the sounds of the night. A chorus of frogs croaked in the water. An owl hooted off to the left. A motorcycle drove by out on Roscoe Boulevard but seemed miles away.

Finally, he stood and offered his hand. She took it and allowed him to help her out of the low-slung Adirondack chair. They dragged the chairs back under the eaves and made their way to the side of the house and slipped out the gate. It was dark there now that the sun had set.

She latched the gate behind her and turned. He stood directly in front of her now—closer than she'd expected. She could sense his presence but couldn't tell if he'd placed himself so close on purpose or if by accident. She took in a sharp inhale.

"We should do this more often," he said, his voice husky and low.

"We should."

His hand reached up to rest on her tricep. His eyes glimmered in the moonlight as her gaze rose to his.

He feathered his fingers along her arm. "Is this okay?"

A soft sound of affirmation escaped her. It was way more than okay.

Then slowly, slowly, he lowered his mouth to hers.

Chapter Twenty-One

Ezra brushed his lips across Mae's, tentative and questioning, as if seeking her approval. The inky darkness beside Halsey's house felt like a cocoon—a special place where her senses were heightened and where Ezra—strong and steady—stood ready to welcome her into his arms.

Her body thrummed with anticipation. She'd lain in bed some nights, wondering what it might be like to be this close to him. To touch him. To feel the hardness of those muscles underneath his shirt.

She took a step toward him as his mouth settled on hers. She stumbled over his foot a bit and mumbled a soft apology. He made a reassuring sound—not really a word—but then words weren't necessary now. This moment was all about their bodies reacting to each other. Her hands glided up his arms to his shoulders. Her breasts pressed against his upper ribcage. He rested his hands on her waist.

The touch of his tongue, the softness of his lips, the firmness of his body made everything else fall away. The only thing she cared about was the here and now.

Slowly, he pulled away, but not before taking a playful nip at her bottom lip.

"Wow. You give a guy a beer and . . ." Her almost inaudible laugh floated away in the night air.

"And what?" His fingers still rested on her waist. He gave her a teasing squeeze.

"He gets a little frisky." Not that she objected.

"Does Halsey know you planned to get the construction crew drunk and seduce them in the dark?"

Her giggle mingled with the sound of the crickets. "First of all, you only had one beer. And secondly, the *crew* isn't here."

"But you haven't denied it was part of your evil plan."

"We really need to go before the Greens get home." Her hands still lay on his chest. She smoothed one over his pec, then pushed away.

Headlights shone out on Roscoe Boulevard, but—luckily—passed the Greens' driveway without pulling in.

She bent and fumbled in the dark until she found the handle to the cooler, then picked it up and turned to walk toward her car. His footsteps brushed the grass behind her. Finally, a motion sensor light came on as they reached the front corner of the house.

He reached out and took the cooler from her, lightening her load. When they reached her car, she used her key to open the trunk, then turned to face him.

"Given what just happened over there"—he jabbed a thumb toward the side of the house—"does that mean you'll go out on a date with me?"

A feeling of warmth cascaded through her body. She tipped her head and grinned at him. "So my evil plan worked."

"Is that a *yes*?"

She nodded slowly. "It's a *yes*."

"I'm driving down to Homosassa this weekend to see my mom and sister."

She wondered about his relationship with his family. Did he *want* to go visit them, or was this trip to the other side of the state out of obligation?

He continued. "I can't really blow them off, so maybe a week from Saturday?"

She nodded. She really didn't want to wait that long, but she wasn't going to stand in the way of any man going to visit his family. She'd always felt like an outsider looking in on all those families that stayed together. That visited each other. That still formed a cohesive unit, regardless of where each person lived.

"Let me think about where we should go. You have any preferences?"

She took the cooler from his grasp and placed it in the open trunk. "I don't know. Somewhere casual."

"It's the beach. Everything is casual."

She glanced toward the mansion. "Oh, yeah? Tell that to Halsey Green."

He grunted out a laugh. "Good point."

She closed the trunk and turned to face him. "Thanks for having a beer with me tonight."

"Thanks for inviting me."

She wanted to kiss him again before they left, but there was a good chance Halsey had cameras on the outside of the house, even if the nanny cams inside no longer worked. Hell, he likely had one out back, too—one that had already captured the two of them sitting on the deck drinking a beer together.

But the side-of-the-house kiss would be their little secret, at least for now. One she would hold for herself, not sharing it with anyone.

***

Mae scrolled through her phone as she sat in the main office of PALM, waiting for Halsey to see her. Barb, the new receptionist, had gotten her a bottle of water and apologized for the delay.

"You might as well get comfortable," said the tattooed twentysomething woman Mae had met during her interview process. She'd come out of her office to pick up something off the printer next to Barb's desk. "Halsey's meetings with the mayor always run long."

"Does he meet with the mayor often?" Barb seemed starstruck.

The other woman shrugged. "Depends on which one." She walked to where Mae sat and held out her hand. "I'm Casey, by the way. I'm the youth minister."

Mae sat up straighter and shook it. "Mae. I'm Halsey's personal assistant."

"Yeah. I know. We met when you were here to interview." Casey returned her attention to Barb. "He meets with the Jax Beach mayor most, but the other mayors want time with him too."

"The *other* mayors?" Mae asked.

"Jacksonville, Atlantic Beach, Neptune Beach. Each town has its own mayor."

"And what do they want with Halsey? I mean, his church isn't even in their town?" The PALM campus sat squarely on the Jax Beach side of the intracoastal waterway, at least a couple of miles south of Neptune Beach. Atlantic Beach sat even farther away, to the north of Neptune Beach.

Casey shrugged. "Halsey's a big name around here. People from all those towns attend his church."

"So what do the mayors want from him?" Barb repeated Mae's question.

Casey glanced down the hall toward Halsey's office and lowered her voice. "I've always assumed it was more for the optics than anything. 'Look at me. I've got an in with the famous pastor.' But they probably want to know his stance on some of the issues too. If he preaches something from the pulpit, his followers tend to listen."

"Do they also want money from the church?" Mae asked. The feud with Bull Williams, after all, had apparently started when Bull wanted Halsey to donate funds toward the school where Bull's daughter taught.

Casey snorted. "*Everyone* wants money from him. They look at his house and his car and his expensive suits and assume PALM is rolling in it."

"Are they not?" Mae asked. "Rolling in it?"

"I guess that depends on who you ask." Casey rapped her knuckles on Barb's desk, as if to adjourn the little gathering, then headed back into her office.

Mae and Barb exchanged a questioning glance.

What the hell did that mean?

Mae wanted to follow Casey back down the hall and into her office. To warn her about not talking so openly about topics that others might prefer to keep quiet. Given her age, Casey couldn't have that much experience in the workplace. But who was Mae to offer guidance to a younger woman? She'd been in her mid-thirties, after all, when the hot mic in Tallahassee had caught her badmouthing her employer's biggest donor. She didn't want Casey to get in trouble, but Mae knew she was hardly a good role model for someone who told too many truths in the workplace.

Finally, Halsey's door opened and he strolled down the hall, walking a middle-aged white man to the reception area. The other man's skin held the healthy tan you might expect on the mayor of a beach community, but Halsey's skin emanated an almost pulsing silver sheen.

The pair exchanged friendly farewells and a firm handshake, then Halsey motioned for Mae to follow him back to his office.

He handed her a thick, sealed, business-sized envelope, along with instructions to hand-deliver it to his attorney in Atlantic Beach. *This afternoon,* he emphasized, though Atlantic Beach was just a few minutes from there. Even Mae knew it sat right up Third Street, and she'd only lived in town for a few weeks.

She hadn't seen him in person over the last couple of days and had hoped to tell him privately about her conversation with Dr. Wisely. But before she could delve into the topic, Barb stuck her head in the door and reminded him that his next Zoom call had started five minutes ago.

He pointed to the envelope in Mae's hand. "This afternoon," he repeated, then sat at his desk, repositioned his ring light, and pasted on a fake smile, ready to charm the world with his brotherly love.

As Mae left the church offices, she wondered again if she should just text Halsey about the fact that a member of the board had approached her about his American Express bills. Surely that would get his attention. Make him stop whatever he was doing to give her a few minutes of his time. But she didn't want to give him a heads up about the conversation, and she didn't want to discuss the topic with him via text or over the phone. She wanted to see his face when she first told him the news. To see his body language—and the silver tone of his skin—as she shared Dr. Wisely's request regarding Halsey's American Express bills. After all, she'd learned in school that more than seventy percent of communication was nonverbal, and she wanted to see Halsey's reaction when she told him about it. There were too many potentially suspicious things going on for her not to gather all the information she could—both verbal and nonverbal.

She moved her fingertips along the edges of the envelope as she walked down the hall toward the exit of the administrative wing. It didn't feel like a wad of cash, so likely not a movement of funds, like with the Flagler Beach errand. Instead, the envelope seemed to hold a thin stack of letter-sized papers, held together by a binder clip. A document of some kind, being hand-delivered to Halsey's attorney.

She pulled her sunglasses from her head over her eyes and pushed the door open to exit the building. Her step stuttered the second she saw her car. She'd gotten one of the few shady spots in the parking lot, and now a man leaned against her driver's side, as if waiting for her.

Forcing herself past the initial surprise, she tucked the envelope Halsey had given her inside her purse and continued walking toward the man. His back was to her, but the closer she got, the more she became convinced it was Rob Lassiter.

The journalist turned as she approached. "Fancy meeting you here," he said.

"That might be funny if you weren't *leaning on my car*." She glared at him as she ground out her words.

He pushed himself off the side of the vehicle. "You said I wasn't welcome at the property on Roscoe Boulevard."

"You're not."

He motioned toward the church. "I'm a potential new member of the congregation. Surely I'm welcome here."

She closed the door, glad the car stood between them. "What do you want?"

"I'd like an appointment with Halsey Green. I can meet anywhere—his house, the church, my office, at a Starbucks somewhere."

"Call the church office. They're in charge of his calendar."

"He's implemented a 'no journalists' rule. At least that's what the new lady, Barb, told me."

Mae wondered if that rule really existed or if Barb had made it up. Maybe the new receptionist had more chutzpah than Mae had initially suspected. If so, good for her. "Then why are you asking me the same question?"

He slid a small notepad out of the back pocket of his khakis and pulled the pen out of the spiral wire at the top. "Do you think Halsey will accept the church's offer of separation?"

She did her best not to show her surprise. A chief rule of public relations was to never appear unprepared. She couldn't let Rob Lassiter—or any journalist for that matter—think she wasn't in the know when it came to her boss. On the other hand, she would *kill* Halsey for not telling her about this new development. Her hand tightened around the envelope he'd handed her a few minutes ago. Did the papers inside have something to do with Halsey perhaps parting ways with PALM?

Moreover, she wondered how this would impact *her*. If Halsey left the church, could he still afford to pay her? A hollowness filled her gut—the awful dread of being back on the job market. The futility of trying to find a position when no one seemed to be hiring. "Personnel matters are confidential, Mr. Lassiter."

"How quickly would the family anticipate moving from the house?"

"From Halsey's house?" His last question made no sense.

Lassiter barked out a laugh. "Is that what he told you?"

She looked at him, still confused.

"It's a hell of a parsonage—that's for sure—but the house belongs to the church. So how quickly would they plan to move?" He poised his pen above the notepad, but she got the distinct impression he knew she didn't have an answer. He was taunting her. Making a point about how uninformed she was. Why the hell did his skin not have the silvery glow when he was clearly up to no good?

Mae immediately thought of Ezra. Bull Williams had indicated that Halsey might not pay Ezra for his work, and if the church really did own the property, didn't that make nonpayment from Halsey more likely? But would a person really rack up big construction bills on a house they didn't even own? "As I said before, personnel matters are confidential."

"If you don't know the answers, then get me an appointment with Halsey Green. That's all I'm asking. Our viewers deserve to know what's going on with the biggest church in town."

She didn't normally manage Halsey's calendar, but she was tempted to try to get Rob Lassiter in front of her boss—to let Halsey be the one to deal with him. Payback for Halsey not keeping her informed about a big new development. For letting her flounder with half-baked information when she was supposed to be his "PR person." A flare of anger heated her chest at the way he'd duped her into accepting that role.

But a zing of smug delight quickly followed the anger. She hadn't yet told him about her conversation with Dr. Wisely. Maybe the unintended delay would work in her favor. If Halsey kept important information from her, then perhaps she wouldn't be so eager to tell Halsey about her encounter with Dr. Wisely. "I will do my best to get you an appointment with Halsey."

"Hot damn." Rob Lassiter slapped his notebook against the other palm—a victorious motion.

She held up one hand. "I make no promises, but I'll at least ask him."

It would serve Halsey right.

Chapter Twenty-Two

Mae let herself in through Halsey's garage door, though she viewed the house differently since her conversation with Rob Lassiter an hour ago. She'd dropped off the envelope with Halsey's attorney, wondering the entire time if its contents had something to do with Halsey's alleged and potential departure from the church.

Now, standing next to Halsey's fridge, she let her gaze move around the large expanse—the kitchen, the great room, the breakfast nook, the formal dining room on the other side of the archway. So the Greens didn't own this house?

That meant Halsey had an even sweeter gig than she'd suspected. He raked in whatever salary he made and didn't even have a house payment? A payment on a place like this would no doubt be substantial. She did some quick Googling and found other homes for sale along Roscoe Boulevard. Those on the intracoastal side of the street started at more than three million dollars and went up from there. The couple of lots that still stood vacant started at 1.5 million. *Damn.* If what Lassiter said was true, she didn't know whether to despise Halsey's greed or admire him for orchestrating such a great deal for himself.

A pill bottle by the oven caught her eye. Probably some antibiotic for one of the kids, but she was tired of being blindsided by Halsey's secrets. Tired of putting herself at risk when she knew so little about him.

She listened for the sound of other people in the house. Klara's car had been out front, but Mae didn't hear anything inside. She crept to the pill bottle and picked it up.

It had Ilma's name on it. The name of the drug: Altretamine.

Mae pulled her phone from her pocket and googled. The words on the screen were like a punch to her sternum. She sucked in a breath, just like she had when she'd fallen off Lucy Wong's porch railing at that party last year and had the breath knocked out of her.

Altretamine was oral chemotherapy. A pill taken to treat late-stage ovarian cancer.

Ilma wasn't hungover all those mornings Mae had judged her. She was *fighting for her life.*

Mae stumbled toward the sink, suddenly in need of some water and vaguely aware of the pill bottle hitting the tile floor behind her. She turned on the faucet and let the cool water run over her hands as she closed her eyes and tried to catch her breath. When she turned to reach for a glass in the upper cabinet next to her, she saw Klara on the other side of the kitchen, glaring at Mae.

Klara held the pill bottle out in front of her. "This is none of your business." Her voice shook with rage. Her skin reddened with anger.

"I . . ." Mae still hadn't gotten a drink of water. She had trouble getting her tongue to work. "I had no idea."

The housekeeper glowered at her. "Because it is none of your business."

Technically, it *was* Mae's business. Klara reported to Mae and Ilma reported to Klara, but Mae wouldn't point that out. Not when self-loathing washed over her like a cascading waterfall. She'd been so judgmental. So quick to form an opinion.

I'd thought she was hungover.

I'd thought the worst of her.

But Mae didn't say those thoughts out loud. Not when they said so much about how awful she was and so little about Ilma. "What can I do to help her?" Her voice was barely audible.

"You do not tell Mr. Halsey about this." Klara shook the pill bottle in front of her, as if to emphasize the point. "Or Miss Dawn. Or anyone else."

"I won't." Mae inched toward the fridge, remembering the stash of water bottles inside. "But why are you not telling them? Maybe they could help." The Greens had money, connections. They probably knew doctors at the nearby Mayo Clinic.

"When Freja's baby was in the hospital, Mr. Halsey fired her for missing work. I cannot let that happen to Ilma."

"He *fired* her? When her baby was in the hospital?"

"Baby was sick for two weeks only." Klara jabbed two fingers in the air. "Then back to stay with Freja's mother every day, like before, but Mr. Halsey said it was too much."

The man really was an ass. "So Ilma comes to work, even when she doesn't feel well." It wasn't a question. Mae now understood what she'd failed to see over the past weeks.

"Lejla and I do the work. We do not mind the extra, but Ilma must be here if Mr. Halsey or Ms. Dawn comes home."

Mae nodded, though based on how Ilma looked last week, Mae wasn't sure anyone would believe she was strong enough to perform any household tasks. But then she'd never seen Halsey really look at the housekeepers. Never in the face. Never in the eyes.

Mae now saw Klara in a new light—and Lejla too. These were *good* women. Far better than the wealthy pastor whose shower they shrubbed and whose carpets they vacuumed. "You cover for her. You do extra work, and you cover for her." Mae's tone was reverent, respectful—but Klara didn't seem to notice.

The older woman tucked the bottle of pills in the pocket of her smock. "You do not tell our secret." Mae now realized the edge in Klara's voice was less anger than it was protectiveness. Klara protected her own. Yes, she misled her employer, but for all the right reasons. Her intentions were good.

"I'm not going to tell them." Mae's voice cracked as shame washed over her. Who had she become that she couldn't see the truth in this woman's condition? That she'd look at someone in Ilma's condition and not see the real human truth of it instead of her own projections? Who had she become that she'd assume the worst of Conrad, for that matter? When the "drug deal" in the parking lot turned out to be Conrad taking on a new dog? Providing a new home to a little being that needed to be housed and fed and loved?

Mae had always prided herself in seeing the truths that others turned away from because they didn't want to see. But here, she'd been the one who'd failed to see the truth—the truth of how many good people there really were in this world.

The sound of the garage door raising made both women's eyes widen. Klara bolted up the stairs, probably to roust Ilma from wherever she lay resting. Mae rushed toward the laundry room, not ready to face Halsey or Dawn in the wake of what she'd just learned.

She turned on the computer and took several long, deep breaths while she waited for it to boot up.

Halsey's voice echoed from the kitchen. He was on a call of some kind. Words like *vendor payments* and *cash receipts* stood out among the rumble of his voice. Was it *cash receipts* she'd taken down to Sherlene in Flagler Beach? Was that how churches categorized their income?

Her shock at learning Ilma's news slowly gave way to anger toward Halsey. The more Mae learned about him, the more wretched he became. Yes, she was paid to be his personal assistant, but that didn't mean she had to respect him. It didn't mean she had to use her hard-earned PR skills to protect his questionable character. And it didn't mean that she had to keep Rob Lassiter away from him.

Finally, his call ended. He got ice from the front of the fridge and puttered around the kitchen a bit, based on the noises she heard. Footsteps sounded from upstairs—the housekeepers at work in the kids' rooms.

Mae scrolled mindlessly through her email, unable to concentrate on it. Instead, her brain played out potential conversations with Halsey about what Rob Lassiter had said. She wanted to talk to Halsey in the laundry room—in private—but there was no guarantee that he'd come to visit her there. She rose and walked into the kitchen.

"Did you get those papers delivered to the attorney?" he asked as she entered the room.

And hello to you too. "Handed them directly to him, per your instructions."

"Good girl." He took a long swig from his glass.

Mountain Dew, she guessed, based on the color of the liquid. "I also had a chat with Rob Lassiter, that reporter from the Channel Ten news."

The muscles in Halsey's throat stilled though the glass remained raised to his mouth.

Mae continued. "He'd really like to get on your calendar. Says he'll meet you anywhere. You name the place."

Halsey lowered the glass and glared at her. "I am not meeting with that man."

"Then you need to tell me what's going on with your job. Because he sure knows a lot more about it than I do. Makes it hard for me to know how to respond to his questions."

Halsey's already silvery skin seemed to pulse with energy.

The rippling sensation underneath Mae's eyebrow ached. She reached up and ran a finger over it, hoping to ease the pain.

He looked around the large great room and down the hall, then grabbed her by the upper arm and steered her toward the laundry room.

She hated being manhandled by him. His grabbing her in that way violated all kinds of societal rules, not to mention pissed her off. If this was how he treated her, then maybe she'd *never* tell him about how Dr. Wisely had approached her at the church the other day. She jerked her arm out of his grasp but continued to follow him to where they could talk in private. She wanted to get to the bottom of this.

"What did he tell you?" Halsey hissed as soon as the laundry room door was closed securely behind them.

"I think he used the term *offer of separation*." Or maybe the board had asked Halsey to resign? Mae couldn't remember the specific words Rob Lassiter had used. She'd been too shocked at the time to recall exactly what he'd said.

Halsey let out a huff of frustration and paced on the other side of the large laundry room island. After a couple of times back and forth, he stopped to face her. "How in *the hell* did he get wind of that?"

"So it's true? They asked you to leave?" She rubbed her arm where he'd grabbed her.

"I *founded* that church. I am the *face* of that church." He jabbed his thumb to the north, in the direction of PALM.

But he hadn't answered her question. She silently met his gaze, willing him to continue.

Instead, he ran his fingers through his thick, perfectly coifed hair and paced some more.

"So if it's your church, can the board really make you leave?" She realized that might sound kind of smart-ass, so she rushed to soften it. "I mean, I'm just trying to understand what's going on."

He stopped to face her, his palms flat on the granite island. "They're supposed to be there for oversight. Not to tell me how to run the damn thing. Once again, it's *my* church."

"And Rob Lassiter says the church owns this house?"

"Jesus Christ." Halsey bit out the words as he thrust his hands in the air. His gaze shot to the ceiling.

Mae couldn't tell if he was cursing or hoping to invoke a higher power. It didn't matter to her which he was doing.

He lowered his head and placed his face in his palms. After staying in that position for several seconds, he lowered his hands and met her gaze. "The house has been part of my compensation package for years. Each month that goes by means I own a little bit more of it. *Outright.* No strings attached. And I founded that church *years* ago, so a lot of months have passed."

"Then why would Rob Lassiter say the church owns it?" She really was trying to understand, though she had zero sympathy for Halsey at this point.

"Who is feeding him this bullshit, anyway? Someone on the board must be talking and . . ." Halsey raised his hand in a fist, then lowered it. He turned to face Mae head on. "*I'll* deal with the board. *You* make Rob Lassiter go away."

"He wants an appointment with *you*. He keeps asking questions that there's no way *I* can answer."

"I don't *want* you to answer them." Halsey moved to the laundry room door and placed his hand on the knob, ready to leave. "My personal affairs are none of his business. Or yours."

Chapter Twenty-Three

Mae lay in her bed, unable to sleep, despite the two glasses of wine she'd had that evening. By herself. In Cole's living room.

She rarely had more than one alcoholic drink at a time for fear she might become her mother, but that afternoon's conversation with Halsey played over and over in her mind, making her angrier and angrier each time she relived it. The man was a shyster, had manhandled her at his house earlier that day, may have made her an accomplice to a crime, expected her to be his PR person, yet told her as little as possible about what was going on. Pretty much the definition of a bad client, which put Mae in an untenable situation.

She'd pulled her phone into bed with her, hoping to get lost in *You've Got Mail*—her favorite comfort movie—but even that didn't help.

Meg Ryan had just figured out that Tom Hanks owned the nearby Fox Books when Mae heard Cole let himself in the front door. She glanced at the clock—a few minutes after midnight. Another long day for him. She had no idea how he switched between early morning and late-night shifts. But she also knew he always took a while to unwind after he got home from the restaurant.

She hit the pause button on her movie, threw a cardigan over her pajamas, and trudged into the living room. "Hey," she said to his back as he leaned into the fridge.

"I brought home some ribs."

"No, thanks. But are you up for some company?"

He stood and turned to face her, a startled look on his face. "Ummmm. Sure?" He opened the can of nonalcoholic beer in his hand with a *kssshhhhh.*

Not exactly the enthusiastic response she'd hoped for, but it wasn't like they'd had a great relationship since she'd moved in. She watched his back as he headed out of the kitchen, remembering all the late-night whisper-sessions they'd had when they were kids. They'd huddle under a blanket and talk for hours—sometimes about real life, sometimes about made-up scenarios involving dragons or winning the lottery or both.

She got a glass of water and joined Cole in the living room, settling onto the couch opposite his big, worn recliner. At least he hadn't turned on the TV, though he held the remote in his hand, like he was itching to use it.

"So what's up?" His gaze was on the blank TV screen.

"I'm going out on a date Saturday night." Best to keep the conversation light, at least in the beginning. Maybe ease into things.

Cole's eyes shifted to her. "With who?"

"His name is Ezra Watts. He owns a construction company here in town."

Cole grunted. "I've seen his trucks around. He probably eats at the restaurant. A lot of construction guys eat there."

Mae was pretty sure Ezra's company had only one truck—singular—but she didn't correct her brother. "He's doing a project out at Halsey Green's house. That's how I met him."

"I'll ask around about him. See if he's a good guy."

"That is *not* why I told you about him. I don't need my big brother checking out any guy I date." And, besides, Cole hadn't given two shits about whom she hung out with when she was younger, when she actually could have used someone looking out for her.

He took a swig of his fake beer. "Then why *did* you tell me?"

She shrugged. "I don't know. Just letting you know what's going on in my life, I guess."

"You couldn't sleep because you're too excited about your hot date?" His grin hadn't changed since they'd been kids. Mae missed that boy. "Has it been that long?" he teased.

"I couldn't sleep because I want to murder Halsey Green."

Cole let out a sarcastic laugh. "Once again, I tried to warn you about that guy." He took an extra-long swig, like a victory celebration.

She hated that he was right. "Even his own board of directors doesn't like him."

"And this surprises you?" At least Cole was no longer looking at the TV.

"But how can he be so . . . famous . . . if nobody likes him?"

"Well, clearly, some people like him. I mean, he fills that gigantic church every Sunday." Cole waved his arm in the general direction of PALM. "And he's got to have some kind of lure, or they wouldn't keep broadcasting the services on TV."

"Do people know him outside of Jacksonville?"

He scoffed. "I have no idea, Pooh Bear. I mean, that's not really my scene."

She stilled. It was the first time Cole had called her by that name since she'd been here—the nickname he'd given her in childhood. Her heart cracked open a bit, wanting to let the old Cole back in. To be as close as they once were, when he'd taught her to fish off the little bridge near their house or when he'd make her breakfast when Mama hadn't come home the night before.

Cole's voice pulled her from her thoughts. "What's he done to you, anyway?"

Mae had trouble getting her bearings. "What?"

He let out an exasperated breath. "Why do you want to murder Halsey Green?"

She went on to tell him a lot of what she knew—the million-dollar-plus home, the firing of the housekeeper whose child was sick, the book collection that focused on building wealth instead of saving souls. The fact that Halsey expected her to defend his image but told her little about any surprises that could pop up in the media. She tried to talk in general terms—knowing that the more specifics she shared, the more she violated Halsey's desire to keep his affairs private.

"So he's a dick," Cole said when she'd finished unloading her big, angry mess onto the living room floor. "A greedy, self-centered dick."

She nodded. "Pretty much so."

Cole got a philosophical look on his face, then took another swig from his can. "But if there's one thing I've learned over the years, it's that we don't ever know all the troubles people have going on in their lives."

"And Halsey *must* have troubles because otherwise, why would he hide—"

Cole held up his hand, which stopped her from speaking. "*Everyone* has troubles, Pooh Bear. And his must be worse because he's on such . . . public display."

"You feel *sorry* for him?"

Cole looked so tired and beat-down—like he had after playing a high school doubleheader in the oppressive Florida heat. "I just think we don't ever really know what's going on inside a person. People have troubles they don't want anyone else to know about."

Mae became suddenly aware that they weren't talking about Halsey Green anymore. "And when did you gain all this wisdom?" No doubt during all those years he'd ghosted her.

He raised his can to his mouth—an attempt to hide behind it, Mae thought. She waited for him to respond.

"You don't get to be forty-years old without seeing a few things," he finally said.

Just tell me, damn it. Stop being so secretive. But Patricia's reprimands about Mae's bluntness shot through her mind. She needed to be . . . softer, more gentle . . . than she wanted to be, especially since he now looked so despondent. "And are those things still . . . troubling you?"

"Like I said, *everyone* has troubles other people don't see. Even people who live in mansions on the intracoastal waterway."

"But we're not talking about Halsey anymore."

He sat forward in his chair, like he was about to stand and leave the room. "Yeah, well, we're not talking about me either."

"I just want to understand . . . what's been going on in your life." Her voice cracked, but maybe that would convey to Cole how much this meant to her. How much *he* meant to her, though she wished that wasn't true. "Where you were all those years?"

He looked at her with eyes so sad it made Mae want to cry. "No, little sister. You really don't want to know."

Chapter Twenty-Four

Mae brushed her hair for the forty-seventh time that evening, knowing that it really didn't change her appearance. She was thirty-four years old, for God's sake. Why was she so nervous about a date?

She'd been okay during most of the week and a half since Ezra had asked her out, especially if she didn't count the erotic dream she'd had about him three nights ago. She couldn't control whatever her subconscious served up in her sleep and, besides, it had been quite pleasant.

But she'd been on edge all day today, hoping that the more they got to know each other that evening, the more they'd like what they found. After Rocco, she had no patience for playing games, and Ezra seemed like a no-games kind of guy.

A knock sounded on the front door. She startled and dropped the hairbrush into the sink.

She rushed to greet him. "Come in," she said as she held the glass storm door open. He looked handsome in his pressed khakis and a peach-colored oxford shirt with the sleeves rolled up. "You want a beer before we get going?"

"You look nice tonight," he said as he stepped into the living room.

She wore her favorite outfit—a deep purple, short-sleeved dress that hugged her body on top and then flared at the waistline. The flounce added a bit of fun and whimsy. "Thanks. You do too."

As he looked around Cole's house, she wondered what he thought of the second-hand furniture, the dated kitchen. But he wasn't a fancy guy himself. Thank God for that. She would never be attracted to someone who lived like Halsey Green.

"Your brother here?" he asked.

"No. He works some nights." She stepped briefly into the bedroom to get her purse, then returned to the living room. "The restaurant business."

"He doesn't work at Palm Valley Fish Camp, does he?"

She frowned. "No. Why?"

"That's where we're going tonight."

"Isn't that just up the road from Halsey's house?" She was pretty sure she passed it every day to and from work.

"Doesn't sound very creative, I know."

"The parking lot is always jammed with cars." She'd actually been quite curious about the place, so she looked forward to going there.

"I've heard it's really good. And watching the sunset over the intracoastal is kind of our thing." He grinned at his own joke.

She gave a quick laugh. "Yes, it is." Their gazes held for a moment or two as memories of the other night danced between them. "Hey, you never told me if you wanted a beer or not," she said.

"Nah. We need to get going if we're going to make our reservation."

She nodded once. "Let's do it." Then she turned to slip her bare feet into the black, high-heeled sandals she hadn't worn since her coworker's wedding in Tallahassee. She'd painted her toenails that afternoon—a light shade of barely-there-lavender that looked almost white.

They made their way out the front door and down the drive to his truck, parked on the street. He rested his fingertips on the small of her back as they walked. She liked the casual way he touched her. Like it was no big deal. Like they were comfortable around each other. Familiar.

Maybe one day they *would* be familiar with each other—know how the other one drank their coffee, what kind of movies they liked, how each other looked when they first woke up in the morning. But those were all things that *might* happen in the future. For now, she needed to concentrate on getting to know him.

He opened the door of his truck and offered a hand to help her up. "Sorry about the farm equipment."

She laughed. "Is that what you call it?" She could tell he'd cleaned the interior prior to their date.

"My Tesla's in the shop."

"Maybe one of us should have stolen Halsey's."

He chuckled, shut her door, and made his way around to the driver's side.

"We need to make a rule," she said as he buckled his seatbelt.

"Uh-oh." He gave her a playful side-eye.

"No talking about Halsey tonight."

"Or his deck and dock project."

She held out her hand, ready to shake. "Deal."

They shook, their gazes lingering a bit longer than necessary as they were turned toward each other. She broke the moment, not wanting him to see in her eyes how important the night was to her. He started the engine and pulled away from the curb.

As they drove toward the restaurant, she asked about his visit to Homosassa. The way he answered her questions, she could tell he loved his family. She respected him for that.

No, he didn't grow up there. He'd grown up in Jax Beach. His mom had moved over there when little sister Lacey had started having children. Lacey had ended up on the gulf coast side of the state when she'd married a guy who worked for a beverage distributor.

Yes, Ezra had a nice visit, but he could only stand so much togetherness. Lacey—four years his junior—was apparently quite the talker. A bundle of nonstop energy that the quieter, laid-back Ezra could only take in small doses.

Mae laughed. "Was it that way when you two were growing up too?"

"I think I . . . wasn't so set in my ways back then," he said slowly. "Like I hadn't quite figured out who I was yet. And, besides, I had to . . . really take care of my mom and my sister once my dad died, so it didn't matter who might annoy me a bit. Lacey was more . . . low-key back then. I think we were all kind of shell-shocked."

Mae wanted to ask how old he'd been when his father had died, but they'd arrived at the restaurant.

"This is fancy," she said as he pulled the truck into the parking lot—a long narrow drive with one row of luxury cars lining each side. Like the homes on this same street, the restaurant sat far back on the lot, close to the intracoastal waterway. A sign read *Valet Parking Only*. They waited for the people in the Volvo in front of them to get out so Ezra could pull up to the valet stand.

"Mine will definitely be the only work truck here." He seemed embarrassed by that fact.

She hoped to ease his discomfort a bit. "They probably have to valet park everyone because it's such a tiny parking lot."

"I hope they have room for this big ole thing," he said.

"Maybe they'll leave it up front. Would be good advertising for you." She slid him a smile. "With the Roscoe Boulevard crowd."

Two clean-cut teenage boys—one white and one Hispanic—approached as Ezra pulled the truck to the valet stand. One opened his door and the other opened Mae's. Again, Ezra placed his fingertips on the small of her back as they made their way the short distance to the restaurant's front door.

The hostess quickly seated them on the outdoor deck behind the restaurant. Only one other table separated them from the intracoastal, and it was a bit below them, on the lawn.

"Is this table okay?" the young woman asked.

Mae smiled. "Perfect."

"It's great." Ezra pulled out a chair for Mae, making sure—she noticed—that she had the best view of the upcoming sunset.

"The sun's pretty warm tonight, so I'll leave the umbrella up," the hostess said. "But you let us know if you want us to put it down."

Ezra nodded his thanks. "Will do. Thank you."

Mae finally felt like she could relax once they each had a drink in their hand—an IPA for him and a sangria for her—and had ordered dinner.

"Have you ever been here before?" he asked.

"This restaurant?" She scoffed. "Not hardly. I don't get out much. And remember, I just moved to Jax Beach a few weeks ago."

"From Tallahassee, was it?" He reached up to tug on one side of the umbrella, angling it so the sun wasn't in their eyes as it made its way toward the horizon.

She nodded.

"Your old job wouldn't let you work remote from here?"

She slid her hands along the tabletop, avoiding his gaze. "My old job no longer required my services." She hoped he'd get the hint that she didn't want to talk about it. She didn't want that episode of her life to seep into tonight's date.

He gave a single, slow nod. "Okay, then."

She was grateful he seemed to understand. "I guess that's one good thing about being your own boss. No one can fire you."

He chuckled. "Yeah, well, it does have its perks. But it has a lot of headaches too."

She slid him a wry grin. "Like Halsey Green?"

"I thought we weren't going to talk about him tonight."

"Touché." She grinned and took a sip of her sangria. "So what surprised you most when you first started your own business?"

He looked out over the water as he thought about her question. "A lot of things, I guess. How much I care about my guys. I mean, I've had a few I had to get rid of, but the core group is like a family to me. I feel so responsible for keeping them working. Their families depend on the wages for mortgage payments and braces and little league uniforms and saving for college."

She tilted her head and smiled. "That's the sweetest thing I've heard a guy say in a really long time."

"Maybe you've been hanging out with the wrong guys," he teased.

She grunted. "That's an understatement."

"Bad boyfriend?"

She stared into her sangria, deciding what to say about that episode in her life. She wanted her conversation with Ezra to be fun and flirty, not mired in her sad past. "I didn't *think* he was bad . . . until I caught him cheating on me."

Ezra's eyebrows rose. "Were you guys serious?"

She finally met his gaze. "I guess one of us more so than the other."

"Yeah. I get it. My girlfriend went to get nachos at a Florence and the Machine concert and ended up leaving with a guy she met in line at the concession stand."

It was Mae's turn to be surprised. She tried not to laugh, but that was a ridiculous story. "Were you at the concert with her?"

Ezra nodded vehemently. "Yes. And we'd been dating for *two years.*"

"Ouch." And she'd thought Rocco's philandering had been bad. "So I guess we've both got our . . . wounds."

"I'm not sure you can get to be our age without them," he said as their server approached the table with a tray full of food.

"Blackened mahi with tasso gravy for the lady," the server said as he placed Mae's dish in front of her.

"It looks delicious," Mae said.

"And shrimp and grits for you." The guy placed a large bowl in front of Ezra. "It's my favorite dish we serve. Can I get y'all anything else?" He circled his forefinger over the table. "Maybe a refill on the drinks?"

Ezra's and Mae's eyes met.

"Sure?" he said.

She shrugged. "Why not."

Mae closed her eyes for a couple of seconds and moaned after the first bite of her fish. "Ooooh. So good."

Ezra grinned at her enjoyment, then slid his fork into the rich, creamy grits. The jumbo-sized shrimp were the largest Mae had ever seen.

"So enough about bad relationships. What else surprised you about owning your own business?" Mae asked, restarting their conversation.

He sat back a few seconds, pondering her question. "I like the money management part of it, which I hadn't expected at all. I always thought I was an outdoors, work-with-your-hands kind of guy, but the budgeting and pricing the jobs and all that turned out to be way more fun than I thought it would be."

"Where'd you learn how to do all that?"

He shrugged. "I learned the business side of things from taking classes, but most of the on-the-jobsite stuff I learned from Joe and people like him."

She frowned. "Joe? That old guy who runs the jackhammer?"

Ezra laughed. "He wasn't always old."

"But *he* works for *you*, not the other way around."

Ezra twirled his fork in his grits a bit, as if figuring out what to say next. "I always hung around my dad when I was little. Like, every day after school and a lot on the weekends. He owned a construction company, and I always thought I'd just follow in his footsteps. Go to work for him when I graduated high school."

Mae had wondered about his father, so she was glad Ezra had brought him up. "Why do I get the impression that didn't happen?"

"Because he died when I was twelve. Heart attack." He snapped his fingers once. "No warning. No nothing."

She set her fork down on her plate and leaned toward him—a show of support.

"I obviously wasn't old enough to take over the company, so my mom had to sell it."

"I can't imagine what she went through, having to deal with selling a company *and* grieving your dad at the same time."

"And raising a couple of kids too. It was pretty hard on all of us."

"Did you get to keep any of your dad's old tools? I mean, for sentimental reasons?"

Ezra swallowed. His eyes misted. "No one's ever asked me that before. People don't seem to understand how much . . . my life changed that day."

She placed her hand on his where it rested on the table.

He continued. "But, yeah. I got to keep his toolbox, so I have his hammer, a few screwdrivers, stuff like that. It never leaves the house because I don't want anything to happen to it."

"And you eventually got into construction yourself." She wanted to know more about how he'd made it through those painful years into adulthood. How those years had shaped him into the man he'd become.

He slid his hand out from under hers and scooped another forkful of shrimp and grits. "As soon as I turned fifteen, I started hustling for work with some of the other companies in town. I eventually found Joe and some of the other guys who'd worked for my dad. They taught me things I hadn't been old enough—or big enough—to do when my dad was alive."

She smiled. "And eventually you started your own company."

He nodded, clearly proud of his accomplishment. "I had to take some classes, had to save some capital, but I eventually made it happen. I was three years older than my father had been when he started his company, but I did it."

"Your dad would be proud."

He squeezed his eyes closed and nodded.

Mae liked how moved he was by this connection to his father. How he wasn't afraid to show emotion. "I didn't mean to upset you."

He opened his eyes and shook his head. "I like talking about him."

"We can talk about him anytime you want," she said softly.

"Thank you," he whispered. He blew out a gusty breath and looked around for the server. "I could sure use that other beer right about now."

She chuckled. "Should we go back to talking about Rocco and the girl who left you at the Florence and the Machine concert?" She took a bite of her mahi.

"Your boyfriend's name was Rocco?"

"He's very Italian."

He chuckled. "I guess."

The server delivered their drinks. Mae grew serious as she swirled the skewer of fruit in her new glass of sangria. "He was the first guy I ever lived with. I thought everything was fine . . . until I came home to find him in bed with Miss Hot-n-Spicy."

"Did *he* call her that? Or did you?"

"It was the signature flavor at the wing joint down the road where she worked."

Ezra blew out a long breath, as if to commiserate with Mae.

"He spent a lot of time there," she said. "Until, apparently, she started making home deliveries. But only to our house." She could tell her humor didn't hide her hurt.

Ezra nodded. "Do you miss him at all?"

"Only his cooking. His spaghetti and meatballs were the best I ever had," Mae said.

Ezra sat forward, leaning toward her. "Oh, yeah? I'll bet mine are better."

"Are you Italian?"

He shook his head. "English and Dutch."

She narrowed her eyes, challenging him. "And you're saying you can out-meatball a guy who learned to cook from his Italian grandmother?"

"I'm saying you should come to my house one day to find out."

"We're talking freshly made sauce and homemade meatballs. Nothing out of a jar or a freezer case."

He put his hand over his heart, as if he'd been wounded. "You doubt me?"

She laughed. "Then it's a deal. I'll bring a salad and some wine to go with it."

Ezra raised his glass in a toast. "To spaghetti and meatballs."

She clinked her glass on his. "*Homemade* spaghetti and meatballs."

She really didn't care how the dish tasted or if Ezra had ever even cooked it before. For now, all she cared about was that he'd already asked her out on a second date.

Chapter Twenty-Five

The stream of headlights along Third Street flashed through the cab of Ezra's truck as Mae sat silently in the passenger seat. As soon as Ezra turned left—away from the beach and toward Cole's street—their near-perfect first date would be over.

But she liked the comfortable silence. The easy way the conversation had flowed between them during dinner, and later as they walked on the beach. The fact that he hadn't asked her back to his house at the end of their date. A guy who tried to move things along too quickly was . . . not a guy she was interested in. She wanted someone who respected her. Someone as interested in establishing a relationship as in sleeping with her. Though if he *had* asked her back to his house, she had to admit, she'd have had a hard time turning him down.

Because . . . look at him.

The man was a walking, talking bundle of testosterone—full of muscle and a deep Southern drawl and that sexy scent that lured her to him. But she'd known all that before tonight. The part that had really gotten to her was how he'd been so vulnerable when he'd talked about his father. How he wasn't afraid to show some emotion.

He was more than just a sexy man. He'd been fun and witty, and he really seemed to want to hear what she had to say—whether it was the kind of books she liked to read or what she'd been like when she'd been younger.

She'd understood his sadness over his father's death and wished—as always—that her own father hadn't been killed in a car wreck when she'd been so young. Ezra had a lot of memories of his dad, but the only thing Mae had was a folder full of pictures and other memorabilia from a man she didn't remember.

They'd talked about all kinds of topics as the sun disappeared over the intracoastal in a blaze of orange and purple, then they'd strolled on the moonlit beach, and now they headed toward home.

He whipped the truck through an opening in the oncoming traffic. The beach community hummed with activity tonight. Or maybe Third Street was this crowded every night. Mae didn't know. She rarely left the house after getting home from work at the end of each day.

"I guess when we're at Halsey's house together, we should act like tonight never happened?" she asked.

He shrugged. "It would probably make things simpler."

"Maybe we should talk to each other in code while we're there. We could give each other Russian spy names. I could be Oksana."

He turned his head and gave her a playful frown. "I don't know any Russian guy names."

"How about Ivan or Igor or . . . oooooh, Alexei."

"Doesn't everyone named Alexei get poisoned by the Russian government?" he said.

She sat back in her seat. "Good point. Maybe we should skip that one."

He pulled along the curb in front of Cole's house. Cole's car was still not in the driveway, but that was typical on a night when he had to work.

"Maybe we should just talk to each other at Halsey's house the same way we always have," he said as he turned off the engine.

"You mean when we're not making out by the side of his house?" She might not have been so bold with her teasing if she hadn't been protected by darkness. Her cheeks burned, and she was glad he couldn't see them turning red.

He chuckled as he opened the door of his truck. "That was all you. I was just an innocent bystander, trying to give you my daily update."

She laughed as she opened her door. "Yeah. Right." He'd clearly enjoyed their moments in the dark the other night as much as she had.

His fingertips were once again on the small of her back as they walked up Cole's driveway toward the front door. She liked it when he touched her like that—intimate and sexy without feeling too pushy or aggressive.

She reached into her purse and took out her key ring, wishing their evening together wasn't over. When she climbed the three steps to the tiny stoop, she rested her back on the side wall, making room for Ezra to join her on the little platform. She hadn't thought to leave the porchlight on, so they were bathed in darkness.

"Are you sure there's room for both of us up here?" he asked.

"It *is* a little tight." Though, truth be told, she wanted him even closer than he already was.

He trailed a finger down her cheek. "You think it's time for another daily update?"

"I thought you were just an innocent bystander."

Their voices were both low. Intimate. Filled with temptation.

"I'm game if you are," he said.

Oh, she was game.

She slid her hands up his chest and to the back of his neck. Their lips met as he took a step closer, pinning her against the house with a solid wall of man and muscle. With someone other than Ezra, she might have felt threatened, but with him, she felt safe. Desired. The way he gently cupped her cheek made her feel almost treasured.

They kissed for a blissfully long time, then slowly parted, like neither of them wanted it to end.

"How long before I can see you again?" he asked, his voice still low.

Tomorrow, she wanted to scream, but she didn't want to appear overeager. "I don't know. Maybe Friday night?"

He trailed kisses along her jawline. "I'm not sure I can wait that long."

Me either.

She let her head fall back against the wall, giving him more access to the sensitive skin along the side of her throat. Her hands moved from the back of his neck to his torso, allowing her to feel the solid expanse of his muscled back.

Me either.

***

Mae lay on the couch on Sunday afternoon, her mind replaying the events of the night before—the nice dinner at Palm Valley Fish Camp, the gorgeous sunset, the way Ezra had held her hand while they walked along the moonlit beach, those blistering hot kisses on Cole's front porch. She closed her eyes, conjuring the heat of those moments, when a loud rap on the door yanked her from her thoughts. Her eyes popped open. Her chest suddenly felt like a large cavern—void of any organs or life-giving activity. She sat up—her body still hovering between thoughts of last night and this new interruption.

The rapping on the front door continued—insistent and aggressive. Cole had left for work hours ago and she wasn't expecting anyone, so maybe she'd just ignore it. But the rapping didn't stop—the storm door rattling against the door jamb.

Mae stood when the sound of the knock deepened—knuckles on wood—meaning the person had . . . opened the storm door? Like she hadn't heard the racket they'd been making before that? What was next? Maybe they'd come right on into the house?

Now she was pissed. She marched the couple of steps across the small living room and jerked at the doorknob. "What do you want?" she said as she swung the door open.

A huge white guy with no neck stood about six inches from her. Beads of sweat covered his bald head.

His eyes widened in surprise, and he took a step back. "I . . . um . . . I'm looking for Cole Montgomery."

Mae took a moment to study him before she spoke. Maybe mid-forties. Sweaty pink skin with no silver tint. The sleeves of his white oxford shirt were rolled up, exposing muscular forearms. A leather portfolio in one hand, tucked near his side. The lanyard around his neck had some kind of nametag on the end of it, but it was turned around so she couldn't read what it said. "He's not here right now."

"Do you know when he'll be back?"

"He's working." She wasn't about to tell this guy that Cole usually got home after midnight when he worked the night shift. She didn't want him to know she was here alone on those nights.

"Still at Bar-B-Que Bill's?"

"Who are you, anyway?" That lanyard around his neck made it look like he was here in some kind of official capacity.

The guy pulled a business card from the pocket of his oxford shirt and handed it to her. "Mike Patterson."

She glanced down and read the card:

Michael R. Patterson

Senior Parole Officer

Florida Department of Corrections

"And?" None of this made sense, plus she still hadn't recovered from the surprise of his visit.

"I'm here to check in with Cole."

She looked at the guy's face, then down at the card again, then back at his face. *Holy shit.* "Cole has a parole officer?"

The guy let out a frustrated sigh, like he was tired of her wasting his time. Despite his impatient demeanor, his skin remained pink. "Can you tell me when Cole will be back, please?"

"Can you tell me why he has a *parole officer*?"

"Are you his . . . girlfriend?"

"Sister." Maybe the family connection would make this guy open up a bit.

He opened his mouth to speak, then closed it again. "Please let him know I came by."

"How often do you have to check on him?"

The guy went down the front steps and turned to face her. "Maybe you should talk to him about that." He gave a single curt nod.

Mae stared at his back as he made his way toward the car parked at the curb. Yes, she was angry. Cole could have at least shared some basic information with her, but she forced herself to confront the truth: Michael R. Patterson wasn't the real villain here.

The real villain—the one at whom her anger *should* be directed—was Cole. Their conversation the other night had made her believe they were close again. She'd started to feel the same camaraderie she'd felt when they were growing up. When they'd steal a few coins out of Mama's purse every time they heard the ice cream truck coming around the corner. Or when he'd rummage through the freezer for frozen lasagna or a pot pie on nights when Mama wasn't home, always making sure his little sister got something to eat. While she ate her portion, she'd often catch him eyeing the bit left in the tinfoil pan—a teenage boy in need of more sustenance but saving it for her. Or for the next night's dinner, in case Mama didn't come home again.

That was the Cole she'd grown up loving. Grown up trusting.

But her brother—the one she'd once trusted—wasn't back at all. He'd been duping her all along. There was nothing special about their relationship. Nothing special about him. Like everyone else in this world, he'd let her down.

Cole's first disappearing act had been when he'd turned eighteen—when he'd taken off, leaving thirteen-year-old Mae behind on the exact week she was supposed to register for high school. He'd been barely an adult. He could have signed all that paperwork for her. Could have helped her figure out what classes to take and how the whole system worked. Because Lord knew Mama wasn't sober enough to help with the process. But instead, Cole had abandoned her. She'd found out later he'd gotten a job as a cook down in the Keys somewhere. He'd been in the same damn state but couldn't even send her a letter or check on her once in a while?

She'd been stupid enough to think he was back for good her senior year of high school . . . until he stole her school-issued laptop and disappeared again. So why would she have trusted him now? Hadn't she learned her lesson about him?

She envisioned a plane plummeting to the ground and bursting into flames upon impact—the perfect metaphor for the few seconds it had taken for her faith in Cole to disintegrate. Again.

Chapter Twenty-Six

Mae had spent hours ruminating about the news she'd learned that afternoon: Cole had a parole officer. A *parole officer*. And he hadn't thought she might want to know that little tidbit? Had he banked on the fact that Michael Patterson wouldn't show up when Mae was home? At least during the three months before Cole's roommate returned and Mae had to go find somewhere else to live? Had Cole thought he could hide it from her forever, despite the now-botched opportunity for her and her brother to really reconnect?

Now she seethed in the darkness, waiting for her brother to arrive home after work. The lights were off throughout the entire house, but the living room sheers allowed in enough moonlight for her to pick up the wine glass on the end table next to her.

She'd guzzled cabernet from this same second-hand Hard Rock Cafe glass back in Tallahassee on the night she'd found Rocco in bed with Miss Hot-n-Spicy. Maybe it was Mae's official my-life-has-gone-to-shit glass. She should throw the albatross away after tonight. Smash it to bits and dump the shards in the trash before anything else bad happened.

She didn't guzzle tonight, though. No, tonight she'd limited herself to only one glass. She'd need her wits about her for the conversation she and Cole were about to have.

The acidic liquid slid down her throat as she took a slow sip, trying to ensure that it lasted until her brother got home.

She stewed in the dark for twenty-five or thirty more minutes before two beams of light moved across the living room wall—a car pulling into the driveway. Her heart leapt as she sat forward, planting her feet on the floor. Ready for battle.

He took a long time to get out of his car, but finally, keys jingled outside the front door. The knob twisted and Cole entered. Even in the dim moonlight, she could tell he'd been beaten down by his thirteen-hour shift. His chef's coat hung unbuttoned on his frame. His shoulders stooped. The smell of smoked meat wafted into the room.

He turned to place his keys in the little basket she'd set on the table near the front door, then startled and gasped. He immediately assumed a defensive posture, like he was ready to take on an intruder.

"It's just me, Cole." She kept her voice low and calm.

"What the fuck are you doing?" He fumbled at the lamp but couldn't seem to find the switch.

"Waiting for you to get home."

The lamp came on. The dim glow cast shadows on the wall and accentuated the dark circles under Cole's eyes.

He motioned toward the table next to her. "Who the hell just sits in the dark, drinking wine with no TV or phone or anything? What're you, a creeper or something?"

"I'm the woman who spoke to your parole officer earlier today."

Even in the dim light, she could see his face go pale. He took two sidesteps toward the recliner and placed a steadying hand on the arm as he lowered onto the cushion. "You talked to Mike?"

She pulled the man's card from her pocket and flicked it toward her brother. It landed on the carpet halfway between them—as isolated and adrift as she felt. "Michael R. Patterson. Senior Parole Officer. Florida Department of Corrections."

Cole ran his fingers through his hair. "I guess you want to talk about it."

She scoffed. "You think?"

He blew out a long breath. "I'm going to need a beer if we're gonna do this."

Never mind that all the beers in his fridge were nonalcoholic.

He placed his hand on the arm of the chair but didn't immediately rise, like he wanted to delay the conversation as long as possible.

"I'll wait." She took a sip of wine. No way was she going to let him out of this. She didn't care how long his shift had been. They were having this conversation tonight. Because—damn it—she needed to know what was going on with him. Why he'd led her to believe she could trust him again.

Finally, he rose and plodded into the kitchen. She heard the refrigerator door open, then the *kusssshhhh* of a beer can releasing its pressure. He returned to the living room, sank into his recliner, and took a big swig. Still, he said nothing.

They sat in silence for two or three minutes before Cole spoke. "What do you want to know?"

"Everything." Anger laced her voice.

He let out a derisive grunt. "I assure you, you don't want to know everything." He took another long drink. "How much did Mike tell you?"

"Nothing. He was pretty much an asshole."

"Sounds like Mike."

She'd considered looking up Cole's name online. Surely the state had a database of convictions, right? Wasn't that kind of thing a matter of public record, viewable by anyone who knew how to google? But she'd decided against any online snooping. She wanted to hear the story directly from her brother. "So it's up to you to tell me the whole sordid tale."

He slid her the side-eye, like he knew she wanted to make this as hard on him as possible. "I used to live over on the westside. We hung out at this country bar called the Silo." He took another drink and sat silently for another couple of minutes, his eyes cast downward.

"The longer you take to tell this story, the longer we both have to stay awake."

He sat back slowly. "Mostly, I hung out with the locals. Shootin' the shit with the same regulars day in and day out, but the weekends got more crowded. Different people, you know?"

No, she didn't know. And none of this told her anything about the crime he'd committed.

"So one Saturday night, there was this guy who kept trying to hit on a couple of ladies. I was playin' pool, and I watched the ladies get up and move to a different table, and he'd follow them and start bothering them there too. This went on through two, maybe three games of pool. Finally, one of my buddies told him to leave them the hell alone." He squeezed his eyes closed.

She could tell the memories were hard on him, but she didn't care. He should have told her about this weeks ago. "And?"

"A little while later, I went out to sit in my buddy's truck with him . . ."

Probably smoking a joint. Or worse. But she didn't want to interrupt him to find out.

". . . and when I was coming back inside, I see the same guy pulling one of the women away from the building and into the parking lot. I mean, she stumbled behind him, trying to keep up because he was walking so fast."

"Had he drugged her drink?"

Cole shook his head. "She was really wasted, but the blood tests they did later didn't show anything other than alcohol." He scoffed. "Probably would have helped my case if he'd slipped her a roofie or something."

This was beginning to feel like more stalling. "What did you do?"

"I tried to get him to let go of her, but he was a really big dude." Cole bowed his arms and shoulders like a muscle man. "He knocked me over and grabbed her again, dragging her toward where all the cars were parked, so I jumped up and grabbed this sign that had a ball of concrete on the end of it where it used to be stuck in the ground . . ." Cole fell silent, letting her fill in the rest.

"You got in trouble, even though you were saving the girl?"

"They said the concrete on the end made it a deadly weapon."

"And what about him?"

Cole grew even more somber. "He fell to the ground the third time I hit him with it. The girl scrambled away."

"Well, that's good."

Cole's gaze slid to her. "I've seen the cell phone video someone took that night. I hit him with that ball of concrete four more times once he was down."

A shiver scuttled down Mae's spine as she imagined what the recording must have looked like, then a thought flashed through her mind like a bolt of lightning. *OMG.* "Did he *die*?"

"No, but he was in a really rough shape for a few weeks. I messed him up pretty bad."

"So you were charged with what? Assault? Battery?" She wasn't sure what the difference was, but neither sounded good.

"Aggravated battery."

"And you went to *prison*?" He still hadn't confirmed what had happened after the fact. And how could all this have happened without her knowing about it?

"Fifteen months."

She tried to imagine her brother cooped up in a cell, with someone else controlling his every move. The total lack of freedom—to eat what he wanted to eat, to shower when he felt like it, to sit in his own ratty recliner whenever he wanted. "Was that why I didn't hear from you for so long?"

"Not exactly the kind of thing you want to put in your Christmas letter to the family."

She could understand why he'd be embarrassed and ashamed, but still, she was his *sister*. His only family, other than Mama—the woman who always put whatever guy was around at the time before her children. "They sent you to prison even though you might have saved a girl from being raped? Or murdered?"

"Because I kept beating and beating on him, even when he was already down." Cole slowly made the motion of wielding the sign every time he repeated the word. "It's like I lost my shit for a few minutes. I just kept seeing Cleo's face and I . . . couldn't stop."

"Cleo? As in Mama's old boyfriend Cleo?" She hadn't thought about that guy in years.

Cole stared down at the worn-out carpet, nodding.

"Why him?"

When Cole's gaze rose to hers, his eyes blazed with contempt. "Because he used to beat me. And Mama too."

Mae sat back, stunned. "How did I not know this?"

"Because we did our best to hide it from you. I mean, what were you? Eight or nine when he lived with us? I didn't want you to think that was how life worked. That adults beat up on little kids when they get drunk or mad or—hell—whenever they just feel like it."

"But how? When? How come I never saw it happening?"

"You used to hang out with that girl who lived down the street." He snapped his fingers a couple of times, like he was trying to remember. "What was her name?"

"Ashlyn Bradley." A warm feeling washed over Mae at the thought of that friendship. The Bradley house had been a haven for her—full of love and family game nights and homemade vegetable soup—none of which had ever appeared at Mae's own home.

"Yeah. You went there every day after school . . . and afternoons were when Cleo was the drunkest. And the angriest."

Mae nodded. She'd always been relieved when she got home from the Bradleys' to find Cleo already passed out. "Did Mama know he beat you?"

Cole grunted. "She tried to protect me at first, but then he'd just beat on her. I think she finally just gave in."

"What do you mean 'gave in'?"

"As long as he was beating on me, he wasn't beating on her." His gaze slid to her. "Or you. And I swear, if he'd ever laid a hand on you, I would have killed him. I might have just been twelve years old, but I'd have found a way to do it."

A pang of guilt sliced through her. Earlier tonight, she'd been convinced Cole didn't deserve her trust . . . and now this?

She rose quickly and grabbed her glass. "I'm going to need another glass of wine." But more than anything, she needed a few minutes alone to absorb what she'd just learned. To reframe a period of her life when she'd found momentary happiness—that is, until Ashlyn Bradley's dad got transferred to Minneapolis and the family moved away. But by that time, she thought maybe Mama and Cleo had broken up? Mae would have to think about the timeline later, but at the moment, it didn't matter.

The timeline that *did* matter: Before six months ago, Mae hadn't heard from Cole in years. She now understood that part of that time he'd been in prison. She'd resented him for so many reasons but now understood at least some of the things he'd been through. The unseen hardships she'd known nothing about. She wished she'd been there to support him through it. It all seemed too much to bear.

She uncorked the half-empty bottle of wine and gave herself a generous pour. So much for sticking to one glass tonight.

But the time alone in the kitchen allowed her to remember how this conversation had gotten started. She stuck the cork back in the neck of the bottle and walked back to the living room. "So did the guy you beat up at the bar go to jail?"

"You know what? I don't even know. I was so sick of the whole thing I didn't want to ever think about it again. I didn't go digging for a final outcome. I wanted the entire thing to just go away." He moved his hand through the air in front of him, as if wiping the memories away.

She returned to her spot on the couch and took a sip of wine, still letting this deluge of new information wash over her. He was supposed to be the guy she looked up to—not the guy who'd been in prison. But given the circumstances, not everything he'd done that night was bad. Sure, he beat the hell out of the other guy, but it wasn't like he'd gone out looking for trouble. And to think he'd tried to protect her and Mama . . .

Mae could almost feel a ragged tear down the center of her chest. It was more than she could absorb in one night.

She and Cole sat in silence for a minute or two, each lost in their own thoughts.

When he spoke, his voice sounded deflated. "And now you know who Angie is."

Her mind flashed to the monogrammed makeup bag she'd found under the bathroom sink the day she'd moved here. "I do?"

His gaze held hers. "She's the woman he was dragging out into the parking lot."

And her makeup bag is in Cole's bathroom?

"You *knew* her?"

He shook his head. "Not before that night, but she tracked me down a couple of weeks later. She didn't remember much about that night 'cuz she was blackout drunk, but her friends told her what had happened, and she wanted to thank me."

"And you two became a thing?"

He shrugged. "We were for a while, but she lived in Daytona, which made it hard. And once I got sentenced, I wasn't going to be around. Mainly, I think she lost interest once the whole you-saved-my-life thing wore off."

"So why do you still have her makeup bag under your sink?"

"I don't know. Because I really liked her. Because it'd be nice to have a woman's things in my bathroom. To have someone around like that."

She smirked. "My things are in your bathroom."

Cole flashed her a not-really-what-I-meant look. "Don't you miss that Rocco guy you lived with in Tallahassee?"

A memory of Miss Hot-n-Spicy straddling her boyfriend flashed through Mae's mind. "Not at all." It was a lie, but she wanted to convince herself it was true.

"How long were you two together?"

"A couple of years. Long enough that he thought I'd take him back, but I promised myself a long time ago that I wasn't ever going to become Mama. I'd never stay with a man who disrespected me."

He nodded. "I'm glad to hear that."

Mae's gaze snapped to his. "Does Mama know? About the prison thing, I mean?"

"Now that you're in Jax Beach, I thought maybe we could call her together."

Yeah, right. "You're on your own for this one, bud." He was a forty-year-old man, for God's sake. He could tell his own mother he'd been to prison. "And, besides, you want to talk to a woman who let her boyfriend beat you? When you were a *kid*?"

"I feel like I should talk to her at least one more time before she's gone."

"I can't believe she's lived this long." At least Mae *thought* Mama was still alive. She hadn't talked to her in years.

"We really should call her. She'd get a kick out of the fact that we're living together."

Mae drained her wine glass and stood, determined to end this tangent of the conversation. "I really do think she should know where you've been, but I have no interest in ever talking to that woman again."

Chapter Twenty-Seven

The glistening of the wide, blue St. Johns River caught Mae's attention out her driver's side window, jarring her mind back to the present. A quick glance out the passenger side showed downtown Jacksonville on her right—confirmation that she'd zoned out and missed her exit.

Diva Dawn had instructed her to pick up a dress from a tailor in the San Marco section of town, but crossing the river meant Mae had gone too far. She'd have to get off the interstate that ran through Jacksonville, turn around, figure out how to get onto I-95 South, then come back across the bridge and down into San Marco. *Ugh.*

And this wasn't her first mistake of the morning. She'd had trouble staying on task since her shower, when she couldn't remember if she'd already shampooed her hair. Her mind still reeled from everything Cole had told her last night—his time in prison, how Mama's boyfriend used to beat him, how Cole had vowed to do anything he could to protect his little sister from the guy.

She took the next exit off the interstate and stopped at the red light at the bottom of the ramp.

She was still pissed as hell that Cole had tried to hide the prison thing from her. Keeping it from her seemed worse than the conviction itself. Another betrayal of the trust that had once existed between them. But she couldn't judge him for his crime. She had, after all, deposited almost four thousand dollars in questionable cash with Sherlene in Flagler Beach. At least Cole had been trying to protect Angie when he'd committed his crime, which was a whole lot better than helping a wealthy evangelist hide cash that might have been skimmed off the collection plate. It wasn't hard to see who the better person was in those two scenarios . . . and it sure as hell wasn't her.

And, besides, the more she learned about people, the more she realized there were very few absolutes. No one was completely good or completely bad. Even Halsey Green, who seemed to be lining his own pockets at every turn, ran an organization that provided support in the community. And Patricia—Mae's boss's boss back at Into the Florida Wilds—had tried to share some words of wisdom to help Mae in the wake of her termination. Hell, even the pretentious donor who'd helped fund that organization had been doing some good in the world . . . at least until Mae opened her big mouth with a hot mic nearby. Yes, people were a messy lot. Sometimes good. Sometimes not so good.

The light turned green, and Mae followed the signs to get back onto I-95 South, toward San Marco.

It was the people in Halsey's orbit who seemed to fall most squarely on the "good" side of things. Conrad and his rescue dogs. Klara and Lejla covering for Ilma. Ezra and his program to employ and train at-risk kids.

The thought of Ezra made her warm inside. They'd exchanged a couple of silly texts on Sunday, then acted stiff and unnatural when they'd seen each other at Halsey's on Monday morning—both apparently not wanting to give away the fact they'd had a make-out session on Cole's porch a couple of nights before.

Finally, she made her way back across the bridge to the *correct* side of the river and took the exit ramp down into one of Jacksonville's historic neighborhoods.

She'd just located the tailor in San Marco Square and found a place to park nose-in along the sidewalk when her phone rang.

"Where are you?" Halsey barked out the second she answered.

"San Marco. Picking up a dress for Dawn."

"How quickly can you get here?"

She wasn't sure where *here* was, but his home in Ponte Vedra sat just a few minutes from the church in Jax Beach. She had yet to go inside the tailor's shop, though. "I don't know. Maybe forty-five minutes?"

"I need you to go to Flagler Beach again."

"Today?"

"As soon as you can get back to the house."

A sense of unease washed over her. "To make a deposit in the bank?"

He let out a frustrated grunt. "Yes. With Sherlene."

Mae hesitated a few seconds, not yet sure how much she wanted to say. So much for having this discussion with him face-to-face, like she'd planned. "Look, I'd be happy to do this for you." *Not.* "But someone from the board approached me the other day. Acted like something illegal might be going on down there."

"Who said that?" Halsey's voice conveyed anger, but—Mae noted—not surprise.

"I'd . . . rather not say." She wanted Halsey focused on *her* risk in this situation, not on whichever board member had sought her out.

"Good God, Mae. Your paycheck comes out of *my* pocket, not theirs."

Yes, but the line between church funds and Halsey's bank account seemed a bit blurry. "There's even a picture of me walking into the bank branch—like a private detective had followed me or staked out the parking lot or something."

"You let someone *see you* when you went down there?" His yelling startled her. She'd never heard him raise his voice that loudly before.

"I didn't know I was supposed to be hiding. All I did was walk into a place of business that's open to the public." *Doing exactly what you told me to do.* "The board member acted like I could get in trouble for all this. Like, *legal* trouble."

"What do you . . . do you meet them at Starbucks for afternoon coffee? To discuss *my* business?"

"No." The word squeaked out of her mouth. She wished she wasn't so intimidated by his anger.

"I stressed the importance of loyalty when you first started working for me. Or have you forgotten that conversation? Those *conversations*—multiple?"

It took Mae a few seconds to recover from the beratement. "Do you think he's right? Could I get in legal trouble for . . . whatever's going on?"

"For making a bank deposit?" He acted like she was an idiot for asking the question, but if nothing underhanded had gone on, then why was he so upset that someone had seen her?

"So everything's above board?"

He let out a long, frustrated breath, like the entire conversation had gotten too tiresome for him. "Yes, Mae. Everything is above board."

"So there's . . . nothing I should know about all this?" she asked.

"When there's something you should know, I'll tell you. But for now, I've got to figure out a different plan for this afternoon."

She hoped to God Plan B didn't involve her.

"I guess I'll have to handle it myself," he said. "Since you couldn't pull the last one off without being *photographed*. Not that I have anything at all to hide, obviously. My personal life is just none of these people's business, and I won't be subject to whatever little witch hunt this *unnamed person* appears intent upon spreading."

"Maybe the picture doesn't even exist. I mean, it's not like I've seen it or anything."

"I've got to go, but this conversation is *not* over." He disconnected the call without saying goodbye.

Mae gripped her steering wheel, glad she'd been parked by the time he'd called. Her hands shook as she eyed the diners at the sidewalk café in front of her. They all looked so carefree, sipping their lunchtime wine and chatting up their friends. She'd bet none of *them* had to worry about being arrested for a crime their boss had conned them into doing.

She closed her eyes and took a few calming breaths. All she had to do was go inside the tailor's shop, pick up one garment, and get back into her car, where she'd have thirty or forty minutes to sort through things while she drove back to the beach.

A bell on the door jingled as Mae entered the shop. An older Black woman came from behind a partition that divided the back of the shop from the front.

"Good afternoon," the woman said with a smile.

"Hi. I'm here to pick up a dress for Dawn Green."

The woman's eyes brightened. "Ahhhh. Yes. The emerald green shift. It will look gorgeous on her."

Mae had too much on her mind to make small talk. Instead, she simply nodded.

"I'll be right back." The woman disappeared behind the partition but came back within seconds, her arm held high so the garment bag she carried didn't drag on the floor. "I hope the gala can still take place this weekend."

Mae had no idea what event Dawn planned to attend . . . and she didn't care.

"But if this storm doesn't turn"—the woman said as she hung the garment bag on a tall hook near the register—"then *everyone's* plans will be cancelled."

Mae hadn't seen a weather report in days. "Storm?"

The woman's eyes widened. "Oh, yes. Landfall somewhere between Daytona Beach and Brunswick, Georgia. At least, that's the current forecast."

That put Jax Beach right in the center of the path.

The woman leaned closer to Mae. "Could be a Category 4."

Well, shit. Even a Category 3 had done significant damage when Mae had lived in Tallahassee—and that was *inland,* after the storm had already lost some of its steam after hitting the shore. She and Rocco had been without power for five suffocatingly hot days, but they were still better off than the neighbor across the street, who'd had a giant live oak fall across both his house *and* his car. An old guy down the block had died of a heart attack while out cutting up downed limbs with a chainsaw.

No telling what a Category 4 could do along the coast. Maybe she should have thought about hurricanes when she considered moving to Jax Beach, but—then again—she hadn't had any other options at the time. "How long until it gets here?"

The woman shrugged. "Three, maybe four days."

More distressing news for Mae to process once she returned to the solitude of her car. She pointed to the dress. "This has already been paid for?"

The woman smiled. "We have a card on file. Miss Dawn is one of our best customers."

Mae lifted the dress from the hook and made her way to her car, not sure which storm she dreaded most—the fallout from Halsey's anger or the Category 4 hurricane headed their way.

Chapter Twenty-Eight

Mae bent sideways, eager to get a look into Halsey's garage as the door raised in front of her. Her shoulders relaxed at the sight of the empty right-hand side. His car wasn't there. Maybe she wouldn't have to see him that afternoon. She feared his anger over her conversation with Dr. Wisely would cause Halsey to fire her, but if she didn't see him face-to-face, maybe he'd do it over the phone or—better yet—via text. Keep the dreaded conversation to a minimum.

She'd thought about her predicament the entire drive from downtown Jacksonville to Ponte Vedra. Cole's roommate would be back in only a few weeks, and Mae still needed to save more money for the security deposit, plus first and last month's rent on an apartment of her own. She'd never really planned to stay in Jax Beach, but her blossoming relationship with Ezra had likely derailed her plans to leave. Besides, she still held out hope that she and Cole could be close again. The problem was, her prospects of a new job continued to be nil. And with a storm approaching, no one in the community would be focused on reviewing résumés.

She held Dawn's dress high—careful to keep it from brushing the floor—and made her way into the house. "It's Mae," she called, not wanting to scare anyone who might be inside.

"I'll be there in a minute," Dawn called from the direction of the owner's suite at the other end of the house.

"You want me to bring your dress back there?" Mae asked because where else was she going to hang it? But joining Dawn in her bedroom felt too intimate. What if the woman had just gotten out of the shower or something like that? Mae didn't want to be any closer to these people than she already was.

Thankfully, Dawn bustled into the kitchen fully clothed. "I'll take that," she said as she reached for the hanger. "Thanks for going to get it."

"No problem." Mae didn't mind errands like that. She liked the alone time, away from the Greens' house.

She made her way to the laundry room, aware this could be her last visit there. At a minimum, she wanted to retrieve her favorite ChapStick, and she'd look for any other personal belongings she might have left.

Dawn pushed open the door as Mae rummaged through the one drawer in the built-in desk.

"Aren't your work hours over for the day?" Dawn leaned against the door jamb and threaded a long, dangly earring through the hole in her ear.

Mae shrugged. "Just seeing what needs to be done tomorrow." She probably wouldn't *work* for them tomorrow, but Dawn didn't seem to know about the Dr. Wisely conversation.

"Well, we've got a dance recital tonight." Dawn rolled her eyes. "Three hours of sitting in the auditorium to watch

Gretchen dance for six minutes. The dancers had to be there an hour ago, but luckily Akira could take her."

"Halsey's going with you?" Mae hoped her question came across as small talk.

"He had to run over to Lake City this afternoon and the recital is in downtown Jacksonville, so he's going to meet me there on his way back into town."

So perhaps Lake City was the new Flagler Beach? And did Dawn ever get suspicious about her husband's random comings and goings? It wasn't like ministers were exempt from having extramarital affairs. But none of that was Mae's business. She didn't *want* it to be her business. But she could keep up this charade with Dawn. "Anything I need to do for you tomorrow?"

"I think I'm good." Dawn stepped fully into the room and stood tall. Her burgundy halter dress hugged her Pilates-thin body and complimented her tanned skin. For once, no tinge of silver colored her face.

Perhaps because Halsey's negative influence wasn't lurking nearby?

"How do I look?" Dawn asked.

She had on way too much eye makeup for Mae's taste, but the rest was impressive. Mae suddenly felt shabby. She wondered if she would look as coifed, manicured, and stylish as Dawn if she had the same financial resources at her disposal. She hoped her smile looked sincere. "You look *spectacular*."

Dawn smiled back. "Thank you. I'll see you tomorrow."

If your husband doesn't fire me first. "See you then," she said as Dawn exited the room.

So what did Mae do now? She still needed to get the daily update from Ezra, and with the Greens gone for the evening, maybe the two of them could chat for a bit after he finished work for the day. She listened until she heard Dawn leave the house, then got up and went into the kitchen to survey the situation in the backyard.

Outside the breakfast nook windows, most of Ezra's crew stooped over newly laid pavers that would lead from the pool deck to the dock. The teenagers who worked for Ezra after school tossed discarded materials into the back of a flatbed trailer. Ezra stood down near the water, deep in conversation with Joe as he pointed to something up high on the new, half-constructed boathouse.

It was ironic how that first day with Ezra had been so maddening and chaotic—having to rescue Billy Graham when he'd escaped from the house—but now Ezra made her feel content. A calming presence one minute, while making her giddy and girlish the next.

And tomorrow, all that could end. Sure, she'd hopefully continue to see Ezra after work. He seemed as crazy for her as she was for him. But it wouldn't be the same as seeing him Monday through Friday at Halsey's house.

Which was why she definitely wanted to wait for Ezra's crew to leave. To have one final "business meeting" with him in case Halsey fired her tomorrow, but she had no work to do for either Halsey or Dawn. She got a glass of water and made her way back to the laundry room.

The job search she'd renewed a couple of weeks ago wasn't going any better than when she'd first arrived in Jax Beach. There didn't seem to be a lot of openings in general, but she'd finally found two that piqued her interest. She'd gotten a computer-generated rejection on one within seconds: *We're sorry, but you don't have the requisite years of experience for this role.* And when she'd followed up on the second one, the recruiter told her the position had been filled by an internal candidate. Why the hell had they posted it externally if they already had the right person in-house?

Each rejection added to her sense of hopelessness. The entire job search process seemed to exist to make candidates feel unworthy. She couldn't figure out which of the three Ds she felt the most—desperate, depressed, or demoralized. The combination of all three felt like a plunger ramming her further and further into a pit of despair.

She pressed the button to turn on her computer in the laundry room. As much as she hated the entire job search process, she had no choice but to engage in it. And since she had time to kill at Halsey's house, she might as well make good use of it.

CHAPTER TWENTY-NINE

A zing of excitement coursed through Mae as she looked out the slider at Halsey's house. Finally, Ezra appeared to be in the backyard alone. She slid the door open and walked toward him. "You done for the day?"

His gaze continued to scan the materials on the ground before him. "Just making sure we got everything secured." He jabbed a thumb toward the back of the Greens' mansion, which was about eighty percent glass. "That house is a nightmare when it comes to the storm turning things into projectiles."

She could see why. She remembered a couple of years ago when the TV news showed a kayak impaled through the outside of someone's house. "The crew's all gone?"

"Yeah. Rodney's older brother texted that he was on his way about a half hour ago, and the rest of the guys left right after that."

"You have time for our update now?"

"Sure." He looked at his watch. "But you're here late."

She held out her hands in an apologetic gesture. "And no cooler full of beer."

He glanced toward the house. "Are the Greens not home?"

She shook her head. "Their daughter has a dance recital in downtown Jacksonville."

He reached out and took her hand, pulling her toward him a couple of steps until only a sliver of air separated their bodies. "So it's our lucky day."

His low, husky tone made her body thrum with anticipation. "I thought so too."

One of his eyebrows quirked upward. "Can I just text you our progress for the day?"

She wanted him to touch her—to more than just hold hands. "Did you have something else in mind for right now?"

He took her hand and gently pulled, urging her to follow him. He led her to the side of the house—away from the security cameras that undoubtedly captured every movement on the pool deck. It was the same little section of privacy where they'd shared their first kiss. "How's this?"

She smiled as she placed her hands on his chest. "Perfect." She rose on her toes to kiss him. Unable to stop herself.

He flattened his palms on the small of her back and pulled her toward him as they deepened their kiss. She lowered her heels to the ground, settling into his embrace. The feel of his arms around her felt like home—like where she belonged. Where she was meant to be. She wanted to be with him constantly—whether that meant grabbing a cup of coffee or running errands together or whatever. As long as she was with him, the rest of the world seemed to fade away.

"Ezra?"

His hands sprang from Mae's back like he'd been scalded. They both spun toward the male voice behind Ezra.

"LaShawn." Ezra wiped his mouth with the back of his hand. "I thought you guys left a long time ago." He acted like a teenager who'd been caught sneaking out of the house or making out under the bleachers during a football game.

The teen jabbed a thumb toward Rodney, who stood beside him. "His brother had a flat tire. Said it would take him a while to get it changed."

Rodney snickered. LaShawn gave Mae an appraising look, as if sizing her up, then looked back to Ezra and nodded his approval.

"Guys . . ." Ezra choked the word out. He cleared his throat and tried again. "Guys, this is Mae." He stepped aside and motioned toward her in awkward, jerky movements, like this was some Chamber of Commerce networking event. He turned to Mae. "This is Rodney and LaShawn."

"She works for Mr. Green, doesn't she?" Rodney asked as if Mae wasn't there.

"I do." Mae stepped forward and shook each of the boys' hands. Since Ezra wanted to teach them the ways of the business world, then she could help out by treating them as colleagues.

LaShawn's face broke into a broad smile. "Ezra's got a girl-friend," he said in a sing-song voice.

Ezra closed his eyes, as if embarrassed that someone had seen him kissing her. After a few seconds, he seemed to have recovered. He opened his eyes. "Do you guys need a ride somewhere?"

Rodney shook his head. "My brother's on his way now. Got the new tire on a few minutes ago."

LaShawn held up his sports bottle. "We just needed to refill our water bottles." He gave a sly grin and fluttered his hand toward Ezra and Mae. "Besides, you two look kinda busy."

Both boys laughed and took off toward the cooler of water lashed to the side of Ezra's truck, playfully jostling each other as they went.

"Shit," Ezra said under his breath as soon as the boys were out of earshot. He paced back and forth in the little corner formed by the fence and the house.

Mae frowned. "I'm sure they've seen people kissing before. I mean, it probably goes on in the hallway at their high school, not to mention they have access to the internet. God knows what they see there."

He ran his fingers through his sweaty hair. "I'm supposed to be setting a good example for them."

"And your workday is over, so . . . ?"

"My dad would have never let something like this happen."

She paused, knowing from the other night how important his dad had been to him. "And?"

"He would have never mixed business with pleasure. He would have never gotten involved with a client." He made a flailing gesture in her direction. "Or someone who represents the client. He would have expected more from me. And I'd never want to disappoint him."

"Maybe you should give yourself a break. I mean, they saw one kiss. It's not like it's going to change the entire trajectory of their lives. And, besides, I'm not sure how much longer I'll be working for Halsey."

"Those boys looked up to me."

"And they'll *still* look up to you. It wasn't like you had me pinned to the ground, forcing yourself on me. It was consensual. Isn't *that* the kind of behavior you want those boys to see?"

His jaw tightened. "They shouldn't see a business owner doing . . . that . . . with his client."

She crossed her arms. "I'm trying really hard not to get offended here."

He clenched his fists by his side. "Those boys need a good role model. The deck is already stacked against them because of their race, and neither one of them has a dad around, and I know what that's like to be a boy without a dad and . . . I'm supposed to be the kind of guy my dad was."

From what Mae had seen, Ezra was already one of the most honorable men she knew, but she was in no mood to argue with him. She marched toward the corner of the house, in the direction of the sliding glass door, then turned. "Don't forget to text me today's update. I'm sorry to have ruined your day."

"I didn't mean . . ." He didn't finish his sentence, which was just as well. Mae had heard enough of what he'd had to say.

Chapter Thirty

Mae groaned to herself as she pulled onto Cole's street and saw his car in the driveway. After that disastrous showdown with Ezra, after the boys had seen them kissing, she'd looked forward to a quiet night of sulking alone.

And why was Cole home in the evening to begin with? He'd told her that morning that he had the late shift that day. Maybe he'd gotten fired. Because why else would someone come home in the middle of their workday? A vision flashed through her mind—Miss Hot-n-Spicy straddling Rocco on the day Mae had come home early because she'd been fired.

And that would really suck if Mae and Cole both got canned in the same week.

"Why are you home?" she asked when she walked in the front door to find him sprawled across the couch in a T-shirt and baggie gym shorts. ESPN droned on about the new college football rankings.

"New schedule at work. Mondays are our slowest day, so the boss wanted me to start taking them off instead of Wednesdays."

Okay. So not fired. There was at least one bright spot in this miserable day. She headed toward her bedroom.

"I bought some bratwurst for us to cook on the grill tonight," he said.

She turned to face him, suspicious. They'd only had a couple of meals together since she'd been here . . . and she'd initiated them both. She'd also done all the cooking. "Don't you spend enough time in front of a grill at work?"

He sat up and muted the TV. "Technically, it's a barbecue pit."

She huffed out an impatient breath. "Same thing."

"And I wanted us to talk about Mama."

Mae felt her shoulders sag—an involuntary reaction to the unwelcome topic. "Cole," she whined.

He stood. "You up for a bratwurst?"

She hesitated, trying to figure a way out, then shrugged. She might as well get dinner out of this deal.

"Good." He walked into the kitchen. She set her purse on an end table and followed him.

"You get started on the salad," he said as he opened the fridge. He took out the packet of sausages, a head of lettuce, a bag of matchstick carrots, a jar of green olives, and some shredded cheese. "There may be croutons in the cabinet, but make sure they haven't gone stale before you put them on our salads."

Thirty minutes later, they sat down at the tiny, scarred table in the corner of the kitchen. She had to admit, eating a home-cooked meal with her brother was better than moping around all night about Ezra. It still pissed her off the way he'd reacted after the teen boys caught them kissing, but hopefully he'd calm down about that soon. Maybe one day she and Ezra would laugh about how that had been their first fight.

As dinner came to an end, Cole brought up the topic Mae had wanted to avoid.

"I had a lot of time to think when I was locked away." Cole pushed his now-empty plate away from him. "I know she wasn't the greatest mom, but maybe we should be the bigger people. Maybe now that I'm clean and you and I are together again . . . maybe knowing that would help her. I know we don't owe her anything, but what if knowing those things made her life a little easier?"

"You really think she spends a lot of time thinking about us?" She snorted. "That would be a first."

"People with addictions are trying to numb themselves. To run away from something that hurts. Maybe what bothers her is knowing what a crappy mom she was."

"Then she could have stopped drinking when we were in elementary school. While she still had time to be a not-crappy mom."

Her brother leaned forward. He placed both palms flat on the table. "You have no idea how hard it is to break an addiction, Mae. I know." He jabbed his thumb into his sternum. "I know what she's gone through for—what—thirty years? I mean, just the guilt of it all can be so . . . destructive."

Mae knew he was right. She avoided the news but had still seen the havoc that drugs and alcohol caused—mugshots of people arrested for DUIs or who had that horrible, scab-faced look of a meth addict. It was epidemic—people addicted to alcohol, to illegal drugs, to prescription painkillers. It seemed their unrelenting grasp could strangle anyone. But that didn't make Mama's neglect hurt any less. "It wasn't just the booze, you know. It was that we always took a back seat to whatever guy was in the picture at the time."

Cole looked down and nodded, like the truth of that statement hurt too badly to acknowledge while he looked into his sister's eyes. After a few seconds, he raised his gaze to look at her. "She's still our mother. She'd probably still like to know we're okay."

Mae narrowed her eyes and leaned toward him. "You're not going to ask me to forgive her, are you? Is that part of whatever program you went through? You have to forgive the people who did you wrong?"

He held up his hands, palms toward her. "Whoa. I'm just suggesting we give her a call. If . . . or when . . . you forgive her is *your* decision. Not mine."

"Have *you* forgiven her?"

He cocked his head to one side. "I'm . . . working on it. I'd even say I'm almost there. And I'd like to make her life easier. I think we owe that to everyone we run across—to show them a little kindness, if we can. To make their life easier."

"Since when did you become all peace and love and . . . ?" She fluttered her hand toward him, unable to find the words to complete her sentence. Unsure what to make of this new version of her brother. She had absolutely no interest in reaching out to their mother, but she envied that Cole seemed to have a softer, gentler outlook on life, even after everything he'd been through.

Mae would give anything to find that same sense of peace. She wasn't sure she'd ever felt that content in her life.

"Will you at least think about it?" he asked. "The two of us calling her together? To let her know we're okay and living together?" he asked.

Her chair scraped across the floor as she stood. She picked up her plate, ready to start the dinner cleanup. "I'll think about it, but I'm not making any promises."

***

Mae's phone buzzed in the dark, waking her from the first bit of fitful sleep she'd had all night. She tried to ignore it, hoping it was part of a dream, but then it buzzed again—an unwelcome intruder in her bedroom. Maybe it was a storm-related alert of some kind, though Hurricane Carly still sat a couple of hundred miles offshore.

Or, better yet, maybe it was Ezra texting to apologize or ask that they get together to talk through what had happened yesterday in the aftermath of the teens catching them in a kiss.

She snaked her hand from under the sheet and lifted the phone from the bedside table. 5:32 a.m. Her bleary eyes eventually focused on the text at the bottom of her home screen.

Are you awake? Can you meet me at my gym at 6:15? We need to talk, but my schedule is full for the rest of the day.

She groaned. Damn Halsey. Did he really have to get her out of bed to fire her at oh-dark-thirty? She rolled onto her back and grasped her phone in both hands.

I don't know what gym you belong to.

If she thought about it hard enough, she might remember the name of the gym from when she paid Halsey's bills, but she didn't want to put that much mental energy into it at such an early hour.

His reply came quickly.

The Ponte Vedra Inn and Club. The gym is right across from the Surf Club.

She rolled her eyes. Of course he worked out at the fanciest club in town. She'd had to meet Dawn and the kids at the pool known as the Surf Club a couple of weeks ago when Dawn had forgotten the birthday gift for one of the kids they were meeting there. Mae'd had to convince the exceedingly clean-cut teenagers working the entrance desk that she was only at the oceanfront club to drop something off and that she'd leave immediately. Once they'd finally let her in, she'd found Dawn and the other moms lounging under giant umbrellas on the Surf Club pool deck while the kids splashed away in shallow end. The waves of the Atlantic crashed on the beach not a hundred yards away. Mae had never felt like such an outsider.

So the gym is on that main street that runs parallel to the ocean? she texted.

Yes. Meet me in the parking lot. 6:15 sharp. Don't be late.

Mae wondered if the sun would even be up at that time of day. And how sketchy would it look—meeting in a parking lot in the predawn hours? Maybe she could just throw on a bra and a T-shirt over her pajama pants. Then she could come home after they met and go right back to bed. A woman didn't need to dress professionally when she expected to get fired, did she?

Are you coming or not? Halsey had apparently lost his patience.

She might as well get this over with. She'd have to face him eventually. Her thumbs flew across the phone screen.

I'll be there.

Chapter Thirty-One

Mae knew she'd entered the Ponte Vedra Inn and Club portion of Ponte Vedra Boulevard because the stately oceanfront homes had given way to a row of uniform villas on the left and a golf course on the right. She eventually passed a two-story building that looked like it probably held the resort's front desk and meeting space. Maybe a bar and a restaurant or two. The street was well-lit—illuminated by both the streetlights and the faint light that hovered along the horizon behind the villas. The rising sun had yet to appear, but a peachy glow announced its impending arrival over the Atlantic.

She coasted along—the only car on the street—until she spotted the awning she'd seen a couple of weeks ago. The fancy scrollwork read *Surf Club*. Across the street, a parking lot with a smattering of cars and a low-slung building that looked like it could be a gym. She pulled in, hoping there wasn't a security gate that would block her from going too far.

Her headlights cast across a tall man at the far end of the parking lot, pacing in front of a dark-colored car.

Halsey.

And he already looked wound up about something.

She drove slowly toward him, past the gym's front door and the few cars parked near the entrance. Halsey had clearly wanted them to meet far enough away so that no one would overhear their conversation.

He stopped pacing and watched as she eased her car into a spot a couple of spaces from his Tesla. The parking lot lights illuminated the silvery glow of his face.

She took a deep breath, opened the car door, and stepped out to meet her fate.

He glanced down at her pajama pants and frowned but didn't say anything.

She crossed her arms, willing him to speak first. Best to let him fire her right away, so as to end this aggravating pre-dawn rendezvous as quickly as possible.

"I appreciate you meeting me so early." His gaze flicked once again to her pajama pants. "My day is packed—everyone trying to squeeze in their meetings before the hurricane arrives—so this was the only time that made sense."

It made sense for *him*, maybe. But then she'd known since her first days of employment that his world revolved around him. She stood there silently, hoping he didn't feel the need to proselytize as much as Patricia had during Mae's termination back in Tallahassee.

He took a step toward her. Both his stern voice and his aggressive demeanor indicated the pleasantries were over. "The more I think about our conversation yesterday, the angrier I get. I want to know more about your interactions with this board member. I mean, how did he contact you to begin with?"

Fine. She'd tell Halsey which board member had approached her so that Halsey could deal with him. All she wanted was for this whole drama to end. "Dr. Greg Wisely approached me at the church. That day I came to deliver the envelope with the concert tickets in it."

"Jesus. That was like a week ago."

Mae couldn't refute the point. Plenty of time *had* passed since her conversation with Dr. Wisely.

"And why would you not tell me *immediately*"—he chopped his hand through the air, emphasizing the point—"when someone like that approached you?"

"I *did* try to talk to you." Multiple times, as a matter of fact. "But you were always too busy. And since Dr. Wisely said I could get in trouble for delivering the cash to the bank, I wanted to figure out what was going on."

"What, exactly, did he accuse me of?" Halsey spoke in a low, menacing tone.

"It had to do with the church paying your personal American Express bills."

A muscle twitched in his silvery jaw, but he didn't say anything.

"And cash perhaps being taken from the offering plate," she added. Cash like *she'd* deposited at the bank in Flagler Beach.

Halsey's eyes blazed with anger, but he didn't seem surprised by either accusation. "First of all, the church has paid my Amex bill *from the beginning*—from the first month the church even existed years ago. But all of a sudden it's an issue because I turned down Bull Williams's request to support his daughter's school? And why would I take money from the church—*my* church—when one of the key tenets is that we help those less fortunate than we are. Why the hell would I work so hard to raise those funds if I wasn't going to use them the way they were intended?"

Because you needed to pay for your kids' private school and your vacation in Aspen?

His rant continued. "But most of all, did it not cross your mind to tell me about this conversation? Even though my *number one expectation* of anyone who works for me is loyalty?"

He stood right in her face, but she refused to back away. She, too, had had time to think about their conversation yesterday. She was no longer the same person she'd been in Patricia's office back in Tallahassee. She would no longer play the victim—enduring the wrath of an angry boss when all she'd done was speak the truth. And she certainly wouldn't play the victim if Halsey had drawn her into some underhanded scheme she had yet to understand. "If you're going to fire me, can you just get it over with so I can go back to bed?"

He cocked his head and studied her face, as if puzzling something through in his head. He looked down at the ground—more thinking. Finally, his gaze rose to hers. "I can't fire you," he said quietly.

Then what was all this bluster and rage? Why the early morning meeting? She almost asked, "Why not?" but thought better of it.

"You've kept Lassiter away from me," he said. "The bank accounts are all in order and the bills are paid and you're helping Dawn and . . . I need you to keep doing all that. There's *way* too much going on in my life right now to have a disruption, and I don't have time to find—much less train—another personal assistant. But for God's sake . . ." He raised both hands toward the sky. "You have *got* to tell me if one of the board members tries to talk to you again. Or if *anyone* comes to you with accusations about—" He stopped himself before finishing the sentence. His voice took on a quieter tone. "About anything."

Mae slumped against her car, not sure if she wanted to continue this unholy alliance. She'd been certain this morning's meeting would be the last time she'd have to answer to him.

But none of her other job prospects held any promise, and as long as she didn't have to do anything sketchy for Halsey, then she couldn't get in trouble, right? Cole's roommate would return in four short weeks, and she'd managed to save enough for one month of rent, but not the security deposit and last month's rent or whatever other bullshit the landlords charged these days.

Maybe Mae's willingness to speak the truth—the trait Patricia had hated so much—could serve Mae well here, especially with Halsey determined to keep her. "I'm not comfortable making any more bank deposits. And if you're doing anything unethical or illegal, I don't want any part of it."

His gaze snapped to hers. He studied her face but stayed silent for several seconds.

She crossed her arms, unwilling to speak until he responded to her last statement.

He let out a frustrated huff. "Fine. No more bank deposits, but I want your *absolute loyalty*. If someone so much as says my *name* to you, I want to know about it. Immediately."

She nodded once. "Agreed."

He opened the back door of the Tesla and took out his gym bag. "And one more thing," he said as he closed the door. "You should tell me if you're dating Ezra Watts."

She opened her mouth, then closed it again, unable to speak. Had he seen them together on a security video at his house? Or maybe at the Palm Valley Fish Camp? During their walk along the beach? After all, Jax Beach *was* a small town. After the issue the other night with the teens catching them in a kiss, she hoped that hadn't been their first and only date.

Halsey hitched his duffel up on his shoulder. "Remember, Ezra is *my* vendor. Those daily updates you get from him are important. Even if the two of you begin . . . fornicating . . . your loyalty lies with me." He jabbed his forefinger into his sternum, emphasizing the point.

Fornicating? Did people really use that word anymore?

Halsey bent down, his face even with hers. "You got it?"

"My loyalty lies with you," she said flatly, knowing it was a lie.

"That's my girl." He gave a smarmy smile and headed toward the entrance of the gym. "Let's touch base at the end of the day. Figure out what this hurricane's going to mean for our workday tomorrow."

***

Fifteen minutes later, Mae pulled into the driveway at Cole's house, knowing there was no way she would get back to sleep. Not after her sunrise meeting in the parking lot of Halsey's gym. Her mind still whirled processing their conversation. On a positive note, she wouldn't be expected to make any more questionable bank deposits, but how the hell had he known about her relationship with Ezra? And did she even care that he knew?

Halsey had doubled down on the need for loyalty, but was he tech-savvy enough to find her internet search history? What would he do if he knew she was looking for another job? On *his* time and using *his* computer?

She'd worry about all that later. For now, she planned to shower and get dressed for work, then maybe make herself some pancakes since she'd woken up so damn early and had some time to kill.

She opened the car door and stepped out. The ever-present humidity hung in the air, but the day's sauna-like conditions wouldn't arrive for another couple of hours. The calm, cloudless sky gave no indication of the miles-wide maelstrom that lurked offshore, headed their way. Even so, an undercurrent of tension permeated the entire region. The sense of agitation, as present and palpable as the humidity.

The calm before the storm had likely become a cliché on mornings exactly like this one.

Everyone Mae had come across in the last forty-eight hours had chattered about the latest spaghetti models and the National Hurricane Center. Had reminisced about how long it had been since Jacksonville had gotten a direct hit. Made the same lame jokes about where the Weather Channel's meteorologists might be setting up and when the Waffle Houses might close.

Schools and universities across eight counties in Northeast Florida had announced closures starting the next day. Cole's restaurant would be open only through lunch tomorrow.

An alert blared from her phone, puncturing the morning's silence. She pulled it from her pocket and read the message—a third reminder from the local emergency management team: *Due to Hurricane Carly's impending arrival, residents who live in flood zones are ordered to evacuate to higher ground no later than 5 p.m. tomorrow.*

Cole's house sat far away from any body of water, but the Greens had the entire intracoastal waterway right outside their back door. Mae wondered if she'd be expected to help the family prepare to evacuate. She made a mental note to suggest to Halsey that she bring her work laptop to Cole's house for safekeeping.

Again, she looked up at the morning sky. The sun had not yet risen above the neighborhoods off to the east, between Mae and the Atlantic Ocean, a couple of miles away. Still, the new day promised to be as blue and clear as she'd ever seen it.

But trouble was undoubtedly on the way.

Chapter Thirty-Two

Mae rushed up the stairs at the Green residence, looking for the housekeepers. Halsey's 5:32 a.m. text that morning had said he had a full day of meetings at the church, so why was he home now?

"Halsey's pulling into the garage," she said to Ilma, who lay curled on the couch in the media room outside the kids' bedrooms. Mae positioned herself to help the sick woman get up but wasn't sure what she should do.

Klara stuck her head out of the bedroom used by the nanny, Akira. "He's here now?" She glanced nervously in Ilma's direction.

"Just pulled in. I didn't know he'd be home so early." Yes, the entire region now hummed with hurricane prep. Why had Mae met him at the crack of dawn that morning if they could have just talked this afternoon?

Ilma stood but wavered a bit. Klara rushed over to steady her as Mae folded the Jacksonville Jaguars blanket Ilma had been using, then spread it across the ottoman, where it normally lay.

Lejla came from one of the other bedrooms and handed Ilma a duster. "Use this."

"We're good?" Mae looked from one woman to the next.

They nodded, so Mae rushed back down the stairs. She'd barely stepped foot on the first floor when the door from the garage opened.

She smiled and tried not to pant from her jaunt up the stairs. "I thought I heard the garage door go up."

Halsey glanced through the mail she'd left on the kitchen counter. "I thought I'd do the daily update with Ezra myself today." He glanced in her direction, as if looking for a reaction. The skin along his brow line turned the color of a thundercloud but laced with silver—a surefire sign that he was up to no good.

She made sure to keep her expression neutral. "Okay."

"I want to make sure they've secured everything the winds could whip around and crash into the house."

She'd assured Halsey yesterday that Ezra's crew had plans to secure everything.

"And I asked them to put all the furniture into the pool," he said.

Mae nodded. Everyone sank their furniture under water to keep it from blowing around, but how was that part of Ezra's construction responsibilities? Could Halsey not do anything for himself? "Do you think we'll be working tomorrow?" she asked.

She'd tossed aside her "no news" rule now that Hurricane Carly barreled toward the Jacksonville area. Her anxiety had caused her to check the local new sites often throughout the day. The entire region was set to shut down—schools, businesses, city services like trash and road repair. Even PALM had been on the list of the closures she'd seen. Only hospitals and first responders would remain open, and even first responders would stop going out on calls once the winds got above a certain speed.

"Did you get all the emails sent out about the Falcon Cup?" he asked.

He and a bunch of his high school buddies apparently got together each October for a golf outing named after their school's mascot, the falcon. He'd volunteered her to disseminate some of the latest logistical information, but did it really have to be done before the hurricane blew through? She nodded. "All of them sent."

"And you figured out why Quicken keeps miscategorizing the payments to the club?"

Again, not something that needed to be figured out before the storm. "I did."

"Then I guess there's no need for you to come in tomorrow."

Ezra passed by outside the breakfast nook windows. Halsey's gaze slid to hers.

"I picked up some extra anxiety meds for Billy Graham," she said, hoping to divert a conversation before it started. "I figured he'd need them during the storm."

"That's probably a good idea. Thank you." He crossed over to where the cat lay on the back of the couch and scratched behind its ears—a rare glimpse of the man's softer side.

Mae couldn't imagine Halsey and Dawn jamming pills down the cat's throat, but maybe they weren't as helpless as they appeared.

"So I'll see you on Thursday or Friday," he said. "Depending on when the storm actually hits." It sounded like a dismissal. Like he wanted her to leave before he talked to Ezra.

She hoped to God Halsey didn't bring up *fornication* to Ezra too. How embarrassing. She jabbed her thumb in the direction of the laundry room. "You want me to take the computer from the laundry room to my house during the storm? You know, to get it away from the intracoastal?"

He nodded. "That's probably a good idea."

"I made sure everything was backed up to the cloud just in case."

"Thank you," he said politely, but the sag of his shoulders seemed to say *Would you get out of here already?*

"So there's nothing else you need?" she asked.

"No, that'll be all."

No *stay safe in the hurricane* or *take care of your family* or any other show of concern. Mae generally didn't pay attention to those niceties—the polite, not-really-heartfelt things people say to each other—but tonight, they seemed to matter. In this situation and with this man, their absence created a noticeable void.

When she passed through the kitchen a couple of minutes later, Halsey stood out on the pool deck face-to-face with Ezra. Halsey's tall, lithe frame looked almost gaunt across from Ezra's broader, more masculine build. Neither man looked angry, but neither looked happy, either.

Mae wondered if their conversation was about the hurricane, the construction project . . . or her.

Chapter Thirty-Three

By the next morning, many of the shelves at the nearby Publix had been picked clean—proof positive that Hurricane Carly would soon barrel ashore in Northeast Florida. Mae unpacked the few groceries she'd been able to snag—a bunch of overripe bananas, four apples, a box of Saltines, a jar of Jif, and a couple of cans of baked beans. Nothing that required refrigeration, that was for sure. She'd learned that lesson after she and Rocco had been without power for five days following the hurricane that had passed over Tallahassee a couple of years ago.

Luckily, Cole had gone to the store four days ago, when jugs of water and loaves of bread were still on the shelves but disappearing fast. Those aisles had been completely bare during Mae's grocery run that morning, giving the place an apocalyptic air.

Mae couldn't imagine how people with more difficult lives than hers could make it through such an ordeal—young families with infants to care for or elderly people whose insulin needed to stay refrigerated. The young mother two people ahead of Mae had shed quiet tears at the cash register when her credit card was declined, but the man between them paid for the woman's groceries—diapers, infant formula, and a package of baby wipes. Mae had wiped her misty eyes as the woman hugged the man and cried on his shoulder, profusely thanking him. Yet another act of kindness, like Conrad with his puppies and Klara with Ilma. Mae had spent so long convinced that people on the whole were basically bad, but all the people in Halsey's orbit had shown her that maybe she'd been wrong.

A knock on the front door pulled Mae from her thoughts. She tossed the plastic grocery bags in the bin in the pantry and headed that way. Her breath caught when she looked through the peephole.

Ezra.

He hadn't called or texted since the other day with Rodney and LaShawn. He'd probably come to tell her they couldn't see each other anymore—that it was unprofessional, and he couldn't set that example for the teens who worked for him. Of course, Ezra would feel like he should tell her that in person. Because he was one of the good guys. Her heart broke a little more as she pulled the door open.

"Hey," she said, bracing herself for the conversation.

He stood down on the sidewalk, a step or two away from the stoop. "Why don't you guys have any plywood over your windows?"

Okay. So not the conversation she'd expected. "Cole texted the landlord a couple of days ago. He told Cole he'd never covered the windows before and he wasn't going to start now."

Ezra grunted. "Nice guy. I guess he doesn't care if your stuff gets damaged when the windows get blown out?" Then he jabbed his thumb toward his truck parked on the street. "I found some old plywood in my warehouse and thought I'd find someone who could use it."

"And you're offering it to us?"

He chuckled. "Don't sound so surprised."

She shrugged. "I just figured you'd give it to one of your guys . . . or maybe Rodney or LaShawn's parents."

He kicked at a weed growing in a crack in the sidewalk. "I didn't want to talk to Rodney or LaShawn's families." His gaze rose to hers. "I wanted to talk to you."

They studied each other, each undoubtedly trying to figure out what came next. She saw a sadness in his dark brown eyes mixed with hope.

"You could have just called or texted," she said.

"I wanted to talk to you face-to-face. About the other day."

She crossed her arms. "I'm listening."

"I may have been a bit of a drama queen."

She snorted. "You think?"

"You know how important my dad is to me."

Present tense, Mae noted. Like the man was still alive. She nodded and stepped out onto the stoop. She sat on the top step and looked up at Ezra, ready to hear what he had to say.

"I just . . . I'm supposed to be setting a good example. Showing those boys how to make their way in the world. How to work hard and show initiative and use their brains to solve problems in the workplace. How to behave in a professional environment." Ezra hung his head.

"And you screwed up because you got caught making out with someone on the jobsite."

He raised his head, a guilty look on his face. "Maybe not the client, but you're, like one degree of separation."

"Did you ever make a mistake when your dad was alive?"

Ezra gave her a quizzical expression. "I was a kid."

"I'm serious," she said. "What was the worst thing you ever got in trouble for with him?"

Ezra looked at the garage door, as if wanting to avoid her gaze. "I got caught stealing a candy bar from the Circle K."

Mae had to keep herself from smiling at how little-boy-pitiful he looked. "And what did your dad do?"

"He grounded me and wouldn't let me hang out with my friend Keaton anymore—he's the guy I was with when we did it—and he made me write an apology note to the manager."

"And now that's all old business." She waved a dismissive hand through the air. "I'll bet you haven't even thought about it in ages."

Ezra stuck his hands in his pockets and gave her a what's-the-point look.

"And your dad would have forgotten about it too. Because you know what? It wasn't a big deal. You did something wrong. You learned your lesson." Kind of like she had after the hot mic fiasco in Tallahassee. "The world didn't come to an end."

He sat beside her on the step but remained silent.

"And the world's not going to come to an end because Rodney and LaShawn saw you kissing me either." She leaned sideways and bumped his shoulder with hers. "They're probably talking about what good taste you have in women."

His shoulder moved with a silent chuckle.

"I've been noticing a lot of kind people lately, and you're one of them. So why not show yourself a little of that kindness? Give yourself a little grace?"

"Yeah, well I pretty much suck at the whole giving myself grace thing."

"It's what your dad would *want* you to do. He wouldn't want you to sit around beating yourself up all the time. Besides, it's not going to hurt the boys to see that grown-ups make mistakes too."

Ezra reached over and took her hand, twining his fingers in hers.

"Sometimes you've got to forgive other people," she said. "And sometimes you've got to forgive yourself."

He turned his head to look at her. "Have you forgiven Rocco?"

Now it was her turn to avoid his gaze. She looked out at his truck parked at the curb. "Not yet." A couple of beats passed before she spoke again. "But he's not the one I need to forgive most."

"Oh, yeah?"

She stood, not yet willing to talk to Ezra about Mama. Mae's heart ached for the lonely little girl who never quite felt safe. Who never quite felt loved. "I was promised some plywood for my windows. And that hurricane isn't going to stay offshore much longer."

Ezra seemed surprised by the sudden change in topic, but he, too, stood.

Mae stepped back to look at the house. "Should we ask the landlord before we do this? I mean, is it going to damage the house in any way?"

"The guy who was okay with all your stuff getting rained on or blown away?"

"Good point. Show me what to do."

***

Mae could see Cole's bewildered expression the second he got out of his car. He strode toward her but kept his gaze on Ezra, who had a couple of sawhorses set up on the far side of the yard, where he cut plywood to fit the windows. He had his head down and his safety goggles on as the electric saw whirred in front of him.

"Who the hell is that?" Cole asked, motioning to the other side of the yard.

"Ezra Watts."

"The guy from the other night?"

Mae nodded. She'd told Cole she had a date but hadn't shared any of the details afterwards. She was still figuring out how much she wanted him to know about her life.

Cole let out a low whistle. "Home Depot's been out of plywood for days. You must have really made an impression on him."

She gave him a sideways look, knowing he'd wanted to say something cruder. "He owns a construction company. He had some in his warehouse."

Cole jabbed a thumb in the direction of the main thorough-fare that ran through the beach's communities. "He could have sold it for top dollar up on Third Street."

"He's not that kind of guy." She knew that much about him. If he hadn't given it to them, he'd have used it to help someone else. "You going to jump in and help? Or just stand around and yap about the guy who supplied the materials and is doing all the work?"

Before Cole could answer, the saw quieted. Ezra glanced up, then straightened. He removed his safety goggles as Mae and Cole made their way toward him.

Ezra stuck out his hand. "Ezra Watts."

Even though Cole had filled out in recent years, he looked thin next to Ezra's breadth.

Cole shook Ezra's hand. "Cole Montgomery, Mae's brother."

Technically her half-brother, but they'd never focused on that nuance since neither father had ever been around during their childhoods. It had just been her and Cole, side by side, doing their best to survive the chaos known as Mama.

Cole motioned toward the sawhorse setup. "This is quite a surprise. A good one. Thank you."

Ezra shrugged and pointed to the logo on Cole's chef's jacket. "Pay me back in barbecue sometime."

Cole grinned. "It's a deal. Give me five minutes to change and I'll come out to help you."

"Gives me time for a water break." Ezra slid Mae a smile. "Your sister's been working me like a dog."

Mae looked toward her brother. "You'd be proud of me, hoisting those huge pieces of plywood up to the windows. Those things are heavy." She pointed to one of the sheets already nailed into place.

"And she did it all on her own," Ezra said sarcastically as the two men shared a knowing look.

Once they'd traipsed inside, Cole went to his bedroom to change. Ezra and Mae each got a glass of ice water and sprawled on the couch under the ceiling fan. The heat and humidity were brutal that week. Anyone who lost power would definitely suffer. In Mae's opinion, Florida was uninhabitable without A/C.

Cole's bedroom door clicked open. He came around the corner in shorts, a T-shirt, and some old tennis shoes. But what caught Mae's attention was the ashen look on his face. He held his phone in front of him, the screen facing him.

Ezra must have noticed something was wrong, too, because he sat up quickly.

"What's wrong?" she asked.

"I checked the Weather Channel while I was in there." His eyes looked spooked. "They've upgraded Carly to Category 5."

Chapter Thirty-Four

Mae stood under the stream of the hot shower, washing away the grime of that afternoon's physical labor. She feared her body would ache the next day, but at least their windows were covered. She wasn't convinced a piece of plywood would keep the neighbor's palm trees from bludgeoning their window, but it might act as a shield against random objects flying through the air. People in Florida knew to bring potted plants and porch furniture inside, but that didn't mean that shutters wouldn't rip off houses or that swing sets wouldn't turn into battering rams.

The forty or fifty mile an hour winds in Tallahassee last year had scared Mae. But Category 5 meant the winds had reached a minimum of 157 miles per hour. Next time—without a doubt—she would evacuate. But I-95 was at a standstill from Vero Beach all the way along the Georgia coast and up to Charleston. Florida safety officials had urged those not already on the road to hunker down and protect themselves. They'd be safer inside their homes than in a car on a highway.

Mae closed her eyes and tried to imagine the hot water rinsing away her fear, but the tension was a monster with hundreds of spiny tentacles, each holding fast to her muscles, her bones, her psyche.

Cole pounded on the door. "Don't use all the hot water."

"Almost done," she yelled, though she wished she could stay there for hours.

Thank God her brother had come straight home after the restaurant closed. There was no way she could have held the biggest piece of plywood over the front picture window while Ezra screwed it into place.

Ezra.

The thought of him leaned over the sawhorse—his arm muscles guiding the saw across the plywood—made her woman parts hum. But it was his kindness and his steadfastness that stood out most in her mind.

He'd gotten a call from a former client, an elderly man who feared a loose panel of wooden fencing needed to be secured before the hurricane arrived. Ezra's work for the guy had had nothing to do with the fence, but Ezra set out to help him, anyway—the kind of everyday hero Mae had seen more of in recent months.

She wished she'd thought to ask Ezra where he planned to go after that. Would he go to his own house, where she knew he lived alone? She wouldn't want to sit alone, listening to things batter the house while the storm howled outside. Or maybe Ezra would come back here? No, she couldn't assume that. They'd had one date, for God's sake. Or might he go somewhere else? To be with friends or to assist the next former client who might need his help? Maybe she'd text him after her shower.

Cole pounded on the door again. "Your phone's ringing. It's somewhere in your bedroom."

Mae let out a frustrated breath. So much for hoping to step out of the shower stress free. Unless it was Ezra, she didn't want to talk to whoever had called anyway. Still, she reached down and turned off the water. "I'm coming."

Five minutes later, she was dressed and had secured her wet hair in a towel on top of her head. She opened the bathroom door, surprised by the eerie darkness of the house until she remembered that plywood covered all the windows.

"Whoever was calling really wanted to talk to you," Cole said as she traipsed across the tiny hallway toward her room. "They called like five times."

She wished Cole had looked to see who it had been, but he'd made it clear on Day One that people shouldn't answer other people's phones. But weren't they closer now than they'd been then? She wondered if he'd been afraid she'd answer a call from Michael R. Patterson, his parole officer. Or maybe there were other secrets he had yet to tell her about?

She rummaged around the top of her messy dresser looking for her phone but couldn't find it. She'd had it in her pocket while they'd put up plywood. Her shorts, maybe? They'd been covered in plywood particles and sweat, so she'd tossed them immediately in her laundry basket. She opened the closet door, pulled out the laundry basket, and found the phone, still in the pocket.

She let out a groan the second she saw the screen. Seven missed calls from Halsey. Three voice messages, each with increasing agitation in his voice. The first two were barked orders to call him back right away. The last anger-filled missive held more detail:

"Mae! Where the hell are you? I need you at the church as soon as you can get there. Rob Lassiter is down there stirring up trouble, and this is exactly why I kept you onboard the other day. Please let me know you got this message, then head straight to the church."

She backed up the couple of steps to reach her bed, then plopped down on it, her mind reeling. The mayor had ordered everyone to stay home except for essential travel within the city. Halsey had given her the day off, but now he wanted her to go to the church? A journalist asking questions hardly seemed like essential work. And it would be dark in . . . what? Maybe three hours? She didn't want to be out in a hurricane at all . . . and especially not once the sun went down.

The phone in her hand rang again. She jumped and stared at the screen, trying to decide if she would answer or not.

She finally—begrudgingly—pushed the button after the fifth ring. "Hello?"

"Why have you been ignoring my calls?" Halsey yelled.

"I was in the shower. We've been hanging plywood all day." She wished she could take the last sentence back the second it left her mouth. Halsey Green didn't care what she'd been doing all day. And, frankly, it was none of his business.

"How long until you can get to the church?"

"I need to go *now*? In the middle of a hurricane?"

"Have you not listened to my voice messages?"

"But who's even there for Rob Lassiter to direct questions to? Aren't people either evacuated or hunkered down in their homes?"

"There are news stations there now too. *With film crews.* Why do I employ a PR person if she's not going to be available when I need her most?"

She'd been hired as his personal assistant, and the PR part had been thrust on her with no extra pay. She hated that she'd tacitly accepted the extra responsibilities. She absolutely did not want to go out with the storm so close, but he was right. This was exactly the kind of moment when a PR person jumped into action. "I'll be there in about twenty minutes."

"Look for Conrad when you get to the church," Halsey said. "I've got another call coming in, but stay in touch with me, you hear?"

Mae looked down at her phone. He'd ended the call.

She stood as her brain kicked into business mode. She'd need to change from her comfy riding-out-the-hurricane-perhaps-without-air-conditioning shorts and tank top into something more professional, maybe even camara-ready. She quickly scanned the few business outfits in her closet, trying to determine which would stand up best as she made it through the wind and rain from her car to the entrance to the church. She'd need to blow dry her hair, which seemed ludicrous given the amount of precipitation about to pummel them.

She replayed the conversation with Halsey in her head as she combed out her wet hair.

Look for Conrad when you get to the church seemed like an odd thing for Halsey to say. Why would she do that? Maybe Halsey was hiding out in some back room she didn't know about, and Conrad would take her to him once she got there?

And why would a TV station be at the church when a direct hit from a hurricane—the first Jacksonville had seen in decades—was imminent? This was the kind of event news crews lived for. Their entire staff—from meteorologists to news anchors to photojournalists—would be covering Hurricane Carly's impact on the community.

But Halsey hadn't said *a* TV station was at the church. He'd said TV *stations* were there—plural. One news crew at the church would be unusual, given the circumstances. But more than one of them?

Mae's brush stilled on her scalp as a realization hit her.

Something major was happening at the church.

A wave of anxiety washed over her body.

She was the PR person being sent in to deal with it.

And she had no idea what was going on.

Chapter Thirty-Five

Mae paced through Cole's house, waiting impatiently for him to emerge from the bathroom. She'd heard the shower water turn off a couple of minutes ago. How long did it take a guy to throw on some shorts and a T-shirt?

Finally, the door opened.

Cole's eyes widened at the surprise of her standing so close. "This is creepy."

"I've got to go to the church."

He glanced at the plastic envelope she held in her hand. "Now?"

"There are news stations there, and since I'm Halsey's de facto PR person . . ." She didn't need to complete her sentence. They both knew the rest of it.

She'd tried calling Halsey back to learn more about what was going on, but her calls had gone straight to voicemail. *Coward.*

Again, Cole glanced at the object in her hand. "You want me to go with you?"

She didn't think there was anything he could do to help her there. "No, but if the weather gets too bad, I may stay there. Surely a structure that big would be safe. I mean, it's the same size as the high schools they use as shelters, so it's probably safer there than here, right? Maybe you should come with me, after all."

He shook his head. "One of us should stay here. Make sure everything's okay."

"I hope to be back." She'd much rather be with him as the storm raged through than with whomever happened to be at the church. "I'll call you and let you know what I'm doing."

He pointed to the red plastic folder in her hand. "What's that?"

"Something you need to protect while I'm gone. It's like . . . my most important possession."

"So what is it?"

"And you have to promise not to tell Mama."

He gave her an exasperated look. "I haven't talked to her in years."

No, but he *wanted* to talk to her. He'd said so the other night, but that was more than Mae was willing to do. Mae hated that Mama still had so much power over her. Mae was a grown-ass woman, for God's sake. She'd been making her own way in the world for more than a decade. And it wasn't like Mama was going to come and rip the folder out of Mae's hands. Hurricane Carly might do that, but not Mama.

Cole motioned with his chin toward the folder. "So what is it?"

"They're pictures of my father. And a few other things. A note he wrote me the day I was born." Tears welled in her eyes. "A card he'd made for his mother one year on Mother's Day. A love note he'd written to Mama."

Cole frowned. "I thought she burned all that stuff?"

Mae nodded. "That's what she always said, but I was nosing around in her room one day, looking for something to use on a school project, and I found them."

"When was this?" Cole asked.

"After you left." In Mae's mind, her childhood was divided into two distinct periods—when Cole was there and after he'd gone. She imagined a page from a magazine, ripped haphazardly by hand. A jagged edge beyond repair.

One side of his mouth curved upward. "You look like him, don't you?" Cole had told Mae years ago about a couple of disjointed memories he had of her father, though she had none herself.

Mae nodded. "Same dark hair. Same light eyes."

"Same freckles," he teased.

That similarity was the only reason Mae embraced her freckles.

"Mama doesn't know you have it?" Cole asked.

"I confronted her about it, like 'What the hell, Mama? Why would you keep all this from me?' But she was drunk." *As usual.* "She slapped me across the face and sent me to my room." It was the only time Mama had ever slapped Mae's face. Fifteen-year-old Mae had felt demeaned and mistreated. That night was one of the huge turning points that had caused Mae to believe that people were crap, despite the fact that Mama's skin never, ever held the silvery sheen Mae saw on other people.

"You should have waited to confront her when she was sober."

Mae grunted. "Yeah, no shit." She'd finally learned that lesson, but it had taken awhile. "But her being drunk kind of worked in my favor too."

Cole gave her a questioning look as he stuck a hand inside the bathroom to turn off the fan.

"The reason she hates him so much is that he wasn't alone when he died in that car wreck."

Cole's eyebrows shot up. "He was with another woman?"

Mae nodded.

"Mama *told* you that? And you believed her?"

Mae shrugged. "Liquor's pretty much a truth serum. At least it always was with her."

"Yeah. You're right. So when did she give them to you?"

"She didn't. She threw them in the outside trash, so I waited until she passed out and then I went out there and dug them out." Mae would always remember the sight of Mama staggering down the carport stairs and over to the big blue bin that sat beside their latest rental house—more caught up in her anger than at what her own daughter needed most.

He grinned. "And then you hid them from her? For years?"

"I hid them in all different places around my room, so if she found one, maybe the others would be safe. I was always afraid she'd find them and throw them away again."

"Have you not scanned them in case you lose the originals?"

"I have, but I want the originals. Especially the notes. They're in his handwriting." Again, her eyes misted. She'd spent hours touching the ink when she'd been younger, until she learned that the oils in her fingertips would damage the paper.

"And you're going to trust me to keep it safe?" He reached for the folder, but she pulled it against her chest, protecting it with her splayed hands.

"Anything in there can be replaced." She jabbed a thumb behind her, toward her bedroom. Or, rather, Ryan's bedroom. The latest in a long line of temporary places she'd stayed. She'd never really had a home. "But I want to make sure this folder stays safe. It's the one thing that matters to me."

Cole's Adam's apple bobbed. "You don't want to take it with you?" His quiet tone showed that he understood how important this was to her.

She shook her head. "I don't know what I'm walking into or what I'll have to deal with. And I don't want to leave it in my car." Vehicles flooded, even in tropical storms . . . and Carly was well beyond that. Mae had seen pictures from other hurricanes of big boats blown into people's yards and sitting on roofs and whatnot. No, her car would not be a safe place to store it as Carly blew through.

She had no other choice but to leave it with the on-again-off-again brother who'd only recently come back into her life. "So I'm trusting you."

She handed the plastic folder to him, hoping to God it would still be intact in twenty-four or forty-eight hours.

Cole reached out his hand and took the plastic folder from her. "I'll do my best to keep it safe."

She motioned toward the front door. "I've got to go. I told Halsey I'd get there as soon as I could."

Cole took a step forward and pulled her into a big bear hug. The dampness of his just-showered body surrounded her. He smelled of soap and some kind of musky-scented shampoo.

"I love you, Sis." His voice was strangled with emotion. "Take care of yourself out there."

She wrapped her arms around his back—the first hug they'd shared in years. She squeezed her eyes shut, willing herself not to cry. "I love you back."

After several more seconds, they inched apart, both misty-eyed.

"You sure you don't want me to go with you?" Cole asked.

She shook her head. "Like you said, it's probably best if someone's here."

"Your phone's charged? You've got your charger with you?"

"You're pretty optimistic about us having electricity."

"Be sure to stay in touch," he said.

She pointed to the folder in Cole's hand. "Be sure to take care of my father."

***

Mae pulled into the church parking lot, trying to gather as much information as she could about the scene in front of her. The pounding rain from one of Carly's outer bands made her car wipers nearly useless.

Vans from three TV stations had parked near the main entrance to the sanctuary. Thirty or forty people milled about under the huge porte cochere. Raincoat-clad reporters stood near photojournalists who held big plastic-covered cameras on their shoulders. But who were the other fifteen or twenty people? A TV station van could hold—what? Maybe three or four people max, plus equipment? That would mean twelve people total, if each of the three TV vans had brought four employees, which seemed doubtful.

Mae eased into a parking space and glanced at the other vehicles parked along the row closest to the sanctuary door—a mix of cars, pickups, and SUVs. One corner of a Jeep's soft-cover top flapped violently in the wind. That interior would be filled with water in no time.

So who did all those cars belong to? Who *were* these people and why were they here?

Her first order of business was to get inside and find Halsey. Or rather, to find Conrad, as Halsey had instructed, who would then tell her where their boss was hiding out.

She scanned the scene in front of her one last time. Rob Lassiter would be the only TV station employee who would know her, but the reporter hanging beside his station's van was a white woman. The cameraman was a big burly Black guy about twice the size of Lassiter.

She leaned over the steering wheel and studied the crowd of people under the porte cochere more closely. Her gaze moved methodically from person to person, but she still couldn't identify Rob Lassiter among them. But then the people were too far away, and hoods obscured many faces.

The person in the bright orange raincoat might be Casey, the tattooed youth minister, but Mae couldn't be certain from this distance. There was no sign of Conrad, even though Halsey had instructed her to find the janitor when she arrived at the church. And there was definitely no sign of Halsey, who would have been the center of everyone's attention had he been among the crowd. No, the group was too chaotic, too disorganized.

Most of the people held some kind of satchel—a backpack, a diaper bag, a big canvas tote. A couple might have even had—Mae looked closer—rolled up sleeping bags?

One man did his best to hold on to a toddler who thrashed about in his arms. A woman swaddled what might have been an infant. A couple of older kids—maybe ten-year-olds?—leaned against the sanctuary door, their little hands gripped together between their skinny bodies. A dog in a tiny raincoat dashed out into the rain but jerked backward when it reached the end of its leash.

Though Mae couldn't make out faces, she could feel the tension of the crowd even from this distance. Even through the wind and rain, she could sense the potential combustion of the situation.

She couldn't wade through that crowd, especially not when she didn't know what was going on yet. Anger roiled inside her at the fact that Halsey had expected her to show up here and just deal with whatever faced her, with no background and no knowledge of the circumstances. A PR person needed to be informed. To have a plan for how and why she would answer questions from the media. She shifted from Park into Drive and slowly moved her car from the large sanctuary building to the low-slung building behind it that held the administrative offices. They were two separate structures, connected via an awning-covered breezeway—a necessity given Florida's frequent rainstorms.

Mae didn't have a key to get into the offices, but maybe someone was back there. If the person out front *had* been Casey, then maybe she'd been in the office first and left the door to the administrative building unlocked.

There were a couple of cars near the door to the office, but Mae hadn't visited the church often enough to know what kind of vehicle any of the employees drove. Halsey likely wouldn't bring his Tesla out in this weather, and Dawn's BMW wasn't there either.

Mae got out of her car and ran through the rain to the office door. Mercifully, it opened, but her sigh of relief was cut short at the sight of the one person standing in the reception area.

"Aaahhhh. The perfect person to talk to." Rob Lassiter's sleazy grin said I've-got-you-now, but—strangely—his skin held no silvery glow. Why did this pushy, unscrupulous man always seem to evade her internal alarm system?

The wind caught the door behind Mae, slamming it against the outer wall of the building. She stepped outside, got ahold of the handle again, and pulled it closed tightly behind her as she re-entered the reception area. "What are you doing here?" she asked, not hiding her annoyance. His station had sent *two* reporters to one location? When there was so much going on with the storm?

"Haven't you heard?"

She paused a moment before answering. PR people hated surprises. "Heard what?"

"The shelters are all full. People who hadn't planned to leave their homes have apparently changed their minds now that it's a Cat 5."

Mae listened a moment, trying to figure out if anyone else was in the office area—someone who could come rescue her from this man's inquiries—but the only sounds were the howling wind and pounding rain. "And what does that have to do with the church?"

"People's homes are already flooding, and Carly hasn't even come ashore yet."

Irritation crept up her back. She wished he'd get to the point. "Again, what does that have to do with the church?"

"People want to take shelter at PALM." He barked out a short chuckle. "Kind of poetic, don't you think?"

A shudder crept down Mae's back. She now saw the scene out front in a different light—the children and the little dog and the people under the porte cochere.

Lassiter continued. "I guess someone on the mayor's staff thought the church would be open and they said as much on the Channel Five broadcast and—"

She held up a hand to stop him. "Wait. You mean the church *isn't* open?"

"You don't know, do you?" Lassiter smirked. "Your boss refused to let them in. Told people to go back to their homes—their *flooded* homes—and that God would take care of them there."

"Where *is* Halsey?" She looked down the hallway toward his darkened office.

Lassiter shook his head. "He was here a while ago, but he skedaddled the second I tried to get him on camera. There's a—" Lassiter raised a small pad in front of him and seemed to scan it for information. "—Casey James out front. A Conrad Manalo brought the crowd some snacks from the kitchen. They're being as hospitable as possible, given the fact that Halsey apparently told them not to open the church doors."

Mae let her butt sink onto the reception desk behind her. Halsey Green had this big, huge building—this "house of

God"—and refused to let people inside when they needed shelter? Wasn't helping people a core tenet of Christianity?

Her questions soon gave way to anger. She could contemplate his behavior later, when she didn't have a job to do.

Damn you, Halsey.

He'd thrust her into an impossible situation. She was expected to protect his reputation, yet he'd given her no redeeming information to share with others. No positive spin to build on. No way to make him look good, given the circumstances Lassiter had just described.

She thought of the mother cradling the baby. The toddler crying in his father's arms. The bedraggled adults who carried knapsacks of God knew what—medicine or family heirlooms or beloved books they wanted to save from the storm.

Had Halsey actually *seen* those people? Had he really stood in front of them and denied them access to a building that some of them may have *helped pay for*? He really was a horrible human being.

And he also wasn't there. He'd apparently slunk away, leaving those around him to clean up his mess. Those around him, like Conrad, who were far better—and far kinder—than he was.

She took her phone from her pocket and dialed Halsey's number, no longer caring what Rob Lassiter might overhear. "I'm at the church now," she said when Halsey answered.

"Are all those people still there?"

"The ones in need of shelter?" Sarcasm dripped from her voice.

Rob Lassiter grinned at her impertinence, though he could only hear half of the conversation.

"They need to be sent home," Halsey said. "We can't . . . soil the sanctuary or assume responsibility for their safety or—What if the church floods? It's a few families now, but what if it turns into *hundreds* of people?"

"The sanctuary holds—what? *Six-thousand people?*"

"That's not the point. It'll hold that many for the length of a church service. But our facilities weren't built to handle a crowd like that for a longer period of time. We don't know how much wind it can withstand. And it's a house of worship, for God's sake. Not a homeless shelter."

It also had a commercial grade kitchen and a gym with plenty of showers—both of which would come in handy if housing a crowd. But Mae didn't want to hear any more of his excuses. All she sought was confirmation of his stance. "So you're not going to open the church to evacuees from the storm?"

Halsey paused for a moment before answering, like he knew how the decision made him look. "You need to find a better way to say that when you talk to the media. Maybe tell them the city hasn't authorized us to be a shelter or something like that."

Mae wasn't even a Christian, but she couldn't imagine that Jesus would wait on anyone's authorization before helping others. "Okay. Got it." Her gaze met Lassiter's, who suddenly seemed less like an enemy and more like a compadre. Maybe that's why she'd never seen a silvery tint to his skin. He *seemed* smarmy on the outside, but maybe his intentions were better than she'd expected.

"Keep me apprised of what's going on there," Halsey said.

"Where are you, anyway?" Mae asked.

He let out an irritated huff. "I've got a buddy with a big ranch west of Jacksonville, *away* from the intracoastal and the river."

Both bodies of water would flood from the storm surge, so Halsey had gotten himself to safer ground. "Dawn and the kids are with you? And Akira?" Would the Greens have taken the nanny with them, ensuring that the young woman was safe from the storm?

"Of course they're with me. Now get to work and stay in touch. I don't want to learn what's going on there by seeing it on the news."

"I'll talk to you later." She hit the button to end the call.

Lassiter crossed his arms. "He didn't budge, did he?"

Mae stood and straightened. A plan niggled in the back of her mind but had not yet fully formed. "Any idea where Conrad got off to?"

Chapter Thirty-Six

Mae allowed Lassiter to follow her as she searched for Conrad throughout the building. It would serve Halsey right if a journalist had a firsthand view of what went on inside the church while the hurricane raged outside.

After about ten minutes, she found the janitor outside a storage closet in the classroom wing of the administrative building.

He hoisted a pallet of bottled water onto a dolly, which already held three other pallets. "These were supposed to be for the Parents' Picnic, but I think they'll be of better use now." He paused to look at Mae, a sudden look of concern on his face. "Do you think it's okay?"

She placed a reassuring hand on his arm. "I think whatever decisions you make today will be fine." She lifted her hand from his arm and held it out, palm up. "And I'd like your keys, please."

Conrad's eyebrows rose. He looked from Mae to Lassiter and back again. "Excuse me?"

Her hand remained outstretched between them. "And show me which one opens the front doors of the church."

A surprised look swept across Conrad's face. "Halsey changed his mind? About letting people in there?"

"Halsey's not here." And Mae would be damned if she'd deny those people shelter while a Category 5 hurricane lashed everything in sight. There were *children* out there, for God's sake. Just the thought of them—huddled against their parents as sideways rain pummeled them, even underneath the awning—reminded Mae of her wild and uncertain childhood. How she always feared what might come next. How she rarely felt safe. She would do everything within her power to make sure those kids felt secure and protected. That their parents and siblings were tucked in beside them, inside the church and out of the storm. Halsey could fire her or go to hell or both.

She held the janitor's gaze, willing him to join in on her plan. "What I see out there is a bunch of people in need of shelter," she said. "You wouldn't want one of your dogs out in this storm, would you?"

His eyes widened. "No, ma'am."

"Then let's not keep people out in it either."

Again, Conrad's gaze slid to Lassiter as the janitor weighed the request. Slowly, Conrad's hand moved to the side of his belt. He unhooked the big ring of keys from the carabiner attached there. A grin spread across his face as he handed the key ring to Mae. "You have a good soul, young lady. *You* should be the one in the pulpit on Sundays."

Except I'm not a Christian. But then one didn't need to follow a specific dogma to be a good person. In fact, it hadn't been a minister who'd finally convinced Mae there was good in humanity. It had been Conrad and Klara. Lejla and Ezra.

A janitor, a pair of housekeepers, and a construction company owner.

She grinned as she closed her fingers around the collection of twenty or thirty keys. "I'll tell Halsey I wrestled them from you."

He gave a single nod. "I appreciate that, ma'am. I need this job."

Lassiter spoke up for the first time since they'd found the janitor. "You opening the doors from the inside or the outside?"

Mae had no idea how this should all work. She looked to Conrad for guidance.

He reached over to Mae's palm and lifted one particular key. "I'd go out the back door of this building and under the breezeway into the back of the sanctuary. It's the way Halsey enters before he's about to conduct a church service."

"So she'll open the doors from the inside of the sanctuary?"

Conrad nodded. "Well, from the vestibule, which leads to the sanctuary."

"That big lobby thing?" Lassiter asked.

Mae guessed he wasn't a churchgoer, either.

"That's right," Conrad said.

Lassiter turned his attention to Mae. "You give me exclusive access to you making that trek and opening those doors, and I'll forget all about the conversation I witnessed here." He motioned between Conrad and Mae.

Mae had to protect Conrad, even if that meant partnering with Lassiter. She held out her hand offering him a deal.

The journalist shook it, then pulled out his cell phone. "I need to get my cameraman back here with me."

She gave Conrad's arm a squeeze of thanks but kept her gaze on the journalist. "I'll give you five minutes. And then we head to the sanctuary."

Chapter Thirty-Seven

Mae stood in front of the ornately carved doors in the vestibule of PALM, knowing that her life was about to change. She had no idea *how* it would change—if she'd regret her decision or be proud of her actions—but she doubted it would ever be the same.

Behind her, the bright light of a TV camera flickered on. Rob Lassiter tried to straighten his disheveled Channel Ten raincoat, but to no avail.

She took a deep breath. "You ready for this?"

Lassiter glanced to the cameraman.

"Ready," the stocky man said.

"Ready," Lassiter repeated to her.

She used Conrad's keys to unlock the huge wooden doors, but when she tried to push one open, a mass of people blocked her way. A rustle of voices turned into distinguishable words.

Back up. Back up.

Finally, the crowd had backed away far enough to wedge the door open. A stream of people began filing in, their expressions thankful and desperate and beaten down all at the same time.

Mae stepped aside, eager to let them in. Young parents hugged soaking, scared toddlers against their chests. Teenagers carried younger siblings. A large, middle-aged man spread his arms out wide, making sure that no one knocked into the elderly woman in front of him who used a cane. A trio of little yappy dogs pulled their owner inside. Halsey would *hate* having dogs in the church because where would they go to the bathroom? But Mae didn't care. This was about protecting people—no, all beings—from the hurricane.

Tears filled her eyes as she witnessed the mass of humanity streaming past her—all trying to save themselves, their loved ones, the few belongings that might help them after the storm. She knew in that moment—without a doubt—that she'd done the right thing.

She reached up to wipe her eyes when Ezra burst through the door. A look of relief flooded his face the second he saw her. He quickly took a step to the left—out of the crowd—and swept her into his arms.

"I heard Halsey wasn't letting people in," he said into her hair as he hugged her.

"He had a change of heart." Her voice shook from the emotion of the moment.

He pulled away and looked her in the face as he grinned. "He actually *has* a heart?"

She smiled through her tears. "Who knew?"

"Am I the only one hearing the Grinch music in my head right now?" His hands made the motion of a pounding heart, getting bigger with each beat.

Her laugh was cut short by Rob Lassiter, who came up behind her and cupped her elbow. He pointed toward the large, sweeping staircase that led to the upper level of atrium. From there congregants could access the balcony seats inside the sanctuary. "I thought we'd have you stand on the second or third step over there. Capture all the people behind you."

She nodded, still not happy about having to appear on camera under these circumstances, but it was her best idea for saving Halsey's behind.

"Where's everyone headed?" Ezra asked as he motioned to the long stream of disheveled people walking past the open staircase and disappearing down a corridor in the distance.

Mae had to yell over the din of the crowd. "We're having them sit in the hallways in the classroom wing—away from any windows. The sanctuary's such a big, huge room, we were afraid the roof might cave in or get blown off or something."

"Smart thinking," Ezra said.

Lassiter motioned for Mae to go over to the staircase. "The sooner we get the word out that PALM is open, the more people will be safe."

She turned to Ezra. "How do I look?"

A warm smile spread across his face. He moved a wet strand of hair off her forehead. "You look beautiful."

And she could tell that he meant it. In some demented way, he really thought she looked good in that moment. She laughed. With her rain-tousled hair and the oversized raincoat she'd borrowed from Ryan's, Cole's roommate's, closet, she knew she was a mess. But she'd never felt more alive, more exhilarated.

"Thanks," she said as she squeezed his arm, then she followed Lassiter over to the big staircase. The camera light snapped on, bathing a large swath of the atrium in an unnatural glow. Bedraggled evacuees making their way toward the classroom wing squinted as they looked up at the bold brightness—a sharp contrast in a day filled with menacing skies.

Lassiter showed her where to stand on the third step from the bottom, then did his best to adjust his own rumpled appearance.

He waited until the cameraman counted down with three fingers, then he spoke. "This is Rob Lassiter with an exclusive report from *inside* the Pathway to Abundant Life Ministries, otherwise known as PALM. We were the only station present *inside the church* as evacuees from Hurricane Carly were given access to the building."

He motioned with his hand to indicate his interviewee. "This is Mae Van Dorn," Lassiter said. "Personal assistant to Pastor Halsey Green. Thank you for being with us, Ms. Van Dorn."

Mae smiled and nodded, then chided herself for looking so upbeat when people's homes were being blown away.

"PALM was not initially open to serve evacuees, but as our viewers can see"—Lassiter motioned to the people in the background, visible through the open staircase—"people were let into the building just moments ago. They're settling in to ride out Jacksonville's worst storm in decades."

"That's right," she said.

"Halsey Green had initially told reporters he would not allow his church to be used as a shelter, so what changed?" Lassiter held the microphone in front of Mae's mouth, waiting for her response.

Mae took a breath and launched into the message she'd been forming in her mind since she'd gotten this idea. "Some of Pastor Green's advisors had expressed concern about potential liability over the fact that this building was not set up to be a shelter *or* approved as such by the city of Jacksonville Beach, despite the fact that another television station had announced PALM would open as a shelter. These are all valid concerns, but as you know, Pastor Green's life centers around Christian values. Each person's responsibility to take care of our fellow human beings. So despite the concerns I mentioned a moment ago, Pastor Green opted to help those in need. No insurance company or local government or any other organization over-rides the responsibility we all have to help those around us. And so"—she stepped to the side and swept her arm behind her to indicate the flow of people making their way to the classroom wing—"he opened the doors so that residents and visitors to our area could take shelter from the storm."

So far, so good. She hoped Halsey was watching. She wanted him to see, minute by minute, how she was saving his reputation in the community.

Lassiter moved the microphone back to his mouth. "Where is Halsey Green right now?"

Mae smiled as Lassiter moved the microphone back to her. "In addition to being the founder of PALM, Pastor Green is a family man. He and his wife, Dawn, have two small children. So once he made sure the church staff had everything they needed to make this facility available to evacuees, he went to be with them during the storm."

"Thank you, Ms. Van Dorn." Lassiter faced the camera directly, no longer turned toward her. "And a bad situation it is, with the first direct hit from a hurricane the Jacksonville community has seen in decades. This is Rob Lassiter with Channel Ten in an exclusive report from inside Jacksonville

Beach's newly opened, if *unofficial*, shelter from the storm. And now back to Chief Meteorologist Cameron Schwartz for the latest on Carly's impact on the First Coast." Lassiter stood smiling for several long seconds, apparently waiting to make sure the station's live feed had switched back to the studio.

Mae's shoulders relaxed as soon as Lassiter stirred—his stiff, on-camera disposition replaced with more casual movements.

She stepped off the staircase and walked toward Ezra, hoping for his approval. His being here—his presence—gave her a buoy to cling to. Yes, she'd made the decision to open the church on her own, but she felt stronger, more confident, with him by her side.

He wrapped his arm around her shoulder and pulled her into his side. "You did great."

"Thank you."

"Looks like you've done that before. You were a real pro."

She let out a soft laugh. "It was mainly my bosses who were on camera in the past, but it wasn't like I had a choice today."

"Did Halsey really leave you here? Like, you're in charge of what goes on here?"

"He's on the westside somewhere," she said. "As far away from the storm as he could get."

"And you're in charge here?" he repeated.

"I'm pretty sure Carly's running the show here. She seems very much in char—"

A deafening sound split through the atrium—an explosion of sorts. Mae's body was thrust to the ground. Her head hit the bottom step of the staircase and her vision clouded. For a couple of brief seconds, she heard what sounded like hundreds of shards of glass falling to the floor, followed by gusts of wind roaring through the lobby—an instant cacophony of squalls and noise and sideways rain.

She felt Ezra shield her with his body, lying on top of her but supporting his own weight with his arms. "You okay?" His panicked voice confirmed that he was as scared as she was.

She opened her mouth to answer, then her world went dark.

Chapter Thirty-Eight

Her foggy brain couldn't seem to rise above the surface of whatever sludge surrounded it. She tried to move her painful shoulder, but something warm and unyielding lay on top of her. She tried to roll over, but again, the mass of muscle pinned her into place.

"Oh, my God. Mae?"

A male voice, though it sounded like he spoke underwater. *Ezra?*

The big body rose gently from her, as if she was fragile or broken.

Ezra's face came into focus. His eyes had a wild look about them. "Are you okay?"

"What happened?"

"Some windows blew out." His gaze didn't leave her as he motioned behind him. "But that's not important. Are you okay?" His eyes and his hands scanned her body, as if looking for signs of injury.

She sat up slowly, testing each limb and joint. Only the one shoulder ached a bit but felt better the more she moved it. "I . . . think I'm okay."

He hovered over her, his hands outstretched, ready to help if she needed it.

She peered over his shoulder to a huge, gaping hole, high on the wall of glass. *Holy shit.* "Was anybody hurt?" She imagined shards of flying glass impaling the poor people rushing to seek shelter.

"I don't know. I don't think so."

"Are *you* okay?" A warm sensation slid through her as she realized that the body on top of her had been his. The one protecting her.

"I'm fine, but let's get into the classroom wing before that happens again."

No argument there. Not when there were twenty or thirty more windows—each the size of the ones that had already given way to the high winds.

He helped her as she stood. "You're sure you're not hurt anywhere?" he asked.

"Just a little . . . wobbly." She wondered what a concussion felt like, but she didn't have time to dwell on it.

He wrapped his arm around her waist. "We'll take it slow."

She glanced around the lobby as they walked, hip to hip, toward the classroom wing. The few other people still in the atrium also made their way in that direction. Mercifully, none seemed injured.

Ezra opened one of the two double doors as soon as they reached the entrance to the hallway that led out of the lobby. He kept his other arm around her waist, guiding her.

Conrad rushed to them, his eyes wide. "You two were *out there* when it happened?"

"Yes, but I think we're fine," Ezra said. "Let's get her a place to sit."

They made their way down the crowded hallway, looking for a vacant spot to sit. People lined both sides, their knapsacks and sleeping bags pulled tight against them, as if protecting what could very well be their only belongings left after the storm. Mae hadn't realized how many people had arrived since she'd opened the doors.

Toddlers played in the center of the hallway, their parents pulling them out of the way when someone needed to pass. A middle-aged couple sat solemnly with two elderly people, perhaps their parents. And there appeared to be "found families" too—groupings of young professionals sitting together, some laughing, some staring at their phones, some holding the hands of their scared-looking friends.

A mass of humanity in all its various forms.

Finally, they found a vacant spot to sit. The lights flickered as Mae put her back against the wall and let herself slide downward. The two men remained standing, as if on high alert. Ezra looked down at her and raised his eyebrows. *You okay?* the expression seemed to say. She nodded.

Mae watched as a middle-aged woman they'd recently passed stood and walked across the hallway toward a young mother who seemed to be dealing with three children all on her own—perhaps one of the many Navy wives whose husbands were out to sea. Two toddlers whined to get on the woman's lap where she sat on the floor, but the young mother's arms were filled with a wailing infant. The middle-aged woman bent and held out her arms, as if offering to take the crying baby. The young mother hesitated, then handed the infant to the other woman, who immediately placed the child on her shoulder and bounced gently from side to side—a perfect picture of grandmotherly experience. A look of relief settled onto the young mother's face as the two toddlers climbed onto her lap, each nestling in one of her arms.

Down the hall, the yip of a dog drew Mae's attention—a recently-arrived Pomeranian in a standoff with a gentle black lab who seemed only curious.

Good Lord, what would Halsey say about the fact that there were *animals* in his pristine church? Mae chuckled inwardly at the thought of it.

Conrad looked down at her from where he stood. "You here for the long haul? Or just to open the doors?"

Mae looked to Ezra, who looked at her. She assumed her face held the same questioning expression as his.

"Where's Cole?" Ezra asked her.

"At the house. He didn't want to come with me."

"You should stay here," Conrad said as the lights flickered again. "No one needs to be out on the roads right now."

Mae had been taking it minute by minute. Now that the church was open, she *did* need to take her next action, but the decision seemed overwhelming. And she'd just needed to sit after the scare in the atrium. "What about your dogs?" She couldn't imagine the janitor leaving them—his family—in this situation.

Conrad gave a sly grin and jabbed a thumb behind him. "I got 'em in their crates in the choir room."

Mae let out a weak laugh and held up her hand for a high five. Her arm felt weak, but she was happy to not be the only one crossing Halsey that day.

Ezra stuck out his hand to the janitor. "Ezra Watts. I'm a friend of Mae's."

Conrad looked from Mae to Ezra and back again, as if trying to size up their relationship. He held out his hand. "Conrad Manalo. I work here at the church."

"Nice to—"

Ezra's words were cut short when a female TV reporter approached from behind him. She pushed past him and looked down to Mae, where she sat on the floor. "Excuse me, are you Halsey Green's assistant? The one who let everyone inside the church?"

Mae chin fell to her chest as exhaustion crashed down upon her. She did *not* want to be the center of attention here, especially not when it could take *hours* for the storm to blow through. She'd done what she needed to do—both morally and as Halsey's employee. She'd let people inside the church. She'd kept Halsey from looking like the selfish prick he was. She'd given Rob Lassiter his exclusive interview.

A camerawoman stood behind the reporter. Though she held the camera in her hand instead of on her shoulder, Mae knew that could change at any moment. She struggled to stand, still shaken by the blast in the lobby. Ezra helped her to her feet.

"I'm not taking interviews right now," she said. "Let's concentrate on making it through the storm."

But the woman didn't back down. "Can you at least tell us why it took Pastor Green so long to decide to open the church to evacuees?"

Ezra stepped between Mae and the reporter, as if sensing Mae's unease. He then looked to Conrad. "Is there somewhere she can go that's . . . private?"

Conrad motioned with his head for them to follow him. "Let's go."

Ezra grasped Mae's arm and guided her down the hallway in the direction of the lobby and sanctuary. She followed them willingly, grateful that these two men were working together to get her out of the spotlight, away from any journalists who remained onsite. The reporter tailed behind them, asking questions in their wake.

"You still have my keys?" Conrad asked when they stopped at a door Mae hadn't noticed before.

She reached into her purse and handed him the big key ring he'd given her earlier. He sorted through the keys, unlocked the door, and stood aside so that Mae and Ezra could enter. He followed them inside and shut the door behind them, leaving the reporter on the other side.

Mae looked around the windowless room, which appeared to be some kind of small living room. A couch and one chair formed a little conversation area, while the walls were lined with bookshelves. "What is this place?"

"It's where Halsey waits until it's time for the service to start," Conrad said.

Mae nodded. A greenroom, of sorts.

"And we can lock the door so no one else can come in?" Ezra asked.

Conrad nodded. "And there's a private bathroom through that door. Y'all can stay in here until the storm's blown through."

But Mae didn't feel right leaving Casey and Conrad out there—potential prey for any reporter who wanted more information about Halsey's decision or the church. "But if I'm not out there, they'll just want to talk to you."

Conrad grinned. "I'll be in the choir room with my dogs."

"And Casey?"

Conrad returned the key ring to the carabiner at his hip. "She left a while ago to be with her parents. They have some kind of shelter built especially for hurricanes."

Mae motioned toward the hallway. "So the people will just . . . run rampant out there?" *Unsupervised?*

Ezra held out his hands in a questioning pose. "And what do you think y'all are going to do if you're out there?"

She thought about that for a moment. The crowd had been as calm and orderly as could be expected—a huddled mass of humanity, each person just trying to survive. To make sure those they loved came out alive on the other side.

She thought of the grandmotherly woman who'd offered to help the young, struggling mother. No, that crowd didn't need Mae or Conrad or anyone else policing them. They'd do just fine on their own.

"I'll walk through every now and then to check on things," Conrad said.

They all exchanged cell numbers so they could stay in touch, then Conrad walked to the door. "Stay safe, y'all," he said as he prepared to leave.

Mae rushed to hug him. He returned her embrace and held her for such a long time it made Mae wonder how long it had been since he'd been hugged. "Stay in touch," she said, embarrassed by the tears in her eyes.

He nodded, said goodbye to Ezra, and left the room.

Mae leaned her head against the now-closed door, welcoming the rare moment of quiet in an otherwise chaotic day.

Ezra came up behind her and wrapped his arms around her but didn't say anything. He seemed to know that she needed time to process everything that had happened. Everything that was *still* happening.

The walls of the hidden room muffled the sound of the storm, but the wind still howled outside. Something clunked against the exterior wall—perhaps a large piece of debris driven by the storm. But she took comfort in what was going on inside the room—the light brush of Ezra's breath against her neck, the sound of his breathing, the gentle rise and fall of his chest against her back.

By the time he took her hand and led her to the couch, she finally felt centered again. Less unmoored by the day's event. They sat on one end—hip to hip—and rested their feet on the leather ottoman. He placed his palm on her thigh—a reassuring gesture—and she placed her hand on top of his.

"You know this doesn't count as our second date, right?" she asked quietly.

He let out a soft chuckle. "No, but it's certainly going to be memorable."

Something we can tell our grandkids about one day. After Rocco, she'd been even more cynical about guys, but Ezra made her believe in love again. "Your house is boarded up?" she asked.

"Yep. And all my valuables are in an old Army safe I got from a buddy of mine's grandfather. That thing's so heavy, there's no way it's going to blow away."

She turned to look at him. "You don't seem like the kind of guy who'd have a lot of valuables."

He placed his palm on his chest in mock offense. "What's that supposed to mean?"

"I mean, do you own . . . jewels . . . or expensive artwork . . . or stock certificates?"

His expression grew serious. "Pictures of my father. A couple of notes he'd written to me. Some pictures of our family—the four of us—before he passed away."

She sat back, facing forward once again, her shoulders square on the back of the couch. She laced her fingers in his. "Yeah. I get it. I don't remember my dad at all, so any pictures of him or things that belonged to him are pretty valuable to me too." She wondered if her plastic folder remained safe at Cole's house.

They sat in silence for several more seconds before she spoke again. "I like the fact that you're not a glitzy guy."

"You mean you're not into men like Halsey Green?"

"I'm into . . . whatever the opposite of him is."

He grinned and gave her the side-eye. "I think that would be me."

She turned again to face him. Her heart pounded in her chest as she thought about saying her next sentence out loud. "Then I guess I'm going to have to fall for you."

He turned sideways to face her too. His hand slid to her hip. "You're already way behind."

He held her gaze as the words sank in. She grinned and leaned in to place her lips on his—a soft, tentative kiss that tasted of promise and possibility.

The lights flickered off, then on again. A thud on the wall behind them—another large object blown against the outside of the building.

Mae's undercurrent of nervous energy spiked. "Seems to be getting worse out there."

He put his arm around her and pulled her against his chest. "This room has no windows, but if it will make you feel better, we can go sit in the bathroom—a smaller room, maybe a little more secure."

But before she could answer, the room plunged into darkness.

Chapter Thirty-Nine

Mae opened her eyes, not at all rested from the five- or ten-minute catnap she'd gotten as the hurricane raged outside. She wasn't even sure she could call it sleep—more like an absence of conscious thought, though her body had remained on high alert from the danger that lurked nearby.

She rose from where she lay on the couch in Halsey's windowless greenroom and walked over to where Ezra lay sprawled across the chair. After hours of talking in the dark, he'd insisted she rest on the couch, while he'd settled into the matching wingback.

The electricity was still out, but her eyes had somewhat adjusted to the darkness. She stood over him, watching him sleep—her first opportunity ever to observe him in such a quiet state. He really was a near-perfect specimen of a man—broad shoulders, square jaw, adorably-rumpled hair. This situation—this location—was not at all right for physical intimacy, but she looked forward to being with him in that way—skin to skin, soul to soul. His kind, gentle nature only heightened her attraction to him.

The wind outside stopped howling for a few brief and blessed seconds, allowing the soft sound of his breathing to fill the silence. Maybe one day—she hoped—that sound would be the regular chorus of her mornings. Yes, their relationship was new, but she somehow knew that this was the man she wanted beside her—through life's ups and downs and everyday challenges.

Her phone's ringtone jerked her from her reverie. She dove toward the couch, finding it wedged between two of the cushions. *Cole.* "Hello."

"You still okay?" They'd spoken a couple of times already, so he knew she was staying at the church.

"We're fine, except for losing electricity. You?" She wished they were together. She never should have left him alone.

"Hanging in there. I lost power a couple of times, but it's on now."

"I read on my phone that the hurricane's throwing off some tornadoes. One of them touched down by Mayport. Leveled a couple of buildings on the Navy base."

"Yeah, I moved to the bathtub a while ago. Pulled a mattress over me."

Her heart broke at the thought of something happening to him . . . or to her, for that matter. They'd lost so much time together. He was the one person who knew what she'd been through. What her childhood had been like. How they'd both been shaped by the places they'd lived. And now this storm could snatch away their newfound connection.

"Let's save our phone batteries," he said.

She nodded—afraid she'd cry if she tried to speak—then realized he couldn't see her. Her voice quavered as she said, "I love you."

"I love you, too, Sis."

Ezra's chair squeaked as she pressed the button to end the call. She turned to face him.

He now stood in front of the chair. "Everything okay?"

"Just Cole checking in. He's in the bathtub with a mattress over him."

Ezra blew out a long breath and ran his fingers through his hair, as if the severity of the situation had come crashing back to him after his sleep.

"I'm sorry to wake you," she said.

"No, I'm glad you did. I need to start organizing a bunch of my boating buddies for after the storm."

"For what?" What kind of event could possibly be so pressing when there was no telling what kind of clean-up was needed? And he had a business to run.

"There's going to be a lot of people trapped in their houses. They'll need to be rescued by boat." He let out a wry chuckle. "This is the one time I'm glad to have a small, beat-up, old boat."

"So, like the Cajun Navy?" She remembered news stories about boaters who made their way through the bayous of Louisiana, rescuing people from rooftops while floodwaters filled their homes.

"Except we're not Cajun."

Why had she not seen it back then—the good in humanity? She'd been so caught up in how horrible people could be to see the glimpses of good. Her experiences growing up had taught her how bad people could be, but now that she'd opened her eyes, she realized that good existed all around her. "You need to conserve your phone battery."

"I'll send out a group text. Tell them all to meet at the marina as soon as the storm is over."

Mae nodded, though selfishly, she wanted him to save enough battery so the two of them could stay in touch once they could finally leave their little two-person fortress. It could be days before electricity was restored. Days before people could return to their homes. Days before flood waters would recede.

Ezra sat in the chair, his thumbs flying across his phone screen.

She curled up on the couch, her knees tucked into her chest. She was grateful for her immediate surroundings—the safety of the windowless room—but overwhelmed by the power of Mother Nature. There were so many unknowns.

Ezra's house could be gone.

Cole's house could be gone.

The community at large could be devastated. Families displaced. Schools and businesses destroyed. Loved ones killed.

Emerging after the storm would be like waking up to a whole new world.

And all they could do was sit and wait.

***

Eight hours later, local radar showed that the bulk of the storm had passed, though a few outer bands remained. Conrad and Ezra had made several rounds through the church's classroom wing, making sure that everyone was okay and that no further emergencies had arisen.

Mae gingerly opened the door of the small room where she and Ezra had waited out the storm. She wasn't sure what made her more nervous—the possibility of being accosted by journalists again or the state of disrepair the church might be in. Housing hundreds of people—even well-behaved ones—would undoubtedly take its toll.

Conrad had texted a few minutes ago that Casey had returned and taken charge of the mass of humanity in the classroom wing. Conrad planned to load up the crates and take his dogs home since they hadn't been outside in almost eighteen hours. He'd come back to the church to start clean-up once he'd gotten his "family" settled at his house.

Mae stepped into the classroom hallway and took in the sight. Hundreds of people hunkered on the floor, though some stood, gathering their belongings as they prepared to go back out into the world.

Ezra stood beside her. He placed his hand on the small of her back. "Must feel pretty good knowing you had a hand in keeping them all safe."

She gave him a side-eyed look, tempted to tell him the truth—that she'd made the decision herself. That Halsey had never given her permission to let them in. But that could be her little secret—hers and Conrad's and Rob Lassiter's. "I just hope their homes are intact."

They watched the scene for a few more seconds before Ezra said, "You ready?"

She nodded. "My car's back by the administration building, but I want to go through the lobby."

She scanned the crowd of people mingling about as they made their way to the atrium. No journalists in sight. *Thank God.*

When they stepped into the lobby, the carpet squished under their feet—rain-soaked from where the windows had blown out. She was grateful to see that all the other windows remained intact. Still, the storm had been *inside* the church. Furniture and large urns lay toppled in corners, tossed about by the wind. Bright green leaves covered everything. Palm fronds and Spanish moss lay scattered about. She hoped PALM had good insurance.

The parking lot looked much the same. A carpet of leaves made the pavement look more green than gray. A wooden picnic table hung perilously from a live oak. So many limbs and larger branches littered the ground that Mae wasn't sure how any of the trees still had any.

She once again scanned her surroundings for reporters. Sure, the journalists would prefer to speak to Halsey, but she'd be an acceptable backup if they spotted her. One news station's van sat on the far side of the lot, but the reporter stood with his back to her and there was no cameraperson in sight.

Mae turned her head—hiding her face—and pointed toward a sidewalk that hugged the front of the sanctuary. She'd need to follow it around the building to get to her car. "I need to go that way."

"Get in my truck. I'll take you to your car."

"No, that's okay. You've got important work to do." They'd already talked out their plans—she would head to Cole's and Ezra would get his boat and meet his buddies with theirs at the marina, ready to start their rescue mission.

"I'm not going to leave before I know your car's okay." He motioned to a nearby SUV—its windshield shattered by the large palm tree resting on its hood.

"Good point. Thank you," she said, grateful for this man who'd come into her life. She'd so rarely felt protected, even with Rocco. She'd been on her own ever since Cole had left all those years ago. It felt good to know someone else looked out for her.

They got in his leaf-covered truck, and he drove through the parking lot slowly as they took in the devastation. A large hole gaped on the roof of a house that backed up to the church's property. The home next door seemed to have lost an entire wall.

She let out a sigh of relief when they'd circled the building and reached her car. Soggy leaves covered it—driven against it by the wind—but, mercifully, it remained intact.

"We'll touch base later?" Ezra asked.

She nodded. "Let me know when you've seen your house."

"I will." He leaned over and pecked her on the cheek. "And you let me know about Cole's."

"Be safe out there." No telling what kind of dangers lay in the murky waters he'd boat through. Alligators for sure. Snakes, most likely. Maybe live electrical lines? Dead bodies? She didn't want to think about it. She opened the door and got out of the truck.

"I can help y'all with anything that needs to be done at Cole's house," he said.

She turned to face him. "Thank you. And . . ." She wasn't sure how to express her gratitude. "Thanks for staying with me last night."

He gave her a grin and dipped his chin in acknowledgment. "I was exactly where I wanted to be."

A warm sensation melted through her as she made her way to her car and got in. They might be away from each other for a few days—no telling how long storm clean-up would last or what it might entail—but hopefully normal life would resume again soon. She wondered what a "normal life" with Ezra might look like.

He waited in his truck, making sure her car started, then gave her a one-fingered wave and drove away. She plugged her phone in and pulled out of the parking lot, careful to avoid any branches that might get lodged under her car.

She forced herself to keep her eyes on the road as she made her way down Third Street, when what she wanted was to look around at all the destruction. Thank goodness not a lot of people were on the road since all the stoplights were out. Roofs were missing from many of the strip malls that lined the street. Cars lay overturned. The massive sign of the Whole Foods shopping plaza had crumpled upon itself.

As Mae waited to turn left toward Cole's house, a huge convoy of utility trucks passed her—their home locations emblazoned on the side of each truck.

Edison, New Jersey.

Baltimore, Maryland.

Springfield, Missouri.

Albuquerque, New Mexico.

Baton Rouge, Louisiana.

She'd read online that a staging ground had been created over by Lake City, where crews and equipment from other states had waited, ready to head into the impacted area as soon as it was safe.

Their presence there made Mae want to cry. Strangers who'd come thousands of miles to help them. Men and women who'd left their families and maybe even endangered their lives, all to assist a community most of them had probably never even been to.

The car behind Mae beeped its horn, startling her. She took the turn and headed toward Cole's neighborhood.

The closer she got to his house, the harder her heart pounded. There wasn't just a missing roof here or there. *Most* of the houses had significant damage. A boat leaned against a tree at a forty-five degree angle. A pickup sat on top of a now-flattened Honda. A long-handled tool of some kind—a hoe, perhaps?—was impaled in a palm tree.

Was this hurricane damage . . . or had a tornado touched down here?

She made the next to last turn before Cole's street and gasped. The entire block of houses had been leveled. Only barren foundations remained. There wasn't even much rubble lying about. All the walls and roofs and belongings of the owners had simply . . . vanished.

Bile rose in her throat. At any other time—in any other circumstance—she would have pulled over to vomit, but she didn't have time now.

She needed to get to Cole.

Chapter Forty

Mae gulped in short, shallow breaths as she gunned her car's accelerator through the dystopian landscape that had once been Cole's Jax Beach neighborhood. Only three houses—each made of concrete block, like Cole's—still had walls, though their roofs had been sheared off by the hurricane force winds. Every other house on the street had been reduced to a flat, concrete foundation. Even the trees had been stripped bare—their ghostly branches devoid of leaves.

A local news station had already reported three storm-related deaths. What if Cole had been one of them? What if he'd died, scared and alone, because she'd left him by himself? Six months ago, he'd been someone from her past. Someone she used to know. Someone who'd done her wrong, leaving painful lessons in his wake.

But these last few weeks had proven that he was—once again—a source of security. A person who had her back. Someone whose loyalty and love she could count on. Their long, heartfelt talk in the dark the other night had told her a lot. She now understood that he'd been too ashamed to call her when he'd been arrested, gone on trial, and been sentenced to prison. And that entire dark episode of her brother's life all stemmed from the same crappy childhood that had haunted Mae all these years. He wouldn't have gone apeshit on the guy at the bar if he hadn't endured all the beatings by Mama's abusive boyfriend. If he hadn't been protecting Mae.

Shame washed over her. Why had she not seen it all along? Cole had always been the center of her family. Cole *was* her family.

Her heart lurched at the notion that she might not ever see him again. That the storm might have snatched him away just when she'd come to know him again. Just when she ached to thank him for all he'd done for her.

She rounded the last corner, and his house came into view. The roof had been sheared off, but she couldn't see much else because a large tree trimming truck—no doubt essential personnel following a hurricane—blocked her view.

She punched the gas pedal even harder until she came to a screeching stop on the other side of the large vehicle, right in front of Cole's house. Standing water pooled in the yard. The protective plywood on the front picture window and the plate glass underneath were both missing. The four small windowpanes in the garage door had also been blown out. The front door hung crookedly, held in place by a single hinge. One corner of the tiny front porch sagged where the wrought iron support trellis had snapped in two.

But there sat Cole on the front steps. He looked shell-shocked as he clutched a neon blue bundle—about the size of a laptop—to his chest. Water lapped at the bottom of the concrete stairs, inches from his flip-flopped feet.

Mae flung her car door open and plunged into ankle-deep water, not caring about her shoes or what kind of disgusting sewage might have merged with the storm surge. "Oh, my God. I'm so happy to see you," she said as she sloshed her way toward him.

Cole's eyes—unmoving in a vacant stare—shone with tears. Mae hadn't seen her brother cry since he was about eight years old. Slowly, his shoulders began to shake, as if his brain's protective defenses finally allowed his body to register the impact of what he'd been through. "Our stuff is just . . ." he said, then made a *poof* gesture with the fingers of one hand. "There's nothing left."

"I don't care about our stuff. I was just so worried. I heard there were tornadoes and . . ." She collapsed onto the concrete step next to him and pulled him into her arms, overcome by gratitude that he was alive.

"I saved this." He still stared forward—zombie-like—as he removed the neon blue covering from around the object he held against his chest. Inside was Mae's plastic folder, kept dry by what she now realized was a neon blue windbreaker. "I wasn't going to let you down again."

Her brother had ridden out a Category 5 hurricane—in a bathtub—while winds sucked the interior of the house into a likely funnel cloud, yet her plastic folder had been that important to him? She squeezed her eyes shut at the sheer magnitude of what he must have gone through—the eerie sounds, the unparalleled strength of Mother Nature, the terror at knowing death could happen at any minute.

I wasn't going to let you down again.

Without thinking, she took his hand in both of hers and bowed her head, overcome by the gravity of his words. When she was finally able to speak, she raised her gaze to look at her brother. "What matters most is that you're still alive. Things—even this"—she touched the plastic folder—"don't really matter."

"Everyone deserves to know where they came from."

She nodded, painfully aware that Mama had never even known the name of Cole's biological father. As much as Mae ached to know more about her dad, the hole in Cole's heart must be even larger than hers. She and her brother had so much in common, and no one else could ever understand what it felt like to be so unmoored. So bereft of belonging.

She laid her forefinger on the folder as Cole held it. "The guy in there's my father, but you're my family. You always have been."

He scoffed and finally broke his haunted stare. He looked down at the water at their feet instead of at Mae. "Yeah, well. I pretty much sucked at it most of the time."

She bumped his shoulder with hers. "You did your best in a tough situation. In *a lot* of tough situations."

Forgiveness had wormed its way into her soul as she'd gotten to know her brother again. Like her, he'd been faced with difficult odds. Thirteen-year-old Mae thought he was so old when he'd left at eighteen, but now—years later—she realized he'd been just a kid too. The world had been tough on Cole, but she would do her best to make life easier on him from now on.

"You think your roommate knows how bad the damage is in Jax Beach yet?" she asked.

Cole looked down. He dipped a toe in the water just below his feet. "Yeah . . . ummm. About that . . ."

"What?" she asked.

Finally, her brother's gaze rose to her. He squinted against the sun. "There isn't really a roommate. I made him up."

Okay, so maybe Mae had forgiven Cole a bit too early. "What? Why?"

Cole had a guilty look on his face. "You and I had just been back in touch with each other for—what—maybe two weeks when your boyfriend cheated on you?"

A memory of Miss Hot-n-Spicy straddling Rocco flashed through Mae's mind. She winced. "Yes, and . . . ?"

Cole shrugged. "You needed a place to stay. I had a spare bedroom. But I knew you weren't looking for a permanent move, so I positioned it like a short-term deal. Figured you'd be more likely to take me up on it that way." His gaze held hers as he got more serious. "I wanted to get to know you again."

Mae took a few seconds to examine that period in her life with this new lens. "And if I turned out to be a brat or a bitch or whatever, then you could kick me out when the 'roommate' was on his way back to town." She made air quotes around the word *roommate*.

"I figured having an out would benefit both of us. Less drama if it didn't work out between us."

Mae had to agree with that, but then something else crossed her mind. "What about those clothes in my closet that smell like dead fish?"

"They're gone, along with everything else in our closets. We have no clothes, no food, no furniture."

"But whose stinky coveralls *were* they?"

Cole gave a sheepish look and raised an index finger. "Mine."

She whapped Cole's thigh with the back of her hand. "You made me live in a room that smelled like dead fish so you could *make up* a roommate?"

He shielded himself with his hands. "It worked, didn't it?"

"You're an ass."

Cole chuckled as he surveyed the neighborhood. "I guess we need to figure out where we're going to sleep tonight."

She nodded. They were in a desperate situation, but at least Cole was by her side. Like so many years ago, they'd weather whatever life threw at them. That, at least, made her happy.

Where did one even start when they had to rebuild their entire life from nothing? She pulled out her phone so she could check the local news sites, assuming she could get internet access. They would likely have information about shelters or aid organizations that could help. Didn't the Red Cross swoop in at times like this? But how many people could they handle? Metro Jacksonville had more than a million people. Numbers like that could overload even the best-prepared organizations. Mae also remembered seeing something about how FEMA had provided housing after the hurricane over on the west coast of Florida. But it might be days or weeks before temporary buildings could be brought into the area. She and Cole needed a place to sleep *tonight*. They needed toothbrushes and toothpaste. Shampoo and dry shoes and an extra pair of underwear or two. She had about forty bucks in her purse and another few hundred in the bank. Not enough to rent an apartment on her own—even if there were any available after the storm—but maybe she and Cole could split the costs.

It was all so overwhelming, even for someone young and able-bodied like she was. How would an elderly or disabled person clean up the mess their home had become? How would the young mother she'd seen at the church pick up her family's lives when she had two toddlers and an infant to care for? How would she feed them in the wake of such devastation? It was all too much for Mae to think about. "Have you let your landlord know what's happened to his house?"

"I couldn't concentrate on anything until I knew you were safe, but I guess I should do that now." He stood. "And I should probably get down to the restaurant to see how it fared, since my boss evacuated to Atlanta. Thank God I had my car keys in my pocket, or they might have blown away."

She motioned toward the garage. "Your car's okay?"

"Banged up a bit, but I'm hoping it starts. You want to come with me to the restaurant? Maybe one of my coworkers has a couch we could crash on for a while."

"Or maybe we could stay at Ezra's. I mean, if his house is still there." She hadn't heard from him since they'd parted ways at the church. She needed to let him know what had happened to Cole's house.

Her brother gave her a teasing grin. "You've had one date with this guy, and now you want to move in with him? Did you not learn your lesson with the last one?"

"First of all, Rocco and Ezra are nothing alike." Not even close. "But Ezra just . . . feels right." She couldn't explain it, but she had an inner knowing about him. A certainty that he would be someone important in her life.

Cole gave her a sly grin as her phone pinged in her pocket. She pulled it out, hoping for an update from Ezra.

Instead, it was an all caps message from Halsey.

MY HOUSE. NOW!

CHAPTER FORTY-ONE

All Mae wanted was to be with "her people." To be in a cool, air-conditioned room, burrowed under a soft blanket—Cole and Ezra nearby—as the three of them figured out how to best recover from the devastation of Hurricane Carly.

But instead, each had gone their separate directions—Cole to check on the restaurant; Ezra out on his boat to help people trapped in their homes by rising floodwaters; and Mae, headed toward Halsey's house and whatever fate awaited her there.

Her phone beeped with an incoming text as she started her car and buckled her seatbelt—Ezra asking how Cole's house had fared.

Mae: *A total loss. All our clothes and furniture are gone. Nothing left.*

It broke her heart to type the words, as if putting them into print somehow made it more true.

Ezra: *You can stay with me until you get back on your feet. Cole too.*

Mae: *Your house is okay?*

Ezra: *No, but it seems better than most.*

Mae: *You're out on your boat?*

Ezra: *Intracoastal. All kinds of flooding. We've rescued twenty or thirty people so far. Taking them to shore. The Red Cross takes it from there.*

Mae imagined Ezra standing, broad-chested, at the bow of a boat as it cut through the water—a marsh-dwelling superhero come to save the day. *I'm headed to Halsey's house now, so I'll see how it is,* she replied.

Ezra: *I'm not far from there. I'll meet you there in about thirty minutes. Got to go.*

She closed her eyes and blew out a breath, grateful for the connection. Her world had been . . . obliterated . . . so a friend to lean on felt like a lifeline—the tiny inkling of a path back to normalcy, whatever "normal" might look like moving forward.

She put her car into gear, left Cole's neighborhood, and made her way down Third Street. Jax Beach merged into Ponte Vedra, though the roadside signs announcing each town limit had blown away. She passed a utility truck from Charleston, South Carolina. Two of its crew members chopped up a downed tree with a chainsaw.

She tried to imagine what kind of shape Halsey's house might be in, especially given what Ezra had just texted about flooding along the intracoastal. But what bothered her most was the urgency of Halsey's message—*MY HOUSE. NOW!* She'd texted back to ask what was going on, but he'd ignored her reply. The more she thought about it, the more his terse command irritated her. Her brother's house—the place she'd been living—had been blown away, for God's sake, and Halsey couldn't take even a second to ask how she was?

But she decided to give him the benefit of the doubt. The damage she'd driven by on the way to Halsey's—just three or four miles to the south—wasn't nearly as bad as the devastation in Cole's neighborhood. Maybe Halsey didn't know how badly some homes had been hit.

And perhaps the urgency of his text meant that journalists were at his home, and he needed Mae's PR expertise. They might be reporting about the flooding along the intracoastal or—hopefully not—still following up on PALM's delayed opening to evacuees of the storm.

Of course, there was a pretty good chance that he planned to fire her. She had, after all, defied his wishes about letting people into the church. But Mae had made him look *good* via her exclusive interview with Rob Lassiter. She'd spun an impossible situation in such a way to allow Halsey to save face in the community. He should *thank* her for that. He probably wouldn't, but he should.

The closer she got to Roscoe Boulevard, the more trees were down. Several of the stately, old live oaks that lined the roads in that part of Ponte Vedra had lost limbs or lay toppled over all together. But the local news had said the real danger would come from the storm surge. As Ezra had said, any home near a body of water was apparently at risk of flooding.

As she made the curve onto Roscoe Boulevard, she kept her eyes peeled to the right, where the large houses backed up to the intracoastal. Standing water glistened in the Florida sun in a couple of front yards, which didn't bode well for those homeowners.

Finally, she pulled into Halsey's driveway. Both garage doors were up, showing Halsey's Tesla and Dawn's BMW. Mae pulled in behind Akira's SUV, which stood parked near the front porch steps.

The door from the kitchen to the garage stood open. As Mae got out of her car, Dawn appeared, carrying a stack of soggy papers—kids' art projects, perhaps? The lid to the big blue trash bin already stood open, and Dawn dropped the papers inside. It was the first bit of manual labor Mae had ever seen her do.

"Did y'all sustain a lot of damage?" Mae asked when the two made eye contact.

The other woman shook her hair from her face and raised her nose in the air. "Halsey wants to see you right away. He's in his study."

"Ummmm. Okay." Mae waited for Dawn to enter the house, then followed her inside. Dawn's pink skin showed no sign of silver, but Mae's eyebrow thrummed. Not a good sign. Was it already picking up on Halsey's vibes, even though she had yet to see him?

An inch or two of murky water covered the tile floor of the kitchen. The couch in the adjacent great room showed water damage at about the six-inch mark, meaning the water line had been deeper at some point. The wall of books Mae had admired on her first visit there was largely intact, with only the contents of the bottom shelf showing any signs of water damage. A small, framed picture of Halsey, Dawn, and the kids still leaned against a row of biographies at eye level, untouched, as if the storm had never taken place.

Mae turned to take in the rest of the room. Sludge and parts of drying plants plastered the outside of the wall of windows in the breakfast nook, but the glass had withstood the force of the wind. A gaping hole stood where the sliding glass door had once been—probably how all the water had gotten in.

"I didn't call you out here to gawk at our misfortune."

Mae startled at Halsey's stern tone. She turned toward where he stood in the doorway to his study. The sun from the large windows of the living room glanced off the silver glare on his face.

"Is everyone okay?" she asked. She'd seen Dawn and Halsey so far, but what about the kids? What about Akira? Mae shuddered at the thought of Klara and Lejla and Ilma—*poor Ilma*—being expected to clean up the majority of the mess.

As if in answer to Mae's question, the sound of children running pounded on the floorboards above them.

Akira scampered into the great room from down the first-floor hall, an apologetic look on her face. "Sorry. I'll get them. I was just putting some wet towels in the laundry room." She rushed up the steps toward the children.

Halsey watched as Akira's bright red Chucks disappeared up the staircase. He waited about ten beats—as if wanting to make sure the nanny was out of earshot—then turned an angry glare at Mae. "What in *the hell* were you thinking?" His voice boomed from across the great room.

"Excuse me?" She was grateful to be in the kitchen, a good distance from where he stood. She rubbed her aching eyebrow. The rippling underneath her skin felt like needles jabbing directly into the bone.

He marched toward her, all the while jabbing his forefinger in her direction, as if to make his point. "I specifically told you we were *not* going to open the church. Yet, you still let them in?"

She felt herself back away, though it hadn't been a conscious thought. "I . . . I had to. There was a Category 5 hurricane on the way, and all the official shelters were full. Plus, I needed to paint you in as positive a light as possible. I mean, you were already getting a bunch of negative press for not letting people into the church."

"But you *defied* my orders."

"I . . . I thought it was the best decision in the moment." She hated the way her voice quavered. "My job is to make you look good, and . . . that's what I did."

"*Was*, Ms. Van Dorn. Your job *was* to make me look good."

She gripped the edge of the kitchen counter, waiting for more. Was he saying she'd failed in that particular situation . . . or that she was fired?

He now stood about three feet in front of her, his chest rising and falling with each angry breath. His furious gaze bore into her. His skin seemed to pulse with silvery energy.

"You're fired, Ms. Van Dorn." His voice was louder than she'd ever heard it. "Effective immediately. I want your keys to the house and any lists of passwords, bank account numbers—that sort of thing—that you have in your possession. *Now*." He held out his palm. "I'll change all the passwords once the electricity comes back on, but *do not* access any of my accounts in the interim. Do you hear me? You're not to speak or act on my behalf ever again. On anything." He sliced his hand through the air—a final severing of their relationship. "We're done."

Her anger flared as she dug into her wallet for the list of accounts.

What a charlatan.

A hypocrite.

She took the key off her key ring but then tucked it back inside her purse, along with the list of accounts. This conversation was not over.

Her gaze rose to meet Halsey's. She didn't even try to hide the contempt she knew shone in her eyes. "But you're a *minister*, for God's sake. The people of your community needed help and you had the means to help them."

"Do you know how much it costs to build and maintain a facility like that? Do you know what kind of clean-up is going to be needed now?"

But had he even been to the church since the hurricane had blown through? "The bulk of the damage would have happened anyway. Two of those big windows in the lobby burst and—"

"You had *no right* to let those people into *my* church." His voice boomed, as if at the height of a passionate sermon.

"*Those people* helped pay for that church. They're members of your congregation."

"Some of them, yes. But probably not all of them."

As if that made a difference. "How can you call yourself a Christian yet not help people when they needed it most? When their *lives* were in danger?"

He puffed out his chest, as if making an important proclamation. "I rely on God to direct me, and he clearly didn't direct me to open the church."

His haughty demeanor infuriated Mae. She waved her arm in the direction of the Atlantic. "The hundred and fifty mile an hour winds weren't enough of a sign that people might need to take shelter?"

He got a smug look on his face. "That's not the kind of sign I get. Mine are more . . . personal in nature. God talking directly to me. But then I wouldn't expect *you* to understand."

"And isn't that convenient? You're the only one who can hear or see these signs, so you can make them out to be whatever suits you best? Is that how it works? Did God tell you to build this huge mansion instead of giving the money to people who might really need it? Was it a sign from God that told you to take that expensive trip to Aspen this winter? Is all that cash—"

"You have no right to judge me. You aren't even a member of my congregation."

"How *do* you convince all those people to join that church? I mean, surely I'm not the only one who sees that everyone around you behaves in a Christian manner . . . except for you?"

"I want those keys and that list of accounts, and I want you gone." He pointed to the door to the garage.

She refused to break eye contact as she reached into her purse and extracted the items that belonged to him. She'd need to ask him about her last paycheck. He owed her for the hours she'd already worked, but she'd call him about that later, once he'd settled down. She'd need all the money she could get to rebuild her life.

But there was one key difference from when she'd last picked up her final paycheck from Patricia in Tallahassee. Back then, Mae had been alone, the way she'd been for so many years. Now she had Cole and Ezra to depend on. Yes, she would have to pay her own way in the world. Yes, her life had been stripped bare of so many things in the last twelve hours. But still, she felt lucky knowing that Cole and Ezra would be there for her. And she knew she'd done the right thing at the church, regardless of what "Minister" Halsey Green thought.

She handed the keys and the list of accounts to Halsey, eager to put an end to the oh-my-God-he's-such-a-hypocrite chapter of her life.

He grabbed them roughly from her hand. "Now get out of my house."

He turned and ran headlong into an end table, knocking a lamp onto the floor, into the standing water. "Damn it," he said as he tromped into his study and slammed the door shut. An almost imperceptible wave of water fluttered across the great room before dissipating.

She turned to go back out through the garage. To leave Halsey Green's house one last time.

And as she did, a glimpse of Akira's bright red sneaker disappeared up the stairs.

Chapter Forty-Two

Mae had just reached her car in Halsey's driveway when her phone buzzed. A text from Ezra.

I just got to Halsey's house. Tying the boat off now.

What a relief. She really didn't want to recap the scene that had just unfolded in Halsey's kitchen word-for-word—not until she'd had time to process it in her brain—but she'd tell Ezra the basics.

Her texted response: *Out front. Go around the house.*

She leaned against her car, grateful for a few moments of reprieve as Ezra secured his boat. Her normal go-get-'em view of life had been replaced by a feeling of defeat and despair.

He came around the house in those tall white rubber boots she'd seen fishermen wear. Mud smudged his faded board shorts and white T-shirt. "I'd give you a hug, but . . ." He motioned up and down his body.

She ran one finger along her eyebrow, hoping it would calm down soon. "Halsey fired me."

Ezra took a couple more steps toward her, closing the gap between them but not touching her. "What? Why?"

"I wasn't supposed to let people into the church. He told me not to, but I did it anyway." She took the final step to him. Her forehead fell to his chest. She didn't care that he was a sopping mess.

He wrapped his arms around her. "I *knew* there was more to that story than you were letting on." He rubbed her back. "But, babe, those people needed your help, and you gave it to them. You did the right thing."

She gave a sarcastic grunt. "Yeah. And look where it got me."

"Sounds like a bold decision to me." He placed his index finger under her chin and raised her face to his. "I think you're a badass."

She smiled and started to speak, but the front door burst open, causing them both to turn toward it. Halsey Green stormed out onto the porch as Mae and Ezra parted in surprise.

"Get off my property, Mae. And you." Halsey pointed at Ezra. "You need to stop fraternizing with my *former* personal assistant."

Ezra stepped between Halsey and Mae—a protective move that Mae appreciated. "It's none of your damn business who I fraternize with." The confidence in Ezra's voice made her proud.

Halsey sputtered for a second—seemingly surprised by Ezra's backtalk. "Well, I don't want her around here. She's not to set foot on my property again."

Ezra looked over his shoulder to Mae. Their eyes met momentarily—confirming they were a team—before he returned his attention to Halsey. "That won't be a problem. Because I quit."

Mae sucked in a sudden, involuntary breath.

Halsey rushed down the front porch stairs. "You can't do that. You've got a job to finish." He waved his arm frantically toward the back of the house. "You've actually got *more* work to do than before. You'll have to do storm clean-up before you can get back to the remodel job."

"I don't *have* to do anything," Ezra said. "That's the beauty of working for myself."

"You work for *me*." Halsey poked his own sternum with his forefinger. He wasn't used to not getting his way. "You do what *I* say and—"

Ezra marched toward Halsey, though Mae doubted Ezra would ever strike the guy. Still, his size was enough to intimidate anyone. Halsey backed against the porch railing, getting as far away from Ezra as possible.

"I can't believe you had that gigantic church," Ezra said. "And you weren't going to let people inside during a *Cat 5* hurricane."

Halsey's eyes flashed. "My church affairs are none of your business."

"You're right, but I also don't have to work for such a hypocrite. How can you preach every week about helping people in need, but then you don't help them? How can you spend that kind of money"—Ezra motioned toward the house—"when there are families struggling to pay the rent and put food on the table? Is that what the Bible says for you to do?"

"If you walk away from the job now, you'll be in breach of our contract."

"Read the paragraph on page five that talks about how changing the project completion date by a significant amount nullifies the contract."

"I'm going to tell everyone in Jax Beach how you shirked your responsibilities." Halsey's words sounded more like a whine than a threat.

Ezra turned and walked away, waving a dismissive hand. "Go ahead. I'll pit my reputation against yours any day of the week."

Halsey stomped up the porch steps and slammed the door behind him.

Mae's heart pounded in her chest as Ezra approached her. "Wow. You're pretty badass yourself. Your dad would be proud."

He blew out a long breath, seemingly dazed by what had just happened. "I didn't put a lot of thought into that before I did it."

That worried Mae. "Do you need to go take it back?"

"No." He shook his head. "I'm not going to work for a guy like that."

"Do you really think you can get out of your contract?"

He paced, as if the adrenaline coursing through his body urged him to move. "I could have invoked that clause the minute he asked me to move the completion date by several weeks. I was just trying to keep the client happy."

She smiled and took his hand. "Well, I'm proud of you."

He gave a happy little laugh. "Thanks. At least there'll be plenty of construction work because of the storm."

The roar of a boat's motor behind the house got louder as another vessel approached. He jabbed a thumb behind him. "I need to get back on the water. We'll connect later?"

She nodded, not sure where she'd go or what she'd do in the interim.

Ezra's eyebrows rose. "Oh, my God. You don't even know my address. 842 Catalpa Street in Neptune Beach. It's the blue house right on the corner." He took out his key ring, removed his house key from it, and handed it to her. "Let yourself in. Make yourself at home. Borrow my clothes. Eat my food. Whatever you need. Cole too."

She clutched the key in both hands and held it to her chest. "Thank you."

She felt grateful for the reprieve. She now had a safe harbor to go to, at least temporarily.

"My phone's almost dead, but I'll let you know when I come in off the water, if I still have any juice left." He gave her a kiss on the cheek.

She touched his arm and nodded toward the intracoastal. "All you boaters out there on the water . . . you're pretty much the heroes of the day, you know."

"There are a lot of people working their butts off today—on land *and* on the water," he said.

"Like I said, your dad would be proud."

He stilled for a moment, then gave a wobbly smile. "Thank you for that," he said, his words barely a whisper. "I'll see you later."

She watched as he walked back toward the intracoastal. When he was almost to the fence that led to Halsey's backyard, he stopped and raised his face to the sky for several seconds, as if communing with his father. He stood at just enough of an angle that Mae could see his strong, resolute profile. After several seconds of standing still, he raised the fingers of one hand to his lips, then—with that same hand—pointed toward the sky. A tribute to the man who meant so much to him.

Ezra was unlike any man Mae had ever meant—strong and gentle at the same time. A badass, yet tender-hearted. Not afraid to show how much his family meant to him.

And in that moment, Mae knew she was falling in love.

Chapter Forty-Three

Mae stood at Ezra's kitchen counter, slathering butter onto slices of sourdough she'd found in the pantry. She'd toast them on the grill, alongside the chicken breasts and pan-roasted carrots that were already out there. After all, Ezra had been out on the water all day rescuing people stuck in their flooded homes. He'd likely be famished when he got home in just a few minutes. And with no electricity, the items from the fridge wouldn't last long.

Cole sat awkwardly at the dinette table in the breakfast nook. He seemed too prim and proper, like he felt out of place in this home that was not his.

Ezra's truck pulled onto the drive outside the small bungalow. Cole sat up even straighter.

"Will you relax?" Mae said. "We could be here for weeks, so you're going to need to get comfortable sooner or later."

Cole held out his palms. "I've met the guy *once*."

"And you liked him, didn't you?"

"As much as I can like any guy who's dating my sister."

Outside, Ezra's truck door closed.

Mae lowered her voice to a whisper. "Well, he's offered you his home, so you need to look like you feel welcome, even if it's an act."

The side door from the carport opened and Ezra stepped inside looking even grimier and more exhausted than when she'd seen him earlier at Halsey's house. Dirt covered his face, his board shorts were caked in mud, and his T-shirt now had a huge rip down one side.

"I'm making dinner," she said. "I hope you don't mind that I used the carrots and the chicken." Most of the grocery stores were still closed, and local news said people had stood in lines at the food banks for hours. She motioned to the other side of the room. "We put the rest of the stuff from the fridge into those coolers."

Ezra nodded a greeting at Cole as he spoke. "Like I said, what's mine is yours. But do I have time to get a shower before dinner?"

Mae's libido sparked as she thought of Ezra naked on the other side of the kitchen wall. "Do we need to get the pressure washer out?"

He and Cole laughed. "Maybe," Ezra said as he pulled the filthy shirt over his head and threw it in the trash under the sink.

Mae tried not to stare at his taut abs. "I'll listen for the water to turn off before I put the garlic bread on the grill." Her phone rang. A local number she didn't recognize.

"Mae, it's Barb." The woman's voice sounded excited. Almost frenzied. "From the office at the church."

Yes, she knew who Barb was, but she really wished Halsey had told the staff Mae no longer worked for him.

Before Mae could figure out how to break the news, Barb launched into a flurry of sentences that poured out too fast, making it difficult for Mae to understand. "Wait. Slow down. I can't understand you," she said.

Ezra, who had started toward his bedroom, stopped and turned to look at Mae. Cole watched her intently.

"I haven't seen the video, but I had *five calls* about it," Barb's voice brimmed with excitement. "The calls came into the church, but I had to wait to call you from my personal cell because there's no way Halsey would want these messages passed on to you."

"The messages are for me?"

"Yes! People are calling after they see the video."

"The video's about me?"

"It's not *about* you. It's a recording *of* you."

"Oh, God." Mae's mind went immediately to the picture Dr. Greg Wisely had of her walking into the bank branch in Flagler Beach. Was there also a recording of the transaction? Probably, yes. Didn't video cameras capture everything that went on inside a bank branch?

"No, it's a *good* thing." Barb's voice dropped to a whisper. "Apparently someone named AkiraAtTheBeach posted it on Instagram, and Channel Ten got it from there."

A picture of Halsey's staircase flashed through Mae's mind. The staircase where she'd last seen Akira's bright red Chucks.

Barb continued to whisper. "It's a recording of Halsey yelling at you for letting people into the church before the hurricane. And he *admits* on tape that he told you not to let them in."

Mae's gaze moved to Ezra, who had a questioning look on his face. There was no way he could guess the contents of what Barb was saying, but perhaps he could gather that something unexpected had happened. Something that could fill Mae's life with unanticipated consequences.

"I can't believe he *fired* you for that," Barb said.

"It's true." And if the video captured her termination, did it also capture what she'd said to Halsey in return?

"And that's why people are calling." Barb's voice picked up speed again. "I mean, a bunch of journalists want to talk to Halsey, but he's dodging their calls. Some of them, though, are calling specifically *for you*. Two are PR firms that want to hire you and another woman wants you to send her your résumé. And no one was at work today because of the storm. These are like the presidents of the companies calling from their *homes*—people who have the *authority* for these on-the-spot job offers. They're using phrases like 'quick on her feet' and 'doesn't sugarcoat the truth' and 'makes good decisions in a crisis.'"

"Really?" Mae couldn't believe what she was hearing. Her last time on TV—in Tallahassee—had gotten her fired . . . and now this time resulted in unsolicited job offers?

"And that doesn't even count the TV stations that want to interview you," Barb said. "Do you want me to give them your personal cell number? Because Halsey's not going to want those calls coming in here at the church."

Mae couldn't concentrate—not with so much new information coming in all at once. "Let me think about that before you do. I'm not sure I want the TV stations to have my personal number." Granted, a PR professional needed to be easily reachable, but she wasn't sure she wanted to go there yet. She needed to have her wits about her before she made that decision. "But can you text me the names and phone numbers of the people with the jobs?" She glanced to Cole and Ezra. Both of them leaned toward her, a look of curiosity on their faces.

"Absolutely." Barb's voice took on an even softer, conspiratorial tone. "And I'll continue to pass them on to you, if more come in." Her short giggle told Mae that Barb would enjoy her role in this covert operation.

"Don't get yourself in trouble. Not on my behalf." Mae no longer felt desperate for a job, even though she didn't have one. Her actions at the church had earned her the respect of at least a few people in the community. "And why were you at the church today if nobody else in town went to work? Didn't you have clean-up to do at your house too?"

"My yard's a mess, but my house is okay. My sons will come over in the next couple of days, after they've dealt with their own places. They'll take down the plywood over my windows and help me clean up my yard. There's not a lot I can do by myself."

"Did Halsey *tell* you to go to work?" That sounded like him, making his employees show up at the office when he likely hadn't even been there himself.

"No, but I figured I should be there. I mean, PALM is a huge organization. We should be able to help a lot of people. Conrad opened the Clothes Closet, even though it wasn't Thursday, and, as you can imagine, people cleared it out within minutes. And the food pantry ran out of food before noon, but people kept dropping stuff off knowing others might need it. I mainly ran around all day, trying to keep things organized."

A sense of happiness settled over Mae as she thought about all the good people around her—Barb and Ezra and the rest of the boaters out on the intracoastal rescuing people. Klara and Lejla, taking care of Ilma. Barb. Conrad. Akira. Oh, God—Akira! How would Mae ever thank her? There was no way Halsey would continue to employ the nanny—not when she'd recorded a private conversation that took place *in his house* and then posted it on social media. Yes, Mae had defied Halsey's orders about opening the church, but Akira had been just as brave.

"You're a good woman," Mae said to Barb. "The world needs more people like you."

"The world needs more people like *you*, Mae Van Dorn. But thank you. I'll keep you posted," Barb said, then they said their goodbyes.

"What was that all about?" Ezra's chuckle told her he could sense her giddiness.

She held up a forefinger. "Two seconds." She swiped to Instagram on her phone, typed in AkiraAtTheBeach in the search bar and motioned for him to step over near Cole. She held the phone so all three of them could watch the screen at the same time.

The unsteady video bounced around, mainly showing the staircase railing and wall of the foyer in Halsey's house, but the voices were clear. Jacksonville and its adjacent beach communities were all too familiar with the minister's unmistakable, booming voice. Akira's phone had captured every word of the conversation. Mae's heart lurched at the knowledge that so many people were now privy to what had been said—both her firing and her calling Halsey out for his hypocrisy.

Once the video was over, Cole turned to her, his eyes asking a string of questions.

"The nanny," Mae said, answering his unasked question. "And people are calling the church, wanting to offer me jobs and interviews."

Ezra laughed and gave her a high five. "So are they good jobs? I mean, ones you'd be interested in?"

"I don't know yet. The church receptionist is texting me their contact information. I guess I'll call them in a day or two, once things start getting back to normal."

Ezra grunted. "That's going to take more than a day or two."

"And, besides." A crazy idea had popped into her head a few hours ago. She hadn't thought it through and certainly hadn't planned to talk to him about it yet, but now seemed like a good time. "I know this really handsome construction guy who might need some help organizing all his new jobs."

Cole rested his head in his hand. "I think I'm gonna puke."

Ezra grinned. "You think he's handsome?"

She laughed at the fact that *that's* what he'd gotten from her statement. "Yeah. And I figure your phone's about to start ringing off the hook with people who need their homes repaired after the storm."

The happiness drained from his face. "But I haven't really budgeted for a project coordinator or whatever you'd be. You need to take one of those other jobs."

"Yeah, I know, but I could help you after work. Kind of a side gig in exchange for letting Cole and me stay with you for a while."

Ezra scrubbed at the side of his mud-caked face. "I may not get much new business if Halsey Green bad-mouths me all over town."

Mae grinned. "Well, I happen to know an *excellent* PR person who would be happy to help you with that."

Ezra cocked his head to one side, still looking at Mae. "You'd do that for me?"

She held out her hands. "You're giving us a place to live, but—yes—I'd do it for you, even if you weren't."

Ezra glanced to Cole and then back to Mae, like he wasn't sure her offer was for real. "It's a deal," he finally said. "I'd appreciate the help."

"And we appreciate the place to live for a while," Cole said. "I can help, too, when I'm not working at the restaurant."

Ezra gave him a dismissive wave.

"But most of all," Cole's voice rose, as if he was about to make his most important point. "Thank you for taking care of my baby sister during the storm."

Ezra looked at her with pride. "I'm pretty sure your baby sister can take care of herself. Or do you need to watch that video again?" He pointed to Mae's phone.

Cole didn't laugh at Ezra's comment. Instead, he looked at Mae and held her gaze. "I haven't always been there for her . . . so I appreciate you looking out for her."

Mae blinked away the tears that welled in her eyes. No, Cole hadn't been perfect, but he was there now, and that's what mattered most.

And, yes, she could take care of herself, at least most of the time. But it sure felt good to be in that cozy little kitchen surrounded by two people who cared for her. Maybe the human race wasn't so bad after all.

But what about her internal alarm system? If people were inherently good, why had she been given "the gift" to see bad intentions shining right on someone's skin?

Maybe it was the universe's way of protecting her. Of making up for a mom who didn't care and a dad who'd died before Mae could remember him. In any case, her gift had ratted out Halsey Green from the get-go and recognized Conrad and Klara and Lejla for what they were—good people who cared for others.

On the other hand, maybe if she hadn't spent so many years paying attention to the silvery faces in her path, she'd have seen the good in humanity more quickly.

She looked around the room once more.

She had Cole, who understood her past like no one else ever could.

She had Ezra, who represented a future on the verge of being built.

She had *strangers*, for God's sake—calling to offer her jobs. People who recognized when someone stood up for what was right.

Maybe Mae would even agree with Cole to give Mama a call. In case Mama might rest easier knowing her children were safe and together.

But for now, this small kitchen held everything Mae needed. She didn't have a house or a job or electricity. Hell, she didn't even have any clothes, other than the ones she now wore.

But her faith in humanity meant the future looked bright. She and Cole and Ezra had made it through the storm, and they would make it through whatever came next.

Chapter Forty-Four

Six Months Later

Mae fidgeted at the table in the courtyard of the Southern Grounds coffee shop at the beach. The warmth of the sunshine felt good on her face, especially given the coolness of the March morning air. Off in the distance—a couple of blocks away—a saw buzzed to life. Perhaps some reconstruction after Hurricane Carly. Jacksonville and its beaches had bounced back, though signs of the devastation still scattered the area.

Mae took a sip of her iced latte. She should have been relaxed in such a beautiful setting and on such a beautiful morning, but Rob Lassiter's request for a meeting had made her suspicious. She hadn't seen or heard from him since a few days after the storm.

He came out of the coffee shop and approached her at the table, a little stanchion holding his customer number in hand. "Good morning." He motioned toward her coffee. "You didn't order any food?"

"Nah. Not hungry." She'd gotten used to eating Ezra's big, hearty breakfasts—the kind fit for a construction worker who'd burn a lot of calories throughout the day. He'd cook and she'd clean up afterwards. She loved the rhythm of their quiet mornings together, before they each headed out to their respective jobs.

Lassiter pulled out a chair and sat. "I never pass up a good bowl of shrimp and grits."

"So what's been going on with you?" she asked, hoping to tease out the reason he'd requested this meeting.

He blew out a gusty breath. "I finally got back into my condo last week. It took them that long to get the lobby fixed, which was so frustrating because my condo's on the seventh floor. It was perfectly fine, but I couldn't get to it because of all the water damage in the lobby."

"Are you oceanfront? Or along the river?" Either way, she was impressed that a reporter could afford a condo in either of those expensive locations.

"It's my grandmother's old place in San Marco." So along the river. "She left it to me when she passed a few years ago."

"That whole time you were at PALM with me during the hurricane, you didn't say a word about being worried about your own place."

He stuck his chest out in a fake haughty demeanor. "Because I'm a professional."

She laughed.

"And what about you?" he asked. "How's your recovery been?"

"My recovery from Halsey? Or from the storm?"

He chuckled. "Good point."

"My brother's rental house was demolished, so we both lived with Ezra Watts for a while."

Lassiter frowned. "That guy who was with you the night of the storm?"

Mae nodded as she took a sip of her latte.

"And what about now?"

Her face heated. "Well, my brother rented an apartment after a couple of months, but I'm still living with Ezra." She gave Lassiter a sly smile.

"Ahhhh. Then it no longer has anything to do with the storm," he teased. "Are you two serious?"

"Like I'm going to tell a reporter all my deep dark secrets." The truth was, she loved the private little cocoon she and Ezra occupied. Yes, they'd discussed marriage. Yes, they'd talked about how—if they decided to have children—they'd need to get started pretty quickly, due to their ages. But for now, they both luxuriated in the fact that they could be together. Just the two of them. A couple newly in love.

Lassiter sat back as a server brought his bowl of shrimp and grits, then removed the customer number from the table.

"Anything else I can get you?" the girl asked.

"No, thank you," the reporter said before returning his attention to Mae. "So what else is going on?" he asked as he scooped up a bite of breakfast onto his fork.

He ate while Mae told him about how she'd bypassed the bigger, downtown-Jacksonville firms that had contacted her immediately following the storm, opting instead to join a boutique PR agency headquartered at the beach. Maybe he could help her in the future if one of her clients needed some media exposure.

"So everything's good?" he asked between bites.

She nodded, unwilling to share the one even more personal part of her life. Cole had finally convinced her last month that they should contact Mama together—to let her know that they'd reunited and that her grown children were now looking out for one another. Mae knew it was the kind thing to do—that it could perhaps help a downtrodden old woman find some small measure of happiness. Even so, Mae had long ago accepted that she needed to remain separate from the woman who'd caused so much harm in her life.

But when Cole had finally tracked down Mama's latest live-in boyfriend, the man told Cole that Mama had died of emphysema three months earlier. She'd had a long, lingering, life-threatening illness and still hadn't reached out to her children. Mae felt sad for herself and for Cole, but sad for Mama too.

But Mae didn't want to think about that now, and, besides, she still didn't know why Rob Lassiter had asked to meet her that morning. "So what did you want to see me about?"

He swallowed the food in his mouth before responding. "I'm about to break a story on Halsey Green and I was hoping you would comment."

Not a chance. She'd put that chapter of her life behind her. Still, she was curious about whatever scoop Lassiter may have uncovered. "What's he done now?"

"The church board is about to oust him. Turns out they've been footing the bill for way more of his extravagant lifestyle than they're comfortable with."

"But hasn't that been happening for years? I mean, how else would a minister live in a waterfront mansion?" This same topic had been part of the very first conversation she'd ever had with Rob Lassiter.

"Yes, but now they have proof. Someone found an old box of American Express bills that he'd been unwilling to show them in the past."

"He was dumb enough to *save* them?"

Lassiter's eyes widened. "So you knew about this?"

She held her hands out in front of her. "No." She did *not* want to get involved in this. Her life was too happy now, too content to be polluted by any of Halsey Green's shenanigans. "I only knew the board suspected it, but nothing more."

"Apparently a work group was cleaning out an old storage unit the church had rented. There were a bunch of bills mixed in with some other papers. But there's more." Lassiter leaned toward her and lowered his voice. "A buddy of mine in law enforcement says Halsey's about to be arrested for stealing thousands of dollars from the PALM offering plate."

Mae did a better job of schooling her reaction than she had before. She hoped to God she wouldn't get dragged into that. Was there a chance she'd get called in as a witness since she'd made a big deposit that may have been cash siphoned from the Sunday service? "Have they caught him? Like on video or something?"

Lassiter shook his head. "My source won't share any details, but it's almost a done deal. He says they've been working on it for months."

She gave a wry smile. "I guess I'd better start watching the news."

Lassiter barked out a laugh. "So you want to comment for the story?"

"No!" Her tone sounded more emphatic than she'd intended.

Lassiter sat up straighter. "Why not?"

"The last thing I want is to be dragged back into Halsey Green's orbit."

Lassiter's phone rang, giving her a reprieve from the conversation. He held up his index finger. "I need to take this call."

He answered the phone as he stood, then walked away to a private spot near one of the not-yet-open-for-the-day clothing shops that lined the courtyard.

Mae looked around the peaceful setting. At the mothers with babies in strollers. The older man with a goldendoodle lounging under his chair. The young professionals in their business casual attire laughing at a colleague's joke. The surfer with his feet and calves covered in sand.

She was grateful to have moved to Jax Beach. Grateful to have reunited with Cole and to have met Ezra.

She hadn't wanted to come there, but she now knew that this was where she belonged.

The brother she'd come to trust again lived fifteen minutes away.

Her new partner was funny, kind, thoughtful, steadfast, and—most of all—as in love with her as she was with him.

And all that goodness was infused with a newfound faith in humanity the old Mae never would have seen, much less believed.

And the funny thing was, she hadn't seen a silvery tinge on anyone in weeks—not on a coworker or an acquaintance or even someone she passed in the grocery store. Her eyebrow hadn't ached since the last time she'd seen Halsey Green.

In the days following Hurricane Carly, she'd started to notice a different phenomenon—a mauve-colored haze that often surrounded those who were helping others. The teenager who coached an elderly woman through ordering a fancy drink at the local coffee shop. The school crossing guard who manned the corner in front of Ezra's house. The coworker who'd invited Mae to lunch on her first day at her new job.

All this made Mae wonder if the good in the world had always been there, and she'd just chosen for years not to see it.

She was a different person now. Life was, indeed, good.

***

Thank you for reading *Mae Van Dorn's Perfect Storm*. Please consider leaving a review on an online review site and/or telling a friend about the book.

To sign up for my newsletter, please visit SheilaAthens.com. Newsletter subscribers are the first to know about new releases, giveaways, and my overall shenanigans.

Acknowledgements

This book came to fruition via a partnership with many wonderful people, including book coach Susan DeFreitas and critique partner Carla Damron. Many thanks to writer D.L. Williams for explaining some intricacies about law enforcement that I needed to understand for the story. Writer Kelly Elizabeth Huston has been both an inspiration and a source of good technical information. I'm especially pleased that the talented Leslie Howard is bringing another of my books to life via her narration of the audiobook.

Many thanks to the writers who act as my support system: the ladies of the bungalow, the writer hikers, the members of the Women's Fiction Writers Association, and the members of the Clubhouse Author Conference. Writer Kristi Leonard belongs to a couple of these groups, but gets a special shoutout because she came up with the name of Halsey's church. The PALM acronym fits this Florida-based book perfectly.

I received insightful input from the beta readers of my manuscript: RA Cook, Aryn Bloom, Debbie Hammer, Terry Hammer, Kim Guzzone Collier and Missi Davis.

Many thanks to the independent booksellers who have been so supportive during my writing journey. I would especially like to recognize The Bookmark (Neptune Beach, Florida), Story and Song Bookstore Bistro (Amelia Island, FL), The Book Loft (Amelia Island, FL), Happy Medium Books Café (Jacksonville, FL), The Bookshelf (Thomasville, GA), San Marco Books (Jacksonville, FL) and E. Shaver Bookseller (Savannah, GA). The bookseller game is strong in the South, y'all!

And finally, I would like to thank the readers out there who not only read my stories, but pass them on to friends via social media posts, word of mouth, online reviews, or by simply shoving my books into the hands of others, imploring them to read them. You have my eternal gratitude.